500

ATLANTIC
OCEAN

ILLINOIS

OHIO

PENNSYLVANIA

INDIANA

W. VIRGINIA

VIRGINIA

SOURI

KENTUCKY

NO. CAROLINA

TENNESSEE

SO. CAROLINA

ANSAS

MISSISSIPPI

ALABAMA

GEORGIA

OUISIANA

Mobile Bay

Mississippi River

St. Marks
(Aute)

(Apalachen)

FLORIDA

St. Marks Bay
(Bahia De Caballos)

APALACHEE
BAY

Tampa Bay

The Journey
of
Cabeza de Vaca

sland

MEXICO

CUBA

Trinidad

July 29, 1988

Beth Pewther 1981   Mary Mace Spradling

Black
Ulysses

Also by Daniel Panger

SEARCH IN GOMORRAH

YOU CAN'T KILL A DEAD MAN

THE SACRED SIN

DANCE OF THE WILD MOUSE

OL' PROPHET NAT

OHIO UNIVERSITY PRESS

Daniel Panger

BLACK ULYSSES

ATHENS OHIO · 1982

Library of Congress Cataloging in Publication Data

Panger, Daniel.
  Black Ulysses.

  1. Estevan, d. 1539—Fiction.   2. Nuñez Cabeza de Vaca, Alvar,
16th century—Fiction.   I. Title.
PS3566.A57B5   813'.54   82-3517
ISBN 0-8214-0660-4   AACR2
ISBN 0-8214-0680-9 (pbk.)

© copyright 1982 by Daniel Panger

MAPS

Book and Jacket designed and illustrated
by Beth Pewther, San Francisco, California

to my wife

Mary Ann Miner M.D.

with deepest love

and appreciation

Black
Ulysses

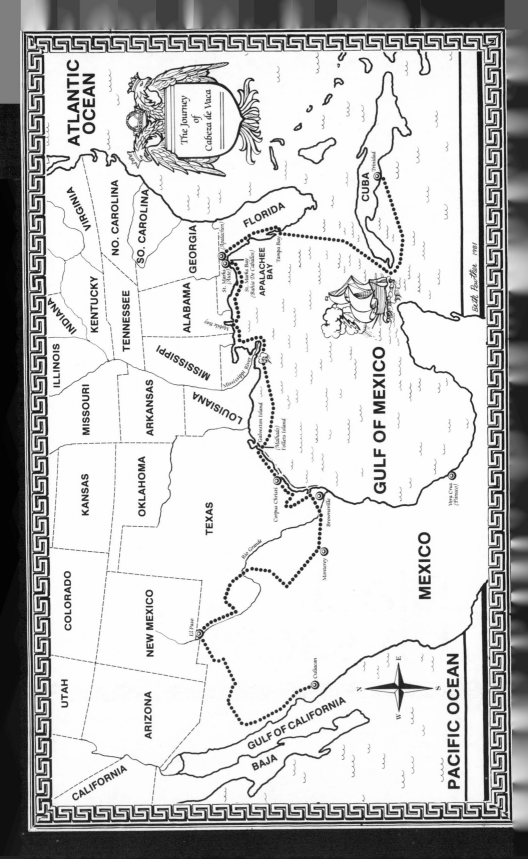

I

I am Estevan, a black man from Azemmour, in Morocco. And this is an account of my journey with Alvar Nuñez, called Cabeza de Vaca. And if there has been a like journey in all the long history of humankind, I have never heard of it. Even the tale of Jason and his courageous Argonauts, although magnificent by any standards, is not its equal. But you be the judge.

Commissioned by His Sacred Caesarian Catholic Majesty, the Emperor Charles V, to seek gold in the land of Florida, Governor Pánfilo de Narvaez at his own expense made ready an expedition. After completing necessary preparations, on the seventeenth day of June, 1527, a Friday, we departed Spain in five ships—six hundred we were, a few more or less— and, except for a score or two who fell sick with the vomits and one lost in the sea, it was a fair and easy voyage to the Island of

3

Santo Domingo, where we rested forty-five days procuring provisions and horses.

There, more than one hundred and forty men were seduced from our ranks by the settlers. When certain threats were made by Governor Narvaez, the colonists gathered near where our ships were berthed and showed an ugly humor that, if further provoked, would have led to loss of life.

Thus it was we departed Santo Domingo reduced in strength by nearly one-quarter, and arrived at Santiago, a port in Cuba, where the Governor, with promises of the riches to be found in the places we were going, supplied himself further with men to the number of half a hundred.

While at the port of Santiago, an hidalgo named Vasco Porcallo de Figueroa approached the Governor and told him of a store of supplies he had in his town of Trinidad, a hundred leagues distant. Several who lived in the town of Santiago and knew of the town of Trinidad warned the Governor that it was a bad port in which many ships had been lost. But the gentleman, Vasco Porcallo, laughed and gave to these the name "old women."

So we sailed for Trinidad. But once at sea, the Governor grew cautious—a warm wind having risen and certain purple clouds having gathered in a corner of the sky—and sought berth in a port halfway to Trinidad called Cabo de Santa Cruz.

The strange warm wind blew all through the night, and in the morning, which was Friday, a great bank of black clouds gathered on the horizon to the east. Several, including Alvar Nuñez Cabeza de Vaca, who commanded the ship on which I served with my master, Andres Dorantes, warned the Governor that to venture to an unsafe port, as Trinidad was said to be, and in such weather, would be a foolish tempt of fate. They then begged the Governor to remain in the secure port of Cabo de Santa Cruz until the weather cleared. This advice he accepted only in part, for he remained with four ships, including

4

one that had been bought at the Island of Santo Domingo, but the other two ships—ours commanded by Alvar Nuñez and another, captained by Juan Pantoja—were ordered to proceed to the port of Trinidad.

Arriving there, Captain Juan Pantoja went with the gentleman, Vasco Porcallo, while Alvar Nuñez stayed with the two ships, which were kept a half league to sea. That night was calm, and we passed it easily. But the next morning rain started falling, and the sea ran high. Alvar Nuñez then granted permission to those who would to go ashore, among which number I was one. Had I not chosen to chance the rain and wind that day and also gone ashore, this account never would have been written.

Shortly before noon, after repeated solicitations from various residents of the town who had need for his authority, and after leaving orders with the pilots that if the south wind started to blow, and if there should be any danger, then they must put the ships on shore some place where the men and horses could be saved, Alvar Nuñez made for the town in a canoe sent for him.

By noon, the sky was as black as a charcoal burner's hands, and the south wind blew as if Satan himself belched across the water.

The two ships were tossed like dogs trapped by a bull, and that night, shattered on the rocks.

During the night and into the next day, which was Sunday, while the wind ripped up great trees and houses, I found refuge in a cave in which were gathered certain Indian slaves, too old to work, sent there to die.

While I stayed safe in that cave, giving whatever comfort I could—some had not touched a morsel in many days—Alvar Nuñez Cabeza de Vaca and several of his companions struggled with the tempest.

All night they wandered, helping those Indians and Spaniards trapped beneath fallen trees or swept away by swollen streams. Not one member of that company escaped injury from the falling branches and wind-tossed stones.

"At times to move upright it was necessary that we should go seven or eight, each holding onto the other," Alvar Nuñez recounted when, after the storm, we gathered to count our losses. "In all my life I cannot remember the equal of this night," he said.

His left cheek was purple, swollen to the size of a plover's egg. And across his nose, in the same place he had once suffered a break from a pikeman's thrust, the split skin dripped blood.

"Sometime shortly after midnight," he continued, "a thing occurred so strange that I have never heard of its like before. So savage grew the storm that earth and air and water all clashed together, stirred by lightning, which is fire. And air was where earth should be; water was in air; earth in water, and everywhere was fire. So mixed were the elements that suddenly, with a roar not heard since Satan was cast out by the Lord, all four were one!"

Alvar Nuñez's eyes were opened wide, but the way he stared I knew he saw something I could not see.

"Above the din," he said softly, "I heard the sounds of timbrels, flutes and tambourines, and voices singing sweeter than the finest Castrada choir. 'The first day of the Thousand Years has come,' I whispered, falling to my knees; and, hugging a broken tree, I offered up a prayer that the Son of God, as He walked again upon this earth, might show me compassion and forgive my sins.

"The sweet sounds grew louder, slowly a blue light formed and where that blue light shone the shuddering trees grew still. More and more blue light was there until all around were quiet trees. Then I knew it was not yet time for Christ to descend, but that it was a sign, a sign His holy vision was upon me and that the storm would end."

All who had listened to Alvar Nuñez were shaken. Several crossed themselves, others murmured Mary's name.

Such dangers he had faced, and then such wondrous happenings; while I stayed safe and dry inside the cave with the Indians sent there to die. Two died that night despite some bread I had placed in their mouths, also dried meat which I first chewed to soften—they died, each singing in a failing voice his song. Fifteen souls were gathered in that cave—nine men, six women. And my heart was leaden when, after the storm, I was forced to leave them. Yet I knew they could not live much longer. Bags of skin filled with brittle bones they were. Their heads—fleshless skulls with sunken eyes. I left with them all my bread and meat and some other things—salt and a good blanket. Then I joined with Alvar Nuñez Cabeza de Vaca.

After Alvar Nuñez had finished with his account, prayers were offered in thanks for those who survived and prayers for the preservation of the souls of those who had died. Then we ate the little bread we had amongst us and roasted our fill of fish— for hundreds lay begging to be taken on the sand. Just as we finished eating, suddenly Captain Juan Pantoja drew the attention of all the others to me. He let off sucking bits of fish from his fingers and called out, "Look at Estevan! Of all of us, he is the only one whose face does not show a break or bruise."

"Hey, Estevanico!" my master Andres Dorantes shouted, "how came you to preserve your beauty? Was it that you found a soldier's wife cowering in her cellar crying out for comfort?" All who heard my master started laughing.

"The poor lady," Alvar Nuñez made a great show of wiping his eyes with the sleeve of his torn shirt, "thinking the one who entered her dark cellar to be surely a Castilian, mayhap an hidalgo or even one of royal blood, allowed her trembling body to be comforted in the way for which Castilian men are justly famed."

"Oh, Estevan," Andres Dorantes wagged his finger, "I

think you must be beaten for taking advantage of the darkness of the night."

"And the present he left for her," Alvar Nuñez slowly shook his head, "when she unwraps it nine months hence . . ."

"When her husband tries to find some resemblance!" Captain Pantoja shouted.

"He will lift the infant and hold it close up to the light," Alvar Nuñez, with much delicacy raised a piece of twisted wood, turning it first to one side then to the other. "See the ear! Certain it is the ear of my mother's father. And the buttocks—a little dark, perhaps, but any who knew my great-grandmother will know . . ." Laughter drowned his words.

"He will give out that it is the climate," Captain Pantoja snatched the twisted wood and hugged it to his breast. "The climate or the water. And at least two learned doctors will agree."

"Tell us truly, Estevanico," Andres Dorantes asked, "were you comforted by a lady's gentle sighs while the rest of us were buffeted by the wind and bruised by broken branches? No man will call you coward, for choosing soft arms against cruel elements."

I tried to tell them it was not in a cellar but in a cave that I had quartered. But before I could explain, Captain Pantoja asked if in that cave there were any women, and I answered, "Six."

"Certain it is you must be beaten, Estevanico," Andres Dorantes raised his fist and shook it before my face. "Five of us you could have succored had you wished. Have you never been instructed of the sin of avarice?"

Although at a different time being the butt of their jests might have caused me distress, this time I took it all in good will knowing how much a moment of levity was needed, for our losses had been severe.

Of all who traveled to that port of Trinidad, no more than

thirty survived the storm. Sixty men and twenty horses aboard the two ships were gone.

After hearing accounts of various ones who had had their nostrils filled with death, although still early afternoon, we separated for sleep.

I found a depression in the sand beneath an overhanging ledge of rock, where different birds had gathered for protection against the storm and were not yet ready to venture forth. Fatigue had closed my eyes, but I could not sleep. The words of Alvar Nuñez telling of the blue light that stilled the trees passed through my mind again and again, and I was seized with an apprehension I could feel in my guts. Each time I had known that fear it had warned of danger. I wanted to rush out and tell my master—but what could I tell him? Yet my brain was filled with remembrances of the times I had known that fear. . . .

In the fourth month of my eleventh year, as I made my way home from the place where I received instruction, I first knew that fear. My life up to that moment had been one of safety, living as I did in my father's house with older brothers to provide protection. That night, judging myself a man, I refused the service of a servant whose charge it was to accompany me, and made my way home alone. A distance of half a league separated my father's house from the house of the Jew, Jacob, who was my teacher. Most of the houses of the city of Azemmour lay between these two dwellings, also several open spaces and the place where the dead were buried. As I walked at an easy pace through the empty streets, my thoughts were with the Jew, who had just shown me how to bind a broken limb—it being my father's wish that I learn from him the art of the physician. The moon cast enough light for me to find my way easily, and I allowed my feet to guide me as I repeated what I had learned, to fix it in my memory. All the houses were locked and shuttered as is the custom in Moorish towns after dark. And except for the distant barking of dogs, all was silent, for the thick walls of the buildings and the heavy shutters allowed neither sound nor the faintest glimmer of a candle to escape. I had covered more than half the distance to my father's house, and was nearing the place where the dead were buried, when I felt a tightening in my guts. I have never known fear of the dead, nor do I now. Rather by a thousand times would I lie all night in any grave-yard than in many roadside inns or stews that soldiers frequent. So, knowing the dead could not harm me, I forced my feet on, although the tightening in my guts made it hard for me to breathe. Ahead was the stone structure in which the corpses were washed. I had sought the coolness of its thick walls surely no less than a dozen times when the summer sun caused the streets to smoke. But as I approached that structure I filled with fear—it was as if a cold hand were thrust inside my body. My feet would not take another step, I shook; my heart beat so I thought it must burst. Then, suddenly, from the entrance to the structure where I would have passed, stepped a jackal, foam dripping from its mouth. I escaped by running, and the next day it was killed, after it bit two women who later died.

How I knew the jackal was there waiting . . . perhaps an odor, or a sound, warned me. Yet it was thirty paces distant, and, when it chooses, a jackal can be a silent creature.

And I remembered another time I felt that tightening in my guts—when my son, a fine and sturdy boy I had by a servant woman of Seville, was stoned to death during a rising against the Moors in that city.

I was at my master's side in the town of Bejar del Castanar, which may be found in the province of Estremadura, the town in which his father, Pedro Dorantes, and other members of his family lived. It was the time to harvest cork, and I worked with a long, curved knife much like the short sword carried by all men in the city of my birth. The odor of a roasting kid filled my nostrils, and my mind was empty of all thought except how its crisping skin should feel between my teeth. I hooked my knife into the thick bark of the oak and pulled it toward me, when a sudden tightening in my guts caused the knife to slip, laying

10

my thigh open. Using an iron needle and sinews pulled from the roasting kid, I closed the wound, but, as I sewed, it was not pain that caused sweat to gather on my brow. Everything was as it should be in that safe place, so why this sense of danger?

Afraid to take up the knife again, I sat away from the rest, my stomach churning, thoughts stinging my brain, my hands and feet, despite the sun, cold as those of a three-day corpse. In this way, I sat until after dark when my master sent his sister's youngest son with orders for me to join the others for the evening meal. But one glance at the round-faced little boy, just the age of my son, and I understood! And so, without asking leave I traveled five days, despite my wounded thigh which oozed blood at every step, sleeping only when I must, until I reached Seville.

My son had been killed that day, as had half a hundred Moors, and his body lay with the others in the marketplace, where I found it late at night, aided only by moonlight.

He weighed less than four stone, so I carried him easily out of the city and buried him before sunrise, in a place hidden behind a hill, where there were trees and a nearby stream of sweet water.

Now, as I lay beneath that ledge of rock, among those birds made fearless of my presence by the fierceness of the storm I wondered of what danger could I warn? Both of our ships and the sixty men were already gone. It would be like a man giving warning of plague with the streets already choked with spotted corpses.

II

Living as best we could, short of provisions, suffering greatly from the weather for we had no warm clothing, we waited where we were in the port of Trinidad until the fifth day of November, when the Governor arrived with his four ships, which had all survived the storm with little damage and no men lost.

There never lived a lover long separated from his maiden who ever greeted his betrothed the way each member of our company greeted every man aboard those four ships, as they stepped ashore.

Several fine widows of the town joined our merrymaking, and although they were few and we many, they promised to reward our patience with a full measure for each man; assuring us that, like the magic golden goblet, no matter how often or deeply their cup was quaffed it would immediately be full again. I danced with a young priest, each of us gripping the other's arms, and he spun around shouting an Andalusian shepherd's song while I shouted back a song of the Moorish fishermen who cast their nets into the river Habid.

One night of merrymaking we had in that place and then days of cold and wet and wind that lengthened into months while we waited for the end of winter.

Cold and damp though it was there on land I felt a certain reluctance when ordered, near the end of February, to board my ship. And I was not alone in my feelings. Knowing from our faces how we felt, the Governor promised fair weather and assured us that our passage through the shoals would be safe, for he had obtained the services of a navigator, one Miruelo, later named "the donkey", who boasted that he knew the northern coast better than the furrows in his mother's face.

The second day at sea, we struck the shoals they call Canerreo, and there we were stuck, the keels of our ships frequently touching bottom, for fifteen days. Had any sudden gale come up, we would have been dashed to pieces, and I do not doubt that the first one to find himself struggling in the water would have been that same Miruelo, for he was a man not well loved as we waited for a sufficient sea to float us free.

Although there was not a single man who did not know of the danger we faced should a sudden storm rise while we rested on that reef, it was not the chance of danger that caused the most distress, but rather boredom. Each day the murmurs grew. Fierce fights bloodied men who, while on shore, had been fast friends. Two were hung by their thumbs for half a day for stabbing another, whose wounds, although at first judged mortal, quickly healed. Three were whipped for stealing a cask of the captain's wine. Although I stayed apart from the others I could not avoid hearing the angry mutterings. Each day the grumbling of the men grew greater with less caution taken to keep these words from the hearing of the officers. More than anyone else they cursed the Governor. "Fool," "devil's spawn," "whoreson," were not the worst words used. In time the officers—my master, Andres Dorantes, not excluded—added their mutterings to those of the men.

Unable to sleep, it must have been the twelfth day of our imprisonment on the reef, I sat in the shadows of the deck where I knew I could not be seen, and watched the moon leaping on the water and the dancing curls of spume. Such an occupation somehow produced a certain peace within me. I must have dozed, for suddenly, not ten feet away, stood Andres Dorantes, Alvar Nuñez Cabeza de Vaca, and the comptroller of the expedition, one Alonso Enriquez, all engaged in earnest conversation; it may be that they had been so engaged for several minutes. I remained silent in the shadows and listened.

"I judge the man a fool," my master spoke, an angry edge to his voice.

"It is not for you to make such a judgment," the comptroller, Alonso Enriquez, answered, his voice also showing an angry edge.

" 'Fool' is a strong word," Alvar Nuñez Cabeza de Vaca said quietly. "A word that can cause a man's blood to spill."

"There are some, Andres," the comptroller spoke slowly, "that would not scruple to carry your words to the Governor's ears."

"Do you not think, if pressed, I would not call him fool to his face and then challenge him to answer me like an hidalgo?"

"He'd have you confessed and hanged within the hour," said Alvar Nuñez. "The only thing your good name would save you would be quartering after you were cut down."

"He would never dare hang an officer for saying to his face what he must know in his heart to be true. You heard him praise Miruelo!"

"Still, 'fool' is a strong word," Alvar Nuñez answered, but there was a certain hollowness in his speech. "He made mistakes. Another in his place might have done no different."

"Mistakes! Pah! You are too charitable, Alvar Nuñez. Who was it that ordered the ships to Trinidad with the sky darkening? The man is a great fool and you know it."

"Let me repeat, Andres Dorantes," said Alonso Enriquez, "there are those—more than you may know—who would show no hesitation in courting the favor of the Governor by reporting your words to him."

"I trust you are not one of them, Alonso, or am I already a condemned man?"

"You have nothing to fear from Alonso," interrupted Alvar Nuñez. "Would that all the other officers were half so honorable."

14

"If he ever dared dishonor an officer and the report got back to the King together with the truth of his mismanagement—he would not risk such a thing," muttered Andres Dorantes.

"He hanged three hidalgos when he was Lieutenant Governor of Cuba; and two officers he hanged on the same tree when he was in Mexico. And there may have been others."

"How do you know of this, Alonso?" my master asked slowly.

"One of the hidalgos I saw hanging with my own eyes; he had turned near black. The Governor refused to let the man's friends cut him down, and he hung a full fortnight. One, Andres, I saw with these two eyes, and of the others I gained knowledge from those who were present at their executions."

"And after doing such terrible things the King granted him the commission to organize this expedition?"

"Andres, by the look of your beard you are no boy," said Alvar Nuñez. "Think! Pánfilo de Narvaez is a man who has powerful friends close to the King. And remember, it was the Governor who undertook the financing of this expedition. I have learned that kings look kindly on those who are willing to undertake ventures which, if successful, can only enrich the royal coffers, and if failures, do not drain the treasury of a single réal. Of such as Pánfilo de Narvaez the King only wants to hear favorable reports. And he who brings unfavorable ones is like as not to be punished for his pains."

"Andres," the comptroller laid his hand for a moment on my master's shoulder, "because I warn of your use of intemperate language does not mean that I too am not without a certain—ah—a certain concern for the safety of this expedition. My rank as comptroller places upon me a heavy burden. Only the Governor himself and Alvar Nuñez have greater responsibility."

"I thought that Friar Xuarez, as commissary, had—" my master failed to finish his sentence.

"Friar Xuarez ranks first in all matters of a spiritual consideration," the comptroller said the priest's name as if suffering from the asthma, "but in matters temporal, my friend, you or even the greenest ensign has a greater authority."

"Alonso is of course correct, Andres," said Alvar Nuñez carefully. "The good father can only advise, not order, in matters not related to the saving of souls."

"You are telling me nothing I do not already know." My master wiped his mouth roughly on the sleeve of his tunic. "But you have not said what you must also know to be true, that our honored Governor will not take a piss without first conferring with his commissary. So what matter if the friar's authority be not his officially—he has it, and that's enough for me."

"Priests who meddle . . . " the comptroller muttered, "and let one who has not taken orders try and interfere with their affairs; he'll have the entire Holy Brotherhood on his back before the day is out."

"It is not uncommon for those in high places to seek guidance in matters other than spiritual from their confessors," Alvar Nuñez said slowly. "More than a few great nations have been guided, if the truth be known, by priests, and some of them not badly."

"Then you approve of the commissary's influence on the Governor, Alvar Nuñez?" said my master.

"You did not hear me say that, Alonso. I only said there have been occasions when priestly influence on secular matters has, all in all, proved beneficial."

"And have there not been occasions, Alvar Nuñez, perhaps even greater in number," my master hesitated a moment, "when the converse has been true?"

"There are things, Andres, that are better left unsaid. I have learned, my friend, and at times to my cost, that prisons are not only built of stone and iron, but can be fashioned from that which escapes our mouths—if we fail in our task as jailers we risk being jailed."

"You have nothing to fear, Andres. from Alvar Nuñez Cabeza de Vaca or from me; but who knows who may be listening." I shrank deeper into the darkness. "The three of us may already be compromised." The comptroller laughed softly.

"We have said enough," Alvar Nuñez lowered his voice. "We understand each other's meanings. I for one will swear that I will not abdicate my authority as second-in-command to any other, be he priest, greybeard, learned bachelor or even tied by sanguineous bonds to the King. There have been mistakes, let us call them mistakes. I will take care that in all future decisions affecting the welfare of this expedition, the Governor, at the very least, first consults with me.

Without another word spoken, my master and the comptroller turned away and left Alvar Nuñez leaning against the bulkhead, his face tilted upward towards the sky.

I was comforted by this promise made by Alvar Nuñez and would have liked, had it been possible, to tell him of my loyalty. I watched the man and saw him pass his hand slowly over his face, then watched the hand as it tugged his beard.

"You may come out of the shadows, Estevan! No need to pretend not to be where for the past quarter of an hour I have known you to have been." I rose slowly, wondering if my ears had played me tricks. "You hear me right—we had been conversing less than five minutes when I descried your black body—it was that silver ring you wear on that leather thong around your neck which caught my eye." I cursed my vanity for not keeping the ring hidden under my shirt. "Come over here," he ordered.

I stepped out of the shadows into the moonlight. Then for a moment, fearing severe punishment, I considered striking the man with a marlin spike that lay close to my hand.

"Do you think, Estevan, if I intended you harm, I would have failed to draw the attention of the others to your presence?" I withdrew my hand. "It was for your protection I said nothing." Had there been a fire near I would have thrust the offending hand into it. "Even your master's affection would not have saved you, considering what was said."

Had I been another sort of man—not a slave—I would have kissed his hand.

"Come closer, where I can see your face," he said gently. I stepped closer, until we were not separated by the length of a short sword, and raised my eyes to his. Although I was by half a head the taller, I felt the shorter man.

"I have no doubt but that I can trust your discretion, Estevan." I nodded. "As payment for being privy to matters not intended for your ears, give me your thoughts on what you overheard." I shrugged my shoulders, not certain of his meaning. "The pig has already fallen into the pit—no need for pretense—your thoughts, black man, on what was said relating to the Governor."

"We are fortunate to have Alvar Nuñez Cabeza de Vaca as second-in-command," was my response.

"You are cautious, Moor," Alvar Nuñez spoke more to himself than to me. "How else should a slave be who would avoid brandings and whippings?"

"I have had a taste of lead-tipped leather. More than a taste."

"You have learned caution Estevanico. Now what of the men; how do they speak of the Governor?"

"They grumble. They call him 'whoreson.' They curse his mother. But I have never known soldiers not to curse. Whether there is a more serious meaning lying hidden in their curses, I cannot say. As slave, I must stay apart from the others."

"Your life is lonely, Négro." It was the first time I heard the word for black spoken in such a gentle way. "Separated by half the world from your home, alone, though amongst men always alone." I strained, but could not see the man's expression.

"If I knew loneliness, my captain," I spoke slowly, "if my

18

need was the nourishment of other men, I must have long since starved and died of my hunger."

"Have you not longed for the comfort of companions?"

"My longing I save for a joint of roasted meat, for a bellyful of wine, for a willing woman, for time enough to sleep."

"It is my belief we will find great quantities of gold, Estevan. Enough to fill our ships so they lie heavy in the water and we must then navigate with caution lest a sudden wind turn them over. And when we gain this gold, black man, you will not be denied a share equal to that granted every soldier. My rank permits me to swear that you will have sufficient to buy your freedom." I nodded, but did not answer.

III

For fifteen days we were stranded on the shoals called Canerreo. At the end of this time a high wind from the south raised such a quantity of water that the ships broke free, but not without great danger to their timbers, which were much weakened. Then, after escaping the shoals, we made for the port of Guaniguanico, where a storm overtook us and we were at one time, as great waves washed over the decks and wind ripped the sails, near being lost. At Cape Corrientes, which is on the southwest coast of Cuba, another storm hit: this one holding us in its grip three days, with every man praying for deliverance. Then, with God's help, having passed these dangerous places, we doubled Cape Anton and sailed with headwinds toward the great port of Havana, where we might secure provisions and repair the damages to our ships. We sailed to within twelve leagues of the city, when a wind came from the south which blew us away from land toward the coast of Florida.

Finally, on the twelfth day of April, 1528, a Tuesday, we came in sight of the land of Florida.

Two days we sailed along this coast, searching for a place where we might anchor safely, and on Holy Thursday we anchored in the mouth of a great bay, to which we gave the name Bahia de la Cruz, within sight of some habitations of Indians. So great was the excitement of the men that surely half, if not restrained, would have risked swimming the quarter league that separated us from the land, despite the fierce crocodiles known to abound in these waters. There were also sharks both white and blue, and other creatures so venomous that they need not bite to kill—the slightest touch being all that is required to bring death.

Although no attempt to land on the mainland was made that day, an expedition of some thirty men, of which number I was one, under the command of the comptroller, visited a nearby island. The island was small, no more than half a league across at its greatest width, and from its size we knew it could support no large number of inhabitants, yet the comptroller took care to choose men with a sufficient reputation for bravery, and ordered each to arm himself either with crossbow or arquebus. Although these precautions were wise, we had no need for our weapons, but we did make good use of a quantity of trinkets we also carried. These were traded for fish and venison with the Indians inhabiting that island, who, by their smiles and gestures showed their satisfaction—which was no greater than ours, for we had not known the taste of fresh meat in more than a month.

Of the two-score Indians there, I counted only five of fighting age, yet they did not appear afraid of us. I wondered at that. Perhaps it was the quiet manner of our disembarking. But the

20

next morning when Governor Narvaez landed a portion of the expedition on the mainland, the Indians all fled and left their village deserted.

Again, I was one of the group of men selected to go ashore. But this time we heralded our landing with trumpet blasts and long drum rolls. Not an Indian remained in that village which, from its appearance, must have served as habitation for more than five hundred. The principal building, around which the others clustered, was large enough to hold three hundred people. And this was not a building the like of which even the proudest city in all of Spain need be ashamed of for it was carefully made of great fire-hardened logs.

That first night spent on the land of Florida, we had little chance to sleep. Fear that the vanished Indians might suddenly appear out of the swampy forest caused a double watch to be set. A dozen, with faces painted red and yellow, did show themselves just before sunrise. These stayed close to the forest and waved clubs fitted with rows of sharpened flints, as they shouted and pointed their arrows at us, which, however, they took care not to notch to bowstring. The discharge of an arquebus caused them to disappear.

The second morning, those who had not yet landed came ashore and brought with them the horses, reduced in number by accident and disease from eighty to forty-two.

Another band of armed and painted Indians showed themselves, and these, Friar Xuarez, flanked by half a hundred men, a great cross in his hand, approached. Again they disappeared, but not before several had thrown their flint-armed clubs, which, however, fell harmless a dozen paces short. That second day was given to raising the royal banner, as Governor Narvaez took possession of the land for the King, then we went into camp, occupying those structures needed for shelter; the rest we pulled down for lumber.

On the third morning in the land of Florida, I became acquainted with one with whom I was destined to share a portion of my life for eight years and more, although I could not have had even a suspicion of this at the time.

A band of forty, led by the Governor, had left to explore to the north, also to seek fresh meat and gain information from the Indians as to cities that might be found in the interior. Those who remained constructed temporary fortifications, or made short forays of no more than a league into the swampy forests to the east and south. I was sharpening the ends of some felled trees with a great doublebladed axe, when Captain Alonso del Castillo, whose face I knew but with whom I had never spoke, ordered me to take my axe and follow him.

Without turning his head to see if I followed, he pushed into the tangled forest, slashing with his short sword at the vines that blocked his way. Of all the captains, Alonso del Castillo was the youngest, not having reached his twenty-third year. Yet it was said he had fought in a dozen great battles. And had those vines been Turks he must have, in that hour he slashed through the forest, dispatched enough to guarantee to Spain a generation of peace. Only when a tree too thick for his sword stopped his progress did he stand aside and motion me to go at it with my axe.

Of all the officers, Captain Alonso del Castillo was the tallest, and in all the company without exception he was the fairest, though had Alvar Nuñez not suffered the break to his nose and the loss of certain teeth, some might have judged him equally fair. But despite his long blond hair and fine features, Captain Castillo was not an easy man. He never smiled, and at times laid a heavy hand on those under his command.

For that first hour, as we cut our way into the forest, he did not speak. Grunts and quick gestures were my only orders, and I had grown so used to his silent ways that my axe slipped and struck a stone when I heard his voice. "Can you smell out fresh water, Négro?" he asked. I did not understand. "We want fresh water—a spring; which way?" I shook my head. He

22

passed his hand over his eyes, a gesture I would come to know well. "I have often heard it said: black Moors and camels can smell fresh water."

"I have known camels to find water a league and more away," I carefully answered. The captain studied my face as I spoke. "I have tasted the water," I motioned to the rear in the direction of our camp, "and would gladly use the power of divination if I had it—for that stuff is sour and tastes of piss."

"It will give the men the fever," the captain muttered. "Perhaps if you tried, Moor," he said slowly, touching my shoulder gently with the flat of his sword. "I never knew I had the gift of singing until called upon a certain night in Granada . . . a man often is unaware of even his greatest gift." A frown that I had never known to be absent from the captain's face suddenly lifted. "Take your time. Sniff the air. It is said there is always a spring of fresh water in a swamp."

Seeing no harm in trying, and judging the captain's patience to be a fragile thing, I wiped my dripping face, tipped back my head and breathed in with loud sniffs. The captain passed his hand across his eyes again and raised his eyebrows; I shrugged, turned a quarter way around and breathed again. The air was heavy with rotting vegetation and with an odor not unlike that of a marketplace where meat and cheese are sold. To my nose, all directions stank the same, but to satisfy the captain, I pointed east, "I cannot know with any certainty," I offered, but he waved me silent and started slashing with renewed vigor.

Another hour we struggled, making slow progress, for the direction I had chosen was a tangle of vines and creepers, with twisted trees whose gnarled branches intertwined with one another so that I must use my axe without relief. Thorns pierced our skins, and liver-colored leeches dropped from the leaves onto our arms and necks so that I must pluck them from the captain and he from me, for their bite was painless and, if undisturbed, they quickly swelled with blood. And yet the cap-

23

tain would not abate his struggle. I do not doubt but that the man would have gone on surely another hour in this way if we had not broken through the wall of vegetation.

A pool, green and still, not more than two-score paces at its greatest width, lay hidden in that forest. So suddenly did we come upon it, for a tangle of vines and leaves guarded it, that we came near pitching headlong into the thick, black ooze bordering that strange water. Not a ripple, not a bubble showed on its slimy surface. The twisted trees that hung over it cast no image, only shadows. And the water, by its stillness and dark green color, told of its poisonous nature. "If this is the quality of your gift of divination, Négro . . ." the captain did not complete his statement.

For a time we stood there, staring down, trying to peer into the depths of those dark green waters. A vile, thick-bodied snake with a mouth white as milk, wriggled through the ooze, slipped soundlessly into the pool and sank from sight.

"How deep?" the captain reached out his sword until its point just touched the water. I could not know, so I shook my head. "A man could fall in, black man, and sink down and down."

"A man could fall from a ship into the ocean," I answered, but I understood his meaning.

"A hundred times would I rather fall into the wildest ocean on the darkest night than . . ." he touched the water with his sword again.

"It is an ugly place," I said slowly.

"A place best not viewed by Christian eyes," was his muttered reply. "Would that we had not found it," but he made no move to turn away. "From such a sink the devil himself might rise," he lowered his voice and made the sign of the cross, "rise up and drag a man down," he whispered, "down into his reeking realm." Still he made no move to leave. "A man who would venture into that pool, Estevan, a man who would dare swim its width—" Alonso del Castillo's face took on a strange and crafty

24

look. "Would not such a man be counted amongst the very bravest?"

"There are snakes in those waters, my captain," I turned my face to the man. "Snakes and, if my guess be true, worse than snakes."

"There can be no bravery where there is no danger, Négro. And what does a man have if he has not bravery?"

The captain's words and, more than his words, the expression on his face, caused me growing uneasiness, and I took a firmer hold of the handle of my axe.

"If a man dare call himself a man, black man, he must prove it when he has the chance, lest he be mocked and called 'woman.' "

I stepped back a full pace and muttered again of snakes and other poisonous creatures that swam in that stinking sump. It had been many years since any had tried to test Estevan, and I determined that it would cost the captain dear if he went on.

But I did not know my man, for his challenge was not for me.

Laying his sword at the foot of a tree, kneeling and saying a prayer to the Blessed Mother Mary, then stripping off his pants and jerkin, the captain plunged into the sink. I made as if to stop him, but he waved me back and struck out for the other side.

My stomach retched as if the pool's green slime had been forced into my throat and my skin grew cold as if a dozen loathsome adders had wrapped around me.

He rose up from across the pool, dripping slime, spat, turned, then plunged in a second time, churning the water with mighty kicks.

Ropes of green ooze hung from his hair and clung to his body as he climbed from the pool. A dozen swelling leeches sucked his blood; black muck stained his hands and feet, and he stank of rot.

We sat together on a flat stone after I had plucked off the

leeches and wiped away the slime. Odorous matter filled his ears and gummed his lashes, which I removed with a coarse cloth I carried for wiping sweat. We sat for a time without talking. The pool had grown still again, but in the silence I could hear soft sucking sounds. The captain pressed his arms down hard on his thighs to keep his limbs from shaking. Had I not been slave and he captain, I would have covered his shoulders with my shirt.

"Speak of this, Moor," Alonso del Castillo said carefully, as he pointed at the water, "and you make an enemy; one whose blood is known to heat with little fuel. Breathe so much as a single word to any man and I swear to cool my choler with your liver."

"I saw nothing, my captain." As I spoke, I turned my eyes back to the water. "Only a poisonous sump inhabited by snakes, by whose banks we rested."

"A sump discovered by a black Moor's sniffing." A smile for the first time softened the man's features. "Pity it is we do not have the services of a camel, or of a Moor properly trained. We must drink piss-tainted water yet another day, I think, and risk the fever."

Weeks later as we struggled northward, each time I chanced to meet the captain, no matter where we met, he would raise his head, sniff the air, and wink.

But I did not see him again for nearly half a month after our day together. For Governor Narvaez returned the next morning with tales of a great bay to the north, and of many Indian villages, and Captain Castillo, together with my master, Andres Dorantes, and more than fifty others, joined the Governor's company for further exploration.

Determined to go beyond the great bay this time and explore inland, they again set out for the north. But before they left the Governor dispatched the brigantine up the coast to seek a certain port the existence of which the pilot Miruelo said he knew, but not its exact location. That donkey when closely questioned by various captains as to where we were, admitted he did not know. Yet even so, the Governor's belief in the man was not shaken. The Governor's company stayed gone some ten or twelve days, but that brigantine we never saw again.

IV

Until the second expedition returned, those of us who remained in camp had an easy time. No one grew fat, for the comptroller, who had command, was careful of the provisions, and we could snare no meat. But there was plenty of fish, and if a man had patience and sat with a hook and line for an hour he could find a tasty supper.

Except for the heat, which grew worse each day, no one had reason to complain. The water, although perfumed in such a way as to bring oaths and wry faces, did not cause the fever. If Indians still lurked in the surrounding forests, they did not show themselves. So peaceful grew our stay in camp that after a week of ease I made my way again through the swampy forest to the pool.

Why I was drawn to that pestilential place I do not know. A hunger to escape the jabber of the others was my excuse, but I could have wandered half a league north or south along the shore and found sufficient peace.

The same rock on which I sat with the young captain again served me as a seat. Some severed vines and broken branches were the only traces of our visit, and I knew that in another week or two in this wet forest these traces would be gone. "And what traces of Estevan will remain after he is gone?" I asked myself. "There is none to mourn his passing. No wife. No son. If there are other ones—parents, sisters, brothers, they must have done their mourning years ago after the Portuguese sacked our town and they found me gone. 'Drowned and washed to sea, or killed in the fighting and dragged into the desert by jackals,' they must have thought. Of those who still live, do any still say my name?" I wondered. "Will I die a slave?" I asked the still, green waters of the pool. "Must I die here in Florida?" My answer was the whine of mosquitos circling about my head. "And when Estevan is dead, what difference will it make?" I stared into the pool, and could see my body lying somewhere in a swamp, clusters of insects clinging to my face and limbs. Then I remembered certain slaves who escaped their condition by seeking death.

Had I not sworn a great oath the day the Portuguese dragged me from my home, I too might have sought escape through death. More than eighty had been trampled at the city gates where I fought with a score of other ill-armed youths against well-armed invaders. A wall of corpses served us as a shield; dead men defending the living. And in that wall was the Jew, Jacob, in death a friend as he had been in life. Ten minutes was all we stayed the rush of the Portuguese fighting with club and knife against broadsword and iron mace. But those ten minutes allowed hundreds to escape.

Of that score of youths, only four survived the battle at the gate, and I alone was left unwounded. The three with wounds, fair-skinned boys, were taken to a tree where their throats were cut and then hanged up by their heels as a warning. But I was judged to be of a certain value if sold as a slave, so they withheld the knife. And as I was dragged down to their ships, tied by neck and wrist to a dozen others, I swore a great oath. An oath to live, to never forget what had happened that day; an oath to remember my teacher, Jacob, that wall of trampled bodies, the three who had been butchered. . . .

That first year as a slave, a dozen times I yearned for death;

the second year, three, perhaps four times my mind turned to thoughts of this dark freedom. Then, one more time, in my third year, after I suffered a branding on my back. And in the years that followed, as memories of my earlier life grew dim, I had no more thoughts of death, and nearly forgot the great oath I had taken.

Yet, strangely, it was at that pool that thoughts of seeking death returned to tempt me. "Sink into the cool waters, let it end," my thoughts whispered.

I searched the surface of the pool for the movement of the snake. I tried to descry the thick, grey body with milk-white mouth along the bank or in the grasses. I knew a single view of that loathsome creature must repel me from those waters. I asked help that I might find the snake before being drawn down into the dark which is its home.

"You stand at the gates of Hell, Estevan!" my mind shouted. "Descend and you will be in the realm of serpents."

For some time I struggled to free myself, begging help from He who it is said is always present. Then, suddenly, this hunger for death was gone. And I looked down and saw a snake curled in the place my feet must first have touched, had I left the stone and started for the water.

V

The expedition headed by Governor Narvaez returned after ten days. And although they had endured various sufferings from the heat and from leeches and insects, none had died, so there was much joy at their return.

I attended my master. The skin on his feet had cracked, and I cleansed them and bound them with strips torn from an old tunic. Then, after resting for a time and after making a good supper of a fat fish I hooked that morning, he joined a small company of men gathered around a smoking fire.

As protection from the swarming mosquitos; we all sat close to the fire, eyes streaming, sweat dripping from our skins. Of the eight or ten gathered there, none had been a part of the expedition. Thus all were eager to hear my master's account.

Andres Dorantes was never one to speak hesitantly or to guard too carefully against giving offense. He was loved by most for his easy friendship, but there were some whose spleen engorged at his blunt words, and he had known his share of challenges. Yet that night he spoke softly, choosing each word with care.

"We were fortunate to lose no men," were his first words. "We captured a great king of the Indians, one who held authority over a dozen villages. But before the Governor would allow his release, he must lop his ears and crop his nose. None understood his language, but from his eyes I know that one will seek an awful vengeance."

"What was his crime?" asked one of the men.

"A crime for a professing Christian, but no crime for a heathen," my master said so softly all leaned close to hear. "He was punished for practicing pagan ways—how should he know the ways of Christians?

"Four Indians we had captured guided us to their village, where we found Spanish-made boxes, each one containing an Indian corpse covered by a painted deer-hide. Friar Xuarez, after consultation with the Governor and after a heated exchange with Alvar Nuñez, ordered the boxes and their contents burned. Later, when we surprised their king, whom we easily captured after a little skirmish, the Governor tried to question him as to where the boxes had been found, and why the corpses, instead of being buried, were preserved in such an idolatrous fashion. Understanding the question about the boxes, the king

30

drew a picture of a vessel we judged to have been lost in the bay, but about the corpses he said nothing.

"Several times I saw Alvar Nuñez and the Governor in a heated exchange; they took care to stay out of earshot, but from their purple faces I knew of their anger. The Governor's blind eye twisted tight until it resembled nothing so much as a withered prune, and the knuckles on both his hands grew white. Half the afternoon they argued, the day the Indian king was to be meted his punishment, then while the deed was being done Alvar Nuñez sat away from the others, his head resting in his hands.

"After treating their king in such a fashion, each hour as we continued northward I expected to be met with a swarm of spears and arrows; but we did not see another one of that nation of Indians on our journey.

"While still in their village, we learned that far inland was a province called Apalachen, where there was plenty of everything we desired, including gold. We had found a gold tinklet in their village, and we gave them to understand that this was the chiefest object of our search.

"With several Indians as guides, we traveled northward twelve more leagues but our provisions running short we then turned back. Why the subjects of that Indian king we had mutilated did not attack us, I do not know. And I was not alone in my belief we must be attacked. The other captains kept their swords unsheathed, and their matches lit. Perhaps it is that we are under Divine protection."

Before leaving the fire, my master again mentioned the bad blood that flowed between Alvar Nuñez and the Governor, and predicted that it would not be long before we saw new evidence of their rancor.

Preparations for abandoning camp and exploring the interior having begun, Governor Narvaez called a council of his chief men. Although only officers joined in that council, not the least soldier was unaware of its nature or of the matters discussed. For there was much shouting and oath-taking, with no effort made for so much as a show of secrecy.

After the council gathered, the Governor declared his intention of breaking contact with the ships and marching inland. The ships, meanwhile, were to sail north along the coast to the harbor of Pánuco, [Veracruz] which the pilot Miruelo had assured him was no more than ten or fifteen leagues away.

"The same Miruelo who guided us so expertly through the shoals they call Canarreo?" Alvar Nuñez asked. The Governor's face reddened. "The same Miruelo who, when carefully questioned before departing with the brigantine, admitted he did not exactly know where we were?" The Governor's breathing quickened. "Will the life of every man in this company again be risked because of belief in the whoreson, Miruelo?"

"Do you say I risk the life of every man in this company, Alvar Nuñez Cabeza de Vaca?" the Governor asked in a rising voice. "Do you have certain charges you wish to make?" Alvar Nuñez turned his face away.

"We have delayed this expedition long enough!" the Governor shouted. "This is no company of nuns, no, nor a gathering of Jew-merchants, greedy to protect their profits. We are soldiers, that must take risks lest we gain the name of 'woman' or even 'Jew' and lose our honor." Many of the officers nodded at the Governor's words.

"Risks, yes, but to foolishly court disaster?" said Alvar Nuñez. "This expedition has suffered enough. Have you forgotten the two ships lost in the storm at the port of Trinidad?" The Governor's hand dropped to the hilt of his sword. "And, if my memory serves me, there were certain warnings given then, about the dangers of that place." Although all knew of the truth of these words, none dared to nod.

"A storm is the will of God!" the Governor forced the words out from between his whitened lips. "A half a year's delay that cost us. And now you preach for more delay."

"You misread my words, Pánfilo, I do not ask delay, only caution. Let us sail with our ships until a harbor held by Spaniards is reached—south rather than north as suggested by that whoreson Miruelo—then, knowing our ships to be safe, where we can find them upon our return, we can strike out for the interior."

"I do not misread your words! Your 'caution' if followed will surely cost us weeks, Alvar Nuñez. Weeks sailing *away* from Pánuco, my friend. Weeks which, if lost, might serve as sufficient opportunity for the Indians of Apalachen to hide their gold. For they, in time, must learn of our coming from those we already met." An uneasy murmuring rose from the assembled officers.

"I am less concerned that the Indians we met will give intelligence of our coming to the inhabitants of Apalachen than I am that these same Indians will prepare such a greeting for us, for the way we entertained their king, that ten-score good Castilian women must needs wear widow's weeds."

"Do you find fault with the way I served that pagan, Alvar Nuñez? Would you have had me heap honors on his head and encourage his idolatrous ways? Friar Xuarez, take note of this one's words; the Holy Brotherhood will, I am certain, be interested in his answer."

"What is past is past," Alvar Nuñez muttered. "I am no theologian, but to expect a pagan to behave other than as a pagan. . . ." He lowered his voice so his words were lost.

"Harsh methods gain respect!" the Governor shouted. "Soft ways are signs of weakness, and weakness invites attack. We have nothing to fear from the Indians; they know our strength—none dared attack us. Not one will venture within ten leagues of us when we travel through their land again. And that I can promise."

"If I had been shaved in such a wise as was their king—the world would not be wide enough . . ." Alvar Nuñez muttered as he shrugged his shoulders. "I pray that you are right, Pánfilo. But even if the Indians do not attack we face a greater danger—starvation. There is less than a pound of bacon for each man and no more than two pounds of bisquit."

"Trust me to learn the location of the Indian's granaries as we travel," laughed the Governor. "And also the places where they store their dried venison. I have learned methods of persuasion.

"Are there others who share Alvar Nuñez's caution?" the Governor turned to the assembled officers with a smile that did not reach his eyes. "Am I alone in my belief that we should depart this day; that the ships can be safely dispatched northward to seek port as we explore in the same direction, not venturing too far inland?"

For a full minute there was no answer. Though many had smiled and nodded as the Governor spoke, some showed doubt in the tightness of their mouths and in their silence. It was Alonso Enriquez who broke the silence.

"We are strangers in a strange and savage land, my Governor. We are uncertain in which direction lies the port of Pánuco, and our only chance of again seeing Christian lands is our ships. We do not know the character of this country. But we do know that the forests are filled with barbarians who have reason to take umbrage at our coming. And we are short of provisions. To venture inland away from our ships. . . ."

"Is it that you are afraid of taking a soldier's risk, Alonso?" the Governor interrupted. "If, instead of exploring, this company was about to enter battle, would you insist we wait until we outnumber the enemy ten to one? Would you have our women plead with their generals to surrender? Would you ask the Pope for intercession? Would you make an offer to buy the victory with a sack of gold?" Most of the soldiers snickered.

"I wish to speak to this matter!" Friar Xuarez raised his wooden cross and took a place alongside the Governor. "I am no soldier," his voice rumbled, and spittle showed on his lips, "I have no weapon; only this!" He pressed the cross to his forehead until the skin grew white. "And I wear no armor." He pulled open his habit, exposing his stained neck around which hung a heavy rosary. "My only protection is the sweet Jesu. But I do not hesitate to follow my Governor. And consider this," the friar softened his voice, "although two expeditions have already ventured into the forest, we have not lost a single man; yet while aboard our ships we suffered adversities. To again embark would be to taunt the Almighty and to risk new storms and the loss of more men." Except for the comptroller, Alvar Nuñez and half a dozen others, all the officers nodded in agreement.

Ignoring the sullenness of the comptroller, who was pulling on his lower lip, the Governor turned to Alvar Nuñez and said in a voice loud enough for all to hear, "Since you so much discourage this expedition, Alvar Nuñez, and since you fear entering the land—I place in your command all the ships and their crews. Sail north, form a settlement at the port of Pánuco, and wait for our arrival."

Alvar Nuñez's face turned white. Twice he opened his mouth to reply, and twice he closed it as he forced his throat free of phlegm. "I must excuse myself from accepting your most gracious offer." His voice whistled and rattled as he spoke. "In another place, at another time—in Spain, in Mexico—such an offer made in such a wise I must take as a challenge to my name and manhood, and must answer in the manner of an hidalgo. But here, in this wild place, my rank as second-in-command compels me not to seek the meaning behind your offer."

"You mistake my meaning, Alvar Nuñez," the Governor said carefully. "I know well enough of your bravery, we differ on a certain matter, that is all. And there is no other to whom I can as confidently entrust the ships. I do not command you to take them; but, knowing how important their safety is to this expedition, I beg you to consider my offer."

"Again I must excuse myself, Pánfilo!"

"Knowing that I mean no disparagement by my offer, my

friend, why do you still refuse?" No penitential pilgrim seeking pardon from the Pope ever sounded more sincere than did Governor Narvaez as he asked this question.

"I reject the responsibility of commanding the ships," Alvar Nuñez chose his words carefully, "because I know that, should this expedition separate from them there will be no finding them again; this I know from the slender outfit we have for entering the country. And rather than have it said that I opposed the invasion and remained behind from timidity and thus my courage be called in question, I prefer to risk my life than put my honor in such a position."

The Governor, in a most serious manner, continued his importuning for many minutes, urging others to reason with Alvar Nuñez. Thus one, and then another, began to entreat him to reconsider—whether they were sincere in their entreaties or were making sport I cannot know. But all fell silent when Alvar Nuñez threatened to judge any further words on the matter as a challenge to his honor, and to respond in a way appropriate to such a challenge.

It was then decided that an Alçalde, whose name was Caravallo, should be lieutenant in charge of ships, and preparations for departure were begun.

The date of this occurrence was Saturday, the first of May—the beginning of an expedition that, almost to the day, would end eight years later.

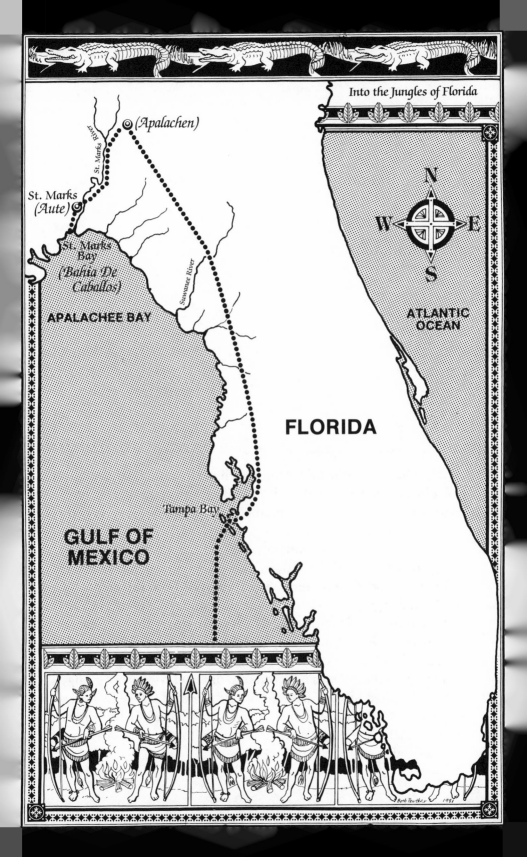

Into the Jungles of Florida

(Apalachen)

St. Marks River

St. Marks
(Aute)

St. Marks
Bay
(Bahía De
Caballos)

APALACHEE BAY

Suwanee River

N
W E
S

ATLANTIC
OCEAN

FLORIDA

Tampa Bay

GULF OF
MEXICO

VI

The men gathered for the march northward. Of those who had sailed from Cuba, three hundred were to make the journey; the rest, a hundred men, remained with the ships together with their crews.

The Governor, mounted and in full armor, flanked by his captains and a dozen hidalgos likewise mounted and arrayed, hesitated for some minutes. Sweat dripped from the men, and black, stinging flies found their way under helmets and between shirts and moist backs. Several times the Governor slapped at his neck and mopped the perspiration on his face, yet still he hesitated. Twice he opened his mouth and rose up in his stirrups as if to shout a final order to those who were not going, then lowered himself without uttering a word. Once he beckoned to Caravallo, the lieutenant in command of the ships, then, as the lieutenant made as if to come forward, he shook his head and waved the man back.

Friar Juan de Palos, the vice-commissary, his head bowed, his hands clasping the shaft of a great cross, was on his knees. He rose to his feet as the order to march was given, and blessed the men with drops of holy water as they passed.

The darkness of the forest, made still darker by contrast with the white sand and burning sun left behind, caused the men to fall silent. It was as if a giant hand had stopped their mouths. Every man had thoughts of the Indians as his eyes searched into the forest. For hours, except for short commands whispered and relayed in whispers from man to man, the only sounds from that company of three hundred marching men were muffled footfalls, an occasional crack of a twig, and the creak of saddles and leather fittings. Even the horses had ceased their whinnying.

A sudden roar, louder than that of a hunting lion, caused all the men to ready their weapons. A second roar, followed by a loud report, was answered by half a dozen discharging their arquebuses into the forest. A third roar, followed by two reports, caused a general firing of weapons and the grouping of men into fighting units.

After the echo of the last gun died away, the forest again fell silent. There were no more roars, and no more reports. When a sufficient time had passed, a company armed with arquebus was chosen to explore in the direction from which the sound had come.

A swamp inhabited by great lizards was discovered by the company before a half an hour. Some who had seen pictures in the Bestiary of the fierce crocodile of the Nile recognized the scaly, loathsome creatures they found crawling in that bog. It was their rutting season, and even as the soldiers watched, two of the larger reptiles came at each other uttering savage roars then striking the mud with their flat tails, producing a sound indistinguishable from that of a small cannon.

Although there was some relief when the company returned with the intelligence that the enemy were beasts, no one was easy. The thought of creatures with gaping mouths filled with rows of sharp teeth crawling through these forests caused much distress, so that, when the march resumed, eyes not only searched into the forest, but also along the ground.

A single bite of bacon, chewed slowly, an ash-cake of flour and water baked hard, was all the supper any man had that night; then, excepting the guards, each, despite the heat, rolled into his blanket seeking protection from the insects, and in moments was asleep.

Soft moans and whimpers rose from the sleeping men. When one or another thrashed and cried out, a guard would come and shake the man into quiet wakefulness. And from the Governor, his one eye fixed unblinking on the fire, came a low mutter. The glow reflecting off his mail shirt caused him to appear covered with a scaly skin. This, and the shadows of the trees and his pointed helmet, changed the appearance of the man into that of a reptile risen from the earth, a reptile staring man-like into the smouldering fire. An endless series of curses was what he muttered—against the heat and insects; the lizards and leeches; curses against the Indians lurking in the forest; against storms and shoals; curses, more softly uttered but with greater venom, against those who had opposed him.

On a far side of the camp, from amongst the sleeping men, Friar Xuarez arose, cast aside his blanket, and advanced carefully toward the Governor. It was almost as if he had learned the ways of silent tread from the Indians, for he moved soundlessly, as did I in the shadows, not a twig or a leaf disturbed. "You do not sleep, my Governor?" were his first words as the other raised his head. "The cares of the expedition lie heavily on your heart?" he went on, his words coming from the deep of his chest. "If you will not sleep, in time the vexations will cause your bile to rise and bring a fever to your brain."

"I will have time and enough to sleep when I am tumbled beneath a grass blanket and tucked in with a spade."

"May the Almighty grant that you do not know such a

sleep for yet half a hundred years, and then that your stay in purgation be a short one."

"Half a hundred years will bring me close to ninety, my good friar. Cut your blessing in half; a score, or twenty-five more years will do. I have no wish to hobble on three legs, my skin flapping on my bones, toothless with no wench willing to warm my shrunk flesh with bosom and belly."

"A man is never too old if he has gold," Friar Xuarez said with a soft laugh. "And you will have enough gold ducats, Pánfilo."

"And the Church will have her share, I promise you, a share equal to that given the King."

"Would that Spain had a thousand more like you, Pánfilo—the Holy Inquisition must then fall into idleness, for how should they find work to do?"

". . . equal to that given the King, I promise you."

"If needless delay does not cause the treasure to be lost, Pánfilo, even the heathen savage can learn the value of yellow metal if he is told."

"And who is to know what Frenchman or pirate might at this very moment be hunting gold in these forests, Father!"

"Or what Indians, Pánfilo, what Indians learning of our interest from our eager questions are headed toward Apalachen to secure for their own use the treasure we seek."

"I will drive the men, there will be no delays." The Governor drew his dagger and slashed through the flames. "If any dare complain, I'll dock their ears—I will not be cheated after all I have already risked."

"Will you turn inland, my Governor, or follow the line of the coast? Turning inland may save us days of travel."

"There are greater dangers if we turn inland," the Governor answered slowly. "Away from the coast we may have our retreat cut off by Indians; and our provisions are short, Father Xuarez. Holding to the coast we can, if need be, snare fish and find clams and oysters."

"Indians are not the danger, Pánfilo de Narvaez. They will retreat in terror when they see our horses and hear the discharge of a single gun. Ten Indians, naked, with simple bows and arrows, are no match for one armed and armored Spaniard. Ten, did I say? Twenty would be a fairer number. No, my friend, the danger is not from Indians. And as to provisions, I will risk my chance of salvation if game does not abound in the interior."

"Indians are not the danger. . . . Behind your words I hear a warning." The Governor leaned toward the friar, who was still standing. "Although no priest, I know how to keep a secret." The priest lowered himself to the ground next to the Governor, so that shoulder pressed against shoulder.

"You are well equipped to deal with the hazards you may meet in the forest, Pánfilo," the friar whispered. "The danger of which I speak you carry in your company." The Governor tested the tip of his dagger with his thumb, then suddenly drove it into a log, where the weapon quivered for a moment then was still. "Professing Christians it is that needs worry you, Pánfilo, not unbaptized barbarians . . . "

"Go on, Father, say their names, I want their names."

"Names, Pánfilo? Do you not still have the sight of one eye? Can you not see? And your ears, are they so stuffed with thoughts of gold you cannot hear? How should it be that I, a friar absorbed in prayer, one whose thoughts are turned constantly towards the One who shed His blood for our sins and toward His Blessed Mother, how can it be that one like me knows of matters unknown to a commander of an expedition whose business it is to know?"

"I demand their names, Father Juan, their names and whatever proofs you have!"

"Proof, my Governor, I cannot give you; that you will obtain in time. But as to names: who was it that accused you of risking the welfare of this expedition? Who was it that defied you before all the other officers? And who was it that rushed to

42

that one's support and mocked you with veiled words—words, my Governor, everyone understood?"

"I will have them watched day and night," the Governor hissed.

"And did you not notice, Pánfilo, that the assessor, Alonso de Solis, stayed glum and scarcely nodded with the others, and that pretty, young captain, Alonso del Castillo, I did not see him respond with overmuch enthusiasm at your plans, nor did our notary, Hieronymo Alainz. And if my eyes serve me right, Juan Velazquez and Soto Mayor both showed false smiles; and all of these have friends, my Governor."

"If they think to betray me or slow this expedition, they misjudge their man. I'll make leggings for the horses from their skins. I'll . . ."

"Alvar Nuñez, your second-in-command?"

"Even he! Let me find a single piece of proof and I'll peel him with these two hands. Peel him and send his head back to the King with the proofs writ on parchment stuck in his mouth!"

Friar Xuarez raised his head and pulled his cowl back; the fire outlined his swollen nose and overhanging brow. Then he slowly rubbed his tonsure with the flat of his hand. "If asked by one whose authority it is to know, what is the principal fault of Pánfilo de Narvaez, I must reply, Excessive gentleness. My friend, you allow others to take advantage of you too easily; being a soldier is a stern business."

"How well I know the truth of your words, Father Xuarez. It is a defect of character I must have gained from my mother; for no sterner man than my father ever drew breath. Again and again I allow my heart to overwhelm my head."

"Beware, lest your tender heart cost your head, Pánfilo de Narvaez."

"One eye it has already cost me. One eye, two years' imprisonment, and the disgrace of appearing before the King and all his court weighted with chains. . . . If, instead of trying to

43

persuade, of showing compassion in respect for his past conquests, I had savagely attacked Hernan Cortez, ordering all my men to do their worst, killing him if I must; I would have a different tale to tell this night—that, and the sight of this useless eye."

"It is a cruel world we live in, Pánfilo. The tender are crushed. Leave compassion to the women. The stone breaks the pot, the hammer breaks the stone, and the anvil in time destroys the hammer. Be the anvil, my friend.

"I, who will not touch a sword, whose only weapon is the sacred Cross, have fought against my flesh and heart since a youth, that I may conquer souls for our Blessed Savior. These legs, Pánfilo," the friar pulled up his habit, exposing limbs deeply pitted and shiny with ridged scars, "these legs I have whipped and gouged ten-score times until they bled like the tortured limbs of our Savior, that they might never falter as they walked His path. And these arms," the friar pulled back his sleeves, showing arms crossed with purple scars, "a hundred times have I pierced them with bodkin—as the cruel hooks pierced the gentle hands of the sweet Jesu; pierced them so that they may never tremble as they struggle with Satan for a sinner's soul. I have fought my flesh and I have fought my heart, and yet must still do battle. A thousand nights I knelt naked in my cell, rejoicing that a cold wind blew through the open window. A thousand nights I scourged my flesh and prayed for my Savior to show Himself that I might grovel at His feet; that I might cleanse His wounds with my tongue; that I might kiss and worship the place where His feet should touch."

As he spoke, the friar's voice grew louder, until several of the sleeping men began to stir. The motion caused the friar to fall silent. He sat for a time next to the Governor, staring into the fire. Then he rose and with a muttered, "Courage, Pánfilo," turned for a moment so the light of the fire fell full on his face, and then walked away.

44

VII

The company turned inland, and for three days we traveled without event. Despite the great heat, little rest was allowed the men while there was yet light enough to guide us through the thick forest. No living creatures appeared that might be fit for food, only lizards, leeches, a plague of insects and, at night, furry bats. The fourth day an event occurred to which Friar Juan de Palos, who was a witness, gave the name: a miracle.

The company was moving through a place less thickly wooded but rutted with deep gullies choked with thorny vegetation. Those afoot, despite fatigue, for it was late afternoon, to save themselves injury stayed alert. But the mounted men, trusting their horses to find a safe way, were less alert. Without warning, a horse suddenly reared up and tossed its rider, an officer named Juan Velazquez, into a gully where he landed face down, his arms and legs spread wide. Several rushed to the man's aid, but pulled back in terror—the arroyo was alive with hissing, venomous snakes, whose thrashing tails, tipped with rings of bone, sounded the leper's rattle. Slowly the officer raised himself to his knees, blood dripping from scores of wounds on his face and hands. Then, taking hold of a lowered rope, he allowed himself to be pulled free while all around him snakes hissed and thrashed, their rattle chilling the blood of all who were near.

Which punctures were made by fangs, which by thorns, no one could know—the man was a mass of wounds. The last rites performed by Friar Palos, we waited for him to expire. But still he did not die. The Governor rode up, a stern look on his face, then turned away when he saw the man. A dozen mounted men he left with that wounded officer with orders to bury him as soon as he should die, then hurry forward.

Two hours later, thirteen mounted men rode up as we were settling into camp. Although Juan Velazquez was sorely wounded, his face and hands resembling those of a victim of the plague, although pale from loss of blood and tortured by the insects crawling on his torn flesh, he was much alive, and greeted his wondering friends with loud laughter, while beating his horse's flank with his leather hat.

Had the venom for some reason been rendered impotent in his blood? "A miracle! A miracle!" Friar Palos kept shouting, waving his cross over the injured man. And the men, despite the hunger that was beginning to gnaw, celebrated with the little wine that could still be found. Scores came up and stared at the wounded man, then wet their fingers in the drops of blood that besprinkled the ground and crossed themselves.

"We have the Almighty's favor!" Friar Xuarez announced after he had examined the officer. "We are under His special protection—one who should by all rights be dead lives, and each minute grows stronger." And his words spread from man to man, until all had forgotten fatigue and hunger and were filled with great joy.

By the seventh day of our journey, all the men were racked with hunger; not one had a crumb of bisquit or a bite of bacon left. Some chewed bark and red berries which made them retch. Strips of deer hide were boiled for their flavor. The starched ruffles some hidalgos still carried were rendered for their sustenance. Many roasted insects for their fat. No food was too lowly even for the highest officers.

That day, a certain slave of Soto Mayor, learning somehow

of a shred of dry venison hid in Captain Juan Pantoja's pack, during the time taken for relief of natural urgings, thinking himself unobserved, extracted the morsel, bit off half, then ran to find his master with the uneaten portion. Captain Pantoja's armorer, who was relieving himself behind a bush, saw the theft, gave chase, and felled the slave before fifty paces with a stone.

When Soto Mayor came up he found his slave trussed like a slaughter pig; a fire to heat the staunching iron already kindled. Captain Juan Pantoja, his face black with rage, was making ready to cut off the thief's right hand, and a score of soldiers had gathered around, nodding their heads at the justice of the captain's actions. The slave, a little man whose size and roundness had brought him the name Chichi, screamed for help, his eyes bulging, his lips bubbling blood-flecked foam, when he saw his master.

"For the love of Christ, save me, my master!" were the words he screamed. "For the love of His Sacred Mother, make them stop!" Piss stained the little man's pants, and mud-darkened snot and tears dripped onto the leathern poncho on which he had been thrown. "With only one hand, how can I serve you?" the slave pleaded. "With only one hand, how can I cook for you? How can I saddle your horse or dress you in your armor?" With each word, the little man's words grew shriller.

Soto Mayor, purple patches showing on his face and neck, turned to Juan Pantoja. "Who intends to lay knife on the slave must first try his master!" He stepped forward until he was between the slave and Captain Juan Pantoja. The watching soldiers muttered angrily, but did not try to interfere.

"A thief must pay for his theft with the offending hand," Captain Pantoja shouted, spittle spraying through his broken teeth.

"For the fifty gold ducats he cost me, you can have both hands and his head as well," answered Soto Mayor, the cords swelling in his neck.

"I will take his hand," Captain Pantoja freed his sword, "and will pay you with fifty ripe turds!"

A moment after Captain Pantoja drew his sword, Soto Mayor's blade was in his one hand, the other gripping a short, curved dagger. Captain Pantoja then pulled the heated staunching iron from the fire with his free hand, and thus armed the two men started circling each other.

With a sudden sweep, Captain Pantoja ducked beneath Soto Mayor's sword and thrust the heated iron against his neck, searing half a span of skin, yet not a grunt escaped Soto Mayor. But a moment later, he lunged forward and, with his dagger, laid open to the bone Captain Pantoja's arm. Each stepped back two paces, then rushed forward, their swords clashing as curses poured from their mouths. The roast-pork stench of burning flesh rose from Soto Mayor's thigh, seared by the heated iron as blood streamed from Juan Pantoja's scalp, sliced open by the dagger. Again each man stepped back two paces. A moan, like that of a calving cow, came from the trussed slave, and the curses of the wounded men had lost their words and were broken screams. Again they raised their swords, but this time they did not come together; for at that moment Alvar Nuñez pushed through the crowd and stepped between them—a great sword in one hand, a studded buckler in the other.

"Whoever is the victor I will kill!" Alvar Nuñez hissed, white showing around his eyes and across the break to his nose. "I swear this in the name of my mother!" Both men held their swords high, but did not try and come together. "And," Alvar Nuñez raised his voice to a shout, striking the haft of his sword against the buckler, "I will lay the flat of this weapon across the shoulders of any idler I still find standing near when I have counted up to ten. One!" He struck the buckler again. "Two!" The soldiers slowly started backing up and the swords of both men began to lower. "Three!" Groups of soldiers turned away. By the time Alvar Nuñez reached ten, all the soldiers and most of the officers had scattered, and the swords of the two combatants were sheathed.

That night, and for several nights after, the men tried to forget their hunger with talk of the clash between the two officers; those who had been witnesses describing again and again the fierceness of the battle, the slashing, the burning, the awful courage of Alvar Nuñez. And with each telling, the battle grew fiercer, the blood and smoking flesh more plentiful, Alvar Nuñez's courage greater.

In the days that followed the men's hunger worsened, until some of the men began dropping by mid-afternoon from weakness. These were dragged by their companions, who quickly fatigued and also dropped.

The tenth day, we found some palmitos, growing like those of Andalusia. They did not satisfy hunger, for they were green and bitter, but they did strengthen the men a little. That night, many sickened with cramps and the vomits. Some screamed that knives were in their bellies and begged to be confessed, for they believed themselves about to die. Two, for no reason, leapt up and tore at each other with nails and teeth— one or both must have surely died had they not been separated. Yet, once separated, they lay down meekly, closed their eyes, and in moments were asleep.

By the fifteenth day, so great was our distress that the company was strung out a full league, men walking singly or in twos or threes, the mounted officers sharing their beasts when there was a need with men who had fainted. Thoughts of Indians were forgotten, each man thinking only of the next step that must be taken and dreaming painful dreams of fresh-baked loaves of buttered bread, roasted joints of meat and thick brown pies bubbling with savory juices. In this way, we reached a great river in the early afternoon. The river's current being too swift for easy fording, and the men crippled with fatigue—all suffered from foot-rot and most showed rashes and open ulcers on the arms and face—the Governor ordered us into camp, although it lacked four hours until dark. Some good, fat fish swam in that river, also eels and turtles, and those who still had strength, using their swords as spears, and their ponchos as nets, secured before nightfall a sufficient quantity that all were able to fill their bellies with boiled and roasted flesh.

Hunger, as is true with all pain, be it from whippings, scorn or the loss of love, once relieved is easily forgotten. With their gullets stuffed, the men began to joke and laugh. Some, despite their bruised feet, made as if to dance; but their antics more resembled the hobble of twisted cripples as they beg for Blancas in the marketplace. Several, to amuse themselves, and to bring laughter to the others, began to tease the little slave, Chichi.

Forming themselves in a circle, with Chichi in the middle, they made grabs for the little man's buttocks, grown less round but still showing the fullness of a woman's rump. "Honey," "dear one," "blushing rose," and a dozen more names used by men to soften wenches, they called him, while he ran squealing around the circle, turning first this way then that. Finally, at a signal, they allowed the slave to escape, and he ran directly to his blanket, which had been prepared with a nest of stinging ants.

Laughter followed the shrieking slave as he ran for the river covered with ants. Even his master, Soto Mayor, laughed and slapped his thigh. A dozen pursued Chichi to the river. But there was no further mischief done the little man that night. Captain Alonso del Castillo came up and silently handed the slave a new blanket, then turned away. After that, none dared molest him.

VIII

Of all that company of three hundred camped by the river, only three stayed apart from the merrymaking and took no notice of the sport made of the slave.

Friar Xuarez, his fire kindled on a flat rock at the bank of the river, sat, eyes closed, with his back toward the camp.

Alvar Nuñez rested against a great uprooted tree, his face in his hands, his neglected fire reduced to smoking ashes.

The Governor, his seat softened by several skins, his back supported by his saddle, sat muttering and scowling before a fire fully as large as the one used by the rest of the men.

Finally when the camp was silent Friar Xuarez rose from the position he had held for hours. He stood for several moments as if listening to the night sounds; then he started in the direction of Alvar Nuñez, taking care that the light of the main fire did not fall upon him.

It was as if Alvar Nuñez expected the visit, for when he raised his head and saw the priest standing not five paces distant, his cowl shadowing his face, he was not surprised and greeted the man with a murmured wish that God might give him good health.

"And may the sweet Jesu grant you His divine protection, Alvar Nuñez," was the soft reply. The friar stepped a pace closer, but did not make as if to sit, and Alvar Nuñez offered no invitation.

"You are troubled, Alvar Nuñez." The priest's words were said in such a way that they could be judged either a statement or a question. There was no reply. "When, after a weary day, one who should be sleeping is still awake, it can only be that he is troubled."

"Then you are troubled, Friar Xuarez?"

"A priest, if he knows his duty, will be the last to sleep and the first to wake, for it is his task to guard men's souls."

"Are they in need of guarding when their owners are asleep? I would think them never safer."

The priest muttered some words about Satan being ever ready to snatch an unwary Christian's soul, then, in a louder voice said, "If you have the need for confession, Alvar Nuñez . . ."

"No need, Father Xuarez," the other interrupted. "Father Palos confessed me when the journey started; since then I have had neither chance nor time to sin."

"I detect a note of apostasy in your words, Alvar Nuñez. Or do I hear you wrongly?"

"Wrongly, Father, wrongly. I intend no apostasy, and will have myself shriven tomorrow by Friar Palos."

"It was not to offer confession that I came up," the priest finally said, after a silence of nearly a minute during which both men remained motionless. "Concern that you may be troubled, that the weight of command lies heavily on your shoulders, and pains your heart . . ."

"May the Almighty reward you for your concern, good Friar."

"Speak freely, Alvar Nuñez. I promise that your words are safe with me and, except for God, will be known by no other."

"I have already shared them with God, Friar Xuarez, and feel no need for recapitulation. Again, I thank you for your concern."

"First a note of apostasy, now a note of mockery. Men of higher rank than you, Alvar Nuñez Cabeza de Vaca, have been examined by the Holy Brotherhood for less. Do not forget, I am commissary of this expedition, and upon return to Spain must make my report. Beware, lest your name be mentioned. When you mock me, you mock the Church."

"Again, Holy Father, I insist I mean no offense, and will ask a proper penance from Friar Palos for any harm my innocent words may have done. Now, if you allow me to be alone I will, I promise, offer up a dozen Hail Marys and an equal number of Pater Nosters as advance payment against the penance Father Palos is certain to levy."—

"Would that your concern was only with men's souls and not temporal matters," Alvar Nuñez muttered softly as the friar walked away. "For that, I would be shriven daily, and gladly," he went on in an angry voice, but one kept soft. "I would walk on dried peas, shave my head, crawl on my knees a full league. For his promise not to further interfere I would cut my beard, wear motly, even ride backwards on an ass."

After leaving Alvar Nuñez, Friar Xuarez walked a dozen paces, until he was hidden by some vegetation, then waited. It was as if he expected the other man to follow him. He listened, cupping his ear with his hand, then, with a nod, gathered his habit so it should not cause a rustle, and started circling the camp in the direction of the Governor.

"God's peace to you, Pánfilo de Narvaez," said the friar in a low voice. "May I sit with you for a little time?" The Governor, still scowling, raised his eyes to the man's face, which was obscured by his cowl, and nodded. Although there was room beside the Governor on the folded skin, the priest chose a patch of bare ground two paces distant.

"Night after night you are awake while others sleep, my Governor."

"They are all asleep?"

"Only Alvar Nuñez is awake. The rest, stuffed with fish, sleep peacefully."

"Another day without food and we must have started butchering the horses!" the Governor's voice was harsh.

"Thanks be to God for guiding us to this river filled with fat, sweet fish!"

"If I do not disremember, Friar Xuarez, you were certain that game abounded in the interior. Or does my memory fail me?"

"The heat has caused the game to hide deep in the dark of the forest," the friar said with a cough.

"Once across the river we may be again forced to travel another fifteen days with empty stomachs. Or will you again offer to risk your chance of salvation that we find abundant game?"

Friar Xuarez frowned and cleared his throat.

"Is a few days of hunger too great a price to pay for treasure, Pánfilo? Can the little discomfort we have known compare with true suffering? He who gave His life for all of us knew suffering; and for His suffering, His reward was death. Yet for pain, not a hundredth part as great as His, our reward will be wealth."

"I do not hesitate to pay a sufficient price for gold, Friar Juan. Nor would any man in this company, I think. Some loss I am prepared to risk; but another fifteen days like those we just have known will cost us all our horses and many dead. And then there may be yet another fifteen days—to a corpse, gold is the same as lead."

"Then it is your intention to alter your plans, my Governor? Return to the place of our departure and wait for the ships to find us?"

"Another fifteen days like those we have just known . . ." the Governor mumbled.

"No man will fault you if you exercise caution. Even if delay should rob us of the treasure, who would dare say that Governor Pánfilo de Narvaez did other than what a prudent man should do?"

"We will not return to the place of our departure! Our bones will whiten here in the forest before I take one step backward. But to again plunge forward . . . I will call a council of my captains."

"And what will be their demands, Pánfilo?—Alvar Nuñez? The comptroller? The assessor? Others?"

"They will advise; not demand! I decide! Only I, Friar Juan."

Friar Xuarez nodded slowly, then reached for his beads. For some moments his lips moved silently. "It is a wise Governor who will confer with his captains," he finally said. "As long as no one forgets who is captain and who the Governor."

"They advise; I decide!" the Governor spat out the words.

"Yet history tells that many a monarch has called a council of his barons which, before the council ended, had stripped away his powers, even made another king."

"I hold a patent from the Crown," the Governor hissed. "It is in my name! In my name," he repeated as he struck his leathern wallet with his fist. Then he said in a softer voice, "I already know what certain ones will say." As he spoke, his fingers toyed with the wallet's stitching. "That whoreson Alvar Nuñez will urge me to turn to the coast and seek the ships. And the comptroller and the assessor will agree. Should I refuse, he will again charge me with risking the welfare of this expedition."

"Then it *is* your plan to turn to the coast, my Governor?"

Governor Narvaez leaned forward, a scowl forcing his eyebrows together, his blind eye twisted into a bulging knot, his good eye peering into the other's face. "You put words in my mouth, Juan Xuarez. I said nothing of turning to the coast. If we had provisions—as little as a fenega of maize for every man—Satan and all that he commands could not prevent me from pressing forward. If I knew we would secure victuals on the other side of the river, even if we must travel two or three days to find them, I would order the company across before daybreak."

"You lack faith, Pánfilo. At the moment of our greatest

extremity, when all appeared black, did we not come to this river God made rich with fish? And have you forgotten how His divine protection saved the hidalgo, Juan Velazquez, when he fell into the snake-filled pit? Have we lost a single man since landing on the coast of Florida? A single horse? We are being tested—the mettle of our faith is being tried. If our mettle proves false, Pánfilo, we will be denied that other precious metal. After guiding us this far, do you believe God will now abandon us?"

"I am second to no man in my faith in God," the Governor answered softly. "Yet, does not God require man to use whatever intellect is given him? Does God expect man to act the blind fool?"

"If the fool truly have faith, yes! And intellect must always be employed in the service of God, not in satisfying human cupidity. By a hundred times would I rather a man be a fool serving God than without faith and of the greatest intelligence."

"I lack faith . . . you judge me lacking in faith, Father?"

"It is God's way to constantly test man's belief. Who will not profess the greatest faith lying at his ease in his vineyard? It is when one stares at the fleshless head of death, when one knows the icy breath of terror, when one is crushed by the boot heel of despair, that one's faith is truly measured. And what man has not doubted? Even Job, that most patient of holy men, cursed the day that he was born. And did not Peter doubt our Lord? And if the prophet and the apostle knew times when their faith was shaken, should not a Spanish governor be allowed as much?"

"The force of your arguments are such, Friar Juan, that they must convince me." The Governor pulled carefully at the lobe of his ear. "I confess to having suffered a loss of faith . . . like the distemper, it crept silently through my veins until, without knowing it, my brain was fevered. But now, your words have cured me. In the morning, under God's protection, we will cross the river and continue northward. May He, in His infinite mercy, provide us with the sustenance we need."

"He will, Pánfilo. As I know Christ died for us, I know He will."

IX

We had not completed the crossing of the river—a hundred men, perhaps, already over, fifty not yet started, the rest in transit—when a dozen soldiers sent forward half a league descried a band of Indians.

Those who had not yet started were urged by shouts and gestures to come on with the greatest haste; those in transit plunged forward, no longer concerned that the packs they carried be kept dry. Several, scrambling over the slippery rocks, tumbled into the current and had to be rescued by their companions, for their armor dragged them under.

Had the Indians attacked us at once, our losses would have been severe, for except eight or ten, the horses were still in the river, and no man had a lit match to fire his arquebus. But the natives held back, two hundred they were, more or less, content to shout, to wave their spears and clubs in a threatening manner, and to shoot arrows which fell short, for they kept close to the trees a quarter of a league distant.

When enough horses had crossed, the Governor formed a band of thirty mounted officers flanked by four-score fully armed and helmeted men; and with this company he advanced half the distance to the trees. In appearance the Indians were more like great birds than men. For they were clothed in mantles stitched of red and yellow feathers, their faces painted blue and white, with plumed hats woven like baskets on their heads. With each step that the company advanced, the Indians grew more frantic. They leapt up and down, waved their weapons wildly, beat their chests and stuck out their tongues.

Several times the Governor attempted to converse with them by signs. He sent a man forward with gifts, but they drove him back with spears and arrows. The Governor laid down his arms, ordered the others to retreat a hundred paces, then beckoned the Indians to send one of their number to meet with him. But their answer was more ugly faces and the discharge of great quantities of spit.

For half an hour, the two forces hesitated, separated by a distance of no more than five hundred paces. Then, being reinforced by ten dozen men, including a number armed with arquebus with matches ready, the Governor attacked. Although most of the Indians quickly retreated into the forest, a few were captured.

Then, employing methods he had used while Lieutenant Governor of Cuba—quantities of water forced down the throat, heavy rocks piled on the chest, wet leather thongs tied tight around the limbs—Governor Narvaez persuaded the captured Indians to lead him to their village.

Although the houses of their village stood deserted, fires still smoked and there were cookpots filled with a thick maize gruel, for which the men were grateful. Close by we found fields of ripe maize, but not a scrap of meat, dried or fresh, was discovered, despite a careful search.

Friar Xuarez blessed the baskets of maize as they were gathered. At different times, when the Governor chanced to pass, the priest nodded and pointed at the grain, and in response the Governor nodded back and crossed himself. One time, the friar murmured behind his hand, "You asked a fenega for each man, but were granted double. May the remembrance of this God-given gift serve to strengthen you when you next are troubled by doubt."

After the maize was gathered, the Governor, without calling a council of his captains, ordered us into camp until both the strength and health of men and horses should be restored. If the Indians, whose place we occupied, lurked nearby, they did not show themselves the seven days we rested in that village. Nor did we even once hear the sound of gourd or drum.

The third day, Alvar Nuñez, the comptroller and the assessor, who were joined by Friar Xuarez, met with the Governor. Supported by the comptroller and assessor, Alvar Nuñez urged that a party be sent out to search for the sea while the company was yet in camp. At first the Governor said that talk of the sea was foolish, for it was remote. Finally, after much urging, the Governor granted Alvar Nuñez permission to take forty men; but they must explore on foot, for he was unwilling to risk any horses.

The next day, before sunrise, Alvar Nuñez departed with Captain Alonso del Castillo and forty men of his company. The Governor accompanied him to the edge of the forest, saying, in a voice loud enough for all to hear, "Go search for your port, Alvar Nuñez Cabeza de Vaca; and if there be one near, I swear by my mother, so soon as I know of your discovery, to fast two days—not a morsel or a drop will touch my lips. But I will be much surprised if upon your return I do not make such a meal of ash-cake and roasted fish that I must expel great quantities of gas all during the time you tell me of your explorations."

There was much laughter at the Governor's words; and after the expedition disappeared into the forest, as he walked up and down drinking a fermented liquor made of maize, the officers gathered around him while he spoke of the great port sought by his second-in-command. "Greater than San Luçar de Barrameda, from which we departed, will be the port of Cabeza de Vaca! Fine Indian ladies, dressed in silks with pointed leather shoes, will he find walking daintily in twos and threes under their umbrellas."

"And surely a hundred ships will be berthed there, taking on and discharging cargo," Captain Juan Pantoja added, laughing.

"What good things will Alvar Nuñez bring us from his port?" asked the notary, Hieronymo Alainz, who rarely spoke.

"Surely a dozen fat swine," snickered Governor Narvaez. "And I hope a bevy of maidens to entertain us."

"For such an entertainment I would give my remaining ear, and gladly!" shouted Captain Pantoja, pointing to his head. "Keep your swine; just grant me a little time with one of the maidens. And she need not be an unblemished maiden. Plump and forty will do, and who shall care if there are a few bristles on her chin. Even fifty, moustached and toothless must I judge fair enough in my condition."

All that day, there was much joking about the port Alvar Nuñez was seeking. Thus it was that, when just before dark the expedition returned, there was not a man in camp who did not leave his cookfire to join with the others in the central compound as the Governor received his second-in-command.

"Did you find the sea?" the Governor asked Alvar Nuñez, a broad grin on his face, his speech thick with drink. "And did you descry a great port?—I think, from the little time you were gone and from the look of you, I have no need to fast."

"Not the sea, my Governor, but a great bay." The grin began fading from the Governor's face. "And further exploration may lead us to a port."

"Further exploration?" the thickness was gone from the Governor's speech.

"Further exploration!" Alonso del Castillo answered, passing his hand quickly over his eyes. "At noon we arrived at sea sands and followed them two leagues. Then, in the distance we saw a great bay. But our further progress was prevented by the same river we crossed a few days since, it being deep and swift at that place."

"If the river be crossed where we once forded it," Alvar Nuñez quickly added, "and then followed, in a little time we must reach the bay. And I have learned where bays empty into oceans there ports are often found."

"There will be no further exploration!" the Governor said in a rising voice. "We depart camp in the morning." Murmurs arose from the officers gathered around him. "There is no port." The Governor's one eye traveled slowly from face to face—except for one or two, all showed troubled frowns. "Another exploration will cost us at least two more days, if not three. We know gold awaits us in Apalachen—only a fool would risk losing a treasure to search for some fabled port."

"If there be a port, my Governor," Captain Pantoja spoke carefully, pulling first his split nose then his remaining ear, "and who can deny that ports and bays are often found together," he grinned and pulled his nose again, "if there be a port, we may gain intelligence of Apalachen from the inhabitants; we may find our ships . . ."

"There is no port!" the Governor shouted.

"But consider, my Governor," Captain Castillo folded his arms tight across his chest, "you yourself ordered the brigantine north to search for Pánuco, of which the pilot Miruelo said he had certain knowledge. Then you instructed Caravello to take the other ships north and search for a port. Have we not traveled in a northernly direction, my Governor?" Loud murmurs of approval escaped the lips not only of the officers but also of many of the men. Heads nodded; and there was much clearing of throats.

"If through God's mercy we should find a port," said the assessor forcing his voice over the sounds of the men, "we may secure fresh horses, meat, other things to speed our journey—the two or three lost days will then be gained back."

"So certain am I that we have not traveled a sufficient distance to find a port," the Governor struggled to control his anger, "that I pledge myself to shave my beard if one is found. But this will be our last delay! I will hang the man—hidalgo, officer, slave or soldier—who counsels further caution."

With that, the Governor ordered a certain Captain Valençuelo, who had not frowned or murmured with the others, to equip an expedition of sixty men and six horses to set out the next morning.

"I will shave my beard," the Governor said again. "But if I find I have no need for a barber, I must laugh until I fall helpless to the ground each time I remember the solemn faces and timid words of you who are gathered here this night."

In two days the expedition returned, reporting they had explored the bay, which was shallow, no deeper most places than to the knee, and, except for five or six canoes of plumed Indians passing in the distance, had discovered nothing.

But this intelligence, despite his earlier words, caused the Governor no laughter. Nor did he again make mention of his beard saved from the barber's knife. And, as he gave orders for the expediton to depart camp, it was noted that he nodded and in other ways showed a certain friendliness toward Alvar Nuñez and the several others who, not three days earlier, had opposed him.

X

Except for hunger, which rode each man's back like a skeleton, for the fresh provisions were soon exhausted, except for galling by heavy armor, except for the foot-rot, for ulcers and for the catarrh, we continued our travel northward without too much difficulty. Each night, after counting our numbers and finding no man missing, all gave thanks. And in the morning, when the captains reported no one taken in his sleep, we again gave thanks. Every man was convinced that we traveled under a special dispensation. Thus it was that, despite our suffering, there was little grumbling. In this way we journeyed through dense forests and treacherous swamps for twenty-six days.

Other than the comptroller, the assessor, Juan Velazquez, Alonso del Castillo and Friar Palos, no man approached Alvar Nuñez for an exchange of friendship during all those twenty-six days. His orders, which he gave in the tersest fashion, were quickly obeyed. None delayed to offer a bit of gossip. At night he unrolled his blanket away from the others, and in the day rode without companion, separated from the nearest man by fifty paces.

When one or another of the few who showed friendship rode up, after a word or two, Alvar Nuñez would wave the man away, returning to his thoughts—which, from his set jaw and his constant frown, must have been deep. Those times when the Governor needed to confer with him, Alvar Nuñez offered no greeting, exchanged no pleasantries, and answered whatever questions that were asked with a minimum of words. Only once in all those days did anyone engage him in lengthy conversation.

We were crossing a great swamp, thick with sharp grasses that grew to the height of a man's shoulder; it being a place hazardous for horses, the officers walked, guiding their beasts as best they could through the soft sand. As had become his habit, Alvar Nuñez traveled separately from the rest. He reached an open place where the grass was grown nearly to the full height of a man, and there found Captain Alonso del Castillo waiting for him. "Do you suffer an indisposition, Alvar Nuñez Cabeza de Vaca?" were the words the frowning captain used to greet him. "Your friends are concerned that you may have contracted an inflammation of the liver." He fell in step with the other man. After a little time had passed, Alvar Nuñez responded with a grunt, whose meaning only he alone could know, for it was not accompanied by any movement of his head.

"I know a little of the art of bleeding, from my father, who served the Court as physician, and will, if you permit, nick a vein in your arm when we go into camp. Letting blood will cause the bile to settle, and should provide relief for your condition."

"I have no need for your services as physician, Alonso del Castillo; I have already been bled enough by leeches and mosquitos."

"Seeing you so solemn, your friends concluded that you suffer from some serious indisposition—that, or are doing the penance of silence."

"My friends?"

"You have friends, more than you know, Alvar Nuñez, not only officers—there are many among the men who love you."

"Tell my *friends*," Alvar Nuñez snorted, "tell all the many who love me they need no longer concern themselves with my health—I do well enough."

"Knowing of the . . ." Captain Castillo passed his hands over his eyes, "knowing of the little differences between you and the Governor, there are some too timid to show their affection."

"Spanish soldiers! Castilian hidalgos! Too timid? I cannot bring myself to believe such a thing, Alonso."

"If not timid, then they are cautious. The Governor . . ." Captain Castillo's words trailed away. "But should the occasion arise, you will see how many are your friends."

"Those who still snicker about a port they call The Port of Cabeza de Vaca. . . ?"

"Those, too, Alvar Nuñez. They find amusement only to

dull the pains of hunger. From my father, who as physician heard things not even for the confessor's ear, I learned there is no one so high that he will not be mocked if he makes a mistake; that those loved best are often the ones jeered most loudly. If a father instructing his son how to shoot should, himself, miss an easy target, will not the son be amused and laugh, even if he loves his father?"

"My father once tumbled from his horse while the beast was standing still—he was so full of wine that he then must be tied to the animal like a sack of wheat."

"Did you laugh, Alvar Nuñez?"

"I ran away a score of paces so none should see."

"And did you love your father, Alvar Nuñez?"

"I loved him enough, and he did me, but had I shown him amusement at his discomfiture. . . ." Alvar Nuñez grinned as he drew his finger across his throat.

"And another thing my father told me," Alonso Castillo lowered his voice, "no one in the Court causes as much amusement as the King. Yet, none dares to let him know it."

"You learned much from your father, Alonso. Perhaps one day when I have the headache, I will let you bleed me."

"It is said, Alvar Nuñez Cabeza de Vaca, that a man, if he be truly wise, must show caution—the rash are never wise. It is further said, it is from the father that one gains wisdom. Knowing his son, I must judge the father of Alvar Nuñez to have been amongst the wisest of men." At that, Alvar Nuñez, with a grin, delivered a blow to the other's shoulder that would have tumbled a lesser man. He received back as good as he gave, also with a grin. Then they separated, and Alvar Nuñez returned to his thinking, but on his face a smile had replaced the frown.

The seventeenth of June, which was the twenty-seventh day of our journey from the place where we camped next to the river, just as we were settling down for our mid-day rest, an

Indian chief, borne on the back of another man, approached us. He was robed in a painted deerskin, his face also was painted, so that one had to look carefully to see where the robe ended and the face began. More than one hundred Indians accompanied him, all feathered and painted, although in different colors than their chief—their colors: yellow, blue and white, his: red and black—and those who walked in advance played on reed flutes. None showed weapons, although some carried sticks to which were affixed shells and feathers and strips of leather.

Seeing their peaceful condition, the Governor ordered that no one molest them. But even as he gave his orders, different ones began to handle the Indian women. A dozen blows from the flat of his sword on the shoulders and backs of these offenders quieted them, and appeared to satisfy the chief, from whose eyes tears had begun to flow. One soldier, who had torn away the skirt of a young maiden, the Governor ordered whipped. His cries seemed to reassure the other women, whose faces at first showed fear.

For an hour the Governor and many of his officers conversed with the chief, whose name was Dulchanchellin, and with his principal men. By means of signs, they were given to understand that we were going to Apalachen, and from those made in return, we gained the information that they were enemies of the people of Apalachen, and would join our company to assist us against them. This news caused much rejoicing among the men, and those who had made most free with the Indian women suffered kicks and blows from others who had shown restraint.

As a proof of friendship, the chief was given a quantity of hawkbells and beads; he, in turn, presented the Governor with the painted skin he wore. Then, in a hundred ways, the Governor showed the chief his friendship. He even offered to have the offending soldier whipped again. But the chief waved both his hands and tossed the bleeding man his stick. By this the Governor concluded he wished the soldier spared.

All that afternoon, we followed the Indians in the direction of their village, for the chief had made known by signs that he wanted to offer us entertainment. The prospect of again knowing the comfort of a full stomach renewed our vigor, even the sickest were much restored, and despite warnings of the Governor, inflamed perhaps by the sight of the nicely made, barebreasted women, there were some that whispered of satisfying other hungers after dark.

Just before dusk, we reached a great river whose depth and current were such that we could not venture to cross until daylight. So we camped on its bank, and shared the little food the Indians carried—scarcely more than a mouthful for each man, yet still most welcome. And, during the night, the men made free with their women, who submitted silently, offering tears but no resistance; some of the more comely being taken by a full score of soldiers before morning.

Since the number of offenders was more than half again as many as those who had obeyed the Governor's orders, since it was evident that amongst the ranks of the guilty were many officers, and since it was whispered that the Governor himself was missing for a time from his blanket, there were no punishments when the Indian chief, his eyes streaming, told by signs and by pictures in the sand what had happened. The Governor listened, frowned, then shook his head; and even when presented with various women showing bruises on their breasts and necks, some with blood dripping from their loins, he continued to evidence disbelief, but then made the chief and his principal men presents of hawkbells and beads.

The river on whose banks we had camped being too treacherous to ford, we constructed in the morning, with the help of the Indians, a great canoe. Then, in small numbers, men and horses were carefully transported. Had any of the Indians at that time chosen to dispute our passage we would have been forced to retire; for even with their help we had great difficulty making it, and our progress was slow.

Juan Velazquez, growing impatient, suddenly rode his horse into the river. A dozen or more times since his escape from the poisonous vipers he had shown his contempt for death: by exploring ahead of the company when Indians were near; by leading the way across swamps where quicksand might be found; by venturing into the forest at night to discover the source of suspicious sounds. But death finally embraced the man when he rode into that river. The violence of the current cast him from his horse; he grasped the reins, pulling the animal's head under, and both man and beast were drowned.

The death of Velazquez caused the company much pain, for he was the first man lost, and many had gained comfort from his surviving the vipers in the pit. A number gathered around his body, discovered wedged between two rocks a half a league down the river. Despite its battered appearance, some yet expected him to open his eyes and grin. But he stayed dead, and his beast provided a taste of meat for all the men that night. Each man, as he chewed its flesh, must have given thought to the one who, not a half day earlier, had sat astride that creature.

"After being spared by the awful mercy of the Almighty," said Alvar Nuñez to a group that had gathered about his fire, "after being granted the gift of life a second time—a gift rarely given more than once, his ways should have been those of the most holy of men; no hooded monk kneeling in his cell should have shown greater devotion. Yet he must risk perdition by lusting with the Indian women." Alvar Nuñez looked slowly around the company. Many lowered their eyes. "He forced his attention on the wives of other men, men who had shown us friendship. Is it any wonder that he lies there dead?" He reached out his hand toward the fresh mound of earth. At these words, many crossed themselves, and several told their beads.

"Further molestation of their women," Alvar Nuñez then said, in a louder voice so that it should not be lost to the Governor and other officers sitting near, "and I fear for the lives of all in this expedition." But again during the darkest hours of that night, certain men made free with the Indian women and sev-

68

eral, captured by Alvar Nuñez while rolling on the ground, were severely beaten.

In the morning, the chief, with tears coursing down his cheeks, led our company toward his village. There was no more playing of flutes; the Indians, as they went, hung their heads and walked slowly, as if every step that brought us closer to their dwelling-place caused them pain.

Before noon we arrived at the village, where the chief ordered maize given us, also a quantity of dried deer meat. That village of the chief Dulchanchellin was little different from the other village we had occupied by the river. But, unlike the other village, we found numerous inhabitants who did not flee at our coming.

A dozen of their houses were acquired for our use. In each thing demanded of him, the chief at once agreed, giving orders in his tongue that our needs be quickly attended. All rejoiced at being so bountifully received after weeks of hardship. By late afternoon, so full of food were all the men, so content from having their feet washed and bound by the women and children, so much at ease lying in the shade on blankets laid on rushes, that most feel asleep, and the few who stayed awake, their lids hanging heavy, took no notice of the Indians departing the village in twos and threes. By nightfall, when a sudden wind stirred most into wakefulness, as clouds of choking dust swirled through the village, it was seen that the place had been deserted, not a child or dog remained.

By daybreak all were so nervous of attack by the Indians, whose sounds were heard all through the night coming from the forest, we departed without so much as a bite to break our fast.

Within an hour a band of Indians came in sight, prepared for battle. In their hands, instead of flutes and gourds, were bows, clubs and other implements of war. The Governor and various officers called out to them, but they would neither come nor wait our arrival. They retired, following from a distance.

In this way we traveled for another hour, the Indians,

whose number must have been not less than two hundred, beating drums and swinging curved sticks attached to thongs that caused a sound like the bellowing of a bull.

The Governor, growing impatient, and seeing that the Indians did not intend to engage us, ordered that some cavalry be left in ambush in the forest. These, bursting forth as the Indians were about to pass, seized four, causing the rest to fall back in much confusion. The four who had been captured were not harmed, and they then served us as guides, conducting us through a country very difficult to travel but wonderful to look upon.

We made our way through forests whose trees were astonishingly high, no man in the company having seen any greater. Many were fallen on the ground, and these so obstructed our progress that our advance was often slowed to half of what it otherwise might have been.

Each night, as we drew ever closer to Apalachen (for our guides gave us to understand that the place we sought was not distant), despite the wet that severely plagued us and our renewed hunger, most of the men showed an increasing levity and excitement. There were few who would not listen, until sleep tumbled them on the ground, to tales told and retold of the vast treasure to be found in Apalachen. With each telling the quantity of gold grew greater: enough so that every horse and man must be laden to the limit; more than the company could carry, so that Indians must be impressed; so much that a portion must be left. "One will carry the load of two!" "We will build wagons and hew a road through the forest!" No man could hear of gold being left without offering his suggestion.

The day after St. John's Day, we came in sight of Apalachen—this was taken as a good omen, for had we arrived a day earlier we would have been forced to fight during a time better given to the remembrance of the one who baptized our Lord. Once in sight of the town, so cautious was our approach—strips of cloth having been tied around the horses' mouths, the leather fittings and armor freshly oiled—that the

70

inhabitants remained unaware of our presence. Seeing ourselves so near, at a sign from Friar Xuarez, all sank to their
knees to give thanks to God for guiding us safely through so
many perils. After we had prayed and after certain ones who
begged it had been confessed, the Governor ordered Alvar Nuñez, together with the assessor, to lead the attack. Taking nine
cavalry and fifty men, all heavily armed, a like number being
sent a half league north to await a signal, Alvar Nuñez then
assailed the town.

Not an arrow was fired at his approach, nor was there any
attempt to bar his passage. And, having got so easily in, and
finding only women and young boys, the soldiers were about to
sheath their swords and start a search for treasure when the
Indian men, who had been absent, returned and began discharging flights of arrows.

The attacking Indians were quickly driven back by the
firing of arquebus. And then, the women and children having
been secured as guarantee against further attack, the Indian
men retired for a time into the forest. The rest of our company
came up in great excitement, rejoicing that the place for which
we searched so long had been so easily taken.

Within an hour, all the excitement was at an end; those
who had rejoiced most loudly now showed in their faces harsh
lines of anger, in their eyes deep despair. For there was no treasure in Apalachen.

XI

Forty houses, small and made low, were all that was in that
Indian town. And there was no order, each set up in a different

place where a mound or a fallen tree might give shelter from the storms. Their material was thatch, and they were built poorer than any we had known. Except for a large quantity of maize, a number of deerskins and a few mantelets of poor thread used by the women, we found nothing.

Two hours after our arrival at Apalachen, the Indian men, who had retreated into the forest, came in peace, begging for the release of their women and children. Some in our camp argued against this, saying that by keeping them imprisoned we were guaranteed against further assault; chief amongst those who so argued was Alvar Nuñez and the assessor. But even these two argued with little spirit, so great was their disappointment at the poverty of the village.

The arguments for their detention not being sufficient, the Governor ordered the women and children freed. But, in order that we might gain information when it should be needed, he took the cacique of the village, whom he then secured with irons.

In consequence of the capture of their chief, the Indians set up a howl during the night, and as soon as it grew light they attacked with such ferocity that they succeeded in setting fire to the houses in which we were. As we joined, they retreated to the lakes nearby, firing flaming arrows and shrieking curses. But, despite our numbers and superior weapons, because of the thickness of the maize fields bordering the lakes and the many fallen trees in the water where they could hide, except for one Indian killed by a crossbowman of Captain Pantoja, we did them little harm.

After the attack had been beaten off, the men wandered about the village in deep dejection. An hour before noon a cold wind suddenly came up; it being summer and we having suffered weeks of heat, this was a strange thing. Some muttered that the wind was an evil omen, many shivered as the cold found its way through their flimsy clothing, but of all that company, not one could bring himself to light a fire.

As the day lengthened to afternoon, the wind grew colder; and had not the Indians of Dulchanchellin we carried as guides built a great fire in the center of the village and several lesser fires, some of our number who were most weakened by sickness must have surely died. And these same Indians later prepared pots of boiled maize and ashcakes for us to eat—the natives of this region being sworn enemies of their people, they must, despite the treatment they had received from us, be our friends.

By late afternoon, had the Indians of Apalachen again chosen to attack, few would have offered any defense, and we would have been easily overrun. Even those ordered to keep watch wandered about aimlessly, their heads bowed, their weapons dragging on the ground.

But the discovery, shortly after dark, of a quantity of fermented liquor in earthenware pots did much to restore the spirits of the men. Although at first taste no stronger than a mild beer, this liquor caused a drunkenness such that even those sick ones who earlier had been willing to die of the cold without a murmur, began to shout and sing and even dance, despite their weakness. And there was no fighting, as so often is the case with drunkenness. All wondered at the bright colors they saw, and the lightness of their hands and feet. Some claimed visions—the place of their birth in Spain; wives awaiting their return; parents who had long since died. There were a few who wept all through the night for their sinful ways, and cried out for Christ to grant them forgiveness.

And the next morning at sunrise the Indians attacked again.

Enough of the company had slept off the effects of the liquor so that a force sufficient to repulse the Indians could be mustered. Yet it was fortunate that the attackers numbered not more than a hundred, for our men shot wide of the mark and behaved with such confusion that it must have cost them the battle had they faced a more numerous foe.

Two more days were to pass before most recovered from

the effects of that potion—we later learned that the liquor was brewed of certain roots and mushrooms and used only at times of great celebration—a few saw colors and walked as if asleep for nearly a week. But although the condition of the men would have brought disaster had the Indians attacked in sufficient number, the potion proved a boon, for it dulled the sharp edge of disappointment, allowing time to balm the wounds already made.

For twenty-five days we stayed in the town, not one of which passed without bands of Indians crossing the lake to harass with shouts and flaming arrows, although they took care not to engage us. Three times expeditions, sent to make incursions into the surrounding country, found it thinly populated and difficult to travel. Everywhere they discovered lakes large and small, all troublesome to ford because of trees fallen along the banks. And in the places between the lakes stood dense forests. In those forests they saw many creatures, although most were so wary of capture that few were taken. Three kinds of deer lived there, also hares and rabbits, bears and lions. An animal with a pocket in its belly was found, a little creature not more than two spans in length. In its pocket its young were kept for their protection, and should they be out feeding and an enemy draw near, the mother will not run until all are safely in. And everywhere were seen great flocks of birds. But, other than a few scattered groups of dwellings, the expeditions could not discover another town.

Before the end of the second week in Apalachen, in consequence of the constant harassment by the Indians who would fire at any that ventured beyond the limits of the village, certain officers began to urge that the expedition move on. The sixteenth day—a servant of the commissary named Don Pedro, once an Aztec prince of the blood from Tescuco in Mexico, having been transfixed by an arrow that morning while carrying water—the principal officers, together with the commissary, approached the Governor.

As had been true ever since his recovery from the effects of the intoxicating brew, Governor Narvaez was separated from all the other officers. He lay half naked on a pile of skins, his face covered by a cloth, a pipe filled with tobacco weed in one hand, a half-empty gourd resting next to the other. Although there was much scuffling of boots, loud talk, coughs and other sounds as the officers came up, it was as if the Governor heard nothing. He lifted his pipe to his lips, puffed, then lowered it as he fumbled for the gourd with the other hand.

"We beg some few minutes of your time for a council, my Governor," Alvar Nuñez spoke out in a strong voice, the others grunting sounds of agreement. "We must report the death of a man killed by an arrow not an hour since."

The Governor pulled away the cloth covering his face and turned his head toward the men. "The one of Tescuco?" his speech was thick. "I have already gained intelligence of the matter. I am sorry for your loss, Father Juan," he nodded in the direction of Friar Xuarez, "I would rather lose a captain than a well-trained servant." A rumbling sound arose from the assessor's chest and the controller forced back his shoulders, causing his sword to rattle in its scabbard. "Take, as a gift, one of the captured Indians," the Governor continued. "With patience you will instruct him to be the equal of the other." He then raised his pipe again.

"It was not to beg gifts that we seek this council," Captain Castillo spoke out, his voice hoarse, his face a mottled purple. "Nor to discuss the merits of servants!"

"Have the rigors of the journey cost you your levity, Alonso del Castillo?" the Governor asked, then sucked up loudly through his nose.

"When I am returned to Cadiz, watching minstrels and mummers at a fair, I will again find my sanguineous humor." The Captain passed his hand over his eyes in a quick gesture.

"But quartered in a village not fit for dogs, shot at should I venture into the open, my mouth having forgotten the taste of meat, tortured with lice, plagued by heat and separated by surely five hundred leagues from the nearest Christian town, you must excuse my lack of lightheartedness, Pánfilo de Narvaez."

As the Captain finished speaking, Alvar Nuñez reached over and gently laid his hand on the man's shoulder. "It has been a difficult time for us all, Alonso," he said slowly. "Near sixty days of struggle through jungle to find a village swine would not endure. But, Alonso, I know no cure for the pain of yesterday. Only for the unspent portion of this day and for tomorrow can we seek to secure relief."

"Spoken like a man of the cloth, Alvar Nuñez," the Governor laughed, then drained the remaining drops from the gourd. "Do you not agree, Friar Xuarez, that my second-in-command, had he taken orders instead of arms, would already wear the bishop's miter, mayhap the cardinal's cap?"

"I have observed much that is priestly in Alvar Nuñez," the friar answered carefully. He hesitated, raised his eyes to those of the Governor, then continued, "And I little doubt that had he chosen church, not king, caution above all other things being deemed desirable in an abbot or bishop, we must find him this day master of some rich monastery or lord of a great cathedral."

"And the reward of rashness, Friar Xuarez?" Alvar Nuñez asked, in a voice no soldier in the furthest reaches of the village could fail to hear. "Master of the swamp and jungle? Lord of the Village of Forty Hovels?"

"Do you seek to mock me, Alvar Nuñez?"

"I? I, mock the Holy Commissary of this expedition? I, mock the one whose great wisdom caused him to urge that ships be abandoned and an unknown forest entered, each man heavily burdened with two pounds of bisquit and a full half pound of bacon?" Several of the officers grinned; those who did not grin wiped their mouths and coughed.

The Governor raised himself to one elbow and blinked his reddened eye against the harsh sunlight. His eye then traveled from face to face of those grouped around him, resting for several moments on each one. "It is not seemly that my commissary and second-in-command should quarrel," he said slowly. "Any who knew of Friar Xuarez's belief in the need for suffering would not deem his advice rash." As the Governor spoke, a look transformed his face that can only be described as one of surprise. It was as if he were listening to the words of another man.

"I have noticed, my Governor," Andres Dorantes started speaking, hesitated, then continued at a nod from the Governor, "I have noticed that a priest will never turn to one not in orders for advice about the Mass, confession or other sacred matters. And if one like me should dare offer a suggestion, he would, I think, before he grew much older, face a judgment of the Holy Inquisition."

"Yet," the assessor added, "this same priest will not hesitate to advise a captain—even a governor—on matters not related to religion."

"When Church councils are called," Captain Castillo offered, in a voice much softened, "are hidalgos or officers ever present? Yet at the councils of captains, clergymen are often found."

"No door can be barred to the Church!" said Friar Xuarez, pointing a quivering finger at the Captain. "The spiritual welfare of man is ever the priest's concern."

"Guard well, then, our spiritual welfare, Holy Friar," Alvar Nuñez crossed himself as he spoke. "I have no quarrel that my soul should be in your keeping; but as for temporal matters, it would be best if these were left to those who better understand them." Without exception, all the officers murmured their agreement, although more than half crossed themselves at the same time. Friar Xuarez looked toward the Governor, but he kept his face turned away as he carefully raised himself to his feet, using an outcropping of rock for balance. Then, still holding on to the rock with one hand, his body swaying slightly, the Governor gestured with the other for whoever had things to say to speak. But the gesture, although it swept a wide arc, stopped before it reached the friar, who stood to the left, away from the rest.

"Not less than a score of men have suffered wounds from the Indians, my Governor, also several horses," Alvar Nuñez said, after glancing quickly at the other officers. "More than two score are sick from louse bites and tainted water. Each day passed in this sad place must bring fresh sorrow. Today we lost the Aztec lord of Tescuco. Tomorrow a soldier? An officer? No one is safe. If there is a tinklet of gold in all of Apalachen it is so well hidden, I'll give my oath, that it will only be uncovered the day the dead again are risen. Let us depart Apalachen, my Governor, and let it be soon."

"Back through the swamps and forests, Alvar Nuñez?" the Governor shook his head from side to side. "Two months more of struggle through jungle in the heat of summer? To again be greeted by the people of Dulchanchellin—embraced by other bands of Indians who have so many reasons to love us?"

"Not back, my Governor, forward!"

"Forward?" The Governor's head stopped shaking and his eyebrows drew together.

"Yes, forward," the comptroller joined in. "There may yet be treasure. . . ."

"Treasure? Do you have knowledge of any treasure, Alonso Enriquez?" The Governor extended his soiled hand toward the comptroller, then let it drop as the other man slowly shook his head.

"A question, Pánfilo de Narvaez," Alvar Nuñez silenced the mumbling men with his hand, "a question. If asked: 'Is there gold somewhere in all the land of Florida?' what would you answer?"

"To such a question I could not make an answer."

"Think on these matters, then, my Governor. Did not Ponce de Leon speak of hoards of treasure, on his return from Florida? And the Indians who kept their dead in boxes under painted deerskins, did they not tell us of the yellow metal, and did we not find a trace of gold in their village? And have we not learned from others—Dulchanchellin, those we captured at the village near the river—of treasure stored in Apalachen?"

The Governor snorted. "You talk in riddles, Alvar Nuñez—treasure stored in Apalachen! If piles of dung are treasure and lice are jewels . . ."

"Hear me through, Pánfilo, before you make your judgment. If you were chief of a certain town where there were quantities of gold—let us call that place by the name: Iscariot—if you were cacique of Iscariot, where fifty or sixty thousand golden ducats lay hidden, would you want a company of Spanish soldiers, well armed and ready to do battle, to know of your hoard?" The Governor wiped his nose, which had begun to drip, then shook his head. Other officers in that company shook their heads also. "Yet these same Spanish soldiers know that there is gold in the land of Florida and are determined to find it. What should the cacique do?" The Governor grinned, then shrugged his shoulders. "To protect the wealth of this town of Iscariot," Alvar Nuñez continued, "we must broadcast it about that another town—the poorest in all the district—is the one where treasure can be found."

"A town like Apalachen!" Captain Juan Pantoja shouted. "Let us seek this other town of Iscariot, my Governor. To return to Spain poorer than we came—dressed in tatters, our toes showing through our boots . . . No! Let us find the town with all the golden ducats."

"As Captain Pantoja says," Alvar Nuñez nodded at the man, "the rich cacique tells all he meets that whoever seeks gold must look for it in a place like Apalachen. And each tells another, until at last it reaches Spanish ears."

"Say on, Alvar Nuñez," the Governor steadied himself so

his body ceased to sway, "your words, I must confess, are the sweetest sounds I've heard in many weeks."

"You may ask: Can we be sure that somewhere in this district—within a hundred leagues—there is a treasure? You may ask: What if all the towns are as poor as Apalachen? And I would answer: Then why the rumor of riches stored in Apalachen? How do Indians three hundred leagues distant from this town come to know its name? Was there ever smoke without somewhere fire? Mayhap the wind has carried the smoke away a little, so that beneath the cloud one will find no fire smouldering. But if that one will seek further . . . Do I convey my meaning, my Governor?"

"The cacique of that town is a clever man," a broad grin showed on the Governor's face. "When I meet that one, I will offer him such a greeting that not an Indian within a thousand leagues will fail to hear of it. I must teach him of the sin of lying and of avarice. . . ."

"He must learn the sweetness of charity!" Soto Mayor shouted as he slapped his thigh.

"And the blessings of poverty," Andres Dorantes added.

"Do not forget chastity or obedience, Pánfilo," Captain Castillo offered.

"He will have no struggle to be chaste after he receives my greeting," the Governor made a cutting motion with his thumb across his middle finger. "As for obedience, Alonso del Castillo, I promise you, in time, he will gain that too."

The day following that of his council with his captains, Governor Narvaez ordered the imprisoned chief of Apalachen brought before him. For many hours, by pictures drawn in sand, by signs and other means, he questioned the man. The four guides taken of the people of Dulchanchellin the Governor also questioned, each away from the others, and always together with his second-in-command. For five days the Governor and Alvar Nuñez either questioned the Indians or conferred. From the Indians they learned that Apalachen was the only village of any size in that region—information already obtained by the three expeditions and now confirmed. But, touching of the region towards the south, they gained intelligence of a town named Aute. Nine days' journeying it would be, through a land of many lakes, was the account of each Indian. And each, separately, portrayed Aute as being greater in size than Apalachen, but did not agree as to how much greater: half again as large, said the oldest one of Dulchanchellin; many times the size, offered the chief of Apalachen. All said there was much maize in Aute, also beans and pumpkins and, being near the sea, there was fish.

The Governor having determined to seek Aute, and orders having been given to make preparations, the soldiers and officers could speak of nothing but the ducats to be found in Aute. For the words of Alvar Nuñez, as they passed from lip to lip, changed from "mayhap" to "yes," and with each new telling the number of golden ducats grew.

Much care was given to the preparations for departure. A quantity of maize was gathered, then baked into cakes—enough to last each man ten days. The sick were washed, their wounds bound, bled if need be, the recovery of many speeded by knowledge of the coming journey. Weapons were sharpened, armor cleaned, fittings and leather oiled, rents in clothing stitched and the horses had the cracks in their hoofs mended with pitch. Nothing that needed to be done was left undone; for, included in the preparation, was the Governor's order that every man be confessed before departure. And it was not a minute's whisper, a muttered blessing, and then the next one. There were no five-quick-Marys-and-two-Paters, but hours of telling beads required, and on the knees, and in the summer's heat with no relief. Nor were the officers spared. Several fell into a faint and must be doused with water. Yet how much louder would the men have prayed, how many more penances would they have begged, could they have seen where the season's change would bring them?

XII

Twenty-five days from our arrival at Apalachen, after a blessing given by Friar Xuarez, who swung his great cross like a sword, and after Governor Narvaez read from the patent granted him by the King, we departed southward, seeking the town of Aute.

Although the Indians of Apalachen had not failed to harass us each day we stayed in their town, the first day of our southward journey, as we sought passages through lakes and around fallen timber, we saw no one. And that night, believing we had escaped the assault of the savages, we held a joyful celebration, with the slave Chichi, dressed as a woman, dancing to a drum made of a hollow tree. Then others danced, with no regard to who was maid or who was man, and some beer, brewed of maize, was passed around. Even the priests, excepting Friar Xuarez, danced. Only he, of all the company, kept apart and prayed, his great cross raised so it reached into the branches of the trees.

With lightened spirits and much laughter after a night of restful sleep, we resumed our journey southward. But within an hour, upon arriving at a broad lake, difficult of crossing, we were attacked by Indians. We answered the attack with crossbow—arquebus being of no effect because of the wet. Men grouped together to protect each other with buckler. But the Indians drove their arrows with such effect that they wounded many men and horses despite the shields.

We forced our way on through the lake, encouraged by shouts from the Governor and others in command who braved grave dangers as they searched out hiding Indians and struck at them with their swords. That none of us came to be killed in that lake was a miracle. But we lost the captured cacique, for he fell amongst his people as soon as he found the chance.

Once across the lake we could not rest, and hurried forward lest the Indians regroup and attack again.

After a league, traveled at a speed that brought anguish to the wounded and caused the bleeding horses to bellow, we came to another lake which appeared to be more dangerous, as it was longer. We plunged in, but were not interrupted in our passage. Perhaps it was that the Indians had exhausted their store of arrows. Whatever the reason, we saw no more Indians that day, and passed a peaceful night, the cooling wind returning without a trace of rain.

But this night there was no celebration, and no dancing, and the slave Chichi did not dress as a woman, for he was wounded in the thigh and lay next to Soto Mayor, moaning. And there were no drumbeats, and no loud talking; the unscathed, as they bathed and bound the injured, whispered. Cloths tied over the horses' mouths kept them silent as their hurts were salved, and a changing guard of two-score men stayed vigilant. Men spoke in soft voices of the miracle that none had died. Many, guided by the priests, gave thanks for gifts already granted, and prayed that all might be spared further suffering. Those more lightly wounded talked, one with the other, of the fierceness of the Indians. They spoke of the Indians' great strength and quickness; how their arrows passed steel armor as if through wood.

In the morning so great was the distress of many that, had not the Governor threatened to hang with his own hands any who defied him, we would not have continued marching. Scores lay about after being ordered to get ready. Dozens muttered curses and pretended not to hear. But when the Governor walked among them, an unsheathed sword in one hand, a rope in the other, with Alvar Nuñez beside him, in his hand a rope also, they began to stir. "Sons of whores," the Governor called them, "sheep without balls," "ancient crones," "turds of swine," and Alvar Nuñez cursed them no less, calling them, "withered cows," "shit-eating dogs," "cowards on whose heads grew horns," and in this way were the men driven to their feet.

By the eighth day of our journey from Apalachen, our condition was much improved. The wounds of many were almost mended. Few of the horses still limped. We had come onto fresh springs of water, which cured the cramp. And, learning that we should reach Aute before nightfall, all showed great excitement. Again there was talk of treasure, and of good things to eat; for, although not suffering starvation, we had had our fill of parched maize and ashcake.

We were within a league of the place to which we were going when Indians fell upon those bringing up the rear. They overran a small number who had lagged behind, then attacked us. They transfixed an hidalgo with an arrow through the neck bringing the number of men we had lost in our journey through Florida to three. Still, although there was sadness as we carried the corpse to Aute, none could say that our losses were too severe—only three men in three months of travel through hostile jungle.

XIII

Except for those who had been the dead hidalgo's friends, the men showed a greater sadness at the condition of Aute than they had at his death. All the houses had been burned; all the inhabitants gone. If there was treasure it too was gone, or well hidden, for we never saw the shine of a single grain of silver or the gleam of a bit of gold. Maize, beans and pumpkins we found in good plenty, all fit for gathering. Also there were palmettos and a sweet nut. On these we feasted, every man having enough to eat, but such was our dejection that there was no celebration as we lay about the fires that night, stuffed with food.

Fearing an attack from the inhabitants of Aute whose howls and drumbeats were heard coming from different parts of the forest, a heavy guard was mounted and, to protect our flank, the Governor ordered a deep trench dug, on whose near side was constructed a great abatis. Those whose disappointment was greatest at finding no gold urged an attack against the Indians. But others counselled restraint—what use would it be to engage the Indians? And might we not suffer great losses of horses and men? Before making a response to the various suggestions brought to him, the Governor first asked the opinion of Alvar Nuñez, who, each time, sided with those who urged restraint.

Having passed, on our way to Aute, a river whose waters tasted salt and having learned from the Indian guides that a great ocean lay close at hand, the Governor, after two days of rest, ordered his second-in-command to take a sufficient company and go search for the sea. Accordingly, the next morning Alvar Nuñez set out with Alonso del Castillo, Andres Dorantes, seven more on horseback, fifty on foot, and the commissary, Friar Xuarez, whose services he had specially requested. There were some who whispered that Alvar Nuñez had begged the company of the commissary to keep his lips away from the Governor's ears.

That same day, just before sunset, knowing perhaps of our weakness, for the men Alvar Nuñez took were the strongest among us, the Indians of Aute attacked. They swarmed in, firing flame-tipped arrows and hurling rocks and spears. Had we not had the protection of the trench and abatis at our rear, we must have been overrun. But they were driven off with the loss of one of our horses, and several of our men wounded. All admired the skill and courage of the Governor, for he stood forward, protected only by his armor, as he commanded the men, and he never flinched, even when arrows flew at him, which he fended off with his buckler.

The following day at sunset, they swarmed in again, setting ablaze with their burning arrows some structures we had made. Again the Governor stood forward; but this time taking an arrow through the thigh. And again, guided by his orders, we drove the Indians back.

Fearing that Alvar Nuñez and his company were lost, or if not lost would not return for many days, the Governor ordered a second trench dug to guard our front. And another abatis was constructed, as well as lesser trenches fitted with sharpened sticks. For half the night, by the light of a dozen fires, we worked. None slept, not even the most sorely wounded. Those who could not walk, driven by the kicks and curses of the Governor and of the officers, crawled, carrying out sacks of earth. Those who could not crawl sharpened sticks with their daggers. When at last all was completed, the Governor walked about, using an Indian spear as a crutch—his wounded thigh having swollen—telling the men that, as they were Spanish soldiers, they must fight bravely as had Spanish soldiers since the days of El Cid. Fight, die if needs be, but no surrender or retreat.

Perhaps it was that his hurt had brought the fever, for as he walked about the camp, blood oozing from his wound, his voice grew louder, his face darker, and his one eye more swollen. "Soldiers of Spain," he addressed the men, "hidalgos, caballeros, Infanzones of His Sacred Caesarean Catholic Majesty, conquerors of the New World: Tomorrow will be tested your right to call yourselves by the name of men. Tomorrow it will be known if lousy, painted savages can frighten the sons of men

86

who drove the Moorish infidel from the soil of Spain. Before the sun is again gone, it will be known if coward will be added to the name given those fathered by your seed. Tomorrow the world will learn if all must laugh when they hear mention of those who journeyed with the expedition of Pánfilo de Narvaez. But this one," the Governor struck his chest, "must first be dead before any who serves with him will disgrace his name. For I will behead, and with these two hands quarter, the man who lays down his arms or turns his back to the enemy. Soldiers of Spain," he thundered, "soldiers of Spain," he said again, his voice breaking, "soldiers of Spain . . ." he said for the third time, then pitched forward on the ground, where he lay in a faint from too much bleeding.

By morning, although much recovered, the Governor was still too weak to stand unaided, and whatever orders he gave were in a whisper.

Many still sick lay exhausted on the ground, yet were afraid to sleep, for at any minute they expected the attack of the Indians. And when the forward guards signaled that a stirring in the forest had been heard, even those most severely wounded raised themselves up and unsheathed their swords.

Never in the several thousand years since Creation had that malign and desolate place known such laughter and such a celebration as when Alvar Nuñez and his men stepped from the forest, for it was their sounds the guards had heard. Not a man of all the ones in camp failed to shed tears. And, of the men in Alvar Nuñez's company, each was hugged as if he were a maiden.

"After a day and you had not returned, Alvar Nuñez Cabeza de Vaca, we despaired of your return," the Governor said in a cracking voice. "If yourselves not destroyed by the Indians —and with there being so many of them and they so savage, we believed that to be the case—if by some miracle you survived, we feared, upon your return, you would find us all slaughtered."

"Again, through the intercession of the Almighty, have we been spared," Friar Xuarez shouted as he made his way through the men. "Have I not told you a hundred times, Pánfilo de Narvaez, that this expedition is under His protection?" Then the friar ordered all to their knees and blessed us, calling on certain saints for guidance.

The Governor, succumbing to his wounds, could not rise when the blessing ended. Twice he tried to force his body up, then, with the sigh of a worn old man, he fell over, his face showing a terrible pallor.

As was his right, Alvar Nuñez assumed command, and ordered preparations to abandon Aute before another hour, our position there being judged too hazardous. And, as the men made preparations for the departure, he conferred with the other officers, telling them where he had been and the nature of the land.

After leaving Aute, he had traveled until the hour of vespers, when he arrived at a road or inlet to the sea. There, he found oysters in large numbers, for which his men rejoiced as they satisfied their hunger. Then, after spending a peaceful night, he had sent twenty men, commanded by Captain Dorantes, to explore along the inlet to learn its direction and the distance to the sea. This party, after two days, returned, reporting numerous inlets and bays, but they did not reach the open sea, it being too distant, and the risk of further exploration being judged too great.

After hearing the account of his explorations, all the officers agreed that the inlet where oysters had been found would be a safer place to camp than Aute. Accordingly, as soon as the gear and horses were ready, carrying as much beans and maize as could be stored in the men's packs, with those too sick to walk tied, like sacks, two to each horse, we departed Aute.

The journey to the place Alvar Nuñez visited, although lasting only that one day, proved difficult. Each hour more men fell sick, until there were not sufficient horses to carry them, and they must be supported by their companions, themselves in a weakened condition. Wounds that had closed tore open from the exertion, and if any sought to find the direction we had gone, they need only follow our trail of blood. Some, too broken in spirit to go on, begged to be left where they might die in peace. But Alvar Nuñez, despite the importuning of several, whose conditions were piteous indeed, ordered that none be left—those who resisted dragged by their arms if needs be. In this way we traveled until, just as the sun was setting, we reached the inlet to the sea.

To detail the suffering of the men that night would be only to repeat things already said. More than a third were very sick. It being already dark, and even the well suffering from severe exhaustion, no food was cooked. Many, too weak to move, lay on the damp ground while mosquitos, ants and gnats made meals of their flesh. Yet, while most passed the hours of darkness in distress, some passed these hours in another way.

Although they had been careful to keep their voices muffled and their actions unobserved, by the next day every man in camp was aware that most of the mounted officers had secretly met to plot desertion of the Governor and the company. Who organized that meeting, no one knew. But, by midnight, except for a few principal officers, all were gathered about a fire built a distance from the camp, where the condition of the expedition was discussed. Most agreed that by abandoning the Governor and the sick, whose prostration must prevent further travel, they would be able to secure a better fate for themselves. "Why should all die when some can be saved?" asked one. "To remain here in this jungle must, in time, cost every man his life," added another. "On horse, keeping close to the coast, we will find our ships or reach a port," offered a third. And so their talk ran, each giving a stronger argument than the one before, to prove the need for desertion.

After a vote of broken straws—a long one saying yes, a short one no—and there being only a few short straws cast into the helmet, they agreed to ask Alvar Nuñez, who was not present, to lead them. He came up from the place he had been sleeping and listened while they told him of their plans.

Then he said, "I see among you certain ones of gentle condition, sons of hidalgos who themselves were sons of noble Spanish men. I see caballeros whose names are honored in every province of Spain for the noble deeds of others who once carried these same names. I see soldiers who fought the Aztec with Hernan Cortez, who served the King against the comuneros, who defended the Faith against the Turkish infidel. And—I hear voices that urge actions whose deformity must disgrace their lineage for a score of generations." Not once as he spoke did Alvar Nuñez raise his voice. "I hear men, whose friendship once brought honor to any so fortunate as to share it, now suggest that their friends be abandoned; their Governor, who carries in his patent the authority of the Crown, be forsaken to perish, a victim to some stealthy savage's knife. I hear certain ones whose bravery I once esteemed, now, to save their lives, speak the words of cowards. I will leave you," he said slowly, "and go back to my sleep. Perhaps in the morning I will find that all I have seen and heard this hour was a dream—that I am dreaming now."

But that night Alvar Nuñez gained very little sleep, for first one, then another of the officers came up to him and swore to remain with the company; that what should happen to one would be the lot of all, until by morning every man who had gathered by that fire had given his oath not to forsake the rest.

The Governor, although knowing of the gathering of the mounted men and of its purpose, pretended things were as they should be. And all through the day he called each officer in turn to ask advice as to what should be done to escape from a country of such miserable condition. Still sick, he lay on a pile of skins and said very little as he listened to his officers' suggestions.

And after each man had his say, the Governor held out his hand to thank him.

All were of the opinion that, unless a means was quickly found to escape this region of northern Florida, in time all must pass out of it through death. A third of the people being very sick, with the number increasing each hour, further travel by land was no longer possible. Thus, the only passage by which we might hope to get away was that of the sea. Yet, for such travel, vessels must be built, and no one could say how such a thing could be done, for we had no knowledge of their construction, no tools and no materials with which to build them. Besides this, offered each officer who consulted with the Governor, there was not sufficient food to sustain those who could labor.

By late afternoon, all who had conferred with the Governor were deeply dejected, although some, encouraged by the priests, turned their thoughts to God, trusting that He would direct things as should best serve Him.

As the sun dipped below the trees, all the camp fell silent, all work was set aside; all but those whose vision was dimmed by approaching death looked up at the sky, streaked crimson and purple with clouds showing orange, black and silver. As all who could still see gazed upward, the little slave, Chichi, died.

The last league from Aute he had been carried by his master, Soto Mayor, his head so weak it rested on the other's shoulder, his arms loose as those of the marionette. Then he had lain without moving, moaning softly; at times, sleeping, but except for sips of water not taking a bite of nourishment, although different ones offered him baked oysters, beans and gruel. Those whose wont it had been to most tease the little man were the ones who most attended him as he lay dying. Some themselves so sick they could not walk without falling, crawled over to offer a moment's comfort. But the slave's eyes stayed closed, his answer a flutter of the lids and a wordless movement of his lips.

Perhaps it was that in the death of Chichi everyone saw reflected his own departure from this earth. Perhaps to each one Chichi was a son or a brother now gone. Or perhaps they loved the man. For, except for those who themselves wrestled with the strangling arms, not a man in that company did not mourn the passing of the slave.

And that night five others also died.

XIV

The next morning, after the dead had been buried Alvar Nuñez and the Governor conferred, with one or another officer coming up at different times for a few words. And all were much surprised when, shortly before the hour of noon, they saw a certain Theodoro, laughingly called "Don Theodoro," a Greek slave captured from a Turkish galley, walk over to the place where Alvar Nuñez and the Governor were conferring. That a slave would dare approach the Governor and his second-in-command without being summoned was a thing that could not escape notice. At first the Governor's face darkened, his veins swelling from his neck; then, after a few words from the Greek, he listened.

"On the Island of Crete, from which I was taken by Turkish pirates when little more than a boy," Don Theodoro told the Governor and Alvar Nuñez, "my uncle Niklos, to whom I was apprenticed, was employed as a builder of boats." The Greek grinned and pulled his ear. "I have not touched an adze in more than twenty years," he said slowly, wiping the perspi-

92

ration from his face with his arm, "and my hands have grown clumsy." He showed his hands, horned with callus from years of pulling galley oars. "But my uncle was a master builder, and the things he taught me he helped me remember with a stick, at different times with his fist." The Greek grinned again. "I know a way we may build the vessels needed to depart this place—with your permission . . ."

"Your uncle, Niklos, you say, was a master boat builder?" The Governor's words were at the same time a question and a supplication. "And you served him as apprentice—for how many years?"

"I was not yet in my twelfth year when he took me, my Governor. He was my mother's brother and came to our village and asked my father for me. I stayed with him until Turkish pirates sacked the town; it was near the close of my sixteenth year."

"In all that time you must have learned much of the art of building boats," said the Governor. The Greek inclined his head. "Again, Alvar Nuñez," the Governor turned to the other man, "we have evidence that we are under Divine protection." Then, with shouts and gestures, he called various officers to him. When most had gathered, after a great laugh which rose up from his belly, he said to them, "Have I not told you many times that this expedition travels under a special dispensation?" Certain officers murmured their assent. "When different ones of you came to tell of your doubts, did I not urge faith?—belief in Him who sent His only son to walk the earth so that we might be saved? Again our faith is answered!" The Governor picked up a stick and pointed it at Don Theodoro. "This one's uncle built boats in Crete," he nodded at Don Theodoro. "Did not each of you separately say to me that only by sea can we escape this place? Now we have a way." The Governor ordered the Greek to stand in the center of the gathering. "For how many years, Greek, were you apprenticed to this uncle of yours who built boats on the island of Crete?"

"For five years, my Governor."

"Five years, do you hear him?" The Governor struck his chest. "And did you learn a little of the craft of boatbuilding in those five years?"

"More than a little, my Governor. Had I not been taken by the Turks, in one, no more than two years, I must have been judged a journeyman."

"In one, no more than two years, he must have been judged a journeyman! Is there any who does not believe that Don Theodoro knows more than a little of the art of fashioning vessels? Tell us, Don Theodoro, how should we prepare for the construction of enough boats to take us from this place? Speak freely."

"We must first have tools, my Governor. I will fashion bellows of pipes made of wood and deerskin. Then build a forge in which to soften iron."

"Iron?" the comptroller turned to the Governor. "Except for a dozen, no more than a score of bars for horses' shoes, we have no iron."

"We have stirrups and spurs, my Governor," Don Theodoro offered. "Sword, halberd, crossbow, pike and mace—all of iron, my Governor."

"Swords!" various captains shouted, their faces darkening. "Crossbows!" Captain Juan Pantoja stepped forward as if to lay violent hands on the Greek. "Give up our weapons?" the assessor turned to the Governor.

"As the Greek has said," the Governor held up his hand to quiet the men, "we need tools, and for tools there must be iron. First stirrups and spurs . . ."

"For nails, and hammers to drive them, my Governor. Then pikes and halberds." The Greek swallowed. "Pikes for axes, that we may fell trees, my Governor, halberds for saws, to saw them into planks."

"And crossbows? Will you need crossbows, Greek?"

"For the adze that must be used to shape the wood, my Governor, I must have a dozen crossbows."

94

"A dozen crossbows, then, but no more. And no swords. We cannot risk giving up our swords."

"I will build your vessels without swords, my Governor. And with the Lord's help I may need only eight or ten crossbows. But before the boats are done, I must have rope for rigging, cloth for sails . . ." The Governor grunted then with an impatient gesture dismissed the man.

With a deep bow, his one hand tugging at his ear, the other wiping perspiration from his brow, the Greek began to back away. But he had not departed half a dozen paces when the Governor ordered him to stay a minute longer. "In all things affecting the building of the boats," said the Governor in a rumbling voice, "until the vessels shall be launched, the slave Don Theodoro is not slave but master. Except for this one alone," the Governor laid his hand on his breast, "all must obey the man." He searched the lowering faces of the officers. "If a she-ass should this very moment appear from the forest with a special knowledge of how to free us from this jungle prison, I would set the beast over all my men, and without hesitation." Several of the officers began muttering to each other. "But to you, Don Theodoro, I have this to say," the Governor beckoned the man closer. "If it should happen that you cannot build the boats and I learn that you play the fool's game with me, and if, within a time which will be agreed upon, the vessels have not been launched, I will have you hung by your ankles from a tree, flayed, slowly roasted, your body quartered then thrown into the jungle to feed the beasts. Do you understand my meaning, Greek?" The slave inclined his head. "But," the Governor said in a softened voice, "if the boats are built and launched as planned, from that day, Don Theodoro, you are a free man!"

After Don Theodoro had been dismissed, the men had much to say to the Governor and he to them. And in these matters it was as if Alvar Nuñez and the Governor were one.

"Never have I known of an officer ordered to obey a slave!" were Soto Mayor's words.

"Rather would I rot here in this jungle than lose my honor!" shouted Captain Juan Pantoja.

"To set a Greek of the galleys over Spanish gentlemen!" said Esquivel in an angry voice, "When, in all the years of our empire, has such a thing been done?"

Even the assessor and the notary showed troubled faces, and all turned to listen as Friar Xuarez stepped forward, many expecting him also to oppose the Governor.

"Cannot a King dub a shepherd knight?" were the friar's first words. "If he please, can he not elevate this same shepherd to be the chiefest lord in all his realm?" The friar paused as he surveyed the men, many of whom still had angry looks. "Another thing," the friar's hand touched his cross, "if a pope choose, can he not lay his hand on the kneeling peasant's head who will then rise a bishop? If the King can make a shepherd, lord, the pope anoint a peasant, bishop, cannot one holding a royal patent raise a slave to be master for a certain time?" Again, Friar Xuarez slowly surveyed the men before taking his place beside the Governor, who made room for him.

"What Friar Xuarez has stated is true," Alvar Nuñez spoke slowly, forming each word carefully. "And you who grumble, rather offer thanksgiving to the Lord for having set amongst us such a one as Don Theodoro. And in your prayers, thank Him so that, through this Greek, we may find a way out of this remote and malign jungle." For several moments there was silence, then grumbling again.

"These, also, are my orders;" the Governor silenced the men by striking his buckler with a mace. "Four times, if needs be five, we will make entry into Aute with all the cavalry and enough others so that we may have maize and beans, and, to nourish those who must work and strengthen the sick, every third day a horse will be killed." Fresh murmurs broke out among the men. "We must have meat!" the Governor shouted. "And there will be no room for horses in the boats." The murmurs grew louder.

"Rather would I rip the hair from that Greek's face than destroy my faithful beast," snarled Andres Dorantes. Others shouted their objections.

"Do I hear words of mutiny?" the Governor hissed. "Before I grow another hour older, must I hang some of my bravest officers?"

"Perhaps they speak in haste, Pánfilo," Alvar Nuñez offered.

"May it be as you say. For it would distress me to see officers dance in the air for the sake of horses."

"Indeed, Pánfilo, it would be a pity if brave officers died for such a foolish thing."

Although there was more grumbling and angry looks, not one again spoke his defiance openly.

By evening of the next day, which was August fourth, all knew that the Greek had spoken the truth to the Governor. After fashioning a forge and a great bellows, which caused such a heat that the hardest iron quickly softened, he then formed half a score of heavy axes and a dozen saws, which were employed the following morning for felling trees.

Before one week, we felled and peeled enough wood for the five boats we needed, each to be twenty-two cubits in length. And so the work went forward—forming planks, cutting poles, shaping wood for ribs, collecting resin from pine trees to be used as pitch, caulking with the fiber of the palmetto, twisting ropes of the manes and tails of horses and stitching shirts together for use as sails.

Four different times, as ordered by the Governor, those soldiers who could be spared, about fifty men, and all the remaining cavalry made entries into Aute to secure provisions. Yet these were not made without contentions with the Indians who opposed them, each time wounding several men. But the Governor deemed these raids vital, for as many as four hundred fenegas of maize were secured every time. To no one's surprise, our raids brought like assaults from the offended Indians, but against these, because of our secure position and our diligence, we made good defense.

But we were not without our losses. So angered had the Indians grown that they stayed hidden in the forest, watching for the unwary Spaniard who wandered too far from the protection of the camp. Not a week passed without one such being found, his head and hands missing, his manly parts cut away, his body transfixed with no less than a dozen arrows.

The twenty-eighth day of our boat-building, despite the danger of lurking Indians, ten men gained permission to seek in the coves and inlets for enough oysters that all in camp might make a supper of that sweet fish. They had traveled less than a quarter of a league, and were still within sight, when the Indians attacked, killing all ten without any in camp being able to offer them relief.

The deaths of these ten men came near to halting all work on the boats, for a dejection spread throughout the camp that had only been equaled when we first entered Apalachen and saw its condition.

"Why sweat any longer in this heat, when we all must die," were the words of one.

"Let us find our peace with God, rather than labor tortured by insects and the burning sun," said another.

"Rather would I face that which must surely come, here on land, than drown at sea," offered a third.

By morning, the depression had grown so heavy that less than half would leave their sleeping places to work on the boats.

Had not Alvar Nuñez and the comptroller held tightly onto the Governor's sword arm and begged him to allow the men two minutes to change their minds, the Governor would have beheaded every man who still lay beneath his blanket, such was his anger. Seeing his fury, the bulging muscles in the arm that held the blade, and how hard Alvar Nuñez and the comptroller struggled to restrain him, those who had refused to work threw off their blankets and ran to the place where the work was being done. Even after they held tools in their hands and were intent upon their work, the Governor kept shouting that he would shorten a dozen before he grew ten minutes older, to teach the rest a lesson. But Alvar Nuñez kept begging him to grant the men mercy in consideration of their months of suffering; and although the Governor made free with his sword among the trembling men, he used its flat and not its edge.

After the death of the ten who had gone to gather oysters, so careful did we all become that we lost no more men at the hands of those Indians. Yet scarcely two days could pass without one of our sick succumbing, until, by the twenty-second of September, when the boats were ready, no fewer than forty were dead of disease.

The night before we were to depart, Alvar Nuñez confronted the Governor in front of all the officers. It was his belief that Pánuco was too far distant to be safely reached in such frail craft. "Turn east, then sail south," he begged the man in a respectful voice, inclining his head a little. "Let us return to Bahia de la Cruz, where we first landed; there our ships, which must be searching along this coast, will surely find us. Do not risk further explorations into unknown territory, my Governor."

"Sail three hundred leagues, Alvar Nuñez?" asked the Governor with a narrowing of his one eye. "To a deserted bay where we must wait, hoping and praying that our ships discover us? Why such a distance to such a place, my friend? Why not westward, fifty, mayhap a hundred leagues, to a Spanish port where we may be properly received?"

"One hundred leagues and we will see Pánuco's smoking chimneys," Friar Xaurez joined in.

Not one of the officers would support Alvar Nuñez. Several declared their agreement with the Governor. At this, Alvar Nuñez gave his shoulders a great shrug, muttering, "May the Almighty guide us and prove me wrong."

It was then that the Governor ordered that the lead boat,

which must find the way through the reefs and rocks, be the one commanded by Alvar Nuñez. "Take the slave of Andres Dorantes," he said to Alvar Nuñez, laying his hand on his shoulder, "he, being the tallest of all the men, can walk ahead of your boat, when needs be, to find passages through the reefs." The Governor then turned to my master, Andres Dorantes, who quickly signaled his agreement.

"Hey, Estevanico," Andres Dorantes called out, "come from behind that tree where I know you to be hiding. Hey, Estevanico," he called again as I stepped from the shadows into the fire's light.

"Always near, yet always hidden, eh, Estevan?" Alvar Nuñez asked with a sly grin.

"At night that one's black skin . . ." muttered Friar Xuarez. "Black as the skin of Satan."

"Moor," the Governor raised his head and examined my face with his one eye, "you are to sail in the vessel commanded by Alvar Nuñez, do you understand?" I nodded, as he continued to stare. "Because of your great size, Négro, you can walk through water that would drown most other men." This was the first time, to my knowledge, that the Governor had more than glanced at me. "You can swim?" I nodded again.

"All of his race can swim," laughed Captain Juan Pantoja. "Throw one of their pups in the water, even one newborn, and he will swim like a baby otter."

"Négro," the Governor tapped my leg with a stick, "you know of the grant of freedom given the Greek, Don Theodoro?" I nodded. "I make you no promises, but . . ." he smiled and winked his sound eye. "But this I do promise you," he smiled and winked again, "if due to your negligence we suffer any loss, I will have for my cloak your tanned skin."

Different officers, encouraged by the Governor's levity— for he went on to detail what sort of cloak would be cut from my skin and how, when he returned to Spain, it would be admired by noble gentlemen—offered ideas of their own. Captain Pantoja then recalled that night in Cuba when I quartered in the cave with the old Indians put there to die.

"Six women this black man enjoyed that night!" Spittle ran down Captain Pantoja's chin as he expelled a laugh. "Six women! For most Spanish men one, at most two, will prove sufficient. I have heard of certain warriors, inflamed by battle, who serviced three. But to enjoy six gentle ladies in one night . . ." the Captain threw back his head and laughed again, showing his broken teeth.

"If you use that one's skin for your cloak, Pánfilo," said Tellez, a captain who rarely spoke, "think what anger you must face upon your return to Spain when different ladies learn of the fate of Estevan." He dabbed at his eyes with the back of his hand. "Such wailing, such anger . . ."

"A dozen must surely attack you with nails and teeth!" shouted Andres Dorantes.

"A dozen?" roared Juan Pantoja. "A hundred, more like."

"Indeed you are a doomed man, my Governor," Alvar Nuñez joined in. "Think of those angry women—long, sharp needles in their hands—waiting on the quay for you to land so that they may give you proofs of their displeasure."

For no less than half an hour the officers continued in this manner. But after a time, as fatigue overtook them, one by one they departed for their blankets, until only Andres Dorantes and Alonso del Castillo remained sitting before that fire. I earlier had retired a dozen paces to my place in the shadows.

It was my master, Andres Dorantes, who broke the silence. "How far do you judge Pánuco to be from this place, Alonso?" he asked.

"How can I know—a hundred leagues, as the friar said, mayhap half again that number."

"My guess would be two hundred—and if we must follow the twists and turns of the shore, fifty leagues more than two hundred." As he spoke, Andres Dorantes raised his arms above his head and yawned. "Did the words of Alvar Nuñez cause you concern, Alonso?"

"About risking further travel—about it being wiser to return to Bahia de la Cruz?" asked Captain Castillo. Andres Dorantes nodded. "I am not one to dismiss the words of Alvar Nuñez lightly," Captain Castillo said evenly. "At times I have taken my stand with him. But . . ." he hesitated and passed his hand quickly over his eyes, "but this time I judge him too cautious."

"Yes, I must agree with you, Alonso, too cautious."

"Yet, who can know with certainty the distance to Pánuco? If it should prove to be not two hundred leagues, but twice that number? Or even four times as far? Six or eight hundred leagues in these frail boats would be no easy matter, Andres."

"We would not survive—three hundred leagues will carry us to our limit, for four hundred we must have a miracle. Not one man will live to set foot in Pánuco if that town lies five hundred leagues away."

"But, as Friar Xuarez said," Alonso del Castillo spoke slowly, "we may see its smoking chimneys before a hundred leagues."

"Friar Xuarez! Pah!" snorted Andres Dorantes. At this Alonso Castillo grinned. Then after a solemn handshake the two men parted for sleep.

Although fatigued, I did not sleep, but stayed by the water. I stretched out and lay my cheek on the moist sand. I listened to the earth sounds, the whispering of the water, to the wind moaning its secrets to the trees and tried to understand.

How long I lay there before I knew I was not alone, I do not know. There are times when the minute becomes an hour, the hour as one minute. I knew another's eyes were upon me, in my throat and in the tightening of my scalp I knew it—not fifty paces distant stood an Indian, his bowstring drawn. His paint-streaked face shone in the yellow light as I held my breath, waiting for his shaft to transfix me. My lungs grew hot, my heart felt as if it must burst, yet still I held my breath, afraid to receive the arrow in an empty chest. I forced my vision through the darkness, feeling for his eyes with mine. Yet I felt no fear, only awareness of the closeness of death. Had there been fear, I am certain the arrow must have pierced my chest. Perhaps it was the color of my skin, darker by many shades than his own that kept him from releasing that bowstring. Perhaps it was because he knew I felt no fear. I turned my eyes to the yellow moon for a moment, and when I turned them back, he was gone.

I did not leave my place on the sand. I lay there, my head resting in my hands, filled with peace. No thoughts of why there had been no fear stirred in my mind. At other times since that night I have wondered, but not then. It was enough that a brother chose to spare me. I watched the moon ripple on the water; again, I tried to understand the sounds. In the muscle of my arms I felt a throb rising up from the earth; my heat beating down. Nothing mattered.

I closed my eyes and saw the young man who had once been me: Freed of the irons that had chained me to the oar and allowed to venture ashore when the galley chanced to lay at berth, I wandered through strange streets of an Italian town, searching but not knowing for what I searched. It was night, and cold, and I leaned forward against the wind. The warm smell of incense drew me to the massive door of a great stone church—never had I been within such a church before. Small wooden ones I had known. One of moderate size, where I had gained the conversion which freed me from the oar. But, before that night, I had not dared to enter such an ornate structure.

I passed the heavy door with its sharp bolts and iron ribs, but found no warmth inside, only relief from the wind. If there were others in that vast place I did not see them—no priest or deacon, no sexton or sacristan, and no one on his knees in the pews or before the altar. I moved forward, drawn by the flames of the many votive lights. Tall, shimmering statues of the holy saints lined the walls and, standing before the cross, Her arms outstretched, a jeweled crown on Her head, Mary, Christ's Mother towered above them all.

Until that moment, that fair-skinned Lady and Her tortured Son held no meaning for me. I had sought conversion only to be free of the shackles. Had swearing allegiance to Satan been the price of freedom, I would have so sworn. Yet I still felt chained during the many months that had passed since the irons had been broken. But at that moment, that moment in the church, I felt free.

All the bitterness of the years drained away, all the pain, all the loneliness. Yet I knew that fair-skinned Lady to be a stone statue and the bleeding Christ an image made of painted clay. But I also knew another thing—as I filled with warmth although still ten paces from the burning candles, as my breath came deeper, as my limbs trembled, as my heart was lightened without reason, as I felt my body rise, I knew that I was one with Him and would never be alone again.

I opened my eyes. The moon still rippled on the water; the sighing trees still spoke of things I did not understand. Then, as I lay there on the sand, deep in the bones of my body I sensed the danger that was to come. Yet there was no fear, for again I was one with Him.

XV

Shortly after the sun had risen, all the men gathered about the readied boats. The water lay at calm, shimmering in the early light—a sheet of polished silver. And the air was still and clear, except for a place across the inlet, where ribbons of mist still clung.

"Hear me carefully, all you hidalgos, caballeros, Infanzones, priests, slaves and soldiers of the expedition commanded by Pánfilo de Narvaez," the Governor, his drink-inflamed face reflecting the rays of the newly risen sun, addressed the assembled men. "In ways equaled only by the early Christian martyrs, have we suffered since the day we departed Spain. Deserted in Santo Domingo by seven score so faint of heart I must call them women. Women!" He struck his buckler a blow with his fist. "For I see here a company of men! Men whose like will not be found even if one should stand in the very midst of the King's own court. . . . Sixty of our number then lost through the fury of the elements off the Island of Cuba. And, as if we must be tested again as to our strength of faith, there came more adversity: New storms, aground for fifteen days on hidden shoals, blown to sea when we sought fresh provisions, driven by fierce winds to a hostile coast. If I were to recount the thousand ways we have been tested, the bitterness of our suffering, the cruel tortures of heat and insects, of disease and Indians, you, the very ones who have lived through this same suffering, must weep to hear tell of it.

"But now, with the Almighty's help, we depart this distant and malign place for the port of Pánuco, and from thence, if it be His will, we return to Spain." The Governor raised his hand and waited several seconds before continuing. "And this one thing I promise you—I swear, whoever shall hear the name of any man who served in the expedition of Pánfilo de Narvaez will know him to be amongst the very bravest of Spanish men. The sons of your sons and all their sons will have honors heaped upon them for the deeds that you have done. No man who shall meet you and know your name will fail to pull off his hat—even if he be a nobleman. And one other thing will I promise," the Governor brought his cross to his lips. "The King himself will hear from these lips what befell the expedition of Pánfilo de Narvaez in the Land of Florida. He will listen and then will grant from his own coffers pensions to all who have so bravely served him.

"And yet one more thing I promise you," the Governor, his eye narrowing, paused and stared at the assembled men. "Be he hidalgo or soldier, slave or priest, whoever shall through cowardice or sloth slow the progress of this expedition will swim for half a day behind my boat with both hands tied." The Governor then grinned. "After such a swim he may find a little difficulty in breathing."

As the Governor finished speaking, Friar Xuarez raised his cross, then ordered all who dared call themselves Christians to fall upon their knees; not a man was left standing. "I have listened to the Governor as he likened the men of this expedition to those holy martyrs in the days of pagan Rome who suffered for their faith. And I, a priest, cannot fault his words, for you all have suffered, and grievously, and may yet suffer; but do you suffer gladly? Those early Christian martyrs—those whose names are legion and those whose names are unknown—for their suffering gained a place before God's very throne. Theirs was no millennium that needs be served in purgation. Already for your service to the Faith the least of you has gained purgation and need not fear descent to Hell." The friar stretched out both arms as he raised his face until it was bathed with the morning light. "For you, no burning sulphur, no boiling lead. For you, no tearing pincers, no horned demons with fire-reddened mauls. For you, no vain shrieks and piteous cries for sins that through all eternity can never be forgiven. But, will you be forced to wait, suffering purgatory's punishment, until Christ's next descent before you gain the gates of Heaven? Only those who here on earth suffer for the Faith and do it gladly—those whose hearts are filled with joy at every added pain—only those will arrive in Heaven without the many torments of purgation." Not one of the kneeling men failed to tell his beads as the friar spoke. "If the sun burns your skin as we travel on the water," thundered the priest, "laugh! If you know great thirst—sing! Should an arrow wound you, rejoice, for that same shaft which quivers in your flesh may be the key that unlocks the door to an eternity of bliss. And if death descends and you should be taken, bless with your last breath the name of the Lord, for your soul must, the moment it is freed, rise to Heaven. But, if anyone amongst you should show by cowardice or by other means a lack of faith—should fail to instantly obey an order, should mutter words of mutiny, should tell another that all is lost—such a one is damned for all eternity to Hell and will suffer those special tortures invented by the devil for the very worst of men. And remember this—for the soul in Hell there is no release through death, no hope for a moment of relief, no chance to make amends for mortal sins done while still on earth.

"What then shall it be?" Friar Xuarez clenched his hands and shook them at the sky. "The devil's sulphur-dripping hands? Purgatory's torments until Christ's descent? Or the golden gates of Heaven?"

No less than two score of the men groveled on the sand sobbing their hope for Heaven. The rest, tight-faced and sweating, hung their heads and prayed. Not one of that gathering of hardened veterans was not shaken by the friar's words.

Then taking with us as much maize as we could carry and using for water bottles skin flayed from the horses' legs which had been tanned; we embarked in the following order: In the boat commanded by the Governor went forty-nine men; in another, under Alvar Nuñez and the assessor, also forty-nine; Alonso del Castillo and Andres Dorantes commanded a craft with forty-eight; two captains, Tellez and Peñalosa captained a vessel with forty-seven; and the comptroller, together with the commissary, commanded one with forty-nine.

The boats, when loaded with provisions and men, sat so deep that less than a span of gunwales remained above the water; and were so crowded that none dared move. There were some who cursed the Greek, for they could not see how we should survive in such craft running through turbulent seas. But from the Governor and from many others, the Greek gained praise, and, as had been promised, was given the grant of freedom and could wear a sword.

Of all the men I alone remained on shore, for I was to guide the boats past reefs and rocks. Alvar Nuñez then tossed me a short sword, to be used against crocodiles and snakes, and a rope to be tied around my waist. I crossed myself, then, as a wind arose which stirred the trees and a cloud passed before the sun, after whispering the Almighty's name and begging His protection, I stepped out into the water.

The Expedition Puts to Sea in Search of Pánuco

GULF OF MEXICO

Beth Pewther 1981

XVI

For seven days we traveled through inlets and passages, seeking the coast. So heavily laden were the boats that we traveled slowly and carefully for fear a hidden rock or modest swell would capsize a vessel and cause the loss of provisions—the water being seldom more than waist deep, there was little risk to the men.

My task proved to be difficult. Sharp-shelled oysters cut my feet, submerged trees bruised; potholes and quicksand trapped me so that I must be quickly freed lest I drown; at different times venomous snakes and brightly-colored stinging jellyfishes came near poisoning me as I slashed at them with my sword, and the mosquitos and black flies were a constant torture.

Not being able to talk or to listen to the men while in the water—at night being overwhelmed with exhaustion—for those seven days we sought the coast I amused myself with my own thoughts. At different times as I struggled to pull the boat clear of a reef or guide it around the rock, I was so fatigued my brain grew leaden and I could not think. But when less fatigued my brain softened and filled with images and thoughts.

Perhaps it was the sun's heat beating on my bare head that caused the memory of my days as a slave in the galley to grow so clear that for a time it was as if I were again there sitting on the bench, more beast than man, roaring with laughter when the master laid his whip on another's shoulder—mine were no longer tickled, for my strength and the power with which I pulled the oar had gained for me the master's affection. It was the day I was freed to fight the black man who kept the beat. "Estevan," the master said, "whoever proves to be the stronger will beat the drum." I nodded. This was a thing I much desired. But before I could lift myself from behind the oar, the other man was upon me, his thick arms around my throat, his teeth sunk deep into my shoulder. Like a beast I struggled and tore at his face with my fingers, trying to rip out his eyes. One eye I dug free and crushed in my hand, the pain causing the man to scream so that his teeth no longer were in the meat of my shoulder. I wrenched around and took hold of his stones and I squeezed with all my strength until the man lay helpless, begging for mercy. Had the master and other officers not held me I would have ripped away his stones and then killed him. But, two holding each of my arms, they dragged me to the drum, while the other man was chained to the oar where I had been.

I began to beat the drum. Had it been covered with less than thick ox-skin I would have burst it, for my anger added power to my arm. I pounded so that the other oarsmen shuddered, so that the officers must escape the din. I pounded, and I laughed as my anger left me; and then I saw the man whom I had fought and beaten. He lay, broken, across the oar and with every movement of the oar he groaned as his crushed stones oozed blood which stained his thighs.

It was when his other eye—the one I had not reached—

looked up that I again became a man. "Estevan," I whispered as that dying eye searched for me, "what have you done? What quarrel had you with that black man that you must kill him?" The words burned my throat. "You have murdered him so that you may beat his drum. Estevan, you have become a vicious brute." Tears I had forgotten formed hot inside my eyes, then spilled down. "Forgive me!" I called out to the dying man, but from his dull searching eye I knew he did not hear. "Forgive me," I called out again, and the eye stopped its searching and rested for a moment on both of mine. Then it closed, and before the day was over he had died, and was thrown into the sea. And as the tears I had known that day in the dim hold of the galley flowed again, I knew that until I drew my last breath, that man's dying eye will stay with me.

Despite wrappings of thick leather, by the seventh day my feet and legs had been so torn by oyster shells and rocks that I despaired of further travel. The water stung my raw flesh, and at each step blood oozed. The rope had rubbed away a portion of the skin around my waist, and my head pounded from the sun. Had we not sighted the coast and come to deep water late in the afternoon of the seventh day, the morning of the eighth would have found me too sick to go on.

Ahead lay a wooded island, a league in length, and Alvar Nuñez ordered all weapons ready as we proceeded toward that bit of land. We were still half a league from that place when from around the end of the island came five large canoes filled with painted savages. Our other boats lying a distance to the rear, there was much uneasiness as the canoes approached. But before we could let fly a crossbow shaft or fire an arquebus, the Indians, seeing us to be a different race of men, fell into wild confusion, leapt into the water and swam for shore, crying out in a piteous manner. Upon reaching land, they dashed amongst the trees where they soon were hidden. There was much rejoicing at our good fortune, as Alvar Nuñez promised that their canoes, which we had secured, would add to our safety and provide more room should we employ them as waistboards—one for each of our boats.

We met no Indians where we landed on that island, but discovered their houses—the ashes in the firepits still warm. And within their houses we found many dried mullet and roes which promised a welcome relief from our distress.

That night, for the first time since we left the place where the boats were built—to which place the name Bahia de Caballos had been given, in memory of the slaughtered horses—that night, for the first time in seven days, we camped in comfort. A point of land at the end of the island made safe by water on three sides was chosen, and there we built our fires and feasted.

Perhaps it was the dried roes and mullet with which the men stuffed their stomachs, perhaps it was the carpet of thick, soft grass which covered the ground, perhaps it was the warm wind that carried with it the taste of the sea, perhaps it was the great fires that our safe position allowed us to kindle, perhaps it was all these things, together with the fact that we had survived so much adversity—whatever may have been the reason, within an hour of our making camp a lunacy or madness swept through the men.

It was the bark of a fox that finally set it off. One of the men, I do not know who, hearing the fox, barked back. Another man answered with a bark of his own—it may have been the fox who answered. Then surely two score more. Someone tried to imitate a lion, but the sound was more that of an ass braying. Another tried the hissing of an angry goose. Then came the crowing of a cock, the quacking of a duck, the mewing of a cat, the chirping of a wren. This was joined by the howling of a wolf and a panther's screams. Before two minutes, the sounds of every beast and bird known to man could be heard in that place. And I, I must confess, tried a peacock's cry, imitated a goat, a sheep, a camel, and surely half a dozen other birds and animals. But the sounds of the creatures were not enough for most. They must then run about on all fours, flap their arms for wings, writhe on the ground like snakes, hang from trees, take bites of grass, lower heads and charge each other. I will swear I saw no fewer than half a dozen squatting on rounded rocks while from their throats came clucks. Surely ten turned horse and begged any who would to ride them. And this madness was not only for the men—the officers ran around like demented creatures. Captain Juan Pantoja, holding the haft of a short sword to his forehead, galloped through the camp as a unicorn. Soto Mayor played the wolf and tried to bite the leg of whomever came too close. And Andres Dorantes, because of his girth, no doubt, bounded about with squeals and snorts. Even the Governor, Alvar Nuñez and the higher officers made animal sounds, although they did not join in the general frolic. And, I am afraid, many practiced sodomy that night.

Of all that company, not excepting the priests, only Friar Xuarez was not affected by this madness. He alone stayed apart from the rest, clutching his great cross as he shouted warnings and imprecations at the sporting men.

So great had grown the madness that Don Theodoro, the Greek, urged on by others, mounted a stump, raised a cross made of two sticks, and started shouting warnings and imprecations of his own. Within moments half the camp had gathered about him, those with enough breath still left making their animal sounds; the rest, purple-faced and gasping with laughter. The sight of the shiny-pated Greek around whose shoulders someone had draped a torn crimson cloak, caused the Governor and his principal officers to try to stop their laughter for fear of offending Friar Xuarez, whose face now was blotched with anger. But when the Greek waved his cross of sticks and then raised his other hand as if to pronounce a blessing, they no longer could resist, and succumbed helplessly to their mirth.

For the seven days since the boats were launched, the men had made much of the Greek, some calling him savior of the expedition. All showed affection for the man, who swelled with pleasure. Standing there on that stump an intoxication over-

114

whelmed him—a drunkenness not of drink but of exhilaration as he tried to match Friar Xuarez's words and gestures.

"Nowhere in all the world is there gathered such a group of men as I see gathered here this night," shouted the Greek as he kissed his cross of sticks. "Men who have shown such fortitude and bravery that those who served with Caesar's legions must be judged craven in comparison." Instead of cheers came grunts and squeals, for the Greek, with all his roundness, bald head and flattened features, resembled nothing so much as a market pig.

"As has been often said," the Greek's voice rose and fell, "we travel under a special dispensation—one granted only to the noblest, the bravest, the holiest of men." Again the soldiers, with their grunts and squeals, cheered him. "How else, if not for the Almighty's special will, would one so obscure as I come to be amongst you, yet one without whose skill this expedition could not have journeyed on." Sternfaced the Greek paused for a long moment.

"If any doubters still know *fear*," Don Theodoro drew the word out as he raised his face to the ringed moon which cast its light down, painting his skin the green of tarnished copper, "if through doubt you still know fear," he prolonged the word "fear" again, "this thing I swear: The vessels built by these two hands," he held out both hands, one of which still grasped the cross of sticks, "hands created and made nimble by the Author of all things, hands ever guided by the Supreme Being, such vessels, I swear, if those who sail in them will but have faith in Him, such vessels can never sink."

To this there was loud cheering, with still some grunts and squeals. And, as the man paused to catch his breath, Friar Xuarez shouted warnings that the Greek and all who listened to his words ran the risk of answering charges of blasphemy.

"I mean no disrespect to the Most Holy," the Greek shouted his reply. "I only speak the truth, and say no more than I have heard you yourself and our noble Governor already say—

that I, a Greek from Crete, am here amongst you by Divine intercession." Uneasy murmurs ran through the men. "And would the Almighty then, after all His efforts, allow the boats—symbols of His intercession—to sink?"

"Hey, Don Theodoro," the Governor called out, "there is strong logic in what you say. And I am relieved to know we need have no fear of the boats sinking no matter how severe the storm." From his tone, it was difficult to judge if the Governor spoke in earnest.

"Let there be waves twenty fathoms high!" The little man of Crete rose up on his toes and stretched to his full height. "Let a wind blow that can crack the mightiest tree; let thunder roll and lightning strike; let the very earth quake, and in the worst of this, set these same vessels upon the sea and steer them away from land. Steer them into the deepest and wildest part of the boiling ocean, and do so with joyful hearts, for there is nothing to fear!"

Then for several moments the Greek, his sweat-streaked face tilted toward the moon, moved his lips but made no sound. The men pressed in closer, some reaching out and touching the garments of the man.

". . . Safe!" The word hissed from the Greek's mouth in a shout that was nearly a scream. "Naked in the midst of battle but girdled with faith I am safer than all your soldiers dressed in their mail and armor. What wooden shaft fashioned by a human hand, what leaden bullet cast by mere man, what sword tempered by a mortal craftsman could harm one shielded by faith in the Creator of all men?"

"He is grown mad!" I heard a certain crossbowman mutter. For this he was punched and kicked by several who stood close. Then without another word the crossbowman quickly withdrew from the swelling throng which by now included all but a handful of the men.

"And he whose heart is truly filled with faith does not ask for a sign, does not wait for proof," the Greek spoke on. Friar

Xuarez, fallen silent, although still on his side of the camp, leaned forward, his face showing a puzzled expression as he listened to the man. "How many times I begged the Almighty for a sign to justify my faith. 'Just a single piece of proof,' I whispered to the Unseen One as I pulled the heavy oar in the darkness of the galley. 'I must be here for some purpose,' I groaned into the darkness. 'Show me for as little as a single second; tell me with but one word, and if I then must serve You twenty years in this cruel place I swear never to doubt again.' And so I suffered, for my faith was tainted by my need for proof. I suffered when I might have known days and nights of the purest joy, unmindful of the tortures to my flesh."

Friar Xuarez now left his place and moved closer.

"Why did it take me thirty years to learn what I already knew the day I was cast into slavery?" The Greek stretched out his arms and opened his hands as if in supplication; the cross of sticks fell and was caught before it touched the ground and then was passed from man to man, with each bringing it to his lips. "As I was dragged in chains from the town where I served as apprentice to my uncle, although frightened, for I was not yet full grown, I knew it all was for some reason. Others the Turks had killed—my uncle and his wife each split like goats while I watched helplessly. Others, who had fought the pirates trussed up like fowl and slowly roasted. The children beheaded; the young women, after raping, strangled. Yet I still lived—loaded with chains but unharmed—not so much as a single blow—and all around my countrymen were dying. I knew in being spared I had been granted His protection for some reason. . . ." The Greek again fell silent, his lips still moving as he raised his face to the moon again.

For a time, as I listened to the man, I wondered if, as the crossbowman said, the Greek was mad. Being given command over all, while the boats were being built, then being granted freedom after so many years of slavery and praised and called savior of the expedition—was this not enough to cause mad-

117

ness? Then, as he went on and spoke of things that struck chords in my memory—in many ways his life was much like my own—as he went on I grew uncertain of what to make of him, but one thing I did know—he was not mad, not that one.

"... And the proof I asked for, the sign—not a vision of an angel in flaming armor," the Greek went on as if the silent words his lips formed had been loudly spoken. "Not a plague of boils visited upon my oppressors, nor water turned to wine. I begged a simple proof, that the slave who kept the beat might miss one time in the next hundred strokes, that a certain rat which nested near when I coaxed it again might come up instead of showing fear. Such were the little proofs I begged, begged because I doubted what I knew.

" 'Sweet Jesus,' I would whisper to the Savior while the others slept, 'one word is all I ask of You so that I may know I am here in this dark place for a reason and am not forgotten,'—of such weak substance was my faith.

"Then came years when I did not care if I lived or died. I had no belief. If I thought at all it was only to wonder if I might find a scrap of meat in the soup they served us or if I might gain the blanket of the next slave who died. What brought back thoughts that it all must be for a reason, that my years of suffering were for some purpose, that I was not forgotten, I do not know. My life in the hold of that galley was the same, nothing in the close darkness had altered; yet one day, I cannot say what month it was, nor can I even be certain of the year, one day, pulling on the oar, it was as if a searing flame had suddenly set fire to my skin. I screamed in agony. My nostrils filled with the stink of my burning flesh. My brain turned liquid and ran from my nose and ears, and I screamed again and was whipped for my screaming; and the whip, like splashes of cool water, brought relief to my fire-tortured skin. Then came such a peace as I had never before that moment known . . ."

More than half the listening men had fallen to their knees,

some so shaken by the power of Don Theodoro's words that they wept. My throat had tightened causing me to swallow again and again.

Tears flowed down the little man's cheeks, but they were not of sorrow, for it was as if his eyes were lit by a torch which blazed within. "Never again did I doubt Him! Never again was my faith shaken. It was enough that I knew that all I had suffered and still suffered was for a certain purpose; that my life was guided by His divine will. And then, at the place given the name Bahia de Caballos, all the events of thirty years came together." The Greek's voice rose again. "A company of Christians—more than two hundred and forty men—serving their Savior and their King, lost in the jungle, unable to travel further. And, of this brave company of men both base and noble, only one—a slave, a galley slave pressed into serving this expedition—only that one could save them. Is there amongst you any who yet doubt Him?"

The Greek did not say another word that night. He walked about, first to the trees, then to the water, with scores following, but not too close, for he waved them back. Those who had practiced sodomy the most vigorously prayed the loudest as he passed amongst them, his face showing the peace of which he had spoken. Some wailed so loudly one must believe their very hearts now were broken in contrition for their sport. And, except for those few who through great carnal appetites had not heard him, never have I seen a group of men so moved by the words of another man.

Friar Xuarez silently withdrew to his place across the camp when the Greek was through speaking. There he sat, his hands stretched out over the embers of his fire as if it were a winter's night. For nearly two full hours he sat, warming his hands and rubbing them despite the mildness of the season. Several times he made as if to rise, but settled down again. What thoughts ran through his mind, no one could know, for he did not answer the several officers who ventured to address him, and, except for the puzzled expression he could not hide, he gave no clue as to his feelings.

And of those in authority, not only Friar Xuarez brooded over the words of Don Theodoro. Alvar Nuñez and the Governor frowned and at different times muttered, but in so soft a voice that no one more than three paces distant could hope to hear them. But from the looks of the other officers, from their gestures of a sacred nature—telling beads, drawing the fish in the sand, making the sign of the cross—it could be seen that they judged the Greek to be a holy man. And by morning he had become more than holy.

Usurping the powers of the Pope, the men of the expedition had canonized the man. And from listening to the men's contented murmurings that morning as we sailed along the coast, I knew that in their minds dwelled the thought—no harm can befall any expedition in whose ranks is found a man as holy as Don Theodoro.

Yet, in my mind there was a different kind of thought. If the Greek should be lost, what then?

After departing the island, we journeyed westward for thirty days. How far we traveled in that space of time I cannot say, for there was so much going in and out of inlets, exploring twisting creeks, hunting for water on barren islands, and tending other necessities that our movement westward must have been no more than two leagues each day. But we had surely traveled no less than fifty leagues, yet still found no evidence that told of the port of Pánuco or if we even moved in the right direction.

The evening of the thirtieth day from our departure from the island, unable to find suitable land for a camp—it all being marsh and infested with snakes—we were forced to spend the night crowded in our boats. We had been without water for more than a day, and, except for a handful of parched maize for each, had eaten nothing since the night before. Because of the

120

crowding, the swarming insects and the heavy heat, most of the men found it difficult to sleep. Some time after midnight—nearly half being still awake, there were enough men to swear to what took place—a great canoe, shining as if made of beaten copper, was descried in the distance. Faster than any canoe ever seen before, it came toward us, the more than two-score Indians in the craft dipping oars as if they were one man, so perfect was their unison. And from the oars dripped drops of silver, and the widening wake of the canoe was of silver too. Not one of those Indian men turned his head as the vessel passed within a crossbow-shot of us. It was as if they did not know of our presence, although the moon shone upon us. Their faces were painted white as corpses, with black around the eyes, giving their heads the look of skulls. All were silent as they passed. Then as that strange craft glided toward the open sea, we shouted and pounded weapons to gain their attention, but it was as if they could not hear us. Past a marsh island—their silver-dripping oar-blades flashing and plunging—the canoe raced for the sea, and within moments scores of our men were screaming for us to follow. Had the Greek not nodded his agreement when the Governor insisted that we wait for daylight, I have no doubt but that the men would have mutinied there and then and put to sea, so powerful had been the effect of that silent craft. But the Greek's wordless nods quieted the men, for he was still deeply revered. Yet, had we followed that craft to the open sea that night, who is there to say but that by so doing we might have avoided the calamity that was to come upon us?

Since that night I have often wondered if that copper craft had been sent to guide us; if the passionate desire of the men to follow it had not been a response to a Will greater than their own.

Before morning, a severe storm of wind, but not rain, was upon us.

As the storm worsened, most gave thanks for the steadfastness of the Governor in refusing to follow the Indian canoe into

121

the open sea. And the belief in the saintliness of the Greek grew. By the second day of the storm, having spent more than forty-eight hours without water some wondered if by risking passage through the open sea we might not have reached a place of equal safety, but one where water might be found. As the storm continued, all the men knew such distress from thirst that there was talk of putting to sea despite the chance of disaster should we pursue such a course. By the fifth day of the storm, so tortured were the men from thirst, that certain ones, defying the orders of the Governor, the importuning of the Greek, and their own intelligence, drank of the sea water. Three or four who did not sufficiently vomit up that vile stuff screamed and writhed for several hours, then died with blood running from their noses and ears. The sixth day of the storm, no one could see how we could survive another day without water. More than a score lay dazed and weak in the scuppers their limbs twitching. "Better a quick death by drowning in the open sea than a slow and horrible death in this malign place," counseled certain officers. But so great is the numbing power of thirst that, as the day drew on, most of the company no longer cared what was to be the course of action. Yet those who still preserved a portion of their reason had lost nothing of their reverence for the Greek, and when he, after an hour of earnest whispering with the Governor, offered that the expedition should commend itself to God and put to sea, they were quick to do his bidding.

Once on our way, not a boat escaped being overwhelmed by the waves as high as houses. Yet somehow the crafts were righted and the men saved. Each minute, as the storm continued in its fury, I expected to be our last. What chance did such frail craft have of surviving the terror of the elements? Yet we refused to abate our struggle as, hour after hour, we grappled with the storm. The course we followed was that taken by the copper-clad canoe, and just before sunset, coming up to a point of land and rounding it, we found shelter with much calm, for we had entered a great bay.

All, except those deprived of their reason by their suffering, gave thanks to God for showing us His favor. And when it was seen, from the many Indian habitations on the shore, that we might soon secure water, the men, not excepting the priests, made obeisance to the Greek. Even the Governor bowed his head and begged of the little man his blessing. At that moment, as Indians in canoes, showing every sign of friendliness approached, I, too, felt a reverence for the man.

Gesturing with their hands, and using pieces of bark on which they drew pictures, the Indians tried to speak to us, then, seeing the difficulty of doing this, still showing their friendliness by smiles and by other means, they made for shore with us following. These Indians were large and well-formed, and of a lighter color than any others we had known. And from the little paint on their faces and the way they received us, we judged them harmless and unfamiliar with men not of their own race.

No fragrant wine pressed of the most perfect grapes and then stored in cool cellars in the finest of oak casks ever tasted as sweet as the water we found in clay pitchers before the dwellings of those Indians.

Having quenched our thirst, we stuffed from crocks of cooked fish, which the Indians freely offered us. Many, grown unused to any quantity of food, vomited up the contents of their stomachs but then stuffed again. In more ways than I could mention, the Indians made us welcome. All their food they shared with us, also a mild beer brewed of acorns. The little maize we still had, we offered them as a poor return, and they, showing us what we supposed to be their gratitude, pressed upon us necklaces nicely fashioned of shells; touched us with their fluttering fingers, making much of the soiled and torn garments that we wore; then beckoned us to follow them to their houses. It appearing that the Indians would be deeply hurt if we did not partake of their proffered hospitality, and none of our number believing that we had anything to fear from such a peaceful band, we accordingly, in groups of ten or twelve, accompanied various ones to their places of habitation, Alvar

123

Nuñez and the Governor followed by the principal officers going hand in hand with their cacique.

Their dwellings were well fashioned of tightly-woven mats affixed to sturdy frames, and were well-kept and clean, not like those louse-infested structures we found in Aute and Apalachen. Not only were their houses clean, but their persons also. Although not handsome in the way that delights most Spanish men, their women, I will confess, I found most pleasing. Long of limb they were, with faces not unlike those of the fairer members of my race. Had they not had flattened heads—from the custom widely practiced by Indians of strapping their newborn to cradle-boards—I would have found them the equal of many who gathered in the marketplace of Azemmour.

Once inside their houses, they again offered us boiled and roasted fish, crocks of beer, bits of wax still thick with honey which they counted as their greatest delicacy and which we made much of, having tasted nothing sweet in many months, and sticks to which were affixed pieces of blackened meat— fierce smelling, but delicate of taste.

So great was the relief of the men to be so gently received after so many weeks of suffering that many suddenly burst into tears. The Indians, both men and women, each time one or another of our number started to cry, would join in. And the sobbing of the Indians caused even those of us most unused to crying to find moisture in the eyes.

By nightfall we were all heavy with the good food we had eaten, and bemused from the great quantities of beer drunk. Except for their dogs, there were no more stirrings in the village; even the wind had ceased. Then the Indians suddenly fell upon us. In each Indian lodging it was the same. And bands that had kept hidden attacked those very sick ones of our company left scattered along the shore, killing three. Knowing that the leaders of our expedition were with their cacique, more than a score of Indians stormed his lodge, sorely wounding the Governor with a stone to his face, and putting the other officers in serious jeopardy of their lives, as they defended themselves with fists and daggers in those close quarters. Alvar Nuñez ordered the cacique seized, but before he could be secured, the Indians attacked again and freed him, leaving behind his robe of civet-marten—a robe with a fragrance equaled only by musk or amber, worth surely a thousand golden ducats in any Christian land.

Commanded by Alvar Nuñez—for the Governor had been deprived of his senses by that rock to his face—we withdrew from the village, leaving some fifty, captained by Juan Pantoja and Alonso del Castillo as a rear guard to withstand the natives. Had the Indians been better provided with arrows, they would have done us great harm, for not one among us escaped injury that night, Alvar Nuñez suffering yet another break to his nose from a thrown club; I, a cut in the meat of my shoulder from a knife, then a dart—not well placed—in the thigh. Although attacked three times with great impetuousity, each attack forcing us to retreat further, not another one of our number was killed. Yet many were so sorely wounded they could no longer fight. Upon reaching the shore, preparations were commenced for putting our boats to sea, when we gained intelligence that the band of fifty men guarding our retreat had been forced into a narrow canyon and were trapped. Although safe for that moment, the canyon being deep and the night dark, the Indians had already lit a number of fires along the lip of the defile so that none should escape, intending, as was plain to all of us, to descend at daybreak to make short work of those fifty men. Never had I seen Alvar Nuñez show greater distress than when he learned how cleverly the Indians had tricked him, and how serious was the danger facing that company of fifty men.

Gathering about him those officers less severely wounded—the comptroller and the assessor, temporarily deprived of their senses from blows to the head, were not of that number—ordering the sergeants and certain other veterans to join him, Alvar Nuñez started to confer. (Although a slave, I was present at that gathering, for my master, Andres Dorantes, judged that I might prove useful.)

"In no more than two hours it will be light," said Alvar Nuñez. "Should those fifty men not be rescued and we not put to sea, our strength will not prove sufficient to withstand further onslaughts." He paused. "Yet if I order a company of sufficient size to attack the Indians and effect the rescue, I must leave the boats and the wounded men without sufficient protection." Again he paused and this time there were murmurings amongst the men. "If there were not almost three score of our number so helpless that the Indian women with the knives they use to gut fish might with ease destroy them, I would say, risk the boats and attack, but can I turn my back on wounded companions? And should we attack and then fail to rescue the trapped men . . ."

"Desperate situations demand desperate measures, Alvar Nuñez Cabeza de Vaca," my master, Andres Dorantes, offered, stepping forward. "Everything you have just said, even the simplest among us must know to be true—we cannot send forward a sufficient company without risking the boats and wounded; yet if we wait for daylight, without the strength of the fifty men we may be overrun, and then for the fifty death is certain."

"Your counsel, then, Andres Dorantes, is that we depart this place at once?" Alvar Nuñez asked in a harsh voice.

"There may be no other choice," Friar Xuarez muttered.

"No, that is not my counsel!" spit sprayed from Andres Dorantes' mouth. "Rather would I be slowly roasted than offer such a counsel."

"Yet you said 'desperate situations demand desperate measures,' " Alvar Nuñez spoke with a question in his voice.

"Desperate measures! Not cowardly measures!" Andres Dorantes lowered his hand to his sword.

"Speak on, Andres, I meant no offense."

With a nod, my master allowed his hand to fall from his

sword. "This is no time for quarreling, Alvar Nuñez. I have a plan." All pressed closer. "What if the fires lit around the canyon should suddenly go out, and then the Indians thrown into confusion? With fifteen men all prepared to forfeit their lives—fifteen the color of my man, Estevan—I think we may be able to pass through their lines, then do them sufficient mischief so that the fifty trapped can find a way to escape. And for those of you who know this one," he laid his hand on my shoulder, "you know that only the cat can see better in the dark. Will you be one of the men, Estevan?" he asked. I nodded, then various soldiers stepped forward, until there were the required fifteen. But as the soldiers were preparing their skins with mud and charcoal, Captain Peñalosa and Captain Tellez also insisted that they join us, counting it a matter of honor to do so.

As we moved through the darkness, we could see the Indians, whose ranks must have surely exceeded eight hundred, dancing about their fires, waving spears and clubs, their women clapping and pounding the ground with bare feet. Two bodies of the three they had killed they had secured, and had severed the limbs and heads. The torsos, dripping fat, hung as sheep or pigs are hung over the coals of a fire built in a pit. And the old ones, both men and women, laughed, showing their toothless gums as they shook rattles, beat drums and rubbed carved bones together.

Crawling on hands and knees, at different times slithering like snakes on our bellies, we found our way through that Indian village, then gathered behind the mounds where their dead are buried. Being in sight of the canyon where our men were trapped and noting six fires along the ridge, each tended by two Indians, with a force of perhaps eighty guarding the open end, Andres Dorantes ordered that each of the fires be approached by two of our number, the Indians tending them silently strangled with leather thongs. Four—the two captains, himself and an old sergeant much experienced in battle—were to ease close to the eighty, then, by beating swords on bucklers, by shouting and by other means, were to draw their attention while I descended into the defile to lead the trapped men to safety. At the moment of the first sounds, the six fires were to be smothered; then, to add to the Indians' confusion, each of the twelve men on the ridge was to depart in a different direction, shouting and, for as long as it might be safely done, waving burning brands saved from the fires.

I was much impressed with the soundness of this plan, as were most of the other men, but Captains Tellez and Peñalosa objected.

"To scatter our meager forces in such a way must surely bring death to each of us with no help to those trapped in the defile," argued Captain Tellez.

"What you urge, Andres Dorantes, is that Spanish soldiers ape the ways of cowardly Indians—ways that must surely lead us to destruction," were Captain Peñalosa's impassioned words.

Captain Dorantes, controlling his rising choler, then asked the two captains what plan they had to offer.

It was their suggestion that we wait an hour until the sky began to brighten, then attack the eighty Indians, counting on surprise to assist us in our task. That we then cut our way through, inflicting severe losses, and, before they had time to recover, lead the fifty trapped men out of the defile and fight our way to the boats, trusting our superior weapons and bravery to gain for us success. Andres Dorantes listened, considered, then shook his head.

"By daylight, more Indians may join the eighty," he said. "Even if not, we may be defeated should we launch an assault upon them—they are already more than four times our number. And even if we are successful in freeing the men, fighting our way through their village in daylight must be judged too hazardous."

"Hazardous!" Captain Peñalosa said, forcing the word through his nose. "Hazardous, and its sister, Dangerous, are words more often heard from women than from men."

128

Without a word, Andres Dorantes felled the man with the haft of his sword, brought with much force against his chin. I and several others then pressed the points of our daggers into Captain Tellez's throat while Andres Dorantes tickled the throat of the fallen man. After two or three moments of deep reflection, both thought better of their plan and agreed that the one offered by Andres Dorantes showed the greater wisdom.

I departed several minutes before the others—Andres Dorantes hoping that I might be able to find my way into the gorge to give Captains Pantoja and Castillo intelligence of what was to come—and made my way past the Indians guarding the entrance, but was stopped a score of paces beyond the canyon's entrance by a seventh fire we had not seen. There was no way for me to pass unobserved. Unlike the six fires on the rim, each tended by two, this fire was tended by four Indians. Crouching in the dark some thirty paces distant, I considered what I must do. Remembering stories told at different times by my father and his brothers of their difficulties with the Berbers—how Berber men had been drawn from their fires into the desert—I made a certain sound in my chest and throat. It was the sound of a young lost goat fearful of the jackals and wild dogs that roamed the desert. And, as had been true with the Berbers, the sound caused the Indians to turn their heads, then drew one from the fire's light into the dark. They were little more than boys, fourteen years would be my guess, and I was saddened by the work that my knotted thong must do. Moving to another place in the dark, I made the sound again, and again drew one from the fire, leaving two. For a little time I watched the actions of these two. First, they strained to listen, then whispered to each other, shifting uneasily from side to side. Still protected by the darkness, I moved a little closer. Then, after fifteen, no more than twenty seconds, they rose, again whispered, and after several moments of hesitation, separated, each slowly moving in the opposite direction. When they had stepped beyond the limits of the light I moved in quickly, doing what must be done to each of them in turn.

129

The closest I came to mishap that night was from the hands of several Spaniards who, as I descended into that defile, struck at me with swords, which I must duck and parry before I could convince them I was Estevan.

As the three captains and the sergeant commenced their din, and the fires along the rim flickered out, the fifty trapped men followed me, at a run, through the entrance of the defile, quenching, as we passed, the fire I had left undisturbed. Then, skirting the band of confused Indians whose attention was drawn in a dozen directions by the shouts and flaming brands, we made for the place behind the burial mounds.

The soundness of Andres Dorantes' plan was attested to by the number who gathered behind the mounds. Not a man had been lost! And the Indians had been thrown into such confusion they could not muster a sufficient force to bar our progress as we made our way through the outskirts of their village to the place where our boats were beached.

In each man, I have heard it said, is hidden an element of the woman; an element infused into our beings while we yet float in the liquid of our mothers. And, as we approached our boats, the first pale light of morning saw, amongst all the men, that womanly element no longer hidden. Not the most hardened veteran could restrain himself from weeping. Soto Mayor and Juan Pantoja, sworn enemies, fell sobbing into each other's arms—would that their tears had washed away their hatred for each other. The Governor, his face swollen, his empty eye filled with blood, hugged Andres Dorantes, staining his neck red. I, too, sought relief by weeping, for the features of those four young Indians had burned deep into my brain, and my tears were to ease the pain caused by their faces.

The Indians of the village for the moment forgotten, scores formed a circle around the Greek, begging for his blessing. Others, gathered into knots of ten or a dozen, spoke of what had happened. The boats in which the wounded rested lay unattended. Then, as if to warn us that our condition was still haz-

130

ardous, a chill north wind came up. As the sun rose the wind grew colder; it was as if in its movement through the night the sun had lost its fire and had become a glistening sphere of ice. At first it was feared that the cold would cause us serious distress, for we had no fuel; but, searching along the shore for pieces of dry wood, more than thirty canoes were discovered hidden in a cove. As we broke these vessels up and built great fires, the Indians, who were ranged a quarter of a league distant began to shout and threaten, but they did not approach.

"Again through Divine intercession our condition is relieved!" Friar Xuarez cried out as he blessed the fires. But of the men, more than half no longer were concerned with an unseen Divine and credited the Greek, whose name they whispered along with that of Christ's Mother, as they told their beads.

Troubled by the faces of the four I had destroyed, I sat a distance from the fires wrapped in my blanket. The youthful faces of the Indians brought from the recesses of my mind old images—my brothers, other companions I had known in the city of Azemmour. "How many men no longer live because of these two hands?" I wondered. Surely half a hundred. Faceless heaps they were. Then I saw the features of the black who had beat the drum. I pressed my hands against my eyes to drive away that one, and saw the body of my dead son. Had he grown to young manhood, would his features have resembled those of the young Indians? "Estevan," I whispered, "you have killed your last man." The cold of my hands passed through my eyes into my brain. "Even if by not killing I must die," I formed each word with care, "even if attacked, I will not kill again."

XVII

Early in the afternoon of the same day, as suddenly as it came, the cold wind ceased. The Indians having reduced their distance from us by nearly a third, and having increased the volume of their shouts and the violence of their threats, Alvar Nuñez determined that our position was precarious and ordered that preparations be made to put to sea. So, although we had but little food and no water, we set sail while there was yet sufficient light to guide us to the mouth of the bay. I went with Alvar Nuñez, for he needed my strength to steer his vessel as his crew had suffered the most and many lay helplessly wounded.

For three days we sailed past barren islands along a coast of marshland and submerged vegetation, until we were reduced to the last extremity from thirst. Yet, despite our suffering, we still retained a portion of our spirit. Then, as it had happened once before, rounding a point of land we entered an estuary where we were met by Indians in canoes, and could see in the distance their numerous habitations. Not being willing to risk another encounter, the Governor, now much recovered, entered into conversation with the Indians, asking for water, but refusing to follow them to the shore.

The Indians, circling in their swift canoes, kept begging us to follow them to their place of habitation, and as they circled, because of the brightness of the sun, the color of their faces kept changing from brown to black to red, then back to brown again. So extreme was our need for water that the Governor offered as payment handfuls of hawkbells and strings of colored beads. But the Indians would not accept payment as they urged us to follow them, promising us, with signs easily understood, to satisfy our needs once on shore. Yet, despite our desperate condition, the Governor could not ignore the painful lesson we had so recently been taught.

We might have waited all that afternoon with no change in our condition and with the Indians still circling, had Don Theodoro not offered to accompany the Indians as hostage to prove our honorable intentions while they went to their lodges for water.

At first the Governor, Alvar Nuñez and the principal officers tried to dissuade the man, urging him to consider the danger a Christian alone and unarmed must face amongst such a company of painted pagans. But to this argument Don Theodoro smiled, then shook his head. "If the Son of God shed His blood for strangers, how should a simple Greek refuse to offer his person for a little time, if in this way he may serve companions now grown as close as brothers? And if there be danger? Will the Almighty deny me His protection just because I go alone and unarmed amongst pagans?" If the Governor had other arguments, he did not offer them. Accordingly, carrying with them all the vessels we had to transport the water, Don Theodoro and one of the guides taken from Dulchanchellin went with the Indians, two of their number, at the repeated insistence of the Governor, being left with us as hostages.

I lay back and listened to the soft lapping of water against the boats after the Greek was gone. The men were quiet, many sleeping. From the forest on the shore I heard the long cry of a bird of an unknown species, then an answering cry. The lowering sun glowed a golden red, and reaching up into the sky from the seaward horizon were mountains of iron-grey clouds whose peaks shone crimson. I tried to descry movement in the dense, dark forest that lined the shore and I searched the surface of the water for the passage of a fish, but all was still.

As the sun dipped to within a hand's breadth of the horizon, the waters of the estuary turned the color of fresh-spilt blood, and the clouds, now stretched halfway across the sky, were stained as if jets had spurted up from a gaping wound. It was then that the Indians returned, holding in their hands the vessels we had given them, mouths downward. In each canoe were surely half again as many men as before, but the Greek and his companion were not among that number. Their cacique called out to the two we held, both of whom tried to plunge into the sea but were restrained. Then, after much shouting and after hurling spears in our direction, all of which fell short, the Indians fled, leaving us burdened with sorrow and dejection.

With the suddenness of the plague that can, in a single day, reduce a robust man to one whose face shows the cast of death, so the loss of the Greek brought to many, in an even lesser time, prostration and a numbness of limb and mind. By morning scores that had withstood thirst and painful wounds now lay hollow-eyed in the boats, unable or unwilling to move, even when threatened with the Governor's sword.

I slept little that night. The boat in which I served pulled close to the craft commanded by Andres Dorantes and Alonso del Castillo, and I listened while they, together with Alonso de Solis and Alvar Nuñez, conferred.

"If the Greek is not returned to us or if we do not effect his rescue, I fear for the welfare of this expedition," Alonso de Solis offered.

"We have survived worse adversities than the loss of a single man," was Alvar Nuñez's reply.

"In your voice, Alvar Nuñez, I fail to detect the ring of conviction," the assessor answered carefully, nodding at the man. "Even the stoutest wall can be breached under a sufficient pounding. The loss of the Greek may be that final blow that shatters the granite of this company." He laced the fingers of his hands together, then squeezed their knuckles white.

134

"Not a week since, there were those of this company who counted fifty of our number as lost, Alonso," Andres Dorantes laid a hand on the assessor's shoulder. "And if we were able to effect the rescue of fifty, why not that of one lone Greek?"

"And do not forget that we yet have two of their number," added Alvar Nuñez in a soft voice.

"For the moment I had forgotten those two, I must confess." Alonso de Solis pulled his hands apart, then rubbed and flexed them until the whiteness had gone out of their knuckles. "If we are careful not to give offense, and if we bargain like crafty Venetian merchants, with God's help, we may be able to make a trade and, as part of the bargain, allow them to keep the Indian of Dulchanchellin. Three for one, what man born of woman could resist such a trade?"

"If we are careful not to give offense," Alonso del Castillo responded by repeating the assessor's words. "And all who know of Pánfilo de Narvaez, and of his gentle ways and sweet disposition know that our Governor is the last one to give offense."

Andres Dorantes snorted.

"Another night of thirst is certain to further sweeten his disposition," Alonso del Castillo continued. "And if the Indians should again shout and throw their spears at us, his mildness will be matched only by the meekest of the Cherubim."

"Knowing what must be the cost should we fail to recover the Greek, he will restrain himself," Alvar Nuñez said after a short silence. "I will speak to him; if needs be, offer to bargain with the Indians in his stead. The wound he suffered is not yet healed—his head still pains him. He may be grateful to save himself the burden."

"With his wound still so fresh any movement of his jaws must cause him agony," the assessor offered in a hopeful voice.

"Only apoplexy will ever stop that one's mouth," was Andres Dorantes' quick response.

"And if by some miracle he should fail to speak," Alonso

del Castillo muttered, "will not his confessor, knowing the Governor's mind better than the man himself, will not the good friar—rather than you, Alvar Nuñez—be the one to bargain?"

"I have reached the limit of my patience with Juan Xuarez. Either the Governor or I will confer with the Indians, no other; this I can promise you."

"Yet, what if the Governor should grant the friar his authority?" asked Andres Dorantes. "What if he . . . "

"Enough of this idle speculation," Alvar Nuñez waved the man silent. "There is a matter of more serious consequence we had best consider while we still have time."

"The effect upon the men should the Greek not be returned?" offered Alonso del Castillo. Alvar Nuñez nodded.

"From that night on the island when I heard Don Theodoro speak," Alvar Nuñez's voice grew harsh, "from that night I knew that should anything happen to the man this expedition must suffer."

"Do I detect traces of despair in your voice, Alvar Nuñez?" asked Alonso del Castillo. "Did I not just hear from your very lips that we have faced and survived worse adversities than the loss of a single man?"

"I own to the words, Alonso; and it is not despair you hear, but thirst-dried anger. My mouth is filled with gunpowder. I fight to keep it safe from sparks."

"Such as those which fall from the Governor's and the friar's lips?" asked Andres Dorantes. To this, Alvar Nuñez made no answer.

"Certain officers, those who travel with him in his boat, whisper they have looked into the Governor's face and have seen madness there," said Alonso de Solis in a lowered voice. Alvar Nuñez brought his finger to his lips. "They say it was the blow he suffered from the Indian's stone," his voice was further lowered, to a whisper.

"They do him a kindness to trace his madness to a stone." Andres Dorantes muttered softly, but not too softly.

136

Forming each word slowly, Alvar Nuñez said, "I do not like this talk of madness." He paused, then, in a full voice, "Was the Governor judged mad when, as I have heard, he stood before all the men in the town of Aute, ordering each man to prove by bravery his Spanish blood, and himself grievously wounded?"

"I know of none who doubt the Governor's bravery, Alvar Nuñez, and I would gladly follow him into battle," the assessor answered. "But it is not a battle that we face when, in a few short hours, it will be morning. And bravery may prove costly if it not be tempered with reason when we bargain with the Indians.

XVIII

Six caciques, wearing their hair loose and very long, were among the Indians whose canoes formed a wide circle around us at the first light of morning. These chiefs appeared to hold more authority and be of a higher condition than any we had yet seen. Each wore a robe of marten such as the one that had been taken, but these robes were made with wrought ties of lion skin, and when they rose to address us, it could be seen that their robes completely covered them as do the ermine robes of kings. The presence of these chiefs, the splendor of their robes, the number of canoes—now not less than three score craft, each with a dozen men—and the boldness of their actions told us that this was no obscure village of Indians, but a great nation.

For the two hostages we held, the chiefs offered vessels

137

filled with water, dried meats, fruits and necklaces fashioned from purple shell. When the Governor replied, with signs, that he would only give up the hostages for the two men they had taken, they beckoned us to come with them; this he refused to do. Again they offered us water and good things to eat in exchange for their two men, but this time to the offering was added two fat deer, newly skinned. Again, the Governor refused, amidst cries and groans of the hunger-tortured men.

Not less than a dozen times the Indians made their offer for the hostages, each time adding to the offering: acorns, ears of maize, baskets used for cooking, bone hooks, other things to eat. And to each offer the Governor made the same reply—their two for our two.

Perhaps it was the teasing sight of water dripping from the proffered vessels and the ease and patience of the Indian caciques, or perhaps it was madness, for suddenly the Governor leapt up, shrieking curses, drew his sword, slashed wildly through the air, and then grabbed a broken pike which he hurled with great force at the nearest canoe. Others, seeing the passion of their Governor, likewise abandoned reason and threw stones, together with weapons they had fashioned from wood and bone. To this barrage, the Indians answered with one of their own. Guiding their canoes in close, they hurled clubs, threw darts, and threatened to shoot arrows, but as they were poorly supplied with bows, this they could not do.

After it grew certain that neither side would gain the advantage, at a signal from one of their chiefs the Indians broke the circle and moved to form a barrier across the estuary. Seeing that should the Indians succeed in gaining a position to our rear we could not escape, the Governor ordered that we make for the open sea. The Indians followed close, several times nearly coming up to us, but just before noon, when the wind began to freshen, judging their position hazardous, for their vessels handled poorly amongst the rising waves, they broke from us.

The sadness of the men as their thoughts turned to the

138

Greek, once the heat of chase was gone, can only be compared with that of withered widows before their husbands' graves. So broken were the men, so certain now that death must surely come, that scarcely a dozen could be mustered in any boat to man the oars. And so we drifted with the current. A squall of rain pouring from the sky as if from great pitchers temporarily eased our burning throats. But then again there was heat and thirst. As night fell and the boats drifted on the blackening sea, most believed themselves doomed, and set up a wail the like of which I had heard only one time before: a galley ripped by a hidden shoal and sinking with all slaves still chained. "Holy Mother!" different ones of our company groaned. "Blessed Father—hear us!" cried out others. "Sweet Jesu, love us!"

Yet a strange thing happened to me that night. Despite the darkness and the wailing of the men, despite my hunger, thirst and a certain weakness that caused my limbs to tremble, despite all evidence which must tell reason that our condition was indeed hopeless, my heart swelled with gladness as my being filled with peace. Never had I known more perfect moments. Only in the nave of the great church of that Italian town, kneeling before the Christ and His holy Mother had there been its equal. And even then the peace and certainty had stayed with me only minutes, then a memory. But this time it did not fade. Waves of the most perfect joy swept through me. I knew, but I did not know. I thought, but I could not think. I had everything and nothing. And thus I floated like Moses in the papyrus boat all through the night. Hunger and thirst forgotten. Alone yet not alone. Thus I floated until I saw again the miracle of the dawn.

It was as if God's hands, fingers spread wide as all the world, reached up from the sea into the sky. And from each finger flowed pale crimson and the sky was the Virgin's heaving bosom. And the bosom glowed with holy blushes as if the Christ Child nestled there. And then the sun rose. A vessel of burning gold, with billowing sails fashioned of flame rising on

139

the celestial wind, which is God's breath. And everywhere was light.

Another day we drifted. Another night. Then again another day, until the middle of the afternoon when the boat which I was in, which was the first, discovered a point made by the land. Rounding an island of sand, we entered a bay formed from a great river, in which there were many islands. There we took fresh water from the sea, the river entering it in freshet. Those who still had strength, and these were no more than a fifth of our number, dipped water into the gaping mouths of the others, then placed cloths soaked with that soothing substance across eyes and brows. As some recovered, they hung arms and heads over the gunwales to soothe their cracked, sun-tortured skin.

How can I describe the taste of that water? My head lowered below the surface, I allowed its sweet substance to flow past my lips into my mouth and over my tongue. It filled my throat until I must swallow. It filled my ears until I could hear only its low, roaring sound. It mixed with my blood and I could feel it coursing through my veins.

Having drunk our fill and soothed ourselves, we gathered in our boats at a sandy island, hoping to parch the little maize we yet carried, and thus ease our hunger. But, other than a few poor sticks cast up by the tide, the island had no wood for fire, and its sandy surface proved treacherous, nearly trapping into its sucking substance one of the men. Thus we determined to try for the mainland no more than half a league away, although from the swift current of the river we all knew this would be no easy matter.

Urged on by the officers, we struck out, all who could sit erect pulling on the oars. Had the men retained even a portion of their spirit, we might have made it. For the officers beat the men savagely on their backs and shoulders and the distance to

140

be traversed was not great. But without spirit we proved to be no match for the violence of the coursing water. First one, then another, finally all five of the vessels, as the crews gave up the struggle, fell victim to the current and were carried out to sea.

Again we drifted with the tides. And that night while all who were in my boat slept, I steered. The wind came up and with it a bitter cold but I did not seek to be relieved. Hours passed and cold numbed my hands and clouded my mind.

"Would that I had half a score like you, Estevanico," Alvar Nuñez's words startled me. "Standing all through the night at the tiller without relief." He rubbed his eyes free of sleep. "With half a score such men," he went on, "with as few as six, I would order this boat turned to sea and risk wind and waves, knowing we must in time reach Cuba or Pánuco." I did not reply, but his words gave me pleasure. "All night you steered, Négro," he said the word for black in such a way that it was no curse, "all night without sleep; denied the little warmth generated by our huddled bodies, guiding this boat and guarding us; Estevanico, who of all the twelve score in this expedition has a better right to call himself man than you? And you a slave!" He reached up and rested his hand for a moment on my arm. "Once before we talked, and I promised you gold, Estevanico." I nodded. "And now I cannot promise you so much as a handful of parched grain." I shrugged. "Who could blame you if you laughed and turned your head away at my promises." I shook my head, but said nothing. "Listen, then, Estevan, slave of Andres Dorantes, for again I will risk making you a promise. Knowing how empty my other promise has been, can you believe me?"

For the space of a dozen heartbeats I waited, then inclined my head.

"I intend to find a way that will take me back to a land governed by the Spanish crown," he then said. "How long this will be with the men so weakened, I cannot know. Many will die—there can be no help for this. But my promise is that some

141

will survive. And of this number, Estevan, if you do not abandon faith, you will be one. This promise I make you, black man. As certain as I am that there is a God in heaven, as certain as my knowledge that Christ died for our sins, you will survive. Do you credit my words, Estevan?"

Again I waited the space of a dozen heartbeats, then nodded. And again Alvar Nuñez placed his hand upon my arm where, until the others began to stir with wakefulness, it rested.

XIX

Three days beyond the sight of land we were carried by the current. With each passing hour, despite the sun which shone bright in a cloudless sky, and despite the calm nights free of all but a little wind, it grew colder. Exhausted so that my breath came in short gasps, I steered, at times relieved by Alvar Nuñez or the assessor, for of the rest of the men not one could muster sufficient strength to stand. Frost formed in my hair and beard, and the hand gripping the tiller numbed then stiffened into a crook. The third night—it still lacking three hours till the end of darkness—I descried in the distance points of light I judged to be fires, and steered for them. The other four boats followed and, standing half a league from land, we all came together. There were great fires along the shore, with clouds of smoke rising high, yet despite our need of warmth none were willing to chance a landing in the dark.

By morning, despite our efforts, the vessels had separated because of the rapid current and we found ourselves alone in

142

thirty fathoms' sounding, a league from land. All that day, keeping well within the sight of the shore, at different times entering inlets, we searched for the other boats. So desperate was our search, that different ones whose weakness caused their limbs to tremble forced their arms to pull on the oars when their help was needed.

As the sun dipped downward in the sky, many of the men, fearing the coming of the night, and we alone on that desolate ocean, began to cry and moan. But at the hour of vespers, rounding a rocky point of land, we sighted two boats—one in the middle distance, the other almost out of sight. Urged on by Alvar Nuñez, we bent our backs, and, while there was still a little daylight left, came up to the nearer boat, which was that of the Governor.

After no more than a word or two of greeting, his hands still gripping the oar which he had been pulling, Alvar Nuñez urged the Governor that both boats join the vessel which went in advance, and that we by no means leave her. With much passion he entreated that our safety lay in all three staying close together. The Governor, instead of making an immediate reply to the entreaty of his second-in-command, turned to Captain Juan Pantoja, with whom he whispered for several minutes. Trying to restrain his rising choler, Alvar Nuñez begged the Governor to give his men the necessary orders without more delay, for the other vessel was nearly out of sight.

"It is already too far away," the Governor muttered as Captain Juan Pantoja nodded his agreement. "In twenty minutes, no more than half an hour, it will be night, and it is my determination to reach the shore." He again whispered to Captain Juan Pantoja, then went on, "If we do not reach the shore while there is yet light, we may be carried out to sea, for the wind is rising."

Seeing the Governor determined to head for land, and judging it best to follow him, Alvar Nuñez ordered that our craft be put around. For nearly a quarter of an hour we followed

143

the Governor's boat, but, despite our efforts, he having the healthiest of all the men, we could not keep up with him. Then, realizing that in another few minutes, with the coming of darkness, we must be separated, Alvar Nuñez called out, begging for a rope so that the two vessels might be joined together. This the Governor refused, saying that tied together neither one should succeed in reaching land.

Not slackening for a single moment on the oar, which he pulled with the power of two men, Alvar Nuñez called out to the Governor, who stood in the rear of his craft holding the tiller: "What of the other boats . . . Dorantes, Castillo . . . Friar Xuarez . . . Tellez, Peñalosa? Which boat—," exertion caused his voice to break, and, freeing one hand, he pointed backwards.

"That is the one commanded by Tellez and Peñalosa," was the Governor's shouted reply. "Of the vessel of Dorantes and Castillo I have no knowledge, perhaps they have found a place of safety and are waiting for us—I cannot know."

"And the one commanded by the commissary," the assessor called out, "what of that vessel?"

"Friar Xuarez begged my leave to turn out to sea and try for Pánuco; we separated this morning."

"You granted him permission to turn out to sea!" Alvar Nuñez bellowed at the Governor, his face blackening with anger. "You freed him from your command; that one?"

"This is no time in which one should command another," the Governor shouted back, his face also showing anger. "You, too, are freed of my command, Alvar Nuñez!"

"Pánfilo de Narvaez! You are the Governor!" Alvar Nuñez let go of his oar and rose up in the boat, both arms raised above his head, his hands tightened into fists. "Your authority was placed with you by the King!"

"We are beyond the authority of the King! Each must do what he thinks best to save his life." With that, the Governor ordered his men to increase their efforts, and before five minutes his craft had pulled away and was lost in the gathering darkness.

Still standing erect, but with his hands, now open, hanging at his sides, Alvar Nuñez, more to himself than to the others, muttered, "Freed of the Governor's authority—that one. He will not last the day at sea. May Christ have mercy . . ." With that Alvar Nuñez ordered the boat turned away from shore and we started in the direction of the vessel commanded by Tellez and Peñalosa.

So great had been the exertion that most no longer had strength to row, but, finding a little wind, in an hour's time we came up to the other craft, which had waited for us.

The condition of the men in that vessel was little different from our own. As their means of persuasion so that the men should not abandon the oars, Captains Tellez and Peñalosa had employed beatings and threats of hanging. But exhaustion and broken spirits finally caused most of the oars to be left unattended. As we came up, only a few men so much as raised their heads.

Judging the sea to be calm enough, the vessels were lashed together and allowed to drift, while all slept and through sleep tried to repair the ravages of exhaustion. But upon awakening we found that we had drifted to sea and were out of sight of shore.

For four days we continued in company, at night tied together, during the day the few that were able rowing. And not once in those four days did we descry the shore.

The fourth day, a storm came up, and because we feared swamping, the ropes joining the boats were loosed. In moments the violence of the storm caused the boats to separate and lose sight of each other. By nightfall, of all in our boat, I and Alvar Nuñez alone were left with the power of speech. Even the assessor had grown so weak he could answer only with nods and little movements of his hands.

Feeling my condition failing—with the sea running high,

someone must steer—we arranged that Alvar Nuñez first would sleep, and then, when sufficiently refreshed, relieve me at the tiller. Never did I know such exhaustion as I did during those hours of darkness. My legs trembled and my vision was blurred. So violent was the beating of my heart that I could not find enough air to breathe. Near the eleventh hour believing myself about to die, I awoke Alvar Nuñez, telling him I could not go on. Then, like one struck with a mace, I fell into the scupper never expecting to rise again. I lay there among the other prostrate men hearing their moans and the harsh sounds of my own breathing awaiting death.

Then suddenly, as if I had become two instead of one, I could see myself lying helpless—a dumb beast chased to exhaustion by a pack of dogs, and now waiting for their fangs. I could see their cruel red eyes, smell their pungent breath. They had chased Estevan, the black beast, howling and snapping at him, keeping him running, knowing they soon would tear at his flesh and crack his bones for marrow. And now Estevan the black beast lay waiting for the yellow fangs.

Swelling with a choking anger, I struggled to my feet. My hands ached to have at those dogs, my feet begged to kick that helpless black beast. I took back the tiller from Alvar Nuñez, then, as I felt the boat respond, and as the cold spray wet my cheeks, the savage dogs began to fade, the helpless black beast dissolved, and again I was Estevan, the man.

My strength restored, I steered through the night, eyes lifted to the stars, ears straining to hear their music. Just before dawn, Alvar Nuñez sat up, saying he could hear the tumbling of the sea and from this he judged us to be near the shore. So absorbed had I been in the stars that I had not heard the change in the roaring of the ocean.

We sounded, and finding ourselves in seven fathoms and fearing to go any closer until light, I tried to put the boat around while Alvar Nuñez pulled strongly on an oar. But the current being too swift for us, we drifted in until, just at the first light of dawn, a great wave took us, knocking the boat up out of the water, higher than twice the height of a tall man. The violence with which the vessel struck aroused even those who appeared to be near death, and finding the shore close and the water shallow, the men crawled on hands and knees to the land.

Helped by the assessor and several others who had regained a portion of their strength, we built fires, then dragged the weakest ones close to the warmth. After a little time, most of the men showed signs of restoration from the heat of the fires and from a meal of parched maize—the first food we had eaten cooked since departing the Indian village. By early afternoon, all but a few were sufficiently recovered, so that they began to exert themselves.

The day on which we arrived, as given by the assessor after some careful calculation, was the sixth of November. I give this date because it marks the end of the journey of the expedition commanded by Governor Pánfilo de Narvaez and the beginning of a different sort of adventure.

XX

The place to which the tide had brought the boat was a rocky cove whose shore was broken by shallow ravines filled with rubble and coarse sand, while to the rear, the land rose thirty or forty fathoms.

After giving thanks for our deliverance, Alvar Nuñez called all the men together for a council. But, although their bodies had been much restored, only a few who gathered for that council were clear enough of mind to answer Alvar Nuñez when he asked, what would be best for us. Of all the men, only Lope de Oviedo, a sergeant, the assessor, Alvano Fernandez, a Portuguese, and one called Astudillo, a native of Cafra, made intelligent answer to the question. All agreed that the weather being boisterous, with good prospects of it worsening, and there being little left to eat, the conditions faced were hazardous. Yet, putting again to sea without sufficient preparation must risk the life of every man. Dejection then caused some minutes to pass in silence. As we sat, gusts of wind whipped clouds of sand into our faces.

"Never have I seen a more desolate place," muttered the assessor, who was the first to break the silence.

"Even the swamps of Florida as we traveled north from the town of Dulchanchellin were less malign," murmured the sergeant, Lope de Oviedo.

"And there it was warm," offered the Portuguese, sighing.

With an angry sound made deep in his throat, Alvar Nuñez gained the attention of most of the men. "In the boat while at sea I heard moans of those who begged that we might again know the comfort of dry land. In the heat of Florida's jungles there were groans for the relief of a cooling breeze. I think that if granted Paradise, a thing not likely to this collection of sniveling whoresons gathered here before me, there would be complaints about the loudness of the heavenly music, the odor of the perfumed breeze, until even the Archangel loses his patience and casts you out that you may join the others of your family who roast in Hell!"

"If this place be Paradise," muttered the assessor softly, but not so softly that he could not be heard, "then give me the other place, where at least I can find some warmth for my frozen bones."

Alvar Nuñez looked hard at the man, a frown darkening his features. "Do you forget who you are, Alonso de Solis?"

148

Although forced low so it should not be heard by most, Alvar Nuñez's voice hissed. "Is 'de Solis' the name of an honored family of Spanish hidalgos? Or is it the name given to the shovelers of shit who live in pens together with pigs?"

The assessor's face turned white.

"Or is it that the one I see here groveling is not Alonso de Solis," Alvar Nuñez went on, his voice cracking from its harshness. "Alonso de Solis was an officer of the King, not some complaining woman dressed in the clothing of a man!"

The assessor's hand moved toward his sword.

"So!" Alvar Nuñez grasped the assessor's wrist and held it with a grip of iron, "is it possible that I am mistaken and the woman is a man?" His teeth bared in fury, Alonso de Solis struggled to free his hand. "If you be an hidalgo, an officer and a man," Alvar Nuñez released the wrist, "you will not prove it with your sword, my friend. Your words, the way you conduct yourself with the men, your every action will say if you be Alonso the hidalgo of an ancient and honorable family, or Alonso the keeper of swine!"

"For what you have said, I will demand satisfaction, Alvar Nuñez!"

"In another place, at another time, you will have your satisfaction, Alonso, not now. First you must again prove yourself to be a man—'frozen bones.'" This last Alvar Nuñez said in a whisper, but with his lips curled down.

Two, perhaps as much as three more minutes passed in silence. Then, forcing his voice not to sound harsh and unnatural, the assessor offered as his suggestion that, rather than staying where we were, engaged in idle speculation, an expedition should be gathered together to explore the land.

"Would that there were sufficient restored to their senses, Alonso," was Alvar Nuñez's answer.

"Then I will go and take with me the slave, the Portuguese and Lope de Oviedo," the assessor proposed.

"The condition of most being as it is," Alvar Nuñez

149

quickly motioned to several who sat nearby, heads bowed, eyes staring at the ground, "with so many unable to defend themselves should we be attacked . . . " the assessor nodded his understanding. It was then decided to have Lope de Oviedo, who was skilled at climbing, climb a tall tree seen at the top of the rise, and from there survey the land.

He returned, running, breathless from exertion and flushed with excitement. "We are on an island," he gasped, "and it may be that this is a land of Christians!" Gaining his breath, he gave his reason for believing we were in a country inhabited by Christians: the land was pawed up in the manner that ground is wont to be where cattle range. Alvar Nuñez nodded vigorously as Alonso de Solis exclaimed, "And I have never known of Indians who keep cattle!"

"Nor have I ever heard of cattle that run wild in this desolate land," Alvar Nuñez added.

"Could it be that you saw the markings left by a herd of browsing deer?" Alonso de Solis asked in the manner of a man who prays that the answer not be 'yes.'

"Would one whose father was herdsman of blooded Andalusian cattle not know which are the pawings of heavy cattle, which of light deer?" answered Lope de Oviedo.

"Heavy cattle?" asked Alvar Nuñez.

"As heavy, I will give my oath, as any I have ever seen— how they should grow so fat in this sparse land . . . "

"I will take the slave and Lope de Oviedo," the assessor said, his voice trembling with excitement. "What have we to fear if this be Christian land . . . " Alvar Nuñez waved the man silent.

"Before parting with my second-in-command," Alvar Nuñez said gently, "even if it be only for a little hour, I must gain more information, Alonso." Then, turning back to Lope de Oviedo, he ordered him to return and carefully examine the countryside, but to range no further than half a league, and at all times to exercise every caution.

150

I will confess to trembling with excitement the first minutes after the man left. How much effort it took not to follow the departing man and join in the exploration, I cannot with any accuracy convey. What if this should prove to be a Christian land and we are saved?—I thought. Warmth, good food, women—in time return to Spain. To see my home again. To sprinkle a little water on the grave of my son. To kneel again in the nave of the great Italian church and face the Mother and Her tortured Son.

Waiting for Lope de Oviedo's return was like a dream— while chained to my oar in the galley, I would often dream that I was free. "You are free, Estevan, go ashore," in my dream the captain would tell me. The shore was that same shore which lies below my city of Azemmour. "Why do you wait, you fool!" the other slaves would say to me, "you are free." "You are free, Estevan," the captain would say again. I had but to swing over the railing—then I would awake, knowing it all had been a dream—a deep ache pulling at my heart and lungs.

Waiting for Lope de Oviedo, I wondered if I would soon awake and find this, too, had been a dream: That there are no Christians. There will be no return to Spain. Never to see my home again.

"Why does that whoreson take so long to return!" the assessor muttered. "He has disobeyed orders and gone beyond a half a league," foam formed in the corners of his mouth.

"It is not yet half an hour, Alonso," Alvar Nuñez answered softly. "Close your eyes and gain a little rest, my friend. I will wake you the moment of his return." To these gentle words the assessor shook his head. Then, squeezing his hands together, he began rocking slowly.

Another fifteen minutes passed. "He is gone too long, Alvar Nuñez!" the assessor shouted above the wind and started to rise.

"A little more patience, my friend; if he does not return before another fifteen minutes I will send Estevan to look for him." In silence, excepting the hissing wind, there again passed fifteen minutes. "Go with the Portuguese and find Lope de Oviedo," Alvar Nuñez then gave as his order. "If he is lost, find him—take care that you are not lost!" I nodded. "If he has been captured by savages, do not attempt his rescue, but return at once. Do you understand my orders, Estevan?" Again I nodded.

Taking up a sword, I climbed the rise, followed closely by the Portuguese, who carried the one crossbow left. I then scaled the tree, but not without difficulty, for my hands were stiff with cold. After a little searching, I descried Lope de Oviedo a quarter of a league distant, walking slowly in our direction. A hundred paces behind, three Indians followed, calling to him. He would take a dozen steps, stop and beckon them on, and they would wave the stout bows they carried and call to him again. Seeing he was in no danger, and fearing to startle the Indians, I waited with the Portuguese until he should come up.

Using these few minutes of time, I surveyed the countryside and, as had Lope de Oviedo, noted that the land had been pawed as if by cattle; yet from the appearance of the three Indians, this was no country inhabited by Christians. Except for breechclouts, they were naked; their underlip was bored through and in it they wore a piece of cane the breadth of half a finger. Also bored was one nipple, from side to side, in which was fastened a cane two and a half palms in length. And they were tall and well fashioned; but, unlike the other savages we had known, wore a full head of hair—wild as a lion's mane—but their faces showed not a trace of hair.

When Lope de Oviedo finally came up, we joined him, beckoning to the Indians. Laying our weapons on the ground and showing open hands, we smiled, nodded, and called to them in gentle voices. Then we started down the rise.

The moment he saw the three Indians, the assessor drew his sword and started forward. And it was fortunate that he was restrained by Alvar Nuñez, for within minutes, as if by magic,

152

the three were joined by surely two hundred more, all carrying bows, who ranged themselves fifty paces distant on the sand.

Speaking softly, Alvar Nuñez ordered that none of the men should rise, that all must smile and wave and nod at the Indians, and most particularly that no hand should move toward sword or other weapon. If these savages were not huge, our fears made giants of them. Their skins were nearly as dark as mine. Their bows were as tall as a man and of a greater thickness than a man's arm, and in their hands they held knives, nicely fashioned of flint, axes of stone, bone-tipped spears and clubs stained red with vermillion which at first we took for blood.

Following orders, all but the most feeble of us grinned, waved and nodded. Two times a grizzled Indian, although advanced in years, straight of back and with clear eyes, stepped forward to address us. In his hands he carried a carved and painted staff from which hung tassels tipped with yellow feathers. But, although we strained to hear him, his voice was lost in the wind, for it held little breath and his speech was made less of words than of sighs. I will confess that as I watched the Indians increase in number until they exceeded two hundred, I despaired of our chances of survival. One flight of their arrows and all would be done. But then, as the minutes passed and nothing happened, I wondered if they might be as afraid of us as we of them. Then came the thought, that having never before seen Christians—men of a different color skin, wearing clothes and with beards—they might be more afraid.

My skin being the most like theirs, I begged permission of Alvar Nuñez to approach them. This granted, I took a quantity of beads and hawkbells and slowly walked forward, and it was as if I had become fifty well-armed men instead of one weaponless man. For the Indians who stood in the place which I approached retreated. I stopped and they stopped their retreat. Then, as I again started forward, they hesitated, allowing me to come within an arm's length of them. Again I waited, moving

153

my hands so that the bells should sound. The grizzled Indian who had addressed us reached his hand out carefully and I gave him two bells and several beads of different colors. Showing a huge grin, he made the bells sound and rolled the beads between his gnarled fingers. Then surely a score held out their hands.

Before five minutes, the Indians had joined us, and we quickly distributed amongst them much of our store of gifts. They then presented each man in our company with an arrow as a pledge of friendship and by signs promised they would return the next day and bring us something to eat. They departed laughing, ringing their bells and saying words that were more like sighs. As they moved away, Alvar Nuñez, in every way he knew, called out that we came in peace and would welcome their return.

All through that night a fierce wind blew. The sea boiled up and spume wet every man. Had we not been able to keep the fires burning we must have lost more than one that first night spent on the island.

As they had promised, the Indians returned, and it was at the first light of morning. Although, as we later learned, they were not well supplied with food, they brought us a quantity of fish and certain roots a little larger than walnuts, which they gather with much difficulty from beneath the water.

As we ate their food, the Indians brought their faces so close their breath was upon us, as is their custom with friends, and, wonder showing in their features, they peered into our mouths, examined our ears, inspected noses and gently tugged our beards. Although not fashioned in the way of Europeans, I did not find the Indians of this nation ugly. Their women, who later came to look at us, I also did not find unattractive, although many of them were worn with toil. Of all in our company, the Indians appeared to be most amazed with me. Perhaps it was my skin, perhaps my size, or it might have been the way my hair curls tight, but whatever their reason, they would not let up from bringing their faces close, stroking my arms and

154

cheeks, feeling the coarseness of my beard, and doing so many other things that in time I felt more like a horse put up for sale than a man. Yet, not to offend them, I suffered their examination.

After they had gone, before we could recover from their attentions, their women and their children came to view us. Amongst these we distributed the remainder of our store of bells and beads, and again were subjected to close examination. In this nation of Indians, all the children go naked except in the most severe weather; the women never cover their breasts, wearing only an apron woven of reeds to preserve their modesty. Not one time did I see these Indians treat their children other than with kindness. Never did they inflict the slightest punishment, and they appeared to love them above all other things.

Twice more the Indian men came with food until we were well supplied. Then having rested three days, Alvar Nuñez ordered that we prepare to embark.

It was the assessor's belief from the distance already traveled that we must be near Pánuco. No more than fifty leagues he gave as his estimate. My thoughts were otherwise though I was not asked. How could a civilized Spanish port be so near and these Indians not know of bearded men with fair skins? How could we be certain we had traveled in the right direction? Yet it was either that Alvar Nuñez agreed with the assessor, or that there were other reasons for pursuing our course again.

With much labor we dug our boat from the sand and found it still seaworthy. This, most took as a good omen, for it had suffered a severe buffeting. Then, after storing in it our provisions as well as all our clothing, for we stripped naked to go through the great exertion required for the launching, all who were able started pushing the craft toward the water. The distance was not great, no more than a score of paces, but we were in such a state that few were not trembling from exhaustion by the time we had her launched.

We had not traveled the distance of two crossbow shots

155

from land, when we shipped a wave that entirely wet us and, being naked and exhausted, and the cold being very great, the oars loosened in our hands. Seeing a high wave coming toward us, Alvar Nuñez and I strained at the tiller, trying to pull the boat around. But the wave struck broadside, capsizing the craft. Most were thrown into the sea, but the assessor and two others held fast to the boat for preservation. Another wave struck and the boat rolled over, carrying the three under and thus they were drowned. The surf being very high and we being close to shore, a single great roll of the sea tossed the rest back on land, close to where we had embarked.

Of all that we owned in this world, the only thing saved was our lives—except for the three who had drowned. Our possessions had been of little value, but we sorrowed at their loss as if they had been all the riches of the Indies. Amongst the more than forty who lay there struggling for breath, there was not so much as a single stitch of clothing. We were the perfect figures of death, privation had caused the skeleton of every man to show through the skin so that each bone might be counted. Then, to add to our misfortune, a north wind began to blow. Another half hour in this condition would have cost all of us our lives, for many already were turning blue. But, thanks to the Almighty, the wind stirred the ashes of our fires, which we believed dead, and showed us sparks. So we made great fires, forming them in a half circle, and lying close to them, covering our bodies with sand, we survived.

We passed the day sorrowing. No one could see how we should last more than a little time, so desperate was our condition. Even Alvar Nuñez could not force his mouth to utter words of encouragement. The death of Alonso de Solis lay heavily upon him, and for many minutes he kept his head bowed into his arms, so that his face could not be seen.

The wind blew increasingly cold, and spume whipped up from the water wet us. Even the ones who lay closest to the fires trembled and could scarcely speak for the chattering of their

156

teeth. Considering our condition, who is there to blame those who then began to weep? I did not weep, yet within my chest I knew such pressure I fought to breathe. It was as if a terrible hand gripped my heart. I said nothing—I could offer no comfort so I stopped my words—but I could not stop my thinking:

"If the Almighty by some miracle does not deliver us before night, by morning not one of us will be alive. Yet how should we be delivered in this desperate and desolate place . . . Will the night that follows the setting of the sun be the darkest night, the last night for Estevan . . . How will it be to die? Close my eyes and drift into the dreamless sleep; or will there be suffering?"

"The Indians will surely come before sunset!" gasped Lope de Oviedo.

The Indians! I had forgotten about the Indians.

"And if they come," said the one called Astudillo, he of Cafra, "what then? Can we make defense against them in our condition—naked, unarmed? If they take us to their huts it will be only to make a sacrifice to their idols." With that, he fell to weeping.

"As Astudillo says!" groaned the Portuguese. "I have been in New Spain. I have seen Christians with their hearts torn from their chests—ripped out still beating—taken by the pagans to feed their famished idols."

"Were we not attacked by those other Indians who first pretended to be our friends," moaned Astudillo. "Rather would I, by a hundred times, be left here to die in peace than suffer tortures at the hands of Indians."

"One more word of tortures," Alvar Nuñez raised his head, his sunken eyes burning with a fierce light, "he who says that word will know the full weight of my fist!" He stared hard at Astudillo and then at the Portuguese. Then he fell silent for a time as he struggled to regain his breath, but he did not let up from staring. "If through the grace of God the Indians should come again," he finally went on, "and I will offer up a hundred

157

prayers this day that they may come, if they come I will beg them to take us with them!"

"I will offer up two hundred prayers, my captain," said Lope de Oviedo. "And if needs be fall to my knees and kiss their feet that they may rescue us." At this, soft murmurs broke out amongst the men.

I marveled at how completely I had forgotten about the Indians. As I earlier lay shivering beneath my sand blanket, it was as if they had never been. Had adversity softened my brain? "Foolish Estevan," I whispered, "the Indians will come and, seeing our condition, they will help us." I closed my eyes so that I might see their faces. Fierce faces—blue tatoos on the cheeks and brow, pierced underlip with its piece of sharpened cane, hair that had never known a comb. Yet their ways were gentle; their touch softer than that of nuns. And the manner of their speaking—sighs and murmurs. Was there a chance of torture, as feared by the Portuguese?

I opened my eyes and saw two hundred warriors, each with his great bow, coming down from the rise. Slowly they came toward us. My limbs trembled uncontrollably. They stopped fifty paces from us, as they had done the first time and stared at us. They whispered to each other. Then they edged backward. Alvar Nuñez, rising from the sand, called out to them, but they moved further backward, their faces showing fear. As he had said he would, he begged them to save us, at length falling to his knees.

Then Lope de Oviedo rose from the sand and fell to his knees, as did others, this one included. Wonder replaced fear on the Indians' faces as they saw us in our nakedness—perhaps they had thought our clothing to be our skins. They cautiously approached; their grizzled chief, his carved staff held forward, leading them. When they learned, by signs, of our loss—three men, the boat, all of our provisions—it was as if the loss had been their own.

All two hundred of those savages squatted on the sand and

began to weep. And this was no false weeping. Tears flowed from each man's eyes, and there were the racking sobs that come only from the deepest grief. As they wept they reached out their fluttering fingers to give us comfort. Not a man amongst us could resist this show of tenderness, and we joined their weeping.

For no less than half an hour the Indians continued weeping. It was not until the sun had set and the wind from the north started to blow again that the weeping finally ceased. Then they made preparations to take us with them. The distance to their village being nearly half a league, and the wind each moment gusting colder, they realized that some of us would die if taken from our fires even for as little as five minutes. Accordingly, after stacking quantities of wood on our fires so they should burn hot, the Indians built four great fires along the way. They then took us, two to each man, and rushed us from fire to fire, so that we fairly flew, our feet scarcely touching the ground, and in this way brought us, without loss, to their village.

There, the very sick were distributed, one or two to a hut, and were cared for with such tenderness that each later swore that he had never known the like since an infant on his mother's teat. Some who could not get warm were wrapped tight in skins together with their women. Those who were too weak to take food were fed a soft gruel. For the rest of us they had prepared a house with many fires in it, and to satisfy our hunger we had boiled and roasted fish, ashcake and dried fruit.

An hour after our arrival, many of us being much restored, the Indians began to dance and hold a great rejoicing, which lasted all through the night and well into the next day. Yet for certain ones of us there was no joy, no festivity, no sleep. These were the ones who were still of the belief that the Indians had saved us only to later make us victims. Of this group of worriers, I, thankfully, was not one.

Having regained much of my strength by morning, and finding that the Indians offered no restriction, I walked about their village. Not less than a score of children followed me, no matter where I went, and in their soft voices called out, "*Ya-an Pal, Ya-an Pal*," which I later learned meant "Tall-Black" in their language; and for all of the time I was amongst them, this, not Estevan, was my name.

Having seen all that could be seen in their village—it being poor, the habitations constructed of sticks covered in part by mats and skins—I joined the inhabitants, who called themselves "Capoques," or at different times, "Cahoques," at their place of celebration. They, as had their children, called me by the name, "*Ya-an Pal*," and from their grins and gentle touches, appeared to be pleased to see me. An old woman, who, if not for her dugs—dried bags of skin—I must have taken for a man, came up and blew her breath first in my one ear then in the other. This, I later learned, was their way of treating those who were sick, or of keeping those who are well free of sickness. It was this same woman, called *Tsol Kuon*, meaning "blue bird," who later, when the Indians lost half their number from an affliction of the bowels, saved Alvar Nuñez and those who were still with him from destruction. Had I known how her affection for Alvar Nuñez would in time be his protection against those who wanted to kill him, would I have suffered a disgust which I must hide as I felt her breath and breathed its stink?

"Toothless crone," was my thought as she breathed into my ears, "I am not yet so desperate from lack of a woman to offer one as withered as you my affection." How should I have known that this woman, held in as great respect as the chief, by her actions, was doing me an important honor? That there was not a warrior of that village who would have not judged it the highest of rewards to be allowed to lay with her?

Led by this same one, whose movements were not those of an old woman, I was given a place to sit where I could view the celebration yet where I was separated from it by the distance of a score of paces. Then she said a few soft words to the children

160

who were clustered about and, as if they were milkweed down and her breath the wind, they drifted away, leaving me alone.

Although as I watched the celebration I could not then know its meaning, later when I gained knowledge of their speech, which was not a difficult task for me, I also learned the language of their dance. All the dancers were men with the younger ones, those wearing reed skirts with yellow ochre markings on their breasts, playing the part of women. The dance was the struggle between birth (the women), and death (the older men). In this dance the woman always won, although as different pairs wrestled it often appeared as if the man, who, being older, stronger and of greater skill, must gain the advantage. When such appeared about to happen, those dressed as women grabbed their bellies and groaned as if in labor, while leaping up and down, and this gave the woman wrestler new strength, and in some mysterious fashion weakened the man. When, after many hours, all the men dressed as women had conquered, for only one pair wrestled at a time, then those who had been vanquished retired, their places taken by all the male children of the village, the littlest ones being carried. The celebration always ended with an old man stealthfully returning, and, before the rest can stop him, stealing away the youngest child. Then all the men dressed as women and all the children searched for the stolen child while the true women, who were watching, set up such a wail that hearing them for the first time one must believe that each one had suffered some terrible bereavement.

I later learned that our arrival amongst them caused certain changes in the dance. Various of the children now had their faces painted white, while the tallest one had his blackened with soot and earth. The celebration, which at first I believed was held to mark our salvation, I later learned was in honor of our birth! These people could not understand how our arrival could be other than through birth. Since we came in a boat from the water, the sea must be our mother. That we might

161

have come from another land was a thing that held no meaning for them.

After an hour of watching their celebration, I was joined by Alvar Nuñez, who was greeted, as I had been, by the old woman. He suffered her breath without flinching, then did a thing I had not thought to do. Showing much gentleness, he offered his breath to her. At this, a murmur rose up from all who were gathered, and their chief came close, that he, too, should benefit from Alvar Nuñez's breath.

Had this dance lasted another twenty hours, I would not have left my place—nor would Alvar Nuñez, I will give my oath. But when the dance suddenly ended as the stealthy old man stole away the youngest child and the women started their terrible wail, Alvar Nuñez, fearing that some harm might befall us, ordered me to follow him to a place of greater safety.

"Only one other time have I heard a wail like that of those Indian women," Alvar Nuñez brought his lips close to my ear as we settled into the dark shadow of an earthen mound. "Italian women, they were, who had come out from their village after the battle to where their men had fallen. Had we been without weapons," Alvar Nuñez made a cutting motion across his throat.

"If the Indians wished to kill us, my captain," I said carefully, "would they not have dispatched us as we lay there on the beach naked and helpless? When the one called Astudillo spoke of the danger from the Indians, your words . . . "

"I remember my words well enough, black man!" I was silenced by the harshness of his voice. But then Alvar Nuñez laid his hand upon my arm. "Will you forgive me, Estevan?" he asked. "It was the sound of the wailing women that unnerved me." Never had a man of rank ever begged my forgiveness. Mayhap in all the history of this world until that very moment, never had an hidalgo begged pardon of a slave.

"As for my words as we lay naked on the beach, they were sprung from our condition," Alvar Nuñez then said slowly. "If not relieved all of us must have died during the night.

162

But now I must again consider the delicacy of our position."
I nodded, to show the care with which I listened. "Of all
my men, by ten times would I rather share these thoughts with
you, Estevanico, than with any other. You know the virtue of
silence, and I have reason enough to trust your bravery.

"Because of the color of our skin, because of our beards
and the strangeness of our speech, to these Indians we are a
curiosity," Alvar Nuñez continued slowly. "When they first
came upon us, when we were yet clothed and armed, they
showed fear. Perhaps it was that they viewed us as creatures
different from themselves, for they made much of our clothing,
as you must remember. But finding us naked and with parts
like their own, they surely know us to be different only as to the
color of our skin. Soon we will cease to be a curiosity, Estevan."
Alvar Nuñez hesitated. "Then, I think, we may be served as we
were by those other Indians, the ones whose peculiar hospitality we shared. But this time we are weaponless and reduced in
number to a helpless remnant." With that Alvar Nuñez fell
silent.

Having waited a sufficient time, and after several clearings
of the throat I said in a voice containing much respect, "If I
may be permitted, my captain." Alvar Nuñez grunted softly.
"I, too, judge our position delicate. But I think we are not in a
desperate situation." I waited for a moment, but hearing no
objection, continued. "Never would I have survived these full
thirty years, my captain, years chained to an oar in a galley,
years filled with fighting in savage wars, years of such adversity
that only one who has known slavery half his life can know my
meaning, had I not possessed a certain sensitivity." I paused,
and Alvar Nuñez grunted for me to continue. "In my bowels
and in my throat, in my hands and in my chest, I have learned
to sense danger. First I know the feeling, my captain, then I
search my mind for its meaning, but always the feeling first."

"And you do not judge our position to be desperate?" Alvar
Nuñez asked slowly.

"Delicate, my captain, but not desperate. We must exercise sufficient caution that we do not offend these simple people. We must show them in a hundred ways that we will not harm them, for it is my belief that, despite our lack of arms and our nakedness, they still fear us. And, from the greatness of their hospitality, from the concern shown by their piteous weeping, and from other things—the celebration we just witnessed—it is my belief that only through fear would they harm us."

"Then we will do all that can be done so they should not fear us!" Alvar Nuñez declared. "Like a plunge into cold water after too much drink, your words have cleared my thinking, Estevan. As you say, in a hundred ways we will show our gentleness and our love for them. I will instruct the men. But, if we possessed a seaworthy vessel or knew where we might get one, or if this was a different season with weather less boisterous for travel . . . "

"In time we may secure such a vessel, my captain. In time the winter will be past."

"Again you offer sound counsel, Estevan. No matter how terrible the winter, there is always the certainty of spring. And with the help of the Almighty, we will live to see it."

After we parted Alvar Nuñez went from man to man, not neglecting those still overcome with weakness, and explained the necessity of our treating our hosts with great delicacy. Remembering how different ones served the women of Dulchanchellin, Alvar Nuñez said to these ones, "You know me to be an honorable man, an officer who, once he gives his word to do a certain thing will surely do that thing. On my mother's grave, I swear to hang any man who dares to disobey my orders!" Then he went on to instruct each man not to take offense, no matter what the provocation; to smile and speak softly; to make no sudden or violent movement; to show affection to the Indian children and not to take so much as a grain of maize without first gaining permission. With Astudillo, he of Cafra, Alvar Nuñez, knowing of his appetites and his savage reputation, added emphasis to his words by seizing that one's throat and squeezing it until the man's face had turned near black. "This is but a taste of the punishment you will suffer should you so much as lay a single finger upon their women or steal a grain of maize."

To the Portuguese, on whose face I thought I saw a certain crafty look after Alvar Nuñez turned away, I softly said a few words dealing with the loss of manly parts—after I had spoken, it took the man several minutes to stay the shaking of his limbs.

XXI

Having finished with his visits to the men and needing, I supposed, a little time alone for thinking, Alvar Nuñez left the Indian village and started north. Knowing that I would cause him anger and be ordered back should my attendance be detected, I followed with discretion for more than half a league keeping well to the rear of the man as he made his way northward.

Having reached a cove of the ocean protected from the gusts of icy wind by a mound of white boulders, Alvar Nuñez found a place on a rotted log and rested his face in his hands. On the far side of the boulders the ocean raged. Several times Alvar Nuñez raised his head and listened as if in the roaring of the water there was a message. Once he rose up, his face drawn and grey, and started for the water; but before twenty paces he stayed his feet, then slowly returned to his place on the rotted log, where, like an old man forgotten by his children, he wrung his hands. That single gesture brought to me the hopelessness of our position. All the brave talk about departing from this savage and lonely place when it should be spring, that hopeless gesture proved hollow. Had tears then flowed from Alvar Nuñez's eyes, I could not have contained those which filled my own.

Who is to know how long we might have remained in that sheltered place—he sitting on the rotted log, grey-faced, staring at the sand, I crouched behind a boulder, an Indian club tightly gripped in my hand—if I had not heard the sound of a band of approaching Indians. Six warriors they were—all armed and, by their markings, of a different nation. I quickly made my presence known to Alvar Nuñez, and, except for a frown that lasted no longer than a moment, he showed no evidence of anger at my having followed him.

Had it been our determination to hide, and had we acted upon that determination, it is my belief we must have been quickly discovered and then judged to be enemies or cowards. Thus it was fortunate that we rose up to meet them. To our astonishment, they showed no wonder at our beards or at the color of our skins, nor did they seem surprised to see us. Then, to our even greater astonishment, as they came up to greet us with sighs and fluttering fingers, we saw that they were festooned with hawkbells and glass beads, the principal one of them wearing on a leathern thong a brass buckle of Spanish manufacture.

After a little time spent trying to converse with us using their soft words and sighs, sounds lost in the roaring of the wind and the sounding of the surf, they departed in the direction from which they came, but not before giving each of us an arrow as a proof of friendship.

"I will risk my chance of salvation, Estevanico, if there are not other Christians on this island!" Alvar Nuñez shouted above the wind. "That, or we are no great distance from the Port of Pánuco." My throat too choked with excitement, I could only nod my agreement. "If I were other than the chief officer of this expedition, I would follow those Indians on the instant." Then he ordered me to remain where I was, and departed, running back to the village.

Not an hour passed before I was joined by Lope de Oviedo, breathless and bug-eyed from running, together with two Indians of the village sent to guide us.

"Had Alvar Nuñez not made the most terrible threats," Lope de Oviedo said between gasps for breath, "every Spaniard, even the most feeble, would have come, so great was the excitement when he told us what he had seen." And so great was my excitement, for my heart had raced and my mind had spun for all the hour I was forced to wait, that I picked up Lope de Oviedo in my two arms and danced with him, and then danced with each of the laughing Indians.

We started northward and had not traveled half a league when we met up with my master, Andres Dorantes, together with Captain Alonso del Castillo and all the others that had been in the boat of their command!

How shall I tell of their emotion? My master hugged and kissed me, as if I had been the ripest of virgins. And Lope de Oviedo, who was not the prettiest of men, knew more caresses than any dozen willing maidens. But then, noting the skins we wore for clothing and our lack of arms, and learning of our loss of possessions and of the three who drowned, they all were much pained.

The day before our landing, a league and a half north of where we met, they had capsized, and although the wetting they received caused them much distress, they lost neither their possessions nor a single man, and had managed, after a struggle, to beach their boat safely on the sand.

Having gained knowledge of our coming from an Indian we sent forward, every Spaniard of our village was gathered at the outskirts. All the Indian men of the village were also gathered, and when we came up, they started weeping in a manner

167

so piteous that before half a minute there was not one of us who was not affected. Then, for surely half an hour, Christian and pagan wept together; officer, soldier, slave and Indian sharing hot tears, hugged and caressed one another. And then, beckoned by the chief, we all followed him to the far side of the village, where the women had built a great fire and prepared a feast of roasted fish. Not only were we given fish, but also ashcake made of ground nuts, strips of dried flesh—black in color but nonetheless most welcome—and a sour berry that causes the teeth to grate one against the other.

Having feasted and being much exhausted from their ordeal, most of the Spaniards would have left the great fire at sunset had Alvar Nuñez not ordered every man in the company to keep his seat. Noting the chief donning a robe of bearskin, then adding fresh streaks of color to his face, and judging that he was preparing himself to speak, and fearing that the departure of any Spaniard might cause offense, Alvar Nuñez gave as his further order that each man must be prepared to stay as long as necessary, and for all that time must also show a good face.

"Rather than give offense to their chief, we will sit here half the night, if needs be," Alonso del Castillo hissed at a few who grumbled. "And he who needs help to stay awake, I will tickle his rump with the point of my dagger, which should prove to be of sufficient help!"

Having completed his preparations, and after having placed a portion of fish and ashcake on a rock close to the fire where in a little time they must be consumed by heat, and after walking slowly around the great circle, followed by the medicine man masked with the horned and furry head of a species of cattle I had never seen before, the chief, still gripping the carved staff, moved to the center of the circle, where the fire's light fell full upon him.

The sun having set, shadows obscured the more than ten score Indians ranged in a half-circle on the other side of the fire. Although muffled, the roar of the ocean could be heard in the

168

middle distance. Trees twisted by years of wind, like a hoard of cripples waiting to descend, crouched on the high ground outlined against the darkening sky. Then the chief started to speak. Yet it was not an oration that he offered as we sat there in the gathering darkness, but rather a sacred tale.

Although at the time I had not yet mastered their language and could only guess at the meaning, at different times in the years I was to live with the Indians of that region, I heard this same tale again.

"Before there was anything," the chief pointed with his carved staff at the trees and rocks, at the fire and ground, "in a time so distant that it is dangerous for any but chief or medicine man to even think about it, there lived the great, white beast —*Ya-an peka téts'-oa*," he pointed with his staff at the cattle-head mask worn by the medicine man. As he pointed, a sound like a groan rose up from all the assembled Indians. "So huge was this beast that all the land of this island and of the mainland across the channel, as far as any man has ever traveled, could have fitted into just one of his eyes. So mighty was this animal that when it bellowed the sky trembled and the sea heaved up in great waves.

"One day, after spending all morning leaping up and trying to hook the sun with its horns, *Ya-an peka téts'-oa* grew hot from coming so close to the sun, so he went to the ocean to cool himself in the water. But as soon as he stepped into the water, the great crocodile—*Ya-an hok-so*—who was hiding there, came up and seized him by the hind leg. *Ya-an peka téts'-oa*, feeling *Ya-an hok-so's* sharp teeth, let out a bellow so terrible that the sun was frightened and hid, so that all was in darkness." With the point of his staff, the chief drew the picture of the great beast on the ground, to which the medicine man added markings with colored sand as the chief continued with his story. "In the darkness, *Ya-an peka téts'-oa* struggled to free himself from the terrible teeth. From his mighty exertions waves rose so high that had the sun not been hiding he surely must have drowned.

169

Then, *Ya-an peka téts'-oa* rose up on his hind legs, turned around and came down with his forelegs on the tail of *Ya-an hok-so*, trapping that one." All the Indians began to laugh and clap, and the women moved their tongues rapidly in and out of their mouths, making a sound like running water. "So there the two great beasts were, each trapped by the other. Needing help, the crocodile opened his breech and brought forth the snake—*Aúd*. Seeing the snake, the great white beast opened his mouth and freed the deer—*Múta*. Then, from the lizard came *Am-tchuta*, the octopus, as the white beast set free *Kíss*, the dog. In this wise were all the creatures of the world born, the last born of the lizard being *Gá'h*, the mosquito, whose sting might have caused *Ya-an peka téts'-oa*'s defeat if at that moment the white beast had not birthed *Yám awe*—man." The skin of a crocodile was tossed on the ground, which the chief then beat savagely with his stick and toward which the assembled Indians discharged quantities of spit. Then the chief declared, "For man's help in saving him, *Ya-an peka téts'-oa* gave as friends all the creatures he had spawned. And since it was man who had caused his defeat, *Ya-an hok-so* presented his offspring to man to plague and to torture him."

Believing the chief to be finished with speaking, for he had squatted down, resting his head in his hands, a number of the Spaniards began stirring, with certain ones asking Alvar Nuñez permission to withdraw. Still fearing that a sudden departure might give offense, he hesitated, but was about to give the order that by twos and threes the men might leave, when the chief rose up and commenced to tell his tale again. The Indians' response was as if they heard the tale for the first time. And it was the same when the chief, after a second brief rest, told the tale a third time.

Perhaps the chief, fearing his people had no more spit, refrained from telling his story for a fourth time. Or perhaps knowing of our fatigue he desisted. Or it might have been the chill of the night and the rising wind that caused him to restrain. But it is my belief that he resisted what must have been a powerful urge to repeat his tale out of awe for the magic number three.

Had the chief again commenced his story, I am not sure that Alvar Nuñez could have restrained certain of the men. For five of our company actually stood up as the Indians were delivering their third offering of spit, and only the most severe threats caused them to sit down. These five were: Sierra, Diego Lopez, Corral, Palaçios and Gonçallo Ruiz. I give their names, for in the coldest days of winter, they met a terrible and most un-Christian end.

After his third narration, the chief hunched down and lowered his head so that his face was hidden, and started drawing certain pictures in the sand. Once when a gust of wind stirred the fire, I saw his face for a single moment, a face twisted by a crafty grin. And, as he drew the pictures on the sand, the Indians, in groups of twos and threes, making angry sounds, departed. Only later, when I learned their language, did I understand the meaning of those pictures, and why the Indians had departed showing anger. The pictures were of another tale, so awful that it could be told only to chiefs, medicine men and certain very old women; for any other one it was too strong. Yet those denied this story hungered for its power. And it is my belief that a certain narration heard by Alvar Nuñez, when in later times he became a medicine man, was this same story.

While the grinning chief crouched, drawing his symbols, the Spaniards, in ones and twos, eased into the darkness until at last I alone remained. Then the chief, as if he waited for all the others to be gone, as if he knew I would remain, beckoned me down; and squatting there beside him, he guiding my hand, I drew the picture of *Ya-an peka téts'-oa* in the sand.

171

XXII

The next day dawning fair with a lessening of wind, and sleep having relieved the fatigue of most, a council of all the Spaniards was called to decide what should be done. The Indians, seeing us gathered and judging, it is my guess, that we held a celebration, brought us pieces of fish and sweet water in their woven pots, for which gifts we were grateful. At this council, it was quickly agreed that we must refit the boat of Castillo and Dorantes and that those with sufficient vigor and disposition to do so should go in her and seek the port of Pánuco. The rest were to remain with the Indians until their strength was restored and then, commanded by Alvar Nuñez, go as best they could along the coast seeking a land of Christians. Those who traveled in the boat, with the help of God our Lord, would secure help in the port of Pánuco and then return along the coast, succoring the ones who journeyed by land.

Directly as our plans were made, those who were fit marched the two leagues northward to the boat. There, remembering what we had learned from the Greek, Don Theodoro, we labored on the boat until, by sunset, she was patched enough to be judged seaworthy.

In the morning, it having been determined that three score of our number should risk the journey, we launched the boat. But as we were too many and the craft too damaged, it could not float. It sank in five fathoms of water and all who were in her must struggle to reach the shore. Yet it was fortunate that we suffered no greater loss than the vessel, for several were nearly drowned by the immersion, and for a time, as they lay on the sand, gave the appearance of death.

Again we held a council of all the Spaniards, to see what should be done. But this time different ones of the company of Castillo and Dorantes murmured against Alvar Nuñez, saying that had the men of his company not crowded into the boat it would not have sunk. To the murmurs of those ones were joined loud mutterings from five of Alvar Nuñez's band, the same five who had shown defiance the night before.

"Had it been God's will that we journey by sea to Pánuco, the boat would not have sunk," the Portuguese then offered. To hear that one speak in such a fashion did much to quiet the men, for the reputation he had gained was not of temperance.

"As the Portuguese says," added Alvar Nuñez, "and by the loss of the boat the Almighty may have saved many lives!" He gestured toward the angry sea.

"Yet a winter in this malignant place may prove fatal!" cried out Lope de Oviedo.

"Fatal is a strong word," answered Alvar Nuñez. "A winter in this place I would judge hazardous, not fatal. But should we secure help from Christians in Pánuco . . ."

"Secure help, my captain?" Astudillo, he of Cafra, said these words as a question, then laughed.

"Yes, help, you great, unwashed, hairy bear of Cafra." At this all laughed. "And you, Astudillo, because of your strength and manliness will be the one to secure this help." There was more laughter, and Astudillo grinned. "But so that you should not suffer from lack of company, I will also send Mendez," he pointed to that man, "Figueroa," again he pointed, "and that evil-smelling, lying whoreson of a Portuguese, Alvaro Fernandez."

All agreeing with the soundness of this plan, the four together with a fifth—an Indian who was to guide them—made ready to depart.

"When you reach Pánuco, you goat-in-man's-skin," Lope de Oviedo shouted at the Portuguese, "do not let the perfume of Spanish women so overpower your senses that you forget your poor companions."

"It will not be their perfume that overpowers," Alvar Nuñez grabbed his nose and turned his head away from the Portuguese. "But I have heard that certain women demand their meat be ripe."

"Then that whoreson of a Portuguese will know all the passionate women of Pánuco," roared Lope de Oviedo.

The preparation for departure proved to be a simple matter, there being no baggage; thus each man had only to wrap a portion of dried fish in a skin, the two with swords to sharpen them, the other two gaining spears from the Indians. Before an hour they were ready, and then after being blessed by Asturiano, the only one of our number left who had taken orders, and after being embraced by Alvar Nuñez, they were gone.

"May the Almighty guide them," murmured Alvar Nuñez as they passed over the rise and were lost from view.

"May He who sent His Son to save mankind from sin hear the prayers of this poor company of men and show us mercy!" cried Asturiano with great passion.

Not one man in all the company showed other than a long face when we again sat in council to decide what must be done. A wind charged with bits of ice and flakes of snow came at us from the ocean, and the sky grew dark as storm clouds gathered.

"Each hour the weather grows more severe," Andres Dorantes muttered.

"It is the season for severe weather," Alonso del Castillo answered.

"We must be prepared to stay here," Alvar Nuñez hesitated, "unless succored by Christians in Pánuco, we must be

174

prepared to stay here until spring." At this a number of the men muttered, and there was much uneasy shifting. "Thus we must gain the hospitality of the Indians, even if this means that we are forced to do different tasks for them."

"Christians serve pagan Indians!" shouted Gonçallo Ruiz—he of the five that had defied Alvar Nuñez. "Rather would I have both arms severed at the elbows."

"If by offering both my arms I could gain shelter, warmth and food without begging these from the Indians, I would gladly have them cut away from my body before I grew another hour older." Alvar Nuñez spoke slowly, controlling his anger. "But I can see no help for it—we must beg protection from the Indians."

"This one will beg protection from no brown-skinned pagan," Diego Lopez muttered in support of his friend. To these words Sierra, Corral and Palaçios vigorously nodded their agreement. Never had I seen Alvar Nuñez so patient. But Alonso del Castillo, his face white with rage, the cords of his neck so tensed I feared they must tear, drew his sword and came at the five men. Had Alvar Nuñez not held his arm and then in a hundred ways tried to calm the man, more than one head must have rolled on the ground that dark afternoon.

The rage of the captain did much to calm the five men, and if there were any further muttering I did not hear them. It was then decided that the two companies should separate, each to its Indian village. Although there was little joy at this prospect, yet there was no help for it, our numbers being too great for both to winter together. It was further decided that as soon as it should be spring both companies would again join and that neither one would depart the island we had given the name Malhado, for it was a place of bad fortune, without the other.

Having grown accustomed to being one of Alvar Nuñez's company, I made ready to go with him, but my master, Andres Dorantes, demanded my return. "I will take my slave, Estevan," were his only words. For a little time Alvar Nuñez hesitated, his features drawn together by a frown. Then, with a single pat on my shoulder, he motioned me to join the other men.

After sharing the weapons so that both bands were equally armed, Alonso del Castillo giving to Alvar Nuñez his own sword, after offering prayers that all might safely weather the winter, and after old friends hugged one another swearing friendship until death, as the wind gusted stronger and snow began whitening the ground, the two companies parted.

If I felt any sadness at being separated from Alvar Nuñez it was only a twinge. For I judged the separation would last three, no more than four months. But it was to be five full years before I was to see the man again. And of what transpired with him and his company during those five years, I only gained intelligence as I sat with him, night after night, after we were re-united and listened to his narration. One that at times was so harrowing it set my stomach churning. Even now as I recount his experiences I am not without distress.

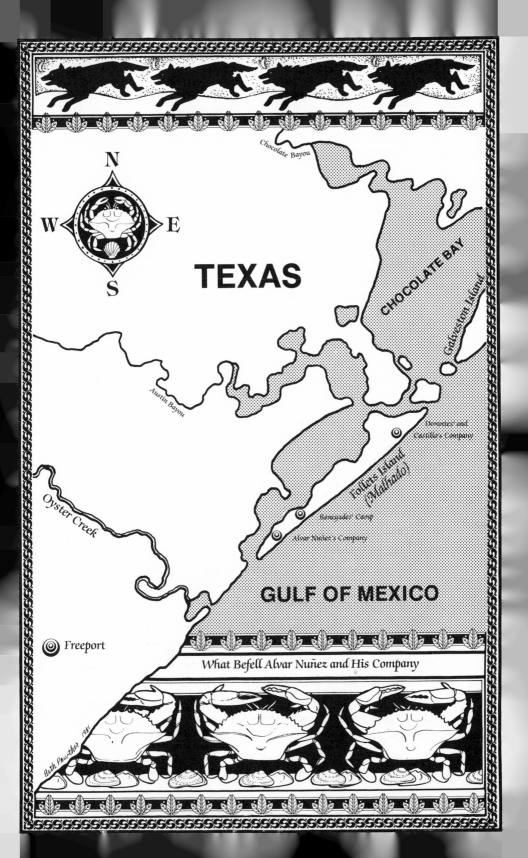

Chocolate Bayou

N
W E
S

TEXAS

CHOCOLATE BAY

Galveston Island

Austin Bayou

Dorantes' and
Castillo's Company

Follets Island
(Malhado)

Oyster Creek

Renegades' Camp

Alvar Nuñez's Company

GULF OF MEXICO

Freeport

What Befell Alvar Nuñez and His Company

Beth Prowther 1981

XXIII

For half the distance back to the Indian village, encouraged by Alvar Nuñez, his men sang. But so severe grew the cold and so violent the wind that for the last quarter of a league the weaker men gasped and stumbled, several tripping on snow-covered roots and falling to the ground. Those who had preserved a portion of their strength then dragged these ones the final several hundred paces.

As they had done once before, the Indians again wrapped the Spaniards in skins, the weakest ones together with their women, and again they fed them a meal of gruel and roast fish. But this time the Indians held no celebration.

In the morning, paying the Spaniards little attention, the Indians gathered in groups, sighing and whispering, their hands and fingers fluttering. The suddenness of the descent of winter and the half-fathom of snow already fallen, with snow still falling, was their chief concern. Never in the memory of even the oldest of the village, a woman who was remembered as old when those now grown were children, had there been such a heavy fall of snow so early in the season.

In each lodge it was the same, every few minutes a boy would rush outdoors for several moments then return, his head powdered, his hands measuring the depth of snow, and each time the faces of the Indians grew sadder, their sighing sounds softer and more prolonged.

Until this sudden change of season, all the Indians had rejoiced at the great quantities of fish caught—so plentiful had been the catch that it was said the fish fought to enter the weirs. The sea, who they all feared and whose name was never spoke except in reverence, had been generous with her fish. "Too generous," whispered the medicine man, "*Bá*, the wind, was angered when he saw how much fish *Gllé-i*, the sea, gave to man." The chief and various of the older men nodded. "Now he brings the cold and snow to show his anger. And if he be not comforted so that his anger lessens, he will cover the land with such a quantity of snow that we cannot find roots or berries and cannot hunt, and he will cause *Gllé-i* to freeze so we cannot fish."

"We must comfort *Bá*," the chief then said, "we must show him we are his friends by giving him good things to eat and skins so that he may be warm." Again all the men nodded.

"But do not make *Gllé-i* jealous," said the very old woman in a soft sigh, "do not forget that one!" With their breaths and with their fluttering fingers, the men told the old woman that they would take every caution.

Then the chief, the medicine man and various of the older men went throughout the village, taking from each lodge a quantity of fish, some dried meat, and also from each a good skin. The meat wrapped in two skins, was carried by the woman who had blown her breath upon Alvar Nuñez to a high place overlooking the ocean. But so violent was the surf and so caked with ice the path down, she did not dare descend, and

179

must make her sacrifice from the cliff. This she did by casting handfuls of meat into the sea, and finally the skin. The fish and the other skins the men offered to the wind, by burning them.

But the fish and flesh would have been better saved for food, the skins for warmth, for the wind did not abate; each hour the depth of snow grew greater and before the next morning the inlets and shallow places where the Indians fished were choked with ice.

Again the Indians made the sacrifice of fish, but this time various of the Spaniards, despite warnings from Alvar Nuñez not to interfere, muttered and showed by their expressions and by gestures how foolish they judged this waste. Chief amongst these mutterers were the same five who twice before had offered defiance. "These whoresons of Indians," said Gonçallo Ruiz, the leader of the five, "if we do not stop them they will destroy all the fish and then we must starve."

His face white with rage, Alvar Nuñez pushed through the men and, coming up to Gonçallo Ruiz, shouted "I will shave you to your shoulders, you bastard spawn of a swine, if you ever again so much as whisper against my orders. My patience is at an end." He freed his sword and brought its haft against the jaw of Gonçallo Ruiz, knocking the man to the ground. Then, waving the weapon, he shouted, "If needs be, I will turn barber and with this lancet bleed any man whose excess of sanguinous humor causes in him a rise of choler. I will bleed him in such a wise, I swear, that he will never again have need of a physician." The friends of Gonçallo Ruiz shifted uneasily. "We are guests of these Indians," Alvar Nuñez then continued in a somewhat softened tone, "guests who depend upon their hosts for their very lives. Have your minds grown so soft," his voice began to rise, "has the little reason God was good enough to give you been so diminished that you cannot see how desperate is our condition? If we are to survive, we must have the love of these Indians, yet certain ones of you mock them." Different men looked angrily at the five friends—even ones who not ten minutes earlier had joined them in their mocking.

180

"But they destroy their fish," Diego Lopez said softly, his voice rising to a question. Alvar Nuñez's sword hand tightened as he searched the man's face, but as he saw that one's lips trembling his hand grew less tight.

"To burn fish is their religion," said Alvar Nuñez slowly, "as we burn votive candles. If they, upon whom our lives depend, are mocked for their religion and for this should drive us from their village . . . "

"Then we are doomed," said Lope de Oviedo. At this, a look of understanding came to the faces of those who had mocked. Even Gonçallo Ruiz, blood oozing from his mouth, nodded his understanding.

That night as the wind blew with such force that the wooden posts which anchored the lodges cracked and groaned, the Indians all pressed tightly together in knots of eight or ten, finger joints cracking, their hands fluttering as they passed around pots made of tightly-woven grasses filled with a thick, bitter liquid of the pulp of a spineless cactus and the juice of certain roots and berries. This potion, which they took in tiny sips, in time caused their eyes to open wide, to bulge, and then to stare without seeing.

At first the pots were passed without the Spaniards being offered any of the potion. But, as the Indians' eyes began to stare they passed the pots of bitter liquid amongst the Christians.

Those Christians whose wont it was to laugh the loudest, those who told the foulest jokes and farted while others ate, those whose actions had gained for them the just reputation of being coarsest, took great sucks of the potent fluid and within moments grabbed their stomachs, gasping that they were poisoned, and then retched. But others, more cautious, those who had noted how the Indians took tiny sips which they slowly swallowed, followed the example of their hosts and although they found the fluid bitter enjoyed its warmth and the way it rose slowly from the stomach, filling the head with whispers, the eyes with colored visions.

As did all the Christians, Alvar Nuñez took a sip when the pot was passed to him. But his was scarcely more than a single drop, which he held for a little time on his tongue and then swallowed. A certain tightness of the throat, as if a woman's arms embraced it, was his first sensation. Then, a fullness behind his eyes, and in his ears the softness of down. Within moments the down in his ears filled his head—shimmering threads of the substance dancing before his eyes. Another sip caused him to gently rise from that dark, close hut filled with reeking savages and to sit in a high place where his hands dipped into streams of flowing stars. Splashes of red drawn from liquid rubies spilled across the sky. Flashes of yellow-blue like the sparks of flint-struck steel danced along the rim of the horizon. Then he saw the One sent by God to earth that He might suffer and so save man from sin. He heard the sound of wine poured from a crystal flagon into a goblet of porcelain and saw the house where he had been born. Its many windows blazed with light, as if in each burned a dozen candles; and laughter of young women like distant goat-bells floated out those windows; and then came the rich laughter of his father and the delicate cough of his mother. "It is I your son, come home," Alvar Nuñez shouted. From the door his mother, dressed in her winding sheet, came out to greet him. And then came his father, grey earth of the grave clinging to his skin.

"It is our son, Alvar Nuñez," the man murmured, wonder showing on his clay-caked face. "Our son we never in this world thought to see again."

"My good, brave son," the woman reached out her arms—now bones, "embrace your mother, for the love you still have for her." He stumbled forward with open arms, then fell to the ground amongst the sighing, swaying Indians.

XXIV

The next day dawned on a world turned white. Snow to the height of a man had piled against the huts; a half-span of snow lay on every branch and snow choked gullies and hid crevasses, so that an unwary man might plunge down and break his bones. The power of the potion still dulling their reason, various of the Christians wandered from the lodges, and had they not been followed by the Indian children who at different times guided them away from danger, more than one would have stumbled and cracked his skull.

With no warning and without reason, Hieronymo Alaniz, the notary, began to run. For all the months of the expedition his cautious counsel and sober ways had shown him to be the most constant of men, yet, suddenly uttering a yell like that made by attacking Turks, he rushed forward, his arms spread wide. Had a tree not blocked his way he would have plunged over the cliff and been killed. As it was, his scalp was split and he lay senseless for a time, his blood staining the snow.

The strange action of the notary sobered many of the Spaniards, who quickly gathered around the fallen man. "A demon must have suddenly possessed him," murmured Lope de Oviedo. "Never have I seen that one show passion; of all the men in this expedition, he is the most temperate.

"It was the potion of the Indians," muttered a soldier named Lachuga, who still staggered from the power of the drink.

"Potion of the Indians!" sneered Gonçallo Ruiz. "I will

risk my chance of salvation if that cautious one drank more than a single drop."

"Never in all the months since we departed Spain did I see him drunk," Corral joined in. "Even in Apalachen, when every man was drunk, that one, whom I always judged to be half woman, stayed sober."

"But did you see the way he ran!" interrupted Lachuga. "Only a man blind with drink would knock himself senseless."

"Blind with drink or possessed by demons," muttered Corral. As Corral spoke, the notary began to stir. "And I, too, will risk my chance of salvation if his demons do not prove to be witches, hags, crones and other fiendish women."

Hearing the commotion, Alvar Nuñez came to the door of the hut. Then, seeing the notary stretched out on the snow, blood oozing from his head, he drew his sword and, roaring a terrible oath, came at Corral, who stood closest to the fallen man. Had Lope de Oviedo not thrown himself between the two men, Alvar Nuñez would have delivered the stroke. "The notary has gone mad and dashed himself against the tree!" Lope de Oviedo shouted as he struggled with his captain.

"Corral has done nothing, my captain!" cried Lachuga, as he tried to secure Alvar Nuñez's sword arm, his lettuce ears, which had gained him the name of that plant, turning a fiery red.

"Have mercy!" Corral screamed, twisting his body away from the gleaming blade, the gunpowder patches on his cheek showing bluer as his skin blanched white.

"I have warned you my patience is at an end!" Spittle dripped from the corners of Alvar Nuñez's mouth.

"Listen, my captain," said Lope de Oviedo, risking with his body the sharp sword, "I saw everything." Alvar Nuñez lessened his struggle. "The notary left the hut, then stood for several minutes—staring. Alvar Nuñez lowered his sword. "Twice I greeted him and asked him how he did, but he would not reply. Then, suddenly throwing his arms wide open, he started running. Ask any of the men. He started to run, as if blind, toward the cliff—had it not been for the tree . . . It was as if he could not see it. He went down like a bullock felled by an axe."

"Struck himself against a tree?" Alvar Nuñez stepped backwards several paces. "If you are playing the fool's game with me, Lope de Oviedo . . . "

"Not this one, my captain—ask any of the men." Others joined in, confirming the man's words.

The notary began to stir again. "Are you doing better, my friend?" Alvar Nuñez asked the fallen man. The notary rolled his head to one side and groaned. This movement caused fresh blood to flow from the wound. "You say he would have gone over the cliff had it not been for this tree?" Alvar Nuñez turned to Corral, who nodded. "Then I will bless this tree." He laid his fingertips for a moment on the place where blood stained the bark. "Yes, I can see that he struck the tree. Forgive me," Alvar Nuñez said hoarsely to Corral. Then he ordered Corral to carry the injured man to the hut. "And do it gently, you speckled ox," he muttered. At this, Corral grinned.

Followed by Lope de Oviedo, Alvar Nuñez walked the less than twenty paces to the cliff. "He would have dashed his brains out against those rocks," said Alvar Nuñez softly, looking down. "He suffers from the fever, poor man—a day's rest . . . "

"And if it is not the fever, my captain?" asked Lope de Oviedo. "If, as Corral says, he is possessed by demons?"

"Demons! Pah! I never thought to hear Lope de Oviedo credit the words of a driveler like Corral. It is the fever."

"As you say, my captain."

Grinning, Alvar Nuñez laid his hand on the other's shoulder. "The little I have learnt of demons, my friend, has taught me that they dwell only where there is passion."

185

"And of all the men, none shows less passion than that one," Lope de Oviedo added, opening his mouth to a toothless grin.

"No, it is certain that our notary never caused the mother of any virgin to know concern."

"The concern he caused, if any, my captain, was amongst whores in the stew hungry for his escudos."

"I'll give my oath that those he spent were few and well bargained for. Any demon who found a home in that one must have soon starved . . . "

A roar of laughter from the hut where they had taken the notary interrupted Alvar Nuñez. This was followed by a hoarse shout. Before the two men could take half a dozen steps, the notary, with Corral holding his one arm and Lachuga the other, reeled out the door.

"He is mad!" shouted Corral, struggling with the man. "He has the strength of ten—I need help." With a lunge, the notary freed himself then started forward. Signalled by Alvar Nuñez, a dozen Spaniards surrounded the man.

"Do not hurt him!" Alvar Nuñez shouted, then ducked as the notary struck out at him. "Stay out of his reach," he warned Lope de Oviedo, but too late, as the notary struck that one full in the face with his fist. For several minutes, like herd dogs surrounding a maddened bull, the men contained the man. The blood gushing from Lope de Oviedo's nose warned them better than any words not to get too close.

Then, as if struck between the shoulders by an iron club, the notary suddenly pitched forward, falling face down in the churned-up snow, where he lay twitching. It was Alvar Nuñez who eased the man over—his wound had opened and his face was a gore of blood. "Is he dead?" Lope de Oviedo asked in a hoarse whisper. "He does not appear to breathe," he muttered. But then the notary let fly a fart. "He lives," Lope de Oviedo grabbed his nose, "and if stink be any guarantee of long life he will live, I will give my oath, to a hundred."

The notary, blood-tinged spittle dripping from his chin, struggled to sit up. Lachuga bent down to help and was bitten on the hand. Bellowing—"Whoreson!" and other oaths, he leapt backwards, his lettuce ears flapping. "Did you see that, my captain!" Lachuga shouted. "He bit me, and he an officer." The notary, unable to sit erect, had fallen over and lay with his mouth and nose buried in the snow, making gurgling sounds.

All around, Indians had gathered, more than half the village, and they grinned and whispered as they watched the struggles of the Spaniards. And then, when the notary lay without moving, making a baby's soft sounds, different Indians came up and with fluttering fingers gently touched him. Cautious lest they be bitten as was Lachuga, the Spaniards hesitated, and thus it was that the Indians, making a litter of their joined arms, carried the notary to the hut of the medicine man.

"He has been visited by the spirits of departed holy men," murmured the medicine man as he treated the gash in the notary's scalp with an evil-smelling balm. Then he bent down and sucked at the wound, spitting from his mouth blood and a black stone the size of a linet's egg. "He will be visited again and then we will learn of their life in the distant place." He extended his arm toward the ocean. The Indians crowding the hut whispered, and the fluttering of their hands like so many fans stirred the fetid air. "Having once been visited by the spirits," the medicine man continued in his sighing murmur, "a man becomes a child and must be guarded lest he fall in the way of harm . . . " And so it was that the notary could not stir from his hut without half a dozen Indians accompanying him.

"It is fortunate for him that he saves his kicks and blows only for his fellow Spaniards," muttered Alvar Nuñez angrily the next day, after receiving reports of attacks by the notary from various ones. "If he served the Indians as he has his brother Christians, I will risk my chance of salvation they would have made short work of him." He muttered something the others could not hear under his breath.

"When we reach Pánuco I will have him examined by a physician," declared Alvar Nuñez to calm Lope de Oviedo who had suffered a second blow to his nose. "And if he is found to be feigning madness . . . "

"I passed the notary as he walked with his Indians," said Lope de Oviedo wiping at his nose and spitting blood between every other word, "I asked him how he did, the whoreson; he nodded and I turned away, and then without warning he struck me—a rock was in his fist. Officer or not, he would have got as good as he gave if not for his accursed Indians."

"I will have him examined by a physician," Alvar Nuñez repeated, "and if he be proved not mad," he hesitated, "I swear you will have as a gift the same fist that offended you," he tapped the scabbard of his sword. "Yet if he is, as I fear, truly mad, then there is no help for it."

Lope de Oviedo nodded his head slowly. "He *is* mad," he muttered softly. "There is no need for a physician, however learned, to confirm what I already know. In all this world is there a place more likely to deprive a man of his reason than this desolate island—quartered amongst savages who worship madness?"

"Do I hear in your words that you, too, feel the first stirring of insanity?"

"Me, my captain?" Lope de Oviedo opened his mouth wide and ran his forefinger along his toothless gums. "For insanity there first must be a brain, or so I have heard. This poor skull has known too many blows for there to be much of that left." He rubbed the stump of an ear lost to the Turks years earlier. Then patted his deeply scarred cheeks. "Would you believe, my captain, that this face was once judged handsome? Before I was fifteen I knew half the milkmaids for the full league around my father's farm. I swear I knew surely half, mayhap more, for they thought me pretty and called me sweet names and begged me to come with them inside the haystack."

188

"War can be cruel to beauty," Alvar Nuñez sighed, his finger touching the deep break to his nose.

"And with each loss of beauty was a loss of brain," laughed Lope de Oviedo. "My skull has been stroked by mace, hammer, sword-haft, pike, buckler and mailed fist. If hanged and given over for dissection, inside they will discover little more than dust." He slapped his head. "There is not brain enough left to produce insanity."

"If Hieronymo Alaniz had only been as fortunate," Alvar Nuñez winked at the other man. "Your words have once again shown that adversity can often prove to be the greatest boon."

"If that be true, my captain, then we are certain to gain the greatest favors ever granted to any group of Christians, for never have I heard of any others who suffered a greater number of mishaps or, you will forgive me for saying this, made more blunders."

"If we are patient," Alvar Nuñez winked again, "and make one or two more blunders, we may then know such benefactions that will make of each member of this expedition a rich man."

"But let them be moderate blunders, my captain. Like one who suffers indigestion from too great a quantity of food, I have no more stomach for the larger blunders." Alvar Nuñez began to laugh. "Will a couple of broken legs from marching backwards do, my captain? Or must we again be found naked in a howling wind? We are without ships to sail upon shoals or to send off without us to Pánuco, thus we are limited as to our blunders."

"I will give this matter my attention, and I order you to refrain from offering another suggestion, for the decision as to blunders, as is true for all important matters, is for an officer to make, and not the concern of an enlisted man."

"Forgive me, my captain," Lope de Oviedo pulled a grave face. "Adversity has caused me to forget my station."

"Yet," Alvar Nuñez also pulled a grave face and spoke slowly, "with the notary's indisposition, your rank as sergeant makes you second-in-command, and as second-in-command, if you demand the right to one or two, no more than three mistakes, how can I deny you?"

"Was there ever a man more just than the hidalgo, Alvar Nuñez Cabeza de Vaca! But you must forgive me, my captain, if I decline your generosity. Habit, that binds tighter than any iron fetter, has accustomed me to low rank and thus I must allow those whose birth and breeding have made them my betters to enjoy the privilege of mistakes, while I, simple man that I am, obey their orders."

"Perhaps when you have grown more accustomed to authority you will try a little one—for, my friend, although you may have judged all my words spoke in jest, I did not jest when I spoke of your being my second-in-command."

"I, my captain, second-in-command . . . Such a thing cannot be, I have not the head for it."

"Truly there are different parts of your head missing!" laughed Alvar Nuñez. "And that portion which is left is not in the best of order. Yet withal you are the best I have."

"But second-in-command, my captain, I am not an officer."

"Then as Governor—Pánfilo Narvaez being lost—and captain of this expedition, I give you the rank of ensign."

"But, my captain, how can such a thing be? I am the son of a man who herded cows."

"Do you forget who I am!" Alvar Nuñez raised his voice and brought his hand to his sword. "Do you dare question my authority?" The other man rapidly shook his head. "If I say you are an ensign, then you are an ensign." The headshakes changed to nods. "You are Lope de Oviedo, son of—son of . . ."

"Cruz Antonio," was the muttered reply.

"Lope de Oviedo, son of Cruz Antonio, herder of cows,

now raised by my authority to ensign. Beware lest I promote you to lieutenant!"

"No, please, no, my captain; it is enough that I am ensign. If my brothers, who are also herders of cows, should ever hear of this! I thank the merciful Almighty that my father is dead and thus is beyond distress."

"I shall watch you carefully, Lope de Oviedo." Alvar Nuñez's brows drew together. "And at the first sign of hesitation or weakness, I swear to promote you before all the men."

"Not one of them would ever speak to me again. I should lose all my friends."

"For the Faith and for the King, men are often required to make sacrifices!"

Lope de Oviedo slowly nodded. "I will serve you as second-in-command, Alvar Nuñez Cabeza de Vaca."

"See how quickly you learn to be an officer; already you call me by my name. And, Lope de Oviedo, I have a desperate need for a loyal officer as my second-in-command."

"I have always been loyal," the man said slowly. "To Hernan Cortez for the more than five years I served in his forces, I was always loyal. Even when for a time he gained the displeasure of the King and others wavered in their loyalty, I never wavered. If needs be I will again swear my loyalty."

"There is no need, my friend, to affirm that which I already know. Gonçallo Ruiz is senior to you in years of service, and also holds the rank of sergeant, yet I did not appoint that one."

"Truly he is senior to me—I had forgotten."

"I did not appoint that one, nor did I consider Diego Lopez, in whose veins flows hidalgo blood despite his bastard birth, because I had no faith in either man's loyalty."

"They both are frightened men, my captain, and they hide their fear with rough words and defiant actions."

"I have never thought of those two as frightened," Alvar Nuñez said carefully. "But you who live close with them . . ."

191

"They are frightened, as are the three others who together make up their little band."

"Palaçios, Sierra and Corral," muttered Alvar Nuñez.

"You know their names, my captain. Of all the men those five are the most frightened. And for this reason, I judge them the most dangerous."

"How quickly you confirm my wisdom at appointing you second-in-command, Lope de Oviedo. I, too, judge them dangerous, and I must confess that yesterday when I saw the notary lying in the snow and Corral closest to him I would not have been loath to reduce the number of that band to four."

"I should have stepped aside and said nothing!"

"You could not have done other than you did. What if I had killed him . . . "

"It would have been of benefit to this expedition. I have heard enough of his mutterings and those of his companions. They stir the others to discontent and they lust after the Indian women."

"Have they lain with the Indian women?" asked Alvar Nuñez in a hoarse voice, both hands tightening.

"To my knowledge, no. Thus far their ardor has been confined to looks, whispered words, wet smiles and gestures with fingers. Not two hours ago I saw the five simpering over several of the maidens."

"I cannot trust myself to speak to them." Alvar Nuñez's voice had grown hoarse. "If any one of those five whoresons were to appear this very minute I must split him crown to crotch—lust after their women! Tell them this, Lope de Oviedo, should I gain even the littlest evidence about further attempts at commerce with the women I will first cut away their parts with my own hands, and then have them slowly burned. Tell them my anger is such that I cannot trust my sword arm, thus you must carry my words."

To this threat made by Alvar Nuñez, Lope de Oviedo added certain touches of his own. Finding the five surrounded by a dozen others, he walked up, boldly shouting, "Beware, lest Alvar Nuñez cross your paths this day, Gonçallo Ruiz, Diego Lopez, Palaçios, Sierra, Corral! He knows of your lustings, and should he see any one of you before he has time to cool his choler, he will run you through before you can croak two words of the Hail Mary." Then he went on to detail the punishment, adding the breaking of bones, the pulling of nails and the tearing out of tongues. Then Lope de Oviedo said, twisting his face into a terrible grin, "As second-in-command, I swear to help Alvar Nuñez inflict this punishment on any who have earned it." At that the five backed away, muttering, their eyes cast on the ground.

There being no fish because of the thick ice, and no way to hunt or gather because of the deep snow, Alvar Nuñez's company ate nothing the third day after the storm, except a thin soup made of fishbones and half a handful of dried berries. The fourth day there were only berries, and the men were much weakened, for the bitter cold robbed them of their strength. Yet the Indians of that village fared little better. Such was their hunger they chewed on strips of untanned leather and consumed a porridge made of deer's dung. These were offered to the Christians but were disgustful to them, and thus refused.

The afternoon of the fourth day, the wind having grown less and there being some warming, the Indians started for an inlet on the far side of the island to dig for roots. Despite much grumbling, Alvar Nuñez ordered all the Spaniards, excepting the notary, to follow him, and to offer whatever assistance that should be needed. Again it was the group of five who grumbled the loudest, muttering that it was not fitting for Christians to wait on pagans. But if Alvar Nuñez heard them he gave no sign of it as he urged the men on with easy punches and friendly oaths. "Aged sheep!" he called them. "Spavinned horses! Farting asses! You hobble like old whores rotted with the clap."

"I have no use, my captain, for horses, sheep or asses," croaked back the armorer, Guzman, the oldest man left of the expedition, "but an old whore, even if she be rotted by the clap . . ."

"Listen to that one!" roared Lope de Oviedo. "He wheezes like a sow in labor—thirty seconds with a whore would kill him."

"Death will come to every man, Lope de Oviedo," gasped the armorer. "And for half a minute's tumble with a juicy wench, I am prepared to die."

"Lope de Oviedo, I fear, suffers from a delicate constitution," laughed Alvar Nuñez, clapping the armorer on the shoulder. "For him, thirty seconds might well prove fatal. But for one made of flint and ox-leather as is the armorer Guzman, such a one can still service the hardiest whore in such a way that she must hobble for a half a week."

For an hour the Spaniards struggled after the Indians through snow that at time reached their paps. When they finally arrived at the far side of the island, all were wheezing and trembling. Another hour of pounding the thick ice with rocks and then feeling beneath the ice for roots left most in such a state of exhaustion that they could scarcely speak. It was then that the armorer Guzman died. One minute he knelt alongside the others, feeling for roots in the chill water, the next he lay sprawled, his head beneath the water.

"Would that he could have had his little minute with a whore," muttered Alvar Nuñez as he gently rolled the dead man over. "Knowing his age, I should have ordered him to stay in the village with the notary."

"To give a soldier such as Guzman such an order would be to insult him," Lope de Oviedo said slowly.

"Better to insult than to kill him!" said Gonçallo Ruiz, stepping back several paces. Alvar Nuñez, still kneeling, raised his head.

"We have listened long enough to your orders, Alvar Nuñez Cabeza de Vaca," snarled Diego Lopez, also stepping backwards. "Because of your orders, a man is dead."

"I hold with the words of Governor Pánfilo de Narvaez." Gonçallo Ruiz's breath rattled in his throat. "Words spoken when his vessel pulled away from ours. He said that this no longer was a time when one man should command another."

Then Palaçios, taking his place alongside the other two, offered: "The Governor said that each should do what he thought best to save his own life."

Alvar Nuñez rose up to his full height as Lope de Oviedo, unsheathing his sword, took his place beside him. After several seconds of hesitation, Corral joined the three who had spoken, followed by Sierra, who moved slowly, being much weakened, and looking as if at any hour he might join the fallen Guzman. Casting off the skin that served him as a cloak, Lope de Oviedo made ready while four of the five unslung axes and drew knives gained from the Indians, Sierra trembling and suffering too much from exhaustion to do more than stand with his companions.

"Draw your sword, my captain, and together we will make short work of them," hissed Lope de Oviedo. But Alvar Nuñez shook his head.

"One dead this day is enough—I have no stomach for killing." At this the five men grinned.

"If we do not kill them you will lose your authority with all the men," Lope de Oviedo muttered softly. "See how they mock you with their grins."

"So, Gonçallo Ruiz," Alvar Nuñez spoke out after waving Lope de Oviedo silent, "you quote the declaration of Governor Pánfilo de Narvaez—that this no longer is a time when one should command another." Gonçallo Ruiz's tiny eyes blinked rapidly as he nodded. "And you, Diego Lopez, son of an hidalgo, you, too, challenge me with the authority of the Governor?" Diego Lopez hesitated, grinding the end of his moustache between his teeth, then he nodded. "And you, Palaçios, and you, Corral." Both men shifted uneasily, but both nodded. "Sierra," Alvar Nuñez's voice softened, "do you, too, seek separation from my command?" Sierra opened his mouth as if to speak, but was silenced by Alvar Nuñez. "Your limbs tremble so you can scarcely stand—consider your condition before you answer."

"If you are a man, Sierra, you will give him his answer!" Gonçallo Ruiz spoke so that no one should fail to hear him. "Being freed of that one's command will in no wise worsen your condition." At the words "that one's," Lope de Oviedo raised his sword and started for the man.

"Lope de Oviedo, do you, too, crave freedom from my command?" said Alvar Nuñez. Lope de Oviedo lowered his sword. "Why should a Spaniard no longer bound by my authority not address me as 'that one'? There must be some advantage. But there also will be some loss. And you, Sierra, had best consider this loss, for it must, indeed, affect your condition." Sierra tightened his fists and pressed his arms against his sides. "All those who renounce my authority will be forced to find their own shelter, for my sword will keep them from the village. The weather is boisterous, Sierra, consider carefully what you do."

"The miserable huts of the Indians offer no better protection than we can procure ourselves," Diego Lopez turned to Sierra.

"We will quarter here," added Gonçallo Ruiz. "Secure

roots from beneath the water as long as needs be, then, when the weather grows less severe, fashion bows and spears and hunt fresh meat.

"How do you say, Sierra?" asked Gonçallo Ruiz. "Do you stay with us or do you crawl back to that village of painted pagans?"

"I stay," Sierra whispered. Then he tried to form other words with his bluish lips, but had not the breath for it.

After again warning the five not to attempt a return to the village, and after directing that several warm skins be left with them, also a short sword, and after weighting the body of Guzman with stones and sinking it beneath the ice, Alvar Nuñez ordered the remaining thirty-three Christians to follow him if they still submitted to his authority. And not once as he led the way back to the village did he turn his head to see that they all followed.

The Christians had scarcely gained the safety of the village when an icy wind suddenly arose, bringing fresh snow and again straining the centerpoles of the huts, which groaned with every gust. After making a poor meal of the few roots they had gathered, most of the Spaniards, numbed by exhaustion, fell over into a deep sleep where they sat.

Alvar Nuñez and Lope de Oviedo, chattering and trembling from the cold, sat away from the Indians who were imbibing the potent juice of their spineless cactus. "A single swallow of their potion," Lope de Oviedo nodded toward the Indians, "and I must fall into such a sleep that only the blessed Gabriel can awaken me."

"In my condition," Alvar Nuñez added slowly, laboring for breath, "half a swallow should be enough to guide me to my final rest."

"Other than that loathsome gruel of deer's dung—the

thought of which makes me want to retch—other than that, they have had no more nourishment than we, yet they sip their potion without ill effect."

"They are a hardy race of men, Lope de Oviedo. I always judged myself sturdy, but I will confess I am near done in."

"And I, my captain, I tremble like an old woman."

"Perhaps a good night's sleep will restore us."

"It will take more than sleep, my captain. A roast of venison, even a joint of some lesser meat—dried mutton, or even half a wheaten loaf would go a long way to restore me. But sleep . . ."

Several minutes passed in silence as both men, with heavy lids, stared at the moving shadows cast by the flickering fire. It was Alvar Nuñez who broke the silence. He sighed, coughed to hide the sigh, then said, "I cannot rid my mind of thoughts of the five men—how will they survive this cold and wind?"

"I, too, have not been able to free my mind of them, my captain. I would have gladly run them through this afternoon, yet now I fear for their condition."

"Even with the skins I gave them, they cannot be warm. Even if they were able to build a fire, the storm must have extinguished it."

"Yet they are hardy men, my captain, excepting Sierra."

"Excepting Sierra! I should have ordered him to come with me. His face held the cast of death."

"Yet it was his wish to remain with his companions."

"His wish. Pah! It was my wish to be rid of him! Of him and of the others. He had a choice only because I gave it to him. I could have ordered the man bound and carried. I could have taught contrition to the other four with the flat of my sword. With my fists, feet and weapon I could have, in ten minutes, made of those men creatures more docile than the cherubim. I have done as much before, Lope de Oviedo, but I wanted to be rid of them."

"There is no one who would fault you for your actions,

Alvar Nuñez Cabeza de Vaca. And if his friends wrap him in the skins, Sierra may yet survive the storm."

"You offer me another 'yet,' Lope de Oviedo," Alvar Nuñez smiled at the man. "You are become a nurse, giving 'yets' instead of sugar-teats."

"I only try to show you the justice of your action, my captain. Another captain would have dispatched them after the first word, yet you . . ."

"Yet another 'yet,' Lope de Oviedo. I have seen many nurses, both dry and wet, but none who had a face like you. Beware lest your charges go into fits when they see it."

Lope de Oviedo grinned, then tapped his finger on his toothless gums. "I will admit I am not a pretty man, but I have a gentle heart. And you are not kind, Alvar Nuñez, to say of the visage of such a gentle one that it will cause fits."

"Now that you smile, my friend, I can see that 'fits' was an exaggeration. A small paroxysm, at most a mild convulsion, for your gentleness shines through."

"Truly I am a gentle man. There have been nights when thoughts of my docile ways caused my eyes to fill with tears— how different ones, because of me, will never have to suffer the despair of growing old or know the pain of infirmity."

"You should have been a priest, my friend."

Lope de Oviedo sighed, "I have often thought I should have taken orders— a monk, sworn to silence, digging in his garden . . ." Several moments passed in silence. Outside the hut, the wind blew in great gusts. From the many breaths, ice formed on the lower posts and a fine powder of snow seeped into the hut.

"I once knew such a garden," Alvar Nuñez murmured. "Capuchin monks they were, and in Castile. My mother's brother was of that order, and I was sent there to recover after an attack of fever."

"There were vines and fruit trees in that garden?"

"Vines bowed with Malaga grapes, trees whose branches

199

bent with golden pears, and everywhere was the heavy odor of sun-warmed lemons."

"It was warm in that garden? It must have been!"

"More than warm, the air danced. But against the north wall was a place cooled by shadows, where I could go and rest when the sun's rays grew too fierce. A quiet place, where the only sounds were of the monks pruning trees and girdling the vines to preserve the sweetness of the grapes."

"Will we ever again see Spain, Alvar Nuñez Cabeza de Vaca?"

"I will see Spain again!" Alvar Nuñez said the words softly, but with great firmness. "I will sit in the shadow of that wall again through the long afternoon."

"Will I see Spain, my captain?"

"If you are determined. Only if you are truly determined."

"Determined?"

"Listen to me, Lope de Oviedo," Alvar Nuñez reached out and laid his hand on the man's shoulder, "I speak to you not as your captain, but as a man to another man. Although well born, I have had little education other than in the use of arms. But one thing I do know with a certainty; one thing I know better than all the bachelors in Granada with their degrees—if a man be determined, he can do whatever he will, for such a man walks in the shadow of the Almighty. I will return to Spain, Lope de Oviedo."

"And I," the man hesitated, "and I—am I determined? Is there a passion within me to return to the place where I was born? More than a score of years have passed since I left. My mother and my father are gone. Who should know me, with my face? I must needs prove to my own sister that the toothless one, scarred and without an ear, who stands before her, is her brother. And my brother, Antonio, whose sons must now be grown, will he and his wife run to embrace me, or will they order the dogs to chase away an ugly stranger? No, Alvar Nuñez, now that I think on it, my determination is not for Spain, but only to survive. No matter how great may be the adversity, I will live, Alvar Nuñez Cabeza de Vaca, of that I am determined."

"You *will* live, Lope de Oviedo. Others will die, but you will live. Mayhap in time you will return to Spain."

"Mayhap in time. How can I know what yearnings the years will bring?"

"If you should ever return, you will be welcome at the house of Alvar Nuñez, son of Francisco de Vera. And you may find this house by asking anyone of Jerez de la Frontera, in the province of Cadiz. With my own two hands I will roast a young kid, and we will feast while my wife plays the lute for us."

"You have a wife, Alvar Nuñez? I did not know this."

"A wife who waits for me, Lope de Oviedo, and will wait for me, if needs be, half a score of years."

"I pray it may be only another half a year, no more than one. If I had a wife who waits for me . . . Until this very minute I believed you to be unwed."

"It is my habit to preserve a silence concerning affairs personal to my life. But I have come to love you as a friend, Lope de Oviedo, and what better proof of friendship can there be than the sharing of private matters. I have a wife I still love, despite her barrenness." Alvar Nuñez drew in a deep breath and held it several seconds.

"Knowing of her husband, I must judge the wife of Alvar Nuñez Cabeza de Vaca to be the gentlest of women."

"More than gentle, Lope de Oviedo, generous, modest, and above all loyal."

"A quality to be cherished in a woman, my captain."

"Or in a friend!"

"Or in a friend! I have been fortunate in the loyalty of my friends, but with my women . . ."

"Would you believe, Lope de Oviedo, the one who is now my wife determined on me as her future husband before the age of ten!" Alvar Nuñez grinned. "And I her elder by a full five years—scarcely aware of her existence. Our fathers were cousins, and two or three times I had seen her at play with her dolls, a gentle child whose face quickly faded from my memory. Yet before she was ten, she had determined on me for her husband."

"If a lady of quality and breeding be once determined . . ." Lope de Oviedo sighed, then rubbed at his fatigue-reddened eyes.

"When she was twelve, I being recently recovered from my fever, her father brought her to the celebration held for my recovery. All I could see of her face were large, brown eyes opened wide." Lope de Oviedo nodded, but his lids hung heavy. "Wherever I wandered that night, I had but to turn my head to see those lustrous eyes upon me. I cannot say I already loved her, for if we spoke at all it was no more than a single word of greeting. But if it was not love from which I suffered, for my bowels were all churned up and my breathing labored, it was the stuff from which love is fashioned." Lope de Oviedo's breathing deepened and grew regular. "I could not sleep that night. And two weeks later, when I chanced to meet that maiden, my hands trembled and I must swallow between every word." Lope de Oviedo's chin dropped to his chest, his mouth opened, and from his mouth there issued a soft snore.

"Have you not learned, Lope de Oviedo," Alvar Nuñez murmured, "that one who is base born cannot be bored by the words of an hidalgo? Yet, from the sound of you, you scarred, old fighting bull, you are well past boredom. What is to be the future of this world when the peasant is lulled to sleep by the speech of the nobleman?" Then, steadying his chilled hands, Alvar Nuñez gently draped a skin over the shoulders of the sleeping man.

Exhausted yet unable to sleep, Alvar Nuñez sat in the corner of the hut staring at the swaying forms of the Indians.

202

Strange shadows cast by the glowing embers of the dying fire flickered on the walls and earthen floor. "Brave words spoken to Lope de Oviedo," he muttered. " 'If needs be she will wait half a score of years!' " A shudder passed through his body. "She will hear reports that the expedition of Pánfilo de Narvaez has disappeared into the jungles of Florida. In time she must judge me lost—and then. . . . Does she already despair of my return? Should another year pass and I not return, will she then not seek to be declared a widow—and as a widow, how long before she becomes the wife of another man?" As if the haft of a sword had been roughly thrust against his breastbone, a pain spread across his chest. The fetid air of the hut ached in his lungs, his head began to spin. He gripped the centerposts, gasping, "I must go out of doors," and forced his body up. "I must walk for a little time beneath the stars." A violent gust of wind shook the hut. Then, as suddenly as it came, the pain was gone. "She will wait for me," he whispered, making the sign of the cross. "She will wait for me," he whispered again, lowering his body to the ground. "She will wait for me," he whispered softly for the third time as he squeezed his eyes shut, trying to recall the features of the woman. But other than dancing whorls of orange and yellow light, he saw nothing. "Her hair is black and glossy," he murmured, trying with words to bring her image. "Her forehead . . ." he pressed his head between his hands. "I cannot see the features—I have only the words." He pressed his head harder. "How can I have forgotten my own wife's features?" his whisper became a groan. He opened his eyes and stared into the grinning face of the Indian woman who had blown her breath upon him. It was seamed and pitted, with sharpened bits of bone fitted into the swollen lobes of her ears; her lips were cracked, and her hair caked with dirt and grease. He stared into her eyes and they opened wide and glistened. Steadily, without blinking, he stared into those eyes and they slowly changed into the eyes of his wife. Then Alvar Nuñez reached out and drew her to him.

XXVI

It was not the sun that awoke the Spaniards in the morning, for its light was hidden by thick coverings of clay-colored clouds but the terrible wailing of an Indian woman. The half-grown son of the chief's brother had wandered from his hut during the night, for some unknown reason, and in the early dawn had been found by his mother, lying frozen in the snow. Her head thrown back, the piercing sound issuing unbroken from her gaping mouth, the woman carried the stiffened corpse through the village. At each dwelling-place she passed, the inhabitants came out to meet her and, seeing the dead child, fell to grieving. Soon there was not an Indian in the village who was not convulsed with sobs. It was as if the child belonged to all of them. And in their weakened condition, how could the Christians be unaffected?

It was to the notary that the child's corpse was finally given. It had been taken from its mother, then passed from hand to hand, each one in turn blowing his breath upon the lifeless form. Even the children must breathe on the child's body. And from the gestures of the chief and medicine man, the Christians knew their breaths also were required, and not one objected. The notary was the last of the Christians. He had been dressed in the finest skins—finer than those worn by the chief or medicine man—around his neck were strings of carved shell and bone, his face had been decorated with streaks of red and black, and on his head was placed a cap of lizard skin, to which the beak and talons of some great hawk were affixed. He took the child in his arms and, resting his cheek against its

204

cheek, softly whispered certain words in Latin. Then he breathed into its face, pressing his lips against its lips. And then he wept. Only the child's disconsolate mother equalled the emotion shown by the notary. No man could have sorrowed more for the son of his own loins than did he for that pagan child. The Indians crowded close, sighing, their fingers fluttering, different ones gently touching the sobbing man, who crouched on the ground, rocking the little corpse.

For the rest of that day, despite fresh snow and bitter cold brought by the rising wind, the Indians wandered aimlessly about. The child's body had been placed outside the village, under a mound of rocks, amidst the lamentations of its family, who cut at their skin with slivers of flint until the blood flowed freely. Then the grave was left to the starving wolves.

Had the cold not grow so severe, despite the falling snow, the Indians might have continued wandering about through the night. But the cold caused such a shortness of breath and numbing of hands and feet that, one by one, they must at last retreat to their huts until only a few of the hardiest still wandered. These few fought the wind and cold, but when the last traces of light were gone, they, too, succumbed to the tortures of the weather and sought the little warmth within their huts.

It was then that a band of two-score marauding warriors descended upon the village. It was as if they knew somehow of the dwelling in which the family of the dead child was quartered—as if they knew that there they would find the least resistance—for they made for that structure, passing silently and unseen the more than a dozen other huts which comprised the village.

The marauders, guided by their chief, gathered close around the hut, their weapons ready. Then, at a signal, uttering terrible shrieks, they slashed open the wall of skins. It would have been a matter of only moments for such a number of armed warriors to have slaughtered all the men and made off with the women and children; the little time needed to do that work was not enough for others of the village to effect a rescue. But instead of splitting skulls and ripping bowels, as had numberless bands of desperate raiders before them, they suddenly stopped as the notary, shrieking curses, plunged his arms into the glowing embers of the fire. Then, gibbering with fear, they scrambled backwards as he faced them, still shrieking, his hands filled with smoking coals. Dropping their weapons, the raiders rushed wildly into the night, seeking escape, as the notary hurled first one then the other hand full of coals in their direction. Two whom the burning coals had hit, dropped as if transfixed by crossbow shots, and were then quickly strangled by the women. One, whose leg was caught by vines that held the centerpole, was dragged to the firepit, where the children forced his head down amongst the smoldering embers. And around the notary, who still stood in the center of the hut, his seared hands hanging by his sides, the Indians piled the weapons abandoned by the raiders.

Of the more than two dozen in that hut, the only one to suffer a hurt was the notary, whose blackened hands dripped a red-tinged fluid. It was as if the fluid he dripped was a sacred substance, for all the Indians of the village must come to that hut and dip their fingers into it and dab it on their eyes and lips. But when the Christians, learning of the condition of the notary, came to the hut they were denied entrance, for the notary was now judged by the Indians too holy.

"It is one thing, my captain, to show these pagans a good face and respect their women," muttered Lope de Oviedo, drawing Alvar Nuñez aside. "But it is quite another to be barred by savages from a Christian and a brother."

"We are poorly armed and weak with hunger, Lope de Oviedo, and they are nearly ten times our number. . . ."

"But where is our honor, my captain, if we abandon a countryman whose condition at this moment may be desperate? And if we have lost our honor, have we anything left?"

Alvar Nuñez motioned with his head, and the two men

moved further away from the others. "You ask—if we lose our honor, have we anything left? My answer, Lope de Oviedo, is that I am no longer certain what is meant by the loss of honor. It may be that what we have often judged to be honor has been only stubbornness, such as shown by the balking ass. It may be that what we have often judged to be honor has been pettiness, such as shown by the hunched crone hawking her barrel of wilted greens. It may be that what *I* have too often judged to be my honor has been viciousness, such as shown by the keepers of stews toward their harlots, or the receivers of stolen goods toward pickpockets and thieves. Enough said about honor, Lope de Oviedo. But of the question: What will we have left? My answer to this is our lives. Our lives, and the chance one day to find the true meaning of honor, if there be one."

"Then we obey the orders of these pagans?" Lope de Oviedo's voice rasped in his throat.

"Obey their orders, please them, if needs be, serve them. We will do what must be done to stay alive. And, as I told you not two nights since, I am determined to survive this malign and desolate place and again see Spain. And if lack of food has not softened my memory, you, too, swore your determination to survive, Lope de Oviedo."

"Being barred by those painted pagans from ministering to a suffering Christian for the moment caused me to forget my determination."

"In truth, you are a kind-hearted man, my friend. But it is my belief that the little we could do to comfort Hieronymo Alaniz would be no match for the attention that the Indians will give him, for they worship him as a holy man. And, considering how cruelly your noble nose was served by that one, your concern again proves you to be the saintliest of men."

XXVII

The raid of the marauders having robbed both Christian and pagan of their sleep, and the lack of food having sapped the will of even the strongest, that morning all the inhabitants of the villages huddled motionless and silent around their fires, different ones sipping from time to time draughts of scalding water to quiet the gnawing in their guts. And all that morning from the father and the mother of the dead child came a terrible moaning as they dug their nails into their mourning wounds to keep them fresh. So hopeless and empty of spirit had different Spaniards grown, that had the wind freshened four or five whose minds were dulled beyond caring must have surely frozen where they sat. But the wind did not freshen, and just before noon the clouds opened and a warming sun shone through. And it was as if the sun's rays were food, for as the minutes passed, those who had appeared nearly lifeless began to quicken. It was then that hoots and laughter were heard coming from the rise just beyond the village.

Outlined against the brightening sky were four of the five who had quartered on the other side of the island. Pulling their mouths open, they distorted their faces into hideous masks. Then they leapt up and down, still hooting, and made insulting gestures with their hands and fingers.

"If I were not certain that those rabbit-livered whoresons would scatter like quail, I would spend the little strength I have left to teach them a lesson in manners such that their backs and shoulders must remember a dozen weeks," Lope de Oviedo growled to Alvar Nuñez.

"To allow those ones to excite your choler is to allow them to gain satisfaction, my friend," Alvar Nuñez gave the man a gentle dig in the ribs. "Rather, enjoy their entertainment—our lives are not so filled with amusements that we must be bored when regaled by four such clowns."

"From the looks of them, my captain, from all their gyrations, they appear in a better condition than any of the rest of us."

"Perhaps they happened on a deer, or took a catch of fish from a break in the ice. If so, it was the work of the Almighty—mayhap to save the life of Sierra."

"I do not see that one with them," murmured Lope de Oviedo. "At least I do not think I see him—the brightness of the sun clouds my eyes."

"It is my guess that he is not yet recovered, and rests in their shelter." Alvar Nuñez shaded his eyes. "Yet I, too, cannot be certain he is not with them. Perhaps he sits amongst the boulders."

"For a taste of their venison—a bone with a bit of gristle, even a scrap of roasted fat—I would join their dance." Lope de Oviedo licked his cracked lips.

"You have but to ask those gentle-hearted fellows, my friend, and, unless I am no judge of men, they will gladly share their meat with you. And when they proffer you your joint of venison, I little doubt but they will provide a like portion for their captain."

"A like portion, my captain? A double portion! How else should they show their love?" Lope de Oviedo paused, and then said in a roughened voice, "How else should they show their love for one who has proved his love by not shaving them to their shoulders, when at different times they begged for the ministrations of the barber."

"You see, my friend, how compassion is rewarded," Alvar Nuñez laughed hoarsely. "I am to enjoy a double portion—mayhap if you whisper to them of our concern for their safety the night of the storm, they will also provide a dish of sauce made of the drippings."

Lope de Oviedo waved his fist in the direction of the cavorting men. "If they would but await my coming, I would offer such a supplication . . ." he drew his sword and slashed savagely at the air.

"Not five minutes have passed since you offered to join their dance for a taste of their food. How am I to trust one whose moods are so uncertain?"

"Do you expect the son of a herder of cows to have the sweet temperament of an hidalgo, my captain? If you promote such a lowly one to ensign, you also promote his churlish disposition."

"What you say is true, Lope de Oviedo!" Alvar Nuñez drew a deep breath. "He who is stained with farmyard dung as a youth reeks of it ever after. I should have trusted Diego Lopez's hidalgo blood and made *him* second-in-command."

Lope de Oviedo slowly sheathed his sword, then squatted back down as the men on the rise, after a final flurry of gestures, retired. "Thus it has always been . . ." he muttered. Alvar Nuñez made a questioning sound. "Since the beginning of time it has always been thus—rascals prosper. . . ."

"And the righteous suffer for their righteousness," Alvar Nuñez interrupted with a harsh laugh.

"Again and again I have seen the just man groan while the rogue got on."

"And of all men, who are more just than Alvar Nuñez Cabeza de Vaca and Lope de Oviedo—men who starve while five of the blackest whoresons ever to cast a shadow fatten on rich venison! Truly I have the right to cry out as did another who once suffered: My God, why hast Thou forsaken me?" Lope de Oviedo snorted and shrugged his shoulders. "Listen to me, my friend," Alvar Nuñez said, touching the man on the arm. "Nowhere in the scriptures does it say that a man's reward will be other than in Heaven."

210

"You do not anger at being denied here on earth while far lesser men enjoy rich rewards?" murmured Lope de Oviedo.

"It is reward enough that the one called Alvar Nuñez was allowed the chance to live," was the soft answer. "And if the Almighty can hear me I say: For the glorious gift of life, my gratitude. As for anything else, *quantum sufficit*—I ask nothing else."

"Nothing else, my captain?" Lope de Oviedo turned so that he faced the other man. Alvar Nuñez shook his head. Then slowly and hesitantly the son of the cowherd reached out his hand until it touched for a moment the shoulder of the nobleman.

The next seven days saw the death of five of the Christians. And it was not only the dwindling band of Christians upon which death's pitiless eyes rested, for eight of the Indians also died that week. The ground being too frozen for burial of the bodies, Christian and pagan were carried beyond the limits of the village and left without even the little protection of a mound of stones.

The seven days that followed must have cost many more deaths had not a band of the Indian warriors happened upon a bull of the species of long-haired wild cattle that inhabit that land. The brute, harried by wolves, had crossed the ice from the main and was first seen on the far side of the island, half a league from where the group of five were quartered. The wolves, weakened by hunger, kept a sufficient distance from the great beast, whose horns and shoulders were stained with bits of gore from more than one of their number who had ventured too close. Driving the wolves backwards with flaming brands, killing several who, frenzied with hunger and seeing their prize about to be lost, tried to attack, the Indians forced the bull into a snow-filled defile where he was trapped. Then, taking care not to spill any of the bellowing creature's blood, they struck at him with clubs until he lay dead.

All the inhabitants of the village came out to meet the warriors as they approached, dragging the great bull and the three slain wolves on a sled made of branches. Then the beast was bled and its blood given as a milk to the starving children. The steaming spleen and liver were cut into small bits and handed to every member of the tribe and to those Spaniards whose hunger drove them to beg for their share of this sanguinous substance.

All that afternoon and through the night, the Indians and Spaniards feasted. The bull, butchered into pieces, was roasted. The wolves, split and skinned, were placed into pits together with heated stones and a certain earth used to sweeten, and there slowly cooked into a thick stew. Careful lest after such a feast they lose the food by vomiting, the Indians forced themselves to eat slowly—it being their custom to stuff their mouths and bolt down with little chewing. But the Spaniards, less accustomed to starvation, swallowed too quickly, and everyone, not excluding their captain, disgorged, much to the amusement of the Indians.

The Indians feasted until they could eat no more, then lay with distended bellies before their fires. Even the couple who mourned their son so lay. The fires and the rich food providing a sufficient warmth, the Indians did not move when fresh snow began to fall, and before the passage of an hour all the inhabitants of the village were besprinkled. The snow, like the finest down, formed a soft blanket which covered the roofs of the huts, clung to branches and piled against stumps and boulders on the ground. The bones of the butchered bull, saved for their marrow, soon were cased with white, and it was as though the creature had become a twisted dragon with a silver skin. The moon, lacking a single night of being full, broke for several moments through the clouds and illumined the score of skulking wolves on the rise above the village. And these starving creatures for those few moments howled their desperation.

It was then that the chief of the village and the medicine man shook themselves free of snow and came carefully to where

Alvar Nuñez lay surrounded by his men. With gentle stirrings of his staff, the chief awoke the man, motioning him to follow. They led him to a place on the far side of the village used only for sacred celebrations. There, in a shelter built of skins and branches, lay a woman swollen with child, who moaned at their approach. Crouched before the fire that guarded and warmed the shelter was the woman remembered as old when those now grown were young. So gnarled and motionless was this creature that Alvar Nuñez took her for a stone until he was almost upon her.

With gestures of his fluttering fingers, with certain sighing words that Alvar Nuñez had come to understand, and with pictures drawn with charcoal, the chief told of the condition of the woman. For five days she had lain suffering the pains of parturition, yet unable to expel the child. "This woman, whose child so loves her that it refuses its freedom, is my daughter," the chief said in his soft sighs. "How should one who has not yet been born know of the consequence of its action? Because you came from the water," the chief gestured toward the ocean, "I know you have great power. Speak in your strange tongue to the unborn one. Beg it to release its hold. Say to it that its love, if not lessened, must destroy the very one it loves. Tell it that once born it will have many to love, and fine presents of soft skins and tightly-woven baskets. Warn it that this woman, its mother, cannot last through another night, and that if she dies, it dies too!" The chief then shared with Alvar Nuñez a draught of the potent potion, which within moments filled his head with passionate whispers.

Kneeling before the suffering woman, Alvar Nuñez laid two twigs on her swollen abdomen so they formed the cross. He then whispered the sacred words of the Hail Mary a full four times. Then, laying both hands on the taut skin, he murmured the Pater Noster, pressing down so that the pressure made the woman groan; fragments of colored visions filled his closed eyes as he intoned. And then he began to speak as the chief had

213

ordered. "If in truth it is your love that keeps you from being born, little one, yours is a peculiar emotion. Too often a belief that certain strange stirrings felt within is love drives us to bring destruction to the very ones we proclaim we love. Release your hold and be born! Do you claim innocence? How can one yet unborn, thus guiltless, be charged with cruelty?" The fragments of the colored visions wove together, then wound close around the mind of the kneeling man. "Too often the face of innocence masks Apollyon's cruelty!" His burning fingers curled into crooks, which he dug into the skin of the groaning woman. "Pink-cheeked priests, with hands softer than a woman's, have caused the blood of innocents to be shed. Doe-eyed ladies with pouty lips have lisped words that led to slaughter. Were not the songs of the Sirens sweet? Release your hold and be born!" His voice had grown harsh and deep. "Release your hold; else I will curse you as a spawn of Satan; else I will damn you so that even in your innocence you are denied your place in Heaven. I warn you, unborn child, that your plea of innocence will prove no protection if because of you this one dies. An eternity as the plaything of the devil's merciless children will be your due." Suddenly his voice took on a pleading tone. "Release your hold on this woman's womb, and in this wise prove the truth of your affection. We must free those we truly love, little unborn one. Too often what is judged love is the agony of loneliness, or fear's clutching desperation." The man's voice grew louder. "How many innocents declared objects of the deepest love have been slain through jealousy? How many Samsons, how many Saint Johns, destroyed by the ones who claimed to love them? Who dares to call this cruelty affection!" The woman groaned louder as the pressure on her abdomen grew greater and the crooked fingers dug deeper into her skin. "Do not transform your cradle to a tomb, little one. As men fear death so must the babe fear birth; are they not both the same? It is your fear, not your love, that keeps you from being born!" shouted Alvar Nuñez. A spasm racked the woman, and the

214

chief and medicine man stiffened. "Hear me, unborn one, you need not fear life which is the love He gave us." The man's voice was almost a scream. "You need not fear love!" A second spasm forced the woman's thighs to open. "You need not fear love!" he screamed again. She shrieked as the child's steaming head appeared. And then the child was born.

The old woman carefully lifted the dripping infant and pressed it to a bosom whose dugs were shrunk to pouches of withered skin. The medicine man cut away the cord which he cast at the feet of the chief, and then seized the glistening mass of tissue which lay between the still-spread thighs of the groaning woman. Sighing and murmuring, the birth tissue in his outstretched hands, the medicine man turned away from the shelter and made slowly for the rise beyond the village where earlier the wolves had been seen.

His eyes burning, his mind reeling from the whirling bits of colored vision, Alvar Nuñez stumbled through the village to the hut where he was quartered.

Like wheat dust within the mill when touched by a spark, the contents of the hut burst around him as he thrust aside the entrance skin. He tumbled into the arms of the Indian woman, fragments of dark faces, of lice-covered limbs falling about him. The woman cradled the head of the fevered man, soothing his burning eyes with her calloused hands, and then, with sighing sounds, she began to murmur words of comfort.

"The dark night passes, my husband; always there is morning. Never in the memory of the oldest one of this village have wolves of winter killed the spotted fawn of spring. Today you must trick your hunger with draughts of scalding water; tomorrow you stuff with meat and roasted fish." Alvar Nuñez allowed his mind to sink into the substance of the woman. The sharp odor of her skin and the roughness of her hands comforted him. "Soon we will cross over to the main and there find sweet roots to eat, and then, in season, feast on prickley pears." She began to rock the man. "So you see, my husband, there is nothing to fear. Each thing is as it should be. To be filled we must first be empty. Without cold there could be no heat. Sleep gives birth to awakening . . ."

The faceless image of his wife floated through Alvar Nuñez's mind. "You are my life," he heard her whispering. "Without you, I am nothing, nothing." His body stiffened.

"Without death, how should there be life," murmured the Indian woman. "Would there be youth if not for age?"

"I will wait for you as many years as needs be," was the whisper of the faceless woman. "So certain am I of your return, no other man shall know me, even if I must wait twice ten years."

"Let the deep of my loins comfort you, my husband," the Indian woman's sighing words filled the ears of the trembling man, and his body softened. "Within this body, a body like that which birthed you, you will be safe from harm."

The faceless woman faded as, groaning, Alvar Nuñez eased beneath the blanket in the arms of the Indian woman.

XXVIII

His mind not yet clear, his chest tight with phlegm, Alvar Nuñez awoke the next morning to learn that three more Christians had died. It was said that too much rich food after so long a period of privation had killed them. But it was not rich food that caused the deaths of another seven. Rather, it was black despair brought on by a savage storm that drove them one by one to wander out alone into the frozen region beyond the village and lie down in the snow.

For five full days the storm howled over the island the Spaniards had named Malhado. Five days with the sun hidden behind masses of boiling clouds. Yet finally the storm abated and there was a brightening in the sky and a warming wind. It was then that Alvar Nuñez, although still suffering chills and fever, called a council of all the Christians to see what should be done.

Coughing and sneezing, with lice, scarcely noticed, crawling in their beards, the men gathered. Eighteen they were, and of that number only Alvar Nuñez and Lope de Oviedo, his second-in-command, would raise their eyes and look into the face of another. They sat in a tight circle on a patch of ground the wind had cleared of snow. And as they sat, the last of the storm clouds lifted and the sun broke through. Forcing his cracking voice through the phlegm that bubbled in his throat, Alvar Nuñez started to address the men. "See how the Almighty has sent the sun to warm this gathering of Christians." A fit of coughing interrupted his speech.

"We are a remnant," Lope de Oviedo then spoke. "Eighteen chosen by the Lord our God to live, while so many other brave men have died."

"Do not forget the notary and the five quartered across the island," muttered the one called Lachuga for his great ears.

"We are nineteen, with the notary!" Alvar Nuñez growled. "Did you not hear Lope de Oviedo speak of brave men? How, then, do you dare include those cowardly five!"

At that very moment three grinning heads appeared above a boulder that topped the rise. "Snot-faced ancient sheep!" shouted the head belonging to Gonçallo Ruiz, gesturing with his fingers.

"Clap-rotted whoresons!" Diego Lopez joined in, sticking out his tongue.

"Cuckold capons!" shrieked Corral, working his arm up

217

and down. "Never have I seen such a gathering of whey-faced men."

"I do not see Palaçios or Sierra," Lope de Oviedo murmured, shading his eyes from the sun. "If they did not survive the storm, here is one who will not mourn them."

"You are no Christian," answered Alvar Nuñez, also in a murmur, hiding a grin. "If they indeed are gone, one who so proclaims his saintliness as you do, to preserve your reputation, must offer a Pater Noster to speed them on their way."

"If I knew for certain that they were gone," Lope de Oviedo said slowly, "if I knew for an absolute certainty, then to prove my sanctity, I would pray. But to pray is not to mourn, my captain."

Shouting and hooting, their fingers making horns above their heads, the three men rose up from their place behind the boulder. Then they briskly rubbed their protruding bellies, licked their lips, and, pulling aside their breech-clouts, pissed.

"For the chance to offer them the services of my sword," muttered Alvar Nuñez, his hands tightening on his weapon, "to provide them with a little trim, I would gladly give up half my lands in Spain."

"Now where is your compassion, my captain?" Lope de Oviedo turned his head to hide his grin. "A gentle Christian would consider their loneliness, separated as they are from their countrymen, and how they sorrow for their deceased companions as they feast on venison and fish."

"Truly, I am chastened by your nobility," muttered Alvar Nuñez softly, "yet, if I could but share a little minute with them . . ."

"We fast while they feast," grumbled Lachuga, as the three again briskly rubbed their bellies. "If we will wait for darkness, then cross the island and descend upon them . . ." Others of the men murmured their assent. As if they somehow knew what was being said, the three, without delivering a parting shot, suddenly turned and disappeared.

218

"If they have a supply of venison, my captain," Lope de Oviedo spoke slowly, "if they have found a place to snare fish . . ."

"For Spaniards to share their food with starving fellow countrymen . . ." Lachuga kept his eyes focussed on the ground.

Alvar Nuñez coughed, ran his fingers through his beard, coughed again, then in a hoarse voice said, "We will cross the island to hunt, but not to steal their venison. Thus there is no need to wait for darkness. If there be fish we will snare them. But it is my order that those quartered on the far side of this island be left alone!"

There being no need for further preparation, those owning weapons having them in their possession, the men, led by Alvar Nuñez with Lope de Oviedo guarding the rear, started for the rise. It was then the Spaniards learned that they were slaves.

Three-score warriors of the village, commanded by the chief, appeared from behind boulders, mounds of snow and fallen trees where they had been hiding, and formed a ring around the Christians. They pressed in close, jabbing their captives with arrow-points as they made their sighing sounds. "You will die if you again try to escape this village," the chief addressed Alvar Nuñez, scratching the man's chest with a sharp stick until beads of blood appeared. "To go from one tribe to another causes great suffering to all our departed holy men." He scratched Alvar Nuñez's chest again. "All tribes are our enemy. Thus we must kill any who will join another tribe."

Try as Alvar Nuñez would to explain that they did not intend to join another tribe, only to cross the island and hunt for food, the chief kept shaking his head and scratching with the stick, until the man's chest bled freely. Then the Spaniards, driven by kicks and jabs, were herded back into the village.

Surrounded by the grinning women and laughing children, the Spaniards were forced to perform different tasks all that afternoon. They must pick up sticks and lay them down

219

again, move heavy stones from one place to another, and, what was most disgustful to them, carry excrement from the pit where the Indians relieved their urgings, to a defile a quarter league away. In this fashion were all the Spaniards employed, not excepting Alvar Nuñez, who sweated and stank with the least of his men. But at sunset, after again warning the Spaniards not to go from one tribe to another, the chief ordered hot water brought, that the befouled men might be cleansed.

Sickened by their noxious task, despite the efforts of the Indian women to clean them, numbed with exhaustion, the Christians stumbled to the hut assigned them by the chief—they no longer being allowed to bed down amongst the Indians. Only Alvar Nuñez was excepted from this order—his woman being the widow of a chief, demanded the right to keep her husband. Yet, despite his being granted an exception, Alvar Nuñez, after whispering with the woman, joined the other men.

Eighteen Christians lay down to sleep, but only seventeen awoke—the eighteenth, Lachuga, he of the ears like the leaves of the lettuce plant, having died—when, shortly after midnight, a terrible wailing was heard coming from other huts of the village.

Fearful lest the sound portend a calamity for his men, Alvar Nuñez instructed them to make ready to defend themselves. Then, cautioning Lope de Oviedo to keep to the shadows, he ordered the man to find out what was happening.

Waiting for Lope de Oviedo to return, the Spaniards steadied themselves by sharpening their weapons. Not one would look at Lachuga, who lay open-eyed, lice in ever greater numbers crawling upon him. Each minute the wailing sounds grew louder.

Not a man of that company did not raise his weapon as the skin guarding the entrance to the hut was roughly thrust aside. Had the face been other than the scarred, one-eared visage of the second-in-command, it would have been skewered and struck by a dozen spears and clubs.

220

"A plague has descended upon the village," gasped Lope de Oviedo, his limbs trembling from the cold. All the men sucked in their breaths. "In each hut it is the same; different ones rolling on the ground, crying that a fire rages in their guts. And it was not only old ones and children I saw suffering. Warriors that drove us back to the village, women who not a dozen hours since laughed as we dug up their dung were amongst those who writhed in agony. Already there are several dead, and if I am any judge, there will be half a score by morning."

"They suffer a burning of the guts?" Alvar Nuñez carefully asked the man. "In all cases, is it the same?"

"All that I saw, my captain, begged for water to quench their fire. All rolled on the ground stained with their puke and shit and drenched with their sweat. It is a terrible plague which has struck this village. May the Almighty preserve us from it." As he spoke, Lope de Oviedo rubbed his numbed hands together, trying to warm them.

It was then, as if drawn by an invisible silken thread, that every pair of eyes turned to the lice-covered corpse of Lachuga. Death had bared the dead man's teeth, and his purplish tongue protruded. "We are doomed," whispered several. "The plague has already descended."

"Did you not hear Lope de Oviedo say, the sick Indians in every case had befouled themselves?" said Alvar Nuñez, anger in his voice. "Will men who have braved so much now act like frightened women? Look carefully at Lachuga. His was no plague death. A stoppage of the breath from an excess of phlegm would be my guess."

"Mayhap the Indians suffer a malady that only strikes down pagans?" Lope de Oviedo raised his voice into a question.

"I have known a pestilence to ravage the ranks of Turkish pirates while not a single Christian fell victim," Alvar Nuñez answered. "And if there be a plague that destroys the Moslem and spares the Christian, who is there to say that there are not plagues solely for these howling savages."

"Then we best prove we are Christians, my captain," said

Lope de Oviedo softly, but not too softly, as he crossed himself. Alvar Nuñez nodded as he, too, crossed himself. With that, such an eruption of Pater Nosters, Hail Marys and crossings broke out within that hut that not the most holy monastery in all of Christendom could have ever known its equal. And in this way the Spaniards passed the night.

Yet it was not only the seventeen Christians of that hut who made the holy sign and prayed. Guided by the notary, the chief, the medicine man, and all of the principal Indian warriors formed the cross with their hands and intoned as best they could the words of the sacred prayers. No Saint Catherine, burning with love for her Savior, ever prayed to the Father with such sighs as did those unbaptized savages. Never were the words of the Hail Mary said with such flutterings of fingers and piteous lamentations, for the Indians wept, as was their wont, openly and unashamedly. And it was as Lope de Oviedo foredoomed. By morning half a score had already exited their life, and an equal number, by their labored breathing and shrunken features, appeared about to join these ones. It was then that the medicine man, unwrapping the bones of a long-deceased holy man, assumed for a time authority over the village.

Ordering that the notary be led away, the sick be carried to another hut, the children and younger women depart, he beckoned the rest to draw in close. Nearly two score they were: the chief and his son, various proven warriors, certain old women; two who, although men, dressed as women; and the one who had taken Alvar Nuñez as husband.

"Only those who have lived many seasons," the medicine man said slowly as he opened and closed both hands three times, "only those who remember the day when our warriors crossed over to the main and brought back all the women and children of a great tribe, only those ones knew the holy man whose bones I lay here before you." With careful fingers, the medicine man placed the bones on the sand so they formed the outline of a man. "This one from whom I gained my instruc-

222

tion, saw in a vision the place of habitation of the great tribe—and it was as he saw; thus we slew all their warriors with little loss, and gained many women and children."

All who were gathered around the medicine man murmured soft sounds of wonder, reaching out gentle hands to the dried, brown bones.

"This holy one," the medicine man bowed his head so his brow almost touched the ground, "this one whose bones you see, knew so many strong and wondrous things that if he again could walk amongst us, with a single word he would end this sickness, and with a gesture supply us with a plenitude of meat. It was I, then a youth, and the medicine man who served this tribe before me, who preserved these bones as is the custom. Even the greatest chief and bravest warrior must at last be given to the wolves as food. Only the holy man is saved, for in his substance is found great wisdom." The medicine man reached out and picked up a small bone, which he rubbed with a circular motion on his toothless gums. "It is the season for us to take wisdom from this holy man. It is the season for him who had the wondrous vision to tell his people what must be done." Various ones picked up bones, bringing them to their open mouths. "As is the custom, the old women who know of such things must prepare these holy bones." And so the old women ground the brittle bones to powder, which they mixed with water, and then each of that number drank a portion of this mixture, the medicine man imbibing the greatest quantity.

For nearly an hour after swallowing the draught, the Indians, still pressed tightly together, sat in silence. But finally the silence was broken by a hissing sound from the throat of the medicine man. "As the snake crawls stealthily into the nest, there to consume the fledglings, so have sorcerers spawned from the depths of the ocean come into our midst. This I have learned from the bones of the holy man." From the throats of different warriors also came the hissing sound. "These sorcerers formed of ocean foam have come to destroy us, that they may live upon our land; that they may hunt our deer; that they may set weirs to snare our fish; that they may feast upon our prickly pears when it shall be the season." To each of his words all but certain of the women and the two men dressed as women nodded. "Those who yet doubt that these ones are sorcerers have only to consider the hair upon their faces—not the most savage of our enemies have ever worn such hair. And consider the color of their skin—is it not the whiteness of foam? Their speech, rough as the roaring ocean? Who can doubt that these creatures are not men, but dangerous sorcerers!" The two men dressed as women nodded, but certain of the women still doubted—chiefest amongst these the one who had lain with Alvar Nuñez. "And what of this sickness which has descended upon us?" The medicine man took the carved stick from the chief and traced three circles in the sand. These he joined with an arrow whose head was formed in the likeness of a serpent. All who were gathered in that hut pushed back from these strong drawings. "Who but sorcerers could have brought this sudden sickness? Is it not a punishment upon us for the tasks they were forced to do!" All but the woman who had lain with Alvar Nuñez nodded.

"For this sickness they have brought us, these sorcerers must die," the chief said slowly. "But lest they do us a further mischief, we will pretend friendship. We will join with them and laugh when they laugh. When they no longer have suspicion, we will guide them to the cliff and, without warning, throw them down."

"Let the ocean who has spawned them receive these evil ones again." The medicine man bowed down until his forehead touched the sand. Again, all who were gathered in that hut nodded, except for the woman who had taken the chief of the Christians as husband.

"When those who came from the ocean are gone, you shall have my son as husband," the chief addressed that woman. "He is young and strong." He touched the broad-backed youth

224

gently with his fluttering fingers. "Such a one as he will bring new heat to your loins. Such a one as he will mount you three times in the night." The woman listened to the words of the chief, a frown tightening her seamed features. Then she slowly shook her head. "That foam-skinned sorcerer you lie with, whose face is hairy as the wolf, is not fit for one who once bedded with a chief and bore him sons. What if these same sons, now grown to warriors," the chief pointed his staff at two men sitting beside her, "what if they sicken of the distemper of the sorcerers?"

Speaking in a murmur so soft all must strain to hear her, her fingers fluttering, sighing between each word, the woman answered, "They are men as we are, not sorcerers. They came from a far place beyond the ocean; I know this from my husband. I who have lain with that one know him to be a man as was the chief my husband." Certain of the women nodded, also the two men dressed as women. "Coming from such a distant place, these white-skinned men know of many things unknown to even the wisest of this village." At this the medicine man started scratching strong symbols in the sand. "I judge them not sorcerers, but holy. Did not my husband cause the child who too much loved its mother to loose its grip and come forth?" The woman turned her gaze upon the chief. "And what of the one who speaks with departed holy men, is he not of their number?" She shifted her eyes to the eyes of the medicine man. "Is it forgotten that so great was that one's love for us he plunged his hands into burning embers?" All the women and certain of the warriors were now nodding. "As is the custom, having come from a different place, they are our slaves," the woman shifted her gaze back to the chief. "But they have shared our food, they have sheltered in our huts, their chief I have taken as my husband, thus, as also is the custom, although slaves, they are of this tribe and must not be destroyed unless they should go from this tribe to another." All but the chief and the medicine man nodded.

225

"If they are men, then truly they are our slaves, and thus of this tribe," said the medicine man as he passed both hands through the yellow of the fire so that his fingers smoked. "But if they are sorcerers and not men, then they have no right of habitation in this village, and thus must be destroyed, else their power will destroy us." The chief handed his carved staff to the medicine man. "Whoever knew of men wearing shiny skins harder than the shells of oysters?" the medicine man went on. "Yet, were not these ones, called men by the woman who has lain with their chief, were not these ones dressed in such skins when we first saw them? Whoever knew of men spawned of the ocean? Their chief speaks of a distant place beyond the ocean. Yet it is known that there is no land beyond. And are we not suffering a dreadful sickness that has already brought death to ten? This woman has lain with the chief of sorcerers!" He pointed the carved staff at the woman. "Into her hungry loins has been thrust a portion of a demon, which in her hunger she judged part of a man. Can we trust the words of such a woman?"

"They in truth are sorcerers," murmured the chief with deep sighs. "Unless they are destroyed, not one of us will escape their sickness."

"I have listened to many tales of sorcerers," said the woman, "tales told by holy men and by aged women. Yet never did I hear of sorcerers who die as do ordinary men. Such is their power, they need not fear death; yet have not nearly half the ones who came to us from the ocean already died?"

The old woman, she who was remembered as old when those now grown were children, stirred from the skin where she lay. "I have heard tales of demons and sorcerers from the ancient ones," she spoke in a voice grown so thin that all must soften their breathing to hear her. "I have heard tales of their great powers and their terrible deeds. I have heard that they come disguised as beasts and as men. I have heard that when it is their pleasure they will lay with women. But never have I heard that they die; never have I heard that death comes to sorcerers and demons as it does to men."

For several minutes there was silence after the old woman had spoken. Then, in a soft voice, a voice almost as soft as that of the old woman, the medicine man said, "In truth they have died, and in this wise proved that they are men. And if they are men, then they are of this tribe."

XXIX

All that day, the sickness of the bowels raged throughout the village. The setting sun saw a full score dead, and nearly a dozen more perished that night. In each hut it was the same. Warriors who could pull a bow the thickness of a man's arm, whose shaft could transfix a tree, now lay befouled in excrement, writhing and moaning in their agony. Broad-hipped women, whose backs had carried bundled sticks of a weight greater than their own, gasped in helplessness as vomit filled their throats and choked them. Children and old ones shuddered as they expired silently. Again, that they be not judged pagans and struck with this heathen malady, the Christians prayed as they made the cross with sticks, drew it in the sand and formed it with their fingers.

"If we are spared," murmured Lope de Oviedo softly, the skin of his face tight as parchment, "I swear to give my life to the service of Christ. If we are spared, never again will I turn away from Him for even the littlest moment." And again the Christians passed the night untouched by the malady.

Daylight found a third of the Indians of the village struck down by the disease. The wife of the chief and his son lay dying. Both sons of the woman who had taken Alvar Nuñez as husband fought to stay alive, their mother clearing their mouths of choking matter that they might breathe. The very old woman had passed in silence, and lay unnoticed in the shadow. And those not yet fallen victim wailed their terrible mourning for the dead.

Fully half the inhabitants of the village lay prostrated by the plague before the day ended, with nearly a hundred gone. With the coming of darkness, the howls of feasting wolves drowned out the wails of those who mourned. It was then that the malady struck the Christians.

Without warning, one of the praying Spaniards threw up his hands and pitched forward, crying, "Holy Mother, I am on fire!" Within moments the hut was filled with the stench of his purging and the sound of rattling in his throat. So suddenly had he been struck down that the others, as if frozen, did not move, even as drowning gasps came from the man. Another half a minute would have seen him gone, had not Alvar Nuñez forced himself to relieve the man's choking. Yet this relief secured for the man less than another hour of life. And he was not the only Christian afflicted that night. Six sickened, and by morning three were gone. It was then that Lope de Oviedo made an end to praying and broke the crosses made of sticks.

As if inflicted with a special punishment for having at first been spared, the Christians fell victim to the pestilence in greater proportion than the Indians. While half the inhabitants of the village survived, of the seventeen Christians quartered in the hut, only Alvar Nuñez and Lope de Oviedo were still alive when the plague lifted. Yet, in all, three Christians survived, for the notary, although struck down, recovered, and with his recovery a portion of his reason was restored.

With the passing of the disease, there came a warming spell so that the ice melted, and it was again possible to fish and dig for roots beneath the water. But most of the Indians, although grown so thin from hunger their heads were skulls and parchment, would not bestir themselves to fish, so deep was their mourning for their dead. Had it not been for the chief, the medicine man, the two men who dressed as women, the one who had taken Alvar Nuñez as husband, and the three surviving Christians, the Indians of that village would have expired of starvation. For nearly a week, until ice again formed on the ocean, these ones labored: digging roots, setting weirs, trapping birds that came to feast on fish, and in this fashion supplied the others with sufficient food for preservation. And of these eight, no one labored harder than the notary. It was he who offered his back, his hands being useless for digging or setting weirs, and struggled up the steep path from the ocean, bowed double under loads of dripping roots. It was he, using his crooked hands as hooks, who carried firesticks to the different huts. And it was he whose example drew each day a few more Indians away from their mourning. Thus it was that when the winter wind returned to freeze the ocean, enough roots had been dug and fish taken to prevent starvation.

The morning following the night of the return of the freezing wind, the three Christians wandered slowly along the outskirts of the village, there being no more work that must be done. So heavy was the sadness oppressing each man for the loss of companions and the chance of his own death, that scarcely a single word was spoken. The silence was suddenly broken by shouts and hoots coming from the rise.

"Still alive, you clap-rotted sons of whores?!" shouted Gonçalo Ruiz.

"Not sons of whores, Gonçalo Ruiz," laughed Diego Lopez, sucking up his nose, "shit-eating dogs who serve as slaves to Indians."

"How is it, you cow's head, for an hidalgo to kiss the hand

229

of a pagan?" Gonçalo Ruiz threw a stone in the direction of
Alvar Nuñez. "Your whore mother, who it is well known laid
with he-asses, must groan in her grave if she knew her bastard
now waits upon heathen savages."

"So many good men gone, yet such vermin as those two
prosper," murmured Lope de Oviedo.

"The wolves fatten on the corpses of your companions!"
shouted Diego Lopez. "I have noticed different ones of those
false Christians, who once dared call themselves men, lying
torn amongst the rotting carcasses of the pagans."

"To suffer such off-scourings to live when the very flower
of Spain have been struck down I judge to be an act of the basest
villainy," Lope de Oviedo's voice rasped.

"Soon it will be your turn to feed the wolves, turd of a
cow!" shouted Gonçalo Ruiz. "Soon you and that earless
whoreson and that mad one with his crippled hands will know
the tug of yellow fangs tearing at your flesh."

"If there be no greater justice," Lope de Oviedo hissed as
he loosed his sword, "if there be no God to bring them punishment, then this day I am become the judge!" Breaking free of
the grip Alvar Nuñez had taken on his arm, thrusting aside the
notary who attempted to block the way, his sword in his hand,
the man rushed up the rise.

Had the distance been ten paces less, had the two men hesitated for the littlest moment, had Lope de Oviedo been strengthened by so much as a single mouthful of venison, he must have
skewered both men. But, seeing the madness in that one's face
as he came up the rise, the sun flashing from his sword, Gonçalo
Ruiz and Diego Lopez, crying the name of the blessed Mother
Mary, turned and ran. Two times Lope de Oviedo came near
overtaking them. And had he thrust his weapon forward like
the spearman, instead of raising it for the slashing motion, at
least one of the two surely would have fallen.

"As I now know there is *no* God in heaven, I swear to rip up
your bellies with this weapon when next we meet!" Lope de

Oviedo shrieked after the two men, as they disappeared amongst a tangle of fallen trees and large boulders. "Venture across this island again and I will bathe my hands in your blood. This I swear on the grave of my mother!" Cupping his mouth so his voice should carry, he then shouted: "Beware lest I descend upon your den in the night to open a vein in your throats with my knife!"

His eyes narrowed to slits, his sword still in his hand, a wolf's grin twisting the corners of his mouth, Lope de Oviedo turned and started down the rise, but in a direction away from his two companions.

Fearing to further inflame what they judged to be a temporary attack of madness, Alvar Nuñez and the notary did not try to join with Lope de Oviedo again that day. Rather, they retired to their hut, each deep in his own thoughts. But when the descent of darkness and a severe worsening of the weather had not brought the man home, the notary grew uneasy.

"Lacking fire and shelter, even a tough old fighting boar like Lope de Oviedo must freeze on a night like this," he said slowly.

"Lope de Oviedo has been weaned of his mother's teat more than a week, Hieronymo Alaniz, save your concern for those who may need it," Alvar Nuñez forced a grin. "He will return when the wind has sufficiently cooled his passion."

"But if it is more than passion, Alvar Nuñez?" the notary rubbed his twisted hands one over the other. "If he suffers insanity as did this one who sits here with you and thus wanders in the darkness until he freezes . . ."

"Has the recovery of your reason changed you to an old woman, Hieronymo Alaniz?" Alvar Nuñez asked gently. "I have never known a man to wring his hands and moan for the safety of a soldier as you now do. Lope de Oviedo fought in the army of Hernan Cortez, he shows the scars of a score of battles—how should such a one suffer death from freezing?"

"May it be as you say, Alvar Nuñez," the notary spoke

softly, his eyes still fixed on the ground. "I pray to the Holy
Mother that he stays out in the freezing weather only long
enough to cool his passion." He raised his crooked hands so
they formed the cross. "And I pray that he be forgiven for his
blasphemy and guided back to his companions who love him."
Tears ran from the man's eyes. "I pray that morning finds not
two, but three Christians still alive in this desolate village."

That night, as Alvar Nuñez slept, the notary, his helpless
hands aching, prayed for the safety of Lope de Oviedo. In a
whisper so soft only Almighty God could hear, he begged that
the man not be judged too harshly for his profanity. "He is an
untutored man, my Lord, one who has known much adversity.
His features have suffered such scarrings that women revile
him and men must turn away their eyes. Despite his harsh
words to You, my Lord, I know him to be a good Christian. If
You will spare him, I will offer a thousand Hail Marys on my
knees, also the Pater Noster no less than three hundred times."
His hands fixed in the sign of the cross, his lids forced open,
staring into the glowing embers of the fire, the notary prayed
through the night as the howling wind swirled snow and bits of
ice against the hut.

But morning failed to bring the return of Lope de Oviedo.
And so severe grew the winter storm that the two Christians,
lacking sufficient clothing, did not dare leave the safety of their
shelter. When it again was evening, the notary, his skin grown
ashen, left off his praying, having given up all hope.

Seeing the pallor of his companion Alvar Nuñez pulled
gently at the man's ear. Then, forcing his tone to be jovial, after
again pulling at the ear, he said, "From the bleakness of your
looks, my friend, you count Lope de Oviedo as already dead."
The notary nodded. "If in truth he is gone, then as Christians
we must mourn." Again the notary nodded. "But what if he
has not yet departed this life and, at this very moment, is shel-

tered in another hut, mayhap enjoying the embrace of some woman? How would it be if we, as professing Christians, mourned as dead and begged the Almighty's mercy for a lusty fornicator?" The notary's mouth opened as if he were going to reply, but instead he bit down on his lip. "If it were any but Lope de Oviedo who had failed to return, I must join in your dejection. But I cannot believe that one as tough as that old stag would willingly lie down in a storm. And if he be not willing, no storm, however frenzied, can kill him."

"In truth, Alvar Nuñez, he is a tough old stag," the notary's face brightened. "And was there ever one so scarred?" He grinned as he gestured towards his ear.

"The way you served his pretty features in your madness," Alvar Nuñez laid a finger on his nose.

"I, my captain?" the notary raised his eyebrows. "I have never been a violent man."

"Forgive me, Hieronymo Alaniz, you were a dove, one of the cherubim, a new-dropped fawn. It was affection that you showered upon your companions."

"I abused fellow Christians?" The notary's eyes opened wide.

"Abused, my friend? Not abused! Offered proofs of your tender passion. Even I tasted of your love." Alvar Nuñez pressed a palm against his cheek.

"I laid violent hands on the person of my captain?" Crimson suffused the notary's features.

"Let us rather say, you caressed your captain, to show him the depths of your devotion. And, from the caresses you showered upon Lope de Oviedo, you demonstrated a devotion seldom shown by the hidalgo toward the base born soldier."

"I will beg him to forgive me," the notary murmured. "And he whose features have suffered such terrible scarrings . . ."

"Do not condemn yourself, my friend, for what was done in your insanity," Alvar Nuñez again tugged the ear of the man. "Besides, I give it to you as my true opinion, that your ministrations added a touch of order to his much disordered features. It is certain that no one could add to that one's uncomeliness."

But these words of comfort were not enough to relieve the notary's distress, for he had recovered only a portion of his reason. So it was that, as Alvar Nuñez slept, although weighed with fatigue, the notary again passed the night awake and praying.

XXX

The storm having ended, the next day and for the three days after Alvar Nuñez searched the countryside for signs of the missing man. The few times he chanced to meet an Indian of the village—most staying within their huts because of mourning—he sought to gain information. But on each occasion it was the same—the Indian's fingers started fluttering as he shrugged and grinned and then departed, sighing.

It was on the fourth day of his search for his companion—having two days since given up any hope, yet desperately continuing with the search—as he made his way around the portion of the village furthest from the ocean, that Alvar Nuñez heard a sound he never in this world expected to hear again. Coming from the hut which quartered the lesser warriors was the hoarse voice of Lope de Oviedo slowly speaking the Indian tongue. Quickly, Alvar Nuñez pushed past the entrance skin.

His face as bare of beard as his gums had long been free of

teeth, his cheeks and chin showing by the crimson humor oozing from a thousand tiny wounds that his beard would never
grow again, Lope de Oviedo sat cross-legged on a pile of skins as
an Indian woman, holding two blood-stained clamshells in her
hand, knelt before him.

"How does it go with you, my captain?" asked the seated
man, keeping his features immobile. "This one," he nodded at
the kneeling woman, "will offer you relief, I promise, if beard-
lice rob you of your sleep. I have never known a better barber—
she lets blood and shaves all with the same motion." He picked
up several long hairs pulled from his face, dangled them for a
moment, then let them fall again. "This one, whom you must
remember from the night you helped her birth her babe,"
again he nodded at the woman, "has sworn to take me as husband so soon as I am clean-shaven." The corners of his mouth
twisted into a grin, but the pain quickly caused a return to his
former cast of countenance. "Will there be any end to wonders?" Lope de Oviedo slowly winked one eye. "The son of a
cowherd first raised to the rank of ensign, now taken as husband by this fine widow, who is the daughter of a chief."

Alvar Nuñez stood open mouthed just inside the entrance
to the hut. Finally, after sucking in several deep breaths, he
forced himself to speak. "I thought you frozen in the storm."
The other man snorted. "And your beard, my friend!" Alvar
Nuñez raised an unsteady hand. "You have lost your beard."
He brought the hand slowly to his chin. "It is not seemly for a
Spaniard to sacrifice his beard—to pull the hairs so it can never
grow again is un-Christian."

Laying two sticks one on the other, so they formed the
cross, then spurning it with his foot, Lope de Oviedo hissed, "I
am become a pagan, Alvar Nuñez Cabeza de Vaca! Never again
will I pray to an unjust God who cares nothing for me or for any
man. I am become a pagan, my one-time captain, and I will
worship trees and stones, the sun and the ocean, as do these
Indians. I will worship things I can see, not some invisible One
who sits high upon a throne in Heaven."

235

"Do not blaspheme!" Alvar Nuñez quickly crossed himself. "To let such words pass your lips must bring a terrible calamity!"

Ignoring the pain to his face, Lope de Oviedo laughed harshly. "Calamity, my one-time captain, whom I still love as friend; calamity," he said again, "can there be a calamity worse than those we have already known?" Again he laughed. "I have done with the Almighty and His terrible calamities. I have done with His bastard son and the son's whore mother. Nothing that can happen to this one," he struck himself on the chest, "nothing will be terrible enough to suck me back into the ways of the Christian. For I care not the thousandth part of a single Blanco if I live another twenty years or if at this very moment I am taken."

Troubled by the scene he had just witnessed, Alvar Nuñez shuffled like a broken man after he left the hut. He moved slowly, his lips moving, stopping at different times as if uncertain which direction he should go. "My God," he whispered, "help me to know what must be done." The sun shone, but for him it was as if the earth lay wrapped in mourning. "Hear me, hear me, sweet Savior Jesus, tell me what must be done," he again whispered. "Holy Mother Mary, guide me. Here is a Christian grown close to the end of his resolution; excepting one poor cripple, I am alone, alone in this land of pagans."

It was as if the curses of the beardless man had sent forth a noxious contagion. For when Alvar Nuñez entered his hut he found the notary, struck mad, kneeling before the firepit with both hands thrust to the elbows in the glowing embers.

The notary's charred arms still smoked as Alvar Nuñez carried him through the village to the dwelling of the chief. So pitiful was his condition that the inhabitants of each hut they passed fell at once to weeping. And different women, streaming tears, came up to blow their breaths and, with careful lips, place spittle on the wounds.

236

"He curses me and asks to be taken to the habitation of the chief," Alvar Nuñez muttered to himself, his face flushed as if with fever. "He says he is not Christian, but of Indian blood." Alvar Nuñez tilted his face upward, so that it was bathed in sunlight. "Can I deny the wishes of one in his condition? But do not listen to his ravings—I beg You. He is a better Christian than most men—his soul is deserving to be saved. Sweet Jesu, do not listen to his ravings."

With eyes nearly closed, his lip caught tight between his teeth, Alvar Nuñez inclined his head as he handed the moaning Spaniard to the chief. Then, pressing his arms against his sides so they should not tremble, and guiding his feet so they should not stumble, while waves of fever from his inflamed bowels rose to cloud his vision, Alvar Nuñez made his way slowly through the village to the hut of the Indian woman.

XXXI

The weeks that followed saw a gradual warming. Each day more snow melted and in different places there appeared the first green of spring. But Alvar Nuñez knew nothing of this change, for fever so wracked him he could only speak in whispers, and the littlest light falling on his eyes caused great agony. So it was that he knew nothing of the preparations of the tribe to leave the village and cross over to the main. And so it was he knew nothing of the notary's worsening condition, as a corruption of the flesh moved slowly up his arms.

The day appointed for the tribe's departure, the Indian woman wrapped Alvar Nuñez tightly in skins, then lashed him

237

to a litter made of sticks—the fever having so wasted the man that even raising his head when he must drink brought a shortness of breath. The notary, being judged too close to death to bear the rigors of the journey, was given to the care of Lope de Oviedo, who chose to remain on the island—he having gained rank as a warrior of the tribe from his union with the daughter of the chief.

In single file the Indians departed the village. Lope de Oviedo, naked except for a breech-clout, came to the door of his hut as the litter on which Alvar Nuñez lay was dragged past. He hesitated, then, falling in step, his head lowered, he spoke slowly to the prostrate man. "With the coming of spring you must recover your strength, my captain." Alvar Nuñez opened his lids for a moment. "I will do all that can be done for the notary—but I see little hope for that one." The sick man nodded. "Because of my love for you, my captain, I will bury him as a Christian." Again the sick man nodded. Motioning the woman to stop, Lope de Oviedo knelt before the litter. "Farewell, my captain," he whispered, as he brought his lips to the forehead of the man. But then, noting the stares of the woman and the looks of her two sons, he quickly rose to his feet and, with a shrug, hurried off in the direction of his hut.

Only one as fevered as he, lying on a litter as he lay, could have known the agony Alvar Nuñez suffered as the litter was dragged across that island. At different times his lips whispered Christ's name, and when the pain grew too great he gasped the words of the Pater Noster.

Having crossed the island, the tribe rested on the beach. It was then, for the first time since departing the village, that Alvar Nuñez found strength to open his eyes. Squatting by his side was the Indian woman, gnawing at a dried root. Several paces distant, her two sons sat cross-legged, picking lice from their hair. All about were grouped other families. Flashes of

238

sunlight, reflected from the boulders scattered along the beach, stabbed at his eyes like needles. He raised his eyes. Trees, dwarfed and twisted by the wind, clung to outcroppings of the headland they had just descended. On the ridge of the cliff, as if shattered by some giant's hand, lay masses of broken stone. He squeezed his lids shut for a moment, to relieve his vision; when he opened them, a stone had turned into the face of a grinning man.

Tiny eyes sunk deep into their hollows, the bones of his cheek and jaw showing through the skin, his lips pulled back from his blackened gums, the head of Gonçalo Ruiz grinned down at the prostrate man. Forgetting that he was tied, Alvar Nuñez tried to rise from his litter. "Come down," he strained to say. But only a hoarse sound came from his throat.

Noting the agitation of the man, and the direction in which he stared, the woman quickly turned her head, but in that moment the face had disappeared. "Rest, my husband," she whispered, passing her calloused hands over his eyes. "Soon we will cross to the main, where there are many good things to eat, and you will again have your strength." Alvar Nuñez tried to speak, but she pressed her fingers on his lips. "You will have fish," she murmured, "both that which swims and that which lives in its house of bone; you will have the meat of deer, of birds, and the fat tail of great lizards; when it shall be the season, my husband, you will fill your belly until it is swollen with the prickly pear, and I will prepare a cake for you of roots and nuts which will restore your vigor."

But despite his being fed meals of rich food, for having reached the main the tribe found quantities of fish and roots, and took many deer, Alvar Nuñez's condition worsened. Finally, despairing of his life—his stomach retching up everything it was given—Alvar Nuñez begged the woman to send her sons to seek those Christians quartered with the tribe on the north of the island. "Tell them," he whispered to the two young men, "that should they wish to see their captain in this life again, they must hurry. Tell them that I will struggle not to depart until they come. Tell them I wish to be shriven by Asturiano if he be yet alive." Although understanding only a portion of what he said, the two men nodded. Then, so that the Christians should know that the message in truth came from him, Alvar Nuñez drew the head of a cow on a piece of skin.

Determined that he would not die before the messengers returned, Alvar Nuñez forced food down his throat, despite his stomach's retchings. With each bite he took he made the cross. In this fashion, despite much suffering, he clung to life.

Three days from their departure, Alvar Nuñez learned of the messengers' return, when the coat of marten taken by the Spaniards from the Indians who had attacked them was tossed at his feet. But it was as if he had suddenly become a leper, for the two young men, despite his importuning and the questioning sounds of their mother, refused to enter the shelter. And, had it not been for the power of the woman the Indians would have abandoned Alvar Nuñez, so frightened did they become when they learned what the messengers had seen.

After feasting with the Christians quartered on the north end of the island, and after repeating certain words of greeting so that they should be memorized, the two Indians, carrying the coat of marten as a pledge to Alvar Nuñez that he would soon be succored, started back across the island. Darkness overtaking them as they reached the cliff that faced the main, they feared to cross the water without light; thus, they determined to pass the night on the island. It was as they searched for a place where they would be protected from the wind and safe from marauders that they came upon the habitation of the five who had broken with Alvar Nuñez. Seeing no signs of fire within, and listening for sounds and hearing none, they entered. There, on the ground, lay the rotted body of a white-skinned one. And in that hut were the skulls and bones of four others.

240

But these had not been consumed by wolves, for the bones, cracked for their marrow, were roasted black.

How many times Alvar Nuñez cried out for God's mercy after learning the fate of the five men, no one will ever know. How many times he struck his chest with fever-enfeebled hands, only Christ himself can know. Only his wish to once more see his companions and be shriven kept him from locking his teeth against food and seeking death. For he held himself to blame for the terrible happening. "I was their captain," he muttered again and again. "It was I who granted them permission to quarter across the island."

Thus it was that Alvar Nuñez, half mad with grief and wracked with fever, fought to stay alive as he waited for his companions. But his companions did not come. . . .

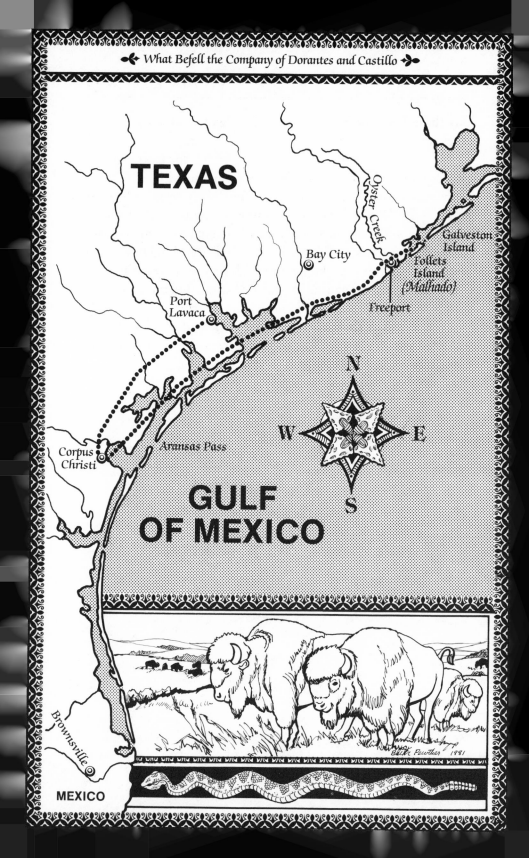

TEXAS

Oyster Creek

Bay City

Galveston Island

Tollets Island (Malhado)

Freeport

Port Lavaca

N

Corpus Christi

Aransas Pass

W   E

S

GULF OF MEXICO

Brownsville

MEXICO

XXXII

It was because Alonso del Castillo and my master, Andres
Dorantes, thought Alvar Nuñez dead that we did not further
seek to find him after we had escaped from the Indians with
whom we quartered, and crossed to the main. Only the vigilance of these Indians prevented us from departing at once
when we gained intelligence of his condition. But knowing
that we would be killed if our hosts believed us ready to abandon their village, for there is no worse crime among them than
to go from one village to another, it was the orders of Alonso del
Castillo and Andres Dorantes that we do everything in our
power to allay their suspicions, the Indians having grown uneasy at the visit of the two messengers. After their departure,
two days passed with every Christian attending to his tasks and
with much laughing and joking when we gathered around the
fire at dusk. But the third night, after bedding with our women,
we stayed awake listening for a fox's bark which was to be the

signal. Then, when it was given, each man in his different hut rose up as if to answer the urgings of his body, took his weapon, and made for a nearby stand of trees.

We were twelve, gathered in that stand of trees from which we made our escape, the rest of our number having died of sickness and starvation. The names of those who gathered there were: Captain Alonso del Castillo, Captain Andres Dorantes, Diego Dorantes, cousin to the captain, Pedro de Valdevieso, also a cousin, Diego de Huelva, these being officers; also a priest called Asturiano, and five soldiers, Estrada, Tostado, Chaves, Gutierrez and Benitez; the twelfth man being the black slave of Azemmour whose narration this is. A thirteenth, Francisco de Leon, was later added to our number when we crossed over to the main, and it was he that falsely told us Alvar Nuñez had died. Yet had it not also been for what Lope de Oviedo told us, who is there to say that Francisco de Leon's report would have been believed, for his information was not first-hand but had been gathered from certain Indians.

His face swathed in bandages made of bruised leaves used by the Indians for healing, Lope de Oviedo greeted us as we entered the village we thought deserted. Surprised by his appearance, for he was naked, the priest questioned him and he answered that he suffered from the itch and clothing tortured him. Then further questioned by Alonso del Castillo as to the fate of the other men, he said all had died, the most recent being Hieronymo Alaniz, and that he had seen Alvar Nuñez, whose condition was so piteous he could not hope to survive. At this information, a heavy depression settled on our company. And if it had not been that we feared that the Indians of our village were following and would come upon us if we delayed, we would have stayed and given full vent to our mourning.

Giving as the reasons for not joining us the itch and attacks of dizziness, and promising that as soon as he recovered he would seek to find us, Lope de Oviedo begged that he be left in

244

the village together with his woman. We parted with the man, but not without some hesitation, for his manner was strange and his appearance was more that of a pagan than a professing Christian.

We crossed over to the main, and it was there we met Francisco de Leon, who had disappeared from our village two months earlier. Although a man not well loved by his companions, for he never bathed, and would first pick his nose then put his fingers in the pot, and was not averse to stealing from his companions, not a man of our company did not rejoice to see him.

"Do my aging eyes deceive me, or is it that evil-smelling goat, Francisco de Leon!" shouted Andres Dorantes as we rounded a pile of rubble and saw the man setting weirs in an inlet of the lagoon.

"We thought you frozen in the storm," joined in Alonso del Castillo, "and long since eaten by wolves."

"Eaten by wolves, Alonso," answered Andres Dorantes, "that one!" he pinched his nostrils.

"What wolf would have the stomach for such rank meat," laughed Diego de Huelva who, himself, had no great reputation for cleanliness.

Coming up to Francisco de Leon, who was grinning broadly, we greeted him with punches to the arms, slaps on the back, beard-pulls, even hugs and kisses despite his mellow fragrance. And, as was his habit when excited, he thrust a forefinger into his nose, sucked his teeth and farted.

"If I doubted that this man truly was Francisco de Leon," roared Andres Dorantes, "he has now given us sufficient proof."

As soon as the levity occasioned by our meeting with a man believed dead had ended, Alonso del Castillo and Andres Dorantes asked if he had any knowledge of Alvar Nuñez. At this, Francisco de Leon pulled a long face, sighed, and nodded his head.

"Well, what is it you know?" Andres Dorantes took a

rough hold of the man's arm. "Do you expect to be coaxed like a maiden—what is it you know!"

"If you will permit me to answer, my captain," Francisco de Leon grinned, but showed in the swelling cords of his neck anger at being used in so rude a fashion. "I heard from different Indians that fish in this lagoon that there was pestilence in his village."

"That we already know, Francisco; what of the man?" Andres Dorantes still kept tight hold of his arm.

"If you only will permit me, my captain," Francisco de Leon said slowly, "I have not used the Spanish tongue since escaping the village."

"Do you mock my cousin, you unwashed son of a whore?" Diego Dorantes took hold of his other arm.

"Give the man a chance to answer." Alonso del Castillo laid a gentle hand on each officer's shoulder. "Two months of disuse must cause even a bachelor embarrassment as he tries to find his tongue—for a peasant raised on a mound of dung, such as this one," he winked at the man, "it must be counted as a miracle if he does not bray or grunt." Their faces softening, both officers released their grip. Alonso del Castillo then nodded at the man to continue.

"After escaping, I was determined to join the forces of the Governor. But I feared capture by those from our village, thus I crossed to the main to wait a sufficient time until it should be safe. It was then I learned of pestilence in his village." The face of Andres Dorantes was again lowering. "Later I saw the Indians of his village cross to the main with the Governor lashed to a litter, but fearing the pestilence, I remained hidden." Francisco de Leon forced a grin, and licked his cracked lips. "But do not think I lacked concern for the welfare of one who was my superior, my captain, do not charge me with neglect of duty as a Spanish soldier. It was that both my mother and father perished of the plague, and I counted myself a dead man if exposed to the contagion."

246

"Sniveling, dung-dipped peasant," muttered Diego Dorantes. "What value is his miserable life, compared to that of an hidalgo!"

"Do not charge me with neglect," Francisco de Leon said again. "Each day I made inquiry from different Indians as to the Governor's condition. Each day I learned of his worsening—and then came a day when the Indian I asked paled and trembled, and I asked if the Governor were dead, and the Indian nodded, then ran away. I inquired of other Indians, my captains, and it was the same—they paled and ran away. All the Christians of that village are dead of the pestilence."

"Excepting Lope de Oviedo," Alonso del Castillo offered.

"That one no longer is a Christian," Francisco de Leon said softly, with rapid lickings of his lips. "From different women who come to fish I learned he is become a pagan Indian." The clergyman, Asturiano, made the cross and started mumbling to himself. "All the Christians of that village are dead of the pestilence," Francisco de Leon said again.

"It will be God's mercy if we, too, are not struck down," Diego de Huelva growled. "With the Governor gone, it must be counted as madness to stay where we may be infected by this contagion."

"To remain another hour in this malignant place, where a breath of wind may bring down upon us the miasma, must be judged as the greatest foolishness," Diego Dorantes urgently added. "It is a pestilence of proven deadliness to Christians— even an hour's delay may be too much."

"My fear of this pestilence, which may have already exhausted itself, is less than of the Indians of our village," Alonso del Castillo then offered. "If it were only the plague we hazarded, my vote would be to try and discover where Alvar Nuñez is buried. But if the Indians of our village should come upon us, our lives would be forfeited."

"As Alonso says," added Pedro de Valdevieso, whose wont it was to seldom speak, "To delay when it is certain that the

Indians of our village follow would be hazardous. There is nothing more we can do for Alvar Nuñez." All the officers being in agreement, and hearing no objection from the priest, we departed, moving south.

That night, I lay apart from the other men, sharing a fire with Francisco de Leon. Urged on by the officers, we had covered no less than four leagues, yet despite fatigue, I could not sleep. So it was with Francisco de Leon. I could not sleep because of thoughts of Governor Alvar Nuñez—would that I could have placed a cross of sticks on his grave and said the Pater Noster for his soul. Francisco de Leon stayed awake oppressed by sadness for the Indian woman he had been forced to leave.

"If I were not a Christian, Estevanico," he finally broke the silence, "I would have stayed with the Indian woman. Lying with her at night, in the day fishing in the lagoon, was not an unpleasant life."

"Do you not yearn for your home in Spain?" I asked, hoping my question might ease him.

"As a Christian, Estevanico, how should I not yearn for a Christian land? But I have no home. I joined with Hernan Cortez before I was twelve—my poncho is my home. And you, Estevanico, a slave who comes from black Afric, how can you speak of home?"

"A slave is a man," I said the words slowly, "and a man, even if he be black, has a home." Francisco de Leon stared into my eyes, the light of the fire caused the saber scar that ran across his brow to shine.

"A man has a home," he said my words carefully as he nodded his head. "A black man has his home in a black land. An Indian in an Indian land—I will find a home in Spain! We will reach Pánuco and when I see Christian women I will forget my Indian." Francisco de Leon lowered his head so his face was in the shadows.

The mention of Pánuco caused a stirring within me. The winter we passed with the Indians had cost three-quarters of our number. Nights as I lay in my hut tortured by hunger, while outside a fierce storm raged, I lost all belief that we should ever reach Pánuco. To stay live until the next day, to find a root to gnaw, were the only hopes I allowed entrance into my mind. Yet, now we were started on the way. Even if it should take many months, I thought, we will be free of boisterous weather. Even if Pánuco lies five hundred leagues distant, we must reach it if we travel south along the coast. How should thoughts such as these not stir me?

I lay beside the fire, listening to the deep breathing of Francisco de Leon, and stared at the brightening that comes before the moon. It was like beaten silver, and deep in my memory I could hear sounds of silversmiths, sitting crosslegged in the entrance to their shops, working with wooden mallets on gleaming plates. In the bazaar of the city where I was born they were, hunched over, spitting, their sweat dripping on the precious metal. Dust stirred by the feet of Arabs, Jews and Berbers filled the air of the bazaar. Everywhere was sound and motion—grunting camels, shuddering their loose skin, snarling dogs, slinking; horses, coughing and pawing at the ground, and everywhere the tapping of wooden mallets. I forced my half-closed eyes to open—the rim of the moon shone over the horizon, the sound in my mind was the lapping of water in the lagoon. Through the darkness I tried to descry the foam along the shore. The lapping water filled me with peace, as had the sound of the pestle in my mother's hands. She squatted close to the fire, pounding nuts in a mortar made of a hollowed stone. Safe within the thick walls of my father's house, I crouched in a corner, my eyes weeping from the smoke, as I listened to my brothers speak of fish taken from the river Habid. And the sound of the pestle brought the river sounds which I used to know as I held the tiller while my father cast the net. Like a heron with outstretched wings, the skiff skimmed over the water, its sails billowing, and I needed all my strength to hold the shuddering tiller. Again, I forced my eyes open—the moon had cleared the horizon. A curl of cold air caused me to shudder—mixed with the lapping of the water I heard another sound.

My body pressed to the ground, I carefully crawled through the bushes toward the lagoon. Parting the tall reeds that grew along the bank, I eased out onto the strip of sand where I lay without moving. Again, I heard the sound, this time more clearly. Straining my eyes, I stared in the direction from which we had come. Then, in the light of the rising moon, I saw three war canoes filled with warriors, coming down.

Taking care that I not be seen I quickly made my way through the reeds and bushes back to where we camped. Bringing my lips to the ear of Alonso del Castillo, my hand cupping his mouth so he should not exclaim, I whispered a warning.

Had we delayed as little as five minutes longer, all would have ended for us that night, for we had not yet fully readied our weapons when we heard the scraping of vessels on the sand. Hurling brands pulled from the fires, shouting and slashing with our swords, we drove the Indians backwards in confusion. Yet if not for dry reeds and bushes along the shore which caught fire, thus dividing us from the attackers, their next onslaught might have destroyed us, they being four times our number.

Guided by Alonso del Castillo, who took command, we retreated inland, a widening wall of flame providing us sufficient time to make our escape. Then we continued inland until morning.

Having traveled no less than three leagues, and having reached a rise which offered a good view of the countryside, we judged it safe to rest—all suffering severely from exhaustion. Yet, fearing the vengeance of the Indians, after two hours' rest,

250

despite there being no sign that they still followed, and despite the grumbling of different men, Alonso del Castillo ordered that we press on. How sound were these orders the grumblers quickly learned.

Not thirty minutes later, as we climbed a second rise, we descried the pursuing Indians gathering where we had been. Straining my vision against the dazzle of the sun, I counted them, and they were not less than two score, each armed with a great bow, their faces painted red and white as is their custom when they go to war. It being certain we must perish if we joined with them—their skill with bows unmatched by any in the world—we pressed on, fear renewing our vigor.

Yet, had it not been for the intercession of the Almighty, it is my belief that we should have perished before another day, for the Indians were immune from exhaustion. It was a storm that saved us. Before midafternoon, despite it not being the season for such things, black clouds filled with thunder boiled up over the horizon, darkening the sky. And with this thunder, which each minute grew louder, came blinding bolts of lightning. It was as though the Lord our God threw down His spears to impale the enemy, for hissing shafts struck to our rear where the Indians followed. The pagans, taking this for a sign of the sky-god's displeasure, crouched, gibbering in terror, while we pressed forward.

Despite exhaustion and the lashing rain, none of our number needed urging as we struggled over the next rise and then down into a chasm. As we again climbed upwards, our feet slipping on the rain-soaked gravel, our hands torn by stones and thorns, there was still no need for urgings. And not a man of our company did not reel, falling against trees and boulders as if drunk, as we traveled the last half league before being overtaken by darkness.

The storm having ended, we feared that the Indians might yet come upon us, thus, while some slept others kept vigil, and in this way we passed the night.

Not one of us having had sufficient rest, chilled from having lain without fire, we again pressed forward at the first light of morning. Only when we had crossed an arid plain and could look backwards two leagues and see that we were not pursued did we slow our forward progress, though we still pressed on. But the hand of the Almighty had saved us, although we did not yet know this, for the storm had provided us a sufficient time to reach a land inhabited by Indians of a different tongue. Upon entering that arid plain, we were safe.

That evening, as we camped in an arroyo, still fearing to light a fire, the two captains asked each man his advisement as to what should be done. Even this one, although a slave, was asked. "This is no time, Estevanico, for slaves and masters," Alonso del Castillo said, when it came my turn. "If agreed by your master Andres Dorantes, from this night you are an equal member of this expedition." Andres Dorantes hesitated, then nodded.

"As Alonso says," he said hoarsely, "this is no time for one to be slave and another master. You are a free man, Estevanico. I declare this before all who are gathered here. Now tell us, as have the others, what should be done."

This grant of freedom having come so suddenly, for a moment I could not find words to speak. But having swallowed several times, and coughed to clear my throat, I offered as my suggestion that we circle back to the coast and then follow the sea, which must in time bring us to Pánuco. This also being the proposal of the two captains, it was so determined, although Diego de Huelva, Diego Dorantes and several other men feared that a return to the shore would again bring us in contact with the Indians of our village.

"They have already traveled a great distance from their women and children," Andres Dorantes answered. "To leave their village unprotected too long a time is not their way. Although I cannot be certain, it is my belief they have even now turned back."

"As Andres says," Alonso del Castillo offered. "And to further travel through such barren country," he gestured with his hands, "will soon bring us starvation—except for snakes and scorpions, what creatures can live amongst these stones and thorns?" At this, all conversation ceased and we lay down for a little time of sleep.

XXXIII

Two hours after sunrise, having traveled a little less than three leagues through what must be some of the most barren wastes in all those Western Indies, we were set upon by a band of Indians of that region. Had they been armed with bows and arrows instead of rocks and spears, they would have overwhelmed us. But, they were so poorly armed, we drove them off despite their superior numbers—thirty would be my guess—yet not without every man of our company suffering painful bruises from their missiles. Benitez, a Moor of my race although not a slave, received a stone the size of a man's fist above his eye, knocking him senseless. It fell to me to carry him, which I did, but with great difficulty, for hunger and hard travel had sapped my strength.

Carrying that unconscious man draped over my shoulder like a sack, I confess I grew bitter. "If this be your grant of freedom," I muttered to myself, "then you are welcome to it." Had he been a friend, rather than one whose wont it was to treat me with contempt, as so often is the case with the free black toward the slave, I would have counted him less a burden. Yet, that day I found in Benitez the greatest of all friendships, although he did not willingly give it.

We had scarcely quit a protected bank where we took the few mouthfuls which passed for our midday meal, when the band of Indians were again upon us. Again, we drove them off, but not before they had cast their spears. All but one of these fell short. The single spear that struck was the one aimed at my back. Thus it was that Benitez proved his friendship, for it was he, draped over my shoulder, that was transfixed instead of me.

Reduced by the loss of Benitez to twelve, we traveled six leagues that day, until we finally reached the water. Those of us who held the belief that upon reaching the sea we would find oysters and take fish—and I was one who so believed—were sorely disappointed. For the place where we came out was a rocky shallow filled with dangerous sands, inhabited only by a species of crab of an indifferent flavor. Thus we were forced to sate our hunger with these fellows, who proved difficult to catch, together with rock weed, which fills but does not satisfy. Then, to add to our discomfort, we found a plague of stinging flies and fleas where we camped. Yet, such was our fatigue that we passed a restful night.

Morning brought a storm fully the equal of the one that had saved us from the Indians of our village. The wind swirled sand and spume into our faces, and the sea came crashing over the rocky beach. It being impossible to travel along the shore in such weather, we huddled together on a sandy point, each man wrapped in his deerskin, which, however, offered little protection. The storm, the hunger gnawing at our bellies, our skin raw from the sun and insects, the loss of Benitez served to bring upon the twelve of us such an attack of despair that had the storm not ended and the sun broken through by noon, that afternoon would have surely seen more than one man end his life by self-destruction. All morning, as the wind blew and the rain beat down, different men muttered: Would it not be better to end it all now? Why suffer any more if death is certain?

254

Human flesh can only bear so much! I, too, found myself weighted with depression, wondering if all this effort was wasted, if fate had not already determined on our destinies. "Forty paces to the east and then the water grows deep, Estevanico," was a thought that teased as I huddled against the storm. "Walk those forty paces, and you will have peace, an end to all pain, no more hunger." And I am certain that others thought as I did. Even Alonso del Castillo showed a long face as he passed his hand again and again over his eyes. And Andres Dorantes, who took great pride in his toughness, frowned and chewed his lower lip. And it took the urging of Andres Dorantes' fist to induce Francisco de Leon to continue on when the storm was over.

"Let me return to my woman and to fishing in the lagoon!" the man begged on his knees. "I have no wish to leave this land. I have no longing to see Spain. Permit me, my captain, to return to the lagoon and to my woman." To Andres Dorantes' urgings were added certain threats by Alonso del Castillo.

We then traveled two days along the shore until our forward progress was obstructed by a bay, or estuary, formed of a river. Finding it too deep to ford, and not wishing to follow the coastline which would have taken us far inland, we determined to build rafts. Our past adventures on the water caused several of the men trepidation, but crossing this bay by raft was judged a lesser risk than venturing inland.

With an hour of light still left, we launched the rafts, and had not traveled a quarter of the distance when a swift current took us, carrying the vessels a full league to sea. One of the rafts, the one holding Estrada, Tostado, Chaves and Gutierrez, struck against a great boulder and broke apart. The rest of us being hard put to save our own lives, and the current swift, the four men were pulled under and so drowned. How it was that the two surviving rafts made land, I find it difficult to remember. All was confusion. Surely a score of times waves broke

255

upon us, pulling the very clothing from our backs. There were reefs and other great boulders, and the light was fast fading, yet somehow we guided the crafts into quiet water, and then sailed for shore. That eight of us survived this tempestuous crossing must be counted as a miracle.

XXXIV

Exhausted to the point of collapse, having lost most of our clothing, weighted with the blackest of depressions, our bruised hands and feet bleeding, we camped on the shore. Clouds of insects descended upon us. So bowed with exhaustion and dejection had we become that the appearance of several Indian warriors on the rise did not cause concern. And had the Indians come down upon us, I doubt if a single man would have offered defense. But such is the buoyancy of man, made as he is in the Almighty's image, that by morning we had regained a portion of our strength and with this came hope, and with hope, determination.

We broke our fast as best we could on crabs of the same poor variety, then each man of the company, not excepting the two captains, was shriven by the clergyman.

An hour past sunrise, after offering a final prayer for the souls of our lost companions, and after binding our bruises, we again started southward. I walked alongside Francisco de Leon, whose appearance was more that of a corpse than a living man. His teeth chattered, and he trembled despite the mild weather. Had I not supported him, he would have fallen before half a league. Only five days had passed since, still filled with vigor, he had spoken of the woman with whom he quartered, and here he was, reduced to this pitiful condition.

"It grows warm, my friend," I said, hoping to cheer him. But his only answer was a shudder. "Ten days, no more than two weeks, must bring us to Christian civilization," I lied. "I have heard Pánuco is a lively place." Again the man shuddered. "Once there, my friend," I gave him my arm for support, "once we are in a land ruled by the Spanish crown, you can gain your discharge from this expedition, even a compensation for your many months of service. Then, if it is still your wish," I turned my head and winked at the man, "if not tempted by the ripe maidens living in that town, you can return to your Indian woman—to setting weirs in the lagoon."

"To my Indian woman," Francisco de Leon answered in a whisper.

In this way, the man leaning on me for support, which proved to be no burden, for he made every effort to stay erect, we traveled four leagues, reaching the estuary of another river in the early afternoon. Had it been necessary to travel half a dozen leagues inland, we would have done so rather than risk another crossing. But, exploring the estuary, we found sand bars and shallows, and the tide being out, it was judged safe enough to cross. It was then that Francisco de Leon, seeking a place to relieve his body urgings, fell into a pit of sucking sand and was lost before we could reach him.

Had I not been restrained by the two captains, I would have jumped into the pit after him, trusting the others to pull me out. But it would have been a futile gesture, for only the man's twitching fingers were seen when we arrived at the pit, and they disappeared a moment after.

As I crossed the estuary, my back could not have been more bent had I carried the living man than it was by his memory. Always in the deaths of others is the warning of your own.

As it was with me, so it must have been with the officers—

all who were left were of commissioned rank. They, too, moved out across the estuary with bowed heads and bent shoulders.

"To be sucked into the mud is no fitting death for a Spanish soldier," muttered Diego Dorantes, who, of all the officers, had used Francisco de Leon the most roughly. "A pike or sword-thrust, a well-placed arrow, even the blow of a mace should have been the way his life was ended. But to be choked to death by sand," the man shuddered.

"The four who drowned made a better end of it than that one," Diego de Huelva added.

"To drown in water or to drown in sand." . . . Andres Dorantes shrugged his shoulders.

"Many an honorable man came to his end in water, my cousin," Diego Dorantes answered. "It is the way of death for most sailors. But to be drawn down into the earth like an insect caught in honey—an ugly death."

"Yet how should one like Francisco de Leon perish in water?" asked Andres Dorantes with half a grin. "Never in his life did he go near that stuff—if ever there was a man destined for sand or mud, it was Francisco de Leon."

"You speak the sad truth," Diego de Huelva sighed, also with a half grin.

"If we need fear only the elements for which we have an affinity," Alonso del Castillo forced his voice to sound stern, "then you, Diego de Huelva, may venture upon the water even in the fiercest storm."

"Alas, my friend," Andres Dorantes pinched his nostrils and made a wry face, "as Alonso says, you mistook your calling when you took arms as a soldier. As a sailor, you could have been certain to die in bed."

"Is it fitting that the living make jests of the dead?" Pedro de Valdevieso, he who seldom spoke, asked in a stern voice.

"Is it fitting!" Alonso del Castillo turned to the man. "Rather by a thousand times would I have my friends make jest of me when I am gone, saying, Do you remember when Alonso

258

did this thing or that, than I should be forgot. For men such as we," he looked at the other man, a frown tightening his features, "for ones so calloused by adversity, the jest may be the only language of affection that is left."

"Then I give my oath to try my hand at wit when you have fallen," Pedro de Valdevieso answered, but in such a way that it could not be determined if he were serious or making sport. "I will recall how, when you were alive, each time you grew excited you passed your hand across your eyes." Alonso del Castillo quickly dropped his hand. "I will mention how you frowned and lowered your features so as not to lose authority—you being such a pretty man." At this, the others laughed, but Alonso del Castillo's face darkened.

"You do not grow angry, my friend?" Andres Dorantes winked at the man. "Pedro only speaks of the affection he will show when you are gone. As you just said, for such as we the jest is affection's language." Alonso del Castillo started to raise his hand, but before it reached his eyes, he forced it down.

I listened to the exchanges of the officers with little amusement. That within another week I, too, might be dead was no idle speculation, and I obtained poor comfort that one or another of my companions would prove their little love for me with ribaldry. Perhaps I gained a certain comfort by sorrowing for Francisco de Leon—to be able to sorrow, if nothing else, is proof that one yet lives. But the ribaldry continued as we made our way through the shallows and across the sandbars, and no one was safe from this sport. Even Governor Narvaez, whose bones must have long since sunk to the depths, fell butt to their amusement as they spoke of his imprisonment by Hernan Cortez and how he lost his eye. The only name they failed to mention was Alvar Nuñez, and I swear, had any one dared, despite my inferior rank, that one would have had me to contend with.

An hour of moderately easy travel across the sandbars brought us to the far bank of the estuary, where we found a boat of apparently civilized manufacture turned bottom-up and half-buried in the sand. How great was our excitement at finding this token that we might be nearing Christian lands cannot be described. The clergyman fell to his knees and started praying. Tears welled from Diego de Huelva's eyes. Andres Dorantes pulled at his beard with such force I could not see how he did not tear it from his chin. And it was as if a cold wind suddenly blew upon us, for the limbs of every man trembled.

Thirty minutes of frantic digging freed the vessel, and each minute our excitement grew, as we became more and more certain that the craft was made by Christian hands. Finally we had the boat free, and we turned it over. It was the boat of Friar Xuarez and the controller, Alonso Enriquez. We knew this from a cross the friar had emblazoned on the port gunwale, and from Alonso Enriquez' family shield that he had inscribed on the other side.

Had the vessel still been seaworthy, we might have been better able to bear our disappointment, but the timbers were rotted beyond use. So it was that each of us wandered off a little distance by himself, each to deal in his own way with his dejection. Had I had an ax or dared to risk my sword, I would have gained a little comfort by splintering that hulk. It was as if some malevolent force had led us to the foundered craft just to tease us. "Have we not suffered enough!" I hissed through clenched teeth at the thorny bushes and crumbling rocks. "If we must die, we must. But to torment us with a moment of hope—that we reached Christian lands." But then suddenly there came the thought—although the craft was lost, the men who sailed it may yet live! It reached this shore in safety; there were no signs of damage. Thus, why should not at least some of the men be yet alive?

It was as if each of us at that same moment had this thought, for as I turned and ran for the boat, shouting, others came running, also shouting.

No roast of venison could have revived our vigor as did this speculation. Diego Dorantes' sallow face suffused with color.

Alonso del Castillo showed such energy that he hopped from foot to foot. Even Pedro de Valdevieso lessened his somberness and eagerly rubbed his hands together.

"As we quartered with Indians, so may those who landed in this boat!" Andres Dorantes shouted. "And if sinful men such as we survived, how should our commissary and his friars, who all are holy men, fail to remain alive?"

"I cannot be certain," Pedro de Valdevieso continued to rub his hands, "but I will risk my chance of salvation if we do not meet up with Spanish Christians before this world grows one week older."

"As soon as that?" excitement caused Alonso del Castillo to relax his features, revealing the comeliness of the man. "Do you truly believe, Pedro, that we will join with our comrades within a week?"

"A week," he answered with great authority, "a week, unless good fortune has guided them on to Pánuco, and then we may expect to find markings and other directions that we can follow."

"Pánuco," Diego Dorantes whispered, making the sign of the cross. "I will light a hundred votive candles—I swear to do this—in the first church we reach." He placed his hand on the cross emblazoned on the gunwale of the hulk. "I will fall to my knees at such time as I first see the spires of the city, and on my knees I will walk the full distance to that church."

Then, as if a portent of good fortune, at that moment a tortoise, greater in size than any I had ever seen, stepped from the ocean. Thus it was we were spared eating those evil-tasting crabs and supped on the tender meat of that blessed creature.

XXXV

The six leagues that lay between the place we found the abandoned boat and the next bay were covered the following day as if we, like the messenger-god of the Greeks, had wings growing on our feet. Yet this was no easy country to traverse, being a land strewn with boulders, choked with cactus, and everywhere we heard the rattle of serpents. But hope, a good night's sleep, and the roast meat of the tortoise had so revived us that even Diego Dorantes, who had appeared to be failing, traveled easily.

Despite the loss of the four men, such was our excitement I am certain we would have again built rafts and risked this next body of water. But another portent of what we judged to be our rising fortunes offered us a better way. For we found a small band of gentle Indians fishing, who, after showing us every mark of friendship, offered to cross us in their canoes.

We then, keeping in sight of the ocean, traveled four days across a barren land cut by arroyos and so thick with cactus that our forward progress was slowed to no more than four leagues a day. Yet we gave thanks that the weather was mild, and that we did not starve, for everywhere we found crabs scurrying along the sand.

No men, except those whose eyes are dazzled with the glories of the Lord, can maintain excitement for four days of hard travel; and so it was with the five officers, the priest and the freed slave of Azemmour. By the second day our excitement flagged. By the third, our spirits began to sink. And by the fourth day, not having come across a sign of the Spaniards, or

262

met up with any Indians who might give us information, our temperament was little different than it had been before discovering the hulk. If any man still possessed a remnant of passion that fourth day, a north wind that began to blow in the afternoon must have taken it from him. So violent did the gusts become, that to save our eyes from blowing sand and fragments of sharp twigs, we huddled in a tight circle, our heads bowed, our faces shielded by our hands.

"I have had my fill of wind and ugly weather!" Diego de Huelva snarled suddenly. "And my feet are so bruised, each step has become a torture."

"Mine, too, are bruised, and also numb," muttered Diego Dorantes. "It is as if my legs ended below the knees. But with me, all the pain has now risen to my back."

"Old women!" muttered Alonso del Castillo. "Crones complaining of their infirmities—and you call yourselves men, pah!"

"If Asturiano will offer a prayer for my cousin's tortured back and that other one's poor feet . . . " laughed Andres Dorantes. "And if this should fail," he made a clucking sound, "then we must prepare a litter. You are strong, Estevanico," he nudged my arm, "will you carry two delicate officers?"

"Two old women hiding in officers' skins," Alonso del Castillo added.

"As Alonso says, Estevanico," laughed Andres Dorantes. "And their being women, mayhap you will have a chance to service them."

"Take care, Andres!" Diego Dorantes' voice took on an ugly edge. "Do not presume upon the fact that we are cousins."

"I am cousin to Diego Dorantes, a soldier who let the blood of a score of Turkish pirates, not to some frail woman who moans of her aching back."

A violent gust of wind interrupted this conversation, and with this gust came a quantity of what appeared to be dry bushes, tumbling across the ground. And not one of us escaped scratches from the sharp twigs.

"What will be next!" shouted Diego de Huelva, as he struggled to free himself of a clinging bush. "Must we expect a plague of toads and then of locusts? Or will the earth just open up and swallow us!"

"If you be swallowed, Diego," laughed Alonso del Castillo, who also struggled with a clinging bush, "you will not be digested, I can promise you. One taste and you must be disgorged—so you are safe."

"As was Francisco de Leon?"

These words caused a silence to descend, and for a time we sat, our heads still bowed, listening to the wind. The silence was broken by Diego Dorantes, whose voice took on a heavy tone.

"If needs be, this one will willingly travel another score of days to reach Pánuco. If needs be, this one will suffer without complaining whatever adversities God, in His greater wisdom, brings upon us, if then we reach Pánuco. But," he paused for a moment and stared at the two captains, "do we travel in the right direction?"

I grew cold as I listened to the man.

"How should we travel, Diego?" Alonso del Castillo asked slowly. "Do you suggest another direction?" Diego Dorantes shook his head.

"Why do you doubt the direction we have taken, my cousin?" Andres Dorantes then asked.

"Cousin, why should I not doubt it? Have we ever, since that day when the Governor ordered the ships to sail north to the port of Pánuco—those ships we never saw again—have we ever since that day been certain in which direction that city lay?"

"Yet we travel south," Pedro de Valdevieso murmured, "and should Pánuco lie to the north?"

"Alvar Nuñez ordered the four to travel south until they came to Pánuco," Alonso del Castillo answered in a strong voice.

"The four?" Diego de Huelva's voice contained a question. "I do not understand."

264

"Has your mind softened, Diego? Have you forgotten, Alvaro Fernandez, Mendez, Astudillo, he of Cafra, and Figueroa?" answered Alonso del Castillo.

"I had forgotten—my mind has softened," the man hesitated. "But how can we know if Alvar Nuñez ordered them in the right direction?"

"He commanded this expedition!" Andres Dorantes snapped at the man. "Do you dare to question your commander?"

"Alvar Nuñez is dead. I cannot question a dead man." Again there was silence, and despite the wind having died down, we still huddled in the tight circle.

After a passage of what must have been nearly five minutes, there being no break in the silence, I determined to test if in truth I was a free man, by offering an opinion. "If I may be permitted." Hearing no objection, I went on. "Pánuco, being a port, must be on the coast." I glanced to see if the officers listened. "We therefore can be certain we are either to the north or to the south of that place." Andres Dorantes nodded. "We have already traveled no less than fifty leagues since departing the Indian village—should we turn north we must again cover those fifty leagues to reach our starting place. Yet, if we had evidence that Pánuco lay to the north, we could do nothing else." As I spoke, I found myself strengthened by my words. "But we have no evidence that Pánuco lies behind us. What little evidence we have goes to the contrariwise." All the officers leaned forward. "If the four survived, they must have, in time, reached Pánuco, or, failing this after traveling a sufficient distance, turned back."

"And we must have met them!" Andres Dorantes added.

"Met them, my captain, or at the very least found their markings, for it is certain they would have left markings," I continued. "And what of the survivors of the vessel that we found?" I allowed myself a smile and gestured with my hands. "Only if we find that death claimed the four and that none from the vessel of Friar Xuarex survived, will we not be certain that

265

Pánuco lies to the south." It took several questions, which I carefully answered, for the others to have my meaning. But before two minutes all, not excepting the clergyman, were grinning, and different ones had clapped me on the shoulder.

When we reached the next bay, fortune led us to an abandoned Indian war canoe; thus, after much exertion, we crossed and continued with our journey. Another three days and twelve more leagues brought us to a rise where, in the middle distance, we saw yet another body of water, the sixth, which must be crossed. As before, dejection and a certain sullenness had settled upon us, and we had traveled in silence since that morning. But when we topped the rise our dejection vanished, for in the league of land that lay ahead we saw evidence of human habitation.

"Yours is the keenest sight, Estevanico," Andres Dorantes said excitedly. "Tell us what you see."

Shading my eyes, I strained my vision—"There are three fires burning along an inlet of the bay, but no dwellings."

"Yes, I, too, can see them!" shouted Alonso del Castillo, hopping from foot to foot. "What else, black man, what else?"

"I cannot be sure if it is the dazzle of the sun," I squeezed my lids shut for a moment, "but I believe there is movement amongst the bushes along the bank, as if from a gathering of human beings."

"It is not the sun's dazzle," Diego Dorantes pounded my shoulder, "I, too, can see the movement."

"What sort of human beings, Négro?" Alonso del Castillo gripped my arm with such strength that, had I not forced myself to remember that he was captain, I must have answered this show of affection with proof of my own.

"If you will permit me, my captain," I forced a laugh and pulled my arm free. "Even for the black Moor, a league is no little distance to distinguish the savage from the Christian." Again I shaded my eyes and strained my vision. "It is certain that some of them are Indians—I can see women with bared breasts."

266

"Christian women do not go about with their breasts bared," Asturiano murmured.

"But there are others," I saw skins that appeared lighter in color than those of the Indians, "if it is not the reflection of the sun . . . " I hesitated.

"Tell us at once what you see, Estevan!" Andres Dorantes ordered as if I were still a slave.

"If it is not the reflection of the sun," I repeated, "it may be that there are different ones with fair skins."

"Christians!" shouted Diego de Huelva. "We have come to the land of Christians."

"Are they Christians, Estevan?" Alonso del Castillo's voice cracked as he asked the question. "If you tell me they are Christians, I will give you a gift of my sword."

Using every atom of concentration, I forced my eyesight— "I cannot say that they are Christians," I finally muttered. "I cannot even say with certainty they have fair skins."

"What does this ignorant black man know!" shouted Diego de Huelva. "Unless he is close enough to sniff, he cannot distinguish between the ass and the horse. They are Christians!"

"May it be God's will that they are Christians," murmured the clergyman. "May it be the will of the Almighty that we have come to the end of our journey." To this every man whispered, Amen.

An hour of cautious travel, each man holding his unsheathed sword in his hand, brought us to the place where the three fires were burning. But our approach, despite our caution, had been detected, and when we arrived, the bushes where we had seen the movement were deserted. A quick search, and we found baskets containing mulberries, and then we knew that the creatures we had seen were not Christians, for the baskets were of Indian manufacture, and why should Christians flee at our approach?

Urged on by Alonso del Castillo, we hurried along the bank of the inlet until we reached the bay. There, we saw several canoes filled with women, putting out from shore; but by the time we arrived at the water they were too distant. Waving our hands and using every sort of word of endearment, we tried to coax them back, but they quickly crossed the bay, which was no more than an arrow-shot in width, and disappeared into the bushes on the far side.

The leaden weight of disappointment had not yet fully settled upon us when, from around a point of land, came a canoe paddled by two men. Twilight having descended, we could not see the features of the men, but the canoe made straight for the place where we were standing.

It was Figueroa, together with an Indian.

XXXVI

We wept. Before the vessel reached the shore all were weeping. Since childhood I had not shed such tears. And how we embraced the man—I must have kissed his cheeks and pumped his hands a dozen times. And how he returned our embraces—his tears mixed with ours, his kisses rained on our cheeks and lips and eyes, and his two hands pumped and pounded. Even the Indian came in for his share of embraces. Then we showered Figueroa with questions, but so great was his emotion several minutes passed before he could make reply.

Yet even before he said his first coherent word we suffered a dampening of our passion, for when asked were we near Christian lands, he shook his head. And he gave this same answer to the question, had he reached Pánuco.

It was as we crossed the bay in his canoe, and then shared a meal of fish and mulberries with the man, that we learned from him what had happened to the four men sent to seek Pánuco, together with other things concerning Governor Narvaez, Friar Xuarez and different members of the expedition.

His hands shaking, his face the color of wet ash, swallowing between every third word, Figueroa attempted to satisfy our questions. He told us how he and his three companions traveled south and had gotten no further toward Pánuco than the sixth bay, when cold killed the Portuguese, also Astudillo, he of Cafra, and the Indian guide. He told us how he and his surviving companion, Mendez, were then taken by the Indians and how, while with them, Mendez fled, going as well as he could in the direction of Pánuco. Then he told of the Indians' pursuit of that man, and how they came up to him and slew him.

It was while living with these Indians that Figueroa gained information of a Christian living among the Mariames, a nation on the far side of the bay. It was from this Christian, one Hernando de Esquivel, that he learned the fate of the other members of the expedition.

From Esquivel, Figueroa learned that the Governor steered his vessel along the coast, after pulling away from the craft commanded by Alvar Nuñez. Arriving at a bay formed by the confluence of two rivers, the Governor discovered Friar Xuarez, the comptroller, and their men camped on a point of land, their vessel having been swamped. When discovered, one-third had already died from the inclemency of the weather, the rest suffering grievously. Crossing the survivors over to the main, the Governor ordered all to go into camp, the weather having grown too boisterous for travel. After declaring Captain Juan Pantoja to be second-in-command, the Governor then went back aboard his vessel, together with the coxswain and a page, offering as his reason an indisposition of the bowels which could only be relieved by the water's rocking motion. In the morning, the craft was gone and the men never knew more of their commander.

Esquivel then told Figueroa of the depression all the survivors suffered when the disappearance of the captain's boat was discovered—even the chief officers walked about with hunched shoulders and bowed heads. He related how, after the passage of several days, it was finally determined to pursue the journey south, the place where they camped being unfit for further habitation. But after traveling little more than another thirty leagues, the onset of winter caused the band to go into permanent camp in a wood bordering a bay where there was fresh water, fuel and some few shellfish and crabs. This wood had been inhabited by Indians who fled across the bay with all their possessions at the approach of the Christians. It was in these woods that the Spaniards began to die, one by one, camped as they were with no shelter except that of their own poor manufacture. And added to this distress was the increasingly severe abuse by Captain Juan Pantoja, who reviled and savagely beat different men with little cause. So severe grew this captain's abuse, from which friars, even officers, were not excepted, that Soto Mayor, who had not forgotten his quarrel with the man over the slave, Chichi, took up a club and struck him, killing him instantly. Thus did the number in the band go on diminishing; the living drying the flesh of those that died for food. The last to die was Soto Mayor, whose flesh was preserved by Esquivel. Feeding on it, that one survived until the first of March, when an Indian tribe that dwelt across the bay found the man and rescued him.

Figueroa's story having ended, we made camp on a point of land across the bay. There I lay, as did the others, staring up at the stars, with the words of the man still whispering in my ears. And bit by bit those few shreds of hope I yet preserved dissolved, and I grew certain we never in this world would reach Pánuco.

XXXVII

The fire crumbled from the lack of wood, yet despite the chill that came with the gathering darkness, not one of us made a move to replenish it. Soon there were only glowing embers, whose dull light scarcely outlined the forms of the huddled men. To the east, past the point of land that formed the entrance to the bay, came the muffled sounds of the ocean. The embers hissed. A crow rose from its perch on a fire-blackened tree and cried out to the darkening sky. It was then that the Indian who had been in the boat with Figueroa signalled to the man to come with him.

With lowered head and hunched shoulders, Figueroa arose and started slowly toward the water. "Where do you go, my friend?" asked Alonso del Castillo, who had not seen the Indian signal. Figueroa hesitated, pointed at the savage, and then nodded toward a wood across the bay. "Rest with us this night; in the morning we will accompany you," the captain spoke in a kind voice, but one that held elements of an order. Figueroa shook his head, and continued walking slowly toward the water.

"Did you not hear a captain order you to stay with us until morning?" said Andres Dorantes, in a rough voice he then softened with a laugh. "Or do you prefer the company of pagan Indians to that of old companions?" This last he said in a gentler manner.

"I cannot stay," Figueroa mumbled, as he continued slowly toward the water.

"Must an old soldier again be taught the meaning of obedience!" this time Andres Dorantes made no attempt to soften the harshness of his voice. "Have these months spent in this wilderness caused you to forget your discipline?" Figueroa stopped, then turned and faced the Spaniards.

"If I do not go with him," he gestured with a quick motion towards the Indian, "others will come and shoot arrows into my legs and arms—mayhap kill me." Alonso del Castillo sucked in his breath. "Mendez ran from them and they caught him, tortured him, then slew him. I do not wish to be tortured, my captains," his voice broke. "I do not want to be slain."

"Tortured! Slain!" Alonso del Castillo hissed, drawing his sword. "You are a Spaniard, Figueroa, a Spaniard and a Christian—as long as we have our weapons . . ." All the others except Asturiano, the clergyman, muttered their agreement.

"You are seven, armed only with swords," Figueroa's voice began to rise. "They are ten score, with bows that will send a shaft through a tree thicker than a man's thigh! Although once a Spanish soldier and a Christian, I am become a slave to Indians." With that, he quickly turned away and continued walking toward the water.

Just as he was about to step into the boat, Asturiano cried out for him to wait. Then, muttering some words about a Christian in peril of losing his immortal soul, about serving Christ where he was needed most, the clergyman snatched up his few belongings and ran toward the water.

It was all a matter of only several moments, during which we were frozen with surprise and confusion. Then the boat pulled away from shore carrying Figueroa, Asturiano and the Indian out into the darkness.

Had the clergyman struck each of us with a club he could not have stunned us more than he did by his abrupt departure. One moment he sat quietly amongst us, now he was gone.

272

"And I did nothing to stop him," murmured Diego de Huelva, turning his face away from the little light cast by the glowing embers. "The best of us, a priest, and I did nothing to stop him."

"A Spanish soldier serving as a slave to Indians," muttered Andres Dorantes, "and now a priest. Christians feasting on Christian flesh . . ."

"Five louse-bitten Spaniards and one Moorish Négro—all that are left of three hundred," Diego Dorantes joined his mutterings to those of his cousin. For several minutes there were other mutterings, then silence as the embers in the firepit turned to ash and grew cold.

XXXVIII

Morning found the six of us still huddled around the firepit. Night dew dripped from our beards and wet our clothing, but no one seemed to care. Although awake for almost an hour, not one of us had stirred; if not for our labored breathing, we might have been stones carved in the likeness of men, staring with empty eyes at the cold ashes. As the night had been signalled by a crow, so was the morning. Again and again the black bird, riding rising currents of air, cried out to the orange sun.

"Black bird of Satan!" croaked Diego Dorantes, droplets of spittle forming on his cracked lips. "We are plagued by the devil's spawn—they will give us no peace." Then, in a passionless voice, he began to curse all creatures sprung from hell, saying their names one by one.

"Do you include amongst your accursed creatures five lousy Spaniards and one giant Négro?" growled Diego de Huelva. "For if it is not from Hell that we are sprung, it is from an even worser place."

"Sprung from Hell, and to Hell we at last return," Pedro de Valdevieso made a sweeping gesture with his arm. "In these woods Christians consumed Christians. . . . " His voice was lost in a low mutter.

A warm wind blowing from across the bay brought to our ears the distant sound of drums. The wind stirred the forest, causing a branch of a rotted tree to fall with a loud report. A cloud floated across the sun, casting a shadow on the clearing where we were camped.

"Have we traveled to a land so distant that we are beyond God's protection?" asked Diego de Huelva, in a dull voice. Except for a single shoulder-shrug by Andres Dorantes, there was no answer. The cloud passed the sun, and the clearing again filled with light.

"Do we go on?" Diego Dorantes' head rested in his hands, and he slurred his words. "Have we come to the end of our journey, or do we again seek to reach Pánuco?"

"If I were certain in which direction Pánuco lay . . . " muttered Alonso del Castillo. "To struggle southward another sixty leagues, and then find that we are sixty leagues more distant. . . . "

"Yet if we should reverse our direction," offered Andres Dorantes, "we must again pass the Indians of the village where we were quartered—and how can we be certain that we then travel in the right direction?"

"You remain silent, Négro," growled Diego de Huelva. For several minutes he had been watching me with narrowed eyes. "If my memory serves me, not many days since you had much to say about this very matter; yet now, when your learned

274

counsel is most needed, you are silent." Knowing of the man's dislike for me, I was careful to offer him no offense. "Tell us, Estevanico, in which direction we must travel to reach Pánuco?" Diego de Huelva's voice took on a dangerous edge, and I eased my hand towards a club I kept hidden beneath my blanket. "Must the officer ask the Négro a question for the second time?" He drew his sword and tested the keenness of its blade. The other four Spaniards said nothing and made no move. "One last time will I beg you for your wise advice, Négro." He rose up until he rested on one knee. "One last time will this one offer you supplication, you ebon-skinned son of Satan who mocks his masters. One last time will I await with gentle patience your answer to my question." As he finished speaking, his lips curled back, exposing his blackened teeth. Having no answer to make, I stayed silent. For several seconds, he stared at me, then suddenly he sprang to his feet and lunged.

Twisting away from his blade, I got to my feet, the club in one hand, my sword in the other. Diego de Huelva's face had turned the color of butchered meat, and his blade quivered in his upraised arm. For perhaps as long as three seconds, we faced each other, then his blade came sweeping down. Leaping backwards and to one side, I caused the weapon to strike harmless. Then, with careful precision, I delivered a blow to the man's chest with my club, tumbling him to the ground, where he lay gasping and moaning.

Uttering a furious oath, Diego Dorantes freed his weapon and came at me. It was only a matter of a single moment before he, too, lay on the ground gasping and moaning. And not one of the remaining three made the slightest move to render assistance to either of the fallen men.

For several seconds I faced the seated men with my weapons ready, uncertain if they intended to help their fallen comrades. But seeing in their faces that their intentions were otherwise, I lowered my sword and club, although my choler still was high. "The time has passed when I will be treated other than as a man," I spoke in a voice which passion caused to crack and hiss. "I have taken an oath never to kill again; do not force me to break this oath."

"As you say, Estevan," Alonso del Castillo made a careful answer. "The time is past when you can be treated other than as a man." He paused for a moment. "And the time has also passed when one man should be captain over another." He slowly brushed his hand over his eyes, "I do not know what you intend to do, Andres," he nodded at the man, "but I resign my commission; and from this moment recognize each one as equal to the other."

"I, too, resign my commission," said Andres Dorantes, but there was a certain hesitancy in his voice. "As Alonso says, it is no longer needful for one to be captain over the other. But to count a black man as equal to a Castilian. . . . " he shook his head slowly.

"From the demonstration this black man has just given, he has proven himself more than equal to the Castilian," laughed Pedro de Valdevieso.

"In another place—in the past—I would have had you flayed for having laid violent hands on Spanish officers, Estevanico," said Alonso del Castillo carefully. "But now, I must thank you for your gentleness with these two mad ones," he nodded at the fallen men. "I would have treated them less gently given your provocation. By only using your club when they attacked with swords, you have earned my gratitude."

"And mine, Estevan," added Andres Dorantes. "When they regain their senses, mayhap they, too, will thank you. But if they should continue to suffer from their insanity and plot to do you harm," he directed his words to the two men, "then I must warn them that any injury done to the one who was once my slave is an injury done to me."

"And an injury also to me," said Alonso del Castillo. He hesitated a moment, then continued, "But I pray that the medicine they just tasted has cured them of their lunacy." He reached out a hand to Diego de Huelva, who had risen to his knees, and rested it for a moment on his shoulder. "We are a remnant of six, lost in this wilderness, my friend," his voice softened. "It is madness for us to quarrel." He then dipped a gourd full of water and passed it to Diego Dorantes, who still labored for his breath. "If we are to survive for even a little time, we must be as brothers." Diego Dorantes took a sip, coughed, then inclined his head. But Diego de Huelva, in the tightness of his features and in the cords of his neck, still showed anger.

A hawk, hovering high above, suddenly plummeted down with a rush of wings, impaling with its talons a hare who uncautiously browsed on the far side of the clearing away from the woods' protection.

"Are we to be like that hare?" gestured Diego de Huelva. Pallor had replaced the tightness of his features. "We are only six!" It was as if he saw the five of us for the first time. "We are lost in this land of savages—and we are only six!" As if to provide an answer, a fresh wind again brought drum sounds from across the bay. The man began to tremble as beads of sweat formed on his forehead. "If ever there was a time we needed your strength, black man, it is now." The man's trembling increased and saliva dripped from the corners of his mouth. "As Alonso said, I suffered from a fit of madness. Can you forgive me, Négro?"

A second hare emerged from the woods, hesitated in the shadows testing the air with its quivering nostrils, then darted to the same clump of vegetation on which the first hare had been feeding. All of us raised our eyes to the sky—there was no hawk.

"Have you not heard of the fate of your brother?" Diego de Huelva addressed the furry creature in a voice that cracked with every word. "Everywhere there is danger—go and hide!" He glanced up at the sky again.

"Some hares escape the hawk," Pedro de Valdevieso said slowly. "There are a few grown so quick and wise that they live

277

to a great age and die peacefully in their beds, surrounded by their children." The man grinned, a thing it was not his wont to do. "Six hundred left Spain, if I do not misremember," his grin grew broader, "and we are six." He slowly nodded, as if this fact contained a special meaning. "Not all hares die and not all Christian soldiers." He winked slyly, his hollow cheeks showing patches of crimson. "Perhaps it is that we are chosen—six, when once there were six hundred," again he nodded.

"If that hare feeding on the very spot where its brother died is not taken, it is a sign," whispered Diego de Huelva. Different ones of us again glanced up at the sky. "We will survive if he safely reaches the woods; but we must do nothing to hasten his departure, else we destroy the sign." Pedro de Valdevieso nodded, as did Diego Dorantes. "See," whispered Diego de Huelva, "he stands on grass stained with the other's blood and is unconcerned."

The hare stood up on its hind legs and pulled down a leaf-laden twig with its front paws. With quick bites, it stripped the twig, then started to comb its whiskers. Rising up again, it pulled down a second twig, this one more heavily laden than the first. "Have you not consumed enough at one sitting, you greedy creature," Diego Dorantes muttered softly. The hare stripped the second twig then hopped away several paces. All of us breathed more deeply.

"Go take your siesta in the woods," Pedro de Valdevieso murmured. "After eating, it is always wise to sleep." The hare again combed its whiskers, then scratched vigorously with one hind leg at the ground. It then raised its head, sniffed in all directions, and hopped back to the clump of vegetation. As if we all were one, the six of us raised our eyes to the sky. In the distance, past the point of land that formed the entrance to the bay, there was a black dot.

"You have eaten enough!" Diego Dorantes hissed at the hare through his clenched teeth.

278

"If you frighten it, you destroy the sign," warned Pedro de Valdevieso, bringing a forefinger to his lips. The hare hopped to one side of the clump of vegetation, sniffed at the twigs, then hopped back to the place where the leaves were thickest. It reached up and started toying with a twig. The spot of black had moved in closer, until it was directly over the point of land. The hare took several bites at the twig, then again scratched with its hind leg at the ground. The black dot hung motionless over the point of land.

"You are in danger, little creature," Andres Dorantes murmured softly. "Move into the shadows, or you will perish before this world grows five minutes older." The hare hopped behind the clump of vegetation where it could not be seen. The spot of black now hovered halfway between the point of land and the clearing.

"The bird is yet too distant to have seen him." Doubt rang in Diego Dorantes' voice. "Not even a hawk has such keenness of vision." The hare appeared from behind the vegetation, chewing on a stalk of grass. It moved out into the full sunlight and started scratching itself.

"You are careless of your life, foolish creature." Alonso del Castillo forced his whispered words through his clenched teeth. "I order you to leave this clearing!" The black dot drifted in the direction of the clearing, taking on the shape of a hawk.

"In the name of the Holy Virgin, begone!" Diego de Huelva mumbled into his cupped hand. "In one more minute . . . " The hawk hovered directly overhead. Suddenly the hare raised its head for a moment, and then as if hurled from a sling rushed for the woods, just as the bird started to descend.

Had the little creature had the chance to make one more leap, it would have escaped. . . .

"Feathered devil!" screamed Diego de Huelva, as he leapt up and rushed at the hawk with his unsheathed sword.

"Skewer the bird, Diego!" bellowed Diego Dorantes. Diego de Huelva hurled his weapon at the rising hawk, missing it by less than the distance of a single span. Then, screaming curses at the disappearing bird, he snatched up his sword and started slashing at nearby bushes, showering twigs and leaves in every direction.

"We have had our sign," murmured Pedro de Valdevieso, "but it was not the one we wished." A bank of clouds risen from the eastern horizon, at that moment, reached the sun. Its first thin wisps passing over the shimmering surface cast faint shadows on the clearing. Moment by moment, the brightness dimmed as denser clouds spread westward. Soon the sun was an orange ball struggling to send its dull light through the thickening cover; then it was gone.

A sudden shift of wind brought the salt smell of the ocean, and caused the drum-sounds to fade until they could not be told from the muffled sounding of the surf. I was certain that a storm was about to break, and warned the other men. But instead of seeking shelter in the woods, it was determined to explore along the shore—my warning of a storm which must bring tides, the others dismissed with shrugs.

We had covered the half league to the rocky point of land which formed the entrance to the bay, and had started toward its far end, drawn by a flock of nesting birds, when the storm broke. On the ocean side of the point of land, the wind whipped up the surf. In moments the waves crashed all around us. How we found our way off that point of land into a cave formed by an overhanging cliff, only the Lord God Himself can ever know.

Not one of us escaped injury. But that not one of us broke a bone or lost his teeth must be counted as a miracle, so severe had been our buffeting. Each of us trembled as blood ran from our nostrils and blood-tinged saliva from our lips. Our hair and beards were matted and our garments so torn we were more naked than clothed. Not one of us had retained his blanket, and Pedro de Valdevieso had lost his sword.

Although no more than three hours earlier I had faced Diego de Huelva's weapon, I could not help feeling for the man when he began to weep. As a hurt child, ashamed to be seen crying by his companions, will bury his face in the ground, so Diego de Huelva hid his contorted features in the mud. It was a piteous sight—a brave officer, one who had served with Hernan Cortez, now groveling, half naked. The rest of us, this one included, made uneasy by the man's actions, pretended not to notice, and offered jests about our naked condition.

The ending of the storm in the early afternoon, instead of providing a measure of relief, brought swarms of insects to torture us. Excited by our open bruises, and little hindered by our torn clothing, they bit and stung until we were forced to coat our bodies with mud for protection. "We all are of your race, now, Estevan." Alonso del Castillo struggled to find lightness in the situation. "If you will allow us, we will crown you king." He picked up a vine and started forming it into a crown.

I smiled and nodded, but then suddenly experienced a sharp tightening in the guts.

I looked up, expecting again to see the clouds gathering for a storm—this one even fiercer than the one before. The sky was clear. My eyes quickly searched the ground for vipers, the underbrush for crocodiles. There were only stinging ants and darting lizards. Then I drew my sword. And it was as if my arm in some mysterious fashion was connected with the arms of all of the other men. For my weapon was scarcely clear of its scabbard when the four with swords had drawn them; Pedro de Valdevieso arming himself with a rock and a heavy stick. "What do you see, black man?" Alonso del Castillo whispered. I shook my head, for I could not give an answer.

"Did you hear something, Estevan?" Andres Dorantes brought his lips close to my ear. I shook my head again, and was searching my mind for a reason for my action, when without warning a hundred or more Indian warriors surrounded us. It was as if each tree had somehow disgorged a savage.

Naked except for the deerskin pouch which concealed their parts, bones piercing their lower lips, coarse matted hair

281

that hung below their waists, armed with clubs and spears, they stood staring at us. And we stared back at them. Taller by half a head than the Spaniard, scarred on foreheads, cheeks and chins, blackened teeth and white paint around the eyes, they resembled nothing so much as demons cast up from Hell.

Had the savages attacked, we could not have withstood them, for they were twenty to our one. And as I waited, staring at those demon men, I counted my life as already over. My only determination was to die quickly, not to suffer torture. But they did not attack, nor did they attempt to come closer; they just continued staring. Then, seeing that they did not intend to harm us, at least at that time, and having learned a little of the Indian language, I attempted to address them. It was as if I were a jester with his bladder, whistling and dancing at a fair. For the savages began to laugh and clap their hands, and soon were creating such a din that they drowned my words, so I fell silent. As soon as I ceased to speak, their noise subsided, until we all were as we had been before—they staring at us, we at them.

Judging from their claps and laughter that they were a gentle people, Alonso del Castillo signalled the rest of us to follow him, and he started to lead us out of the circle of staring savages. But as soon as we came up to them, they pushed us back roughly, scratching at our chests with their spears. Thus it was that we began our slavery.

XXXIX

The village to which the Indians took us was not unlike the one where we had quartered for the winter, except that the houses were less well made and contained greater quantities of filth. Reeking piles of refuse, on which their children played and in which their barkless dogs foraged, were scattered everywhere. And the trench used for body urgings was so located that the slightest wind wafted to us its powerful perfume. Their women greeted us, grinning like she-devils and waving stone knives which they used to make pretend passes at our manly parts. And although not uncomely and quite well-formed, they stank. Later I learned that this odor was due in part to grease from the tails of crocodiles which they used as an unguent to repel mosquitos.

Despite our bruises and weakened condition, and without offering us anything to eat or drink, the Indians immediately put us to work. Even Diego de Huelva, whose legs could scarcely support him, was forced to work with us, gathering sticks for their fires. And as we worked, with gestures and by other means, the Indians informed us that if we did not perform our tasks with vigor we would not eat and would also suffer beatings.

When the Indians were less vigilant, I, Alonso del Castillo and Andres Dorantes assisted Diego de Huelva, the other two of our company having problems enough of their own due to sores on their hands and feet. The sticks we gathered being covered with sharp thorns, and the place where we worked swarming with flies and mosquitos, we passed a difficult afternoon. Yet a belief that our condition of slavery was a temporary one, that as soon as our bruises healed we would escape, served to fortify us.

Perhaps as a reminder that we were slaves, or as a means to encourage us to work harder in the future, the Indians administered a severe beating to each of us when we finished working. Diego de Huelva and Diego Dorantes were unable to remain erect as they received their beatings, and sank to their knees, a painful sight to behold. When my turn came there were moments when it took a strong effort of my will to keep my legs from buckling.

This punishment over, the women again came at us playfully with their knives. Having no experience of metal, the Indians had not taken our swords, and at different times as they administered the beatings, as the women came at us, and then when the children started hurling stones and offal, I considered drawing my weapon and exchanging my one life for more than one of theirs. Only my oath not to kill again restrained me. What restrained Alonso del Castillo and Andres Dorantes, I do not know. For in their faces I saw rage that bordered on insanity. Perhaps they restrained themselves with thoughts of the vengeance they would take upon our escape.

"If I must roast in Hell for all eternity, I will open the bellies of not less than a dozen of their women before I quit this village," hissed Andres Dorantes when they finally permitted us to retire to the louse-infested hut allowed us as a shelter.

"You have your dozen women, Andres," Alonso del Castillo spat his words as if they were bits of wormy fruit, "you have your women; I swear by my dead father to slit the throats of a score of their fiercest warriors. And I will piss in each one's face as he expires."

"In a few days, when I recover my strength," Diego de Huelva murmured, drawing all our attention, for he had lain apparently senseless since entering the hut, "in a few days, no more than a week, I will risk my chance of salvation by skewering every last one of their children before I depart this village. Destroy their pups and you wound them worse than if you cut their throats."

In this fashion did the conversation continue as we ate the poor fare the Indians provided us. It was Pedro de Valdevieso who steered the conversation away from vengeance. "Only if we are able to convince these savages that we are grateful to be their slaves and intend to serve them faithfully will we gain the opportunity to escape. Diego spoke of escaping within a week," he nodded at the man, "would that it were possible." He nodded again, this time in agreement with his own words. "We must

284

be prepared to labor for these savages—and put on a good face—we must be prepared to serve as slaves not less than one full month, even two."

"Two months!" Andres Dorantes raised his fist as if to strike the man. "How I controlled this hand from drawing my sword as they came at me with their whips . . . a week of submitting to their abuses will drive me to insanity."

"Is it truly your belief, Pedro, that we must stay with these savages?" asked Alonso del Castillo. "We escaped easily enough from the Indians of the village where we quartered."

"We escaped after we had lived with them four months," was the man's careful answer. "We lay with their women and played with their children—and we were not their slaves. Yet they pursued us and came near taking us; and we were twice our present number—clothed and better armed." To these words of Pedro de Valdevieso all nodded.

Exhaustion, and all that we had suffered, caused the others to sink into sleep moments after the conversation ceased. And had I been able, I would have joined them in that blessed state, for weariness caused my very bones to ache and my muscles to tremble. But I could not sleep. The close darkness and swarming lice of the hut oppressed me, so I eased out of the shelter. Not meeting with any objection—the Indians scarcely seemed to notice me—I walked slowly through the village until I found a place away from the piles of reeking refuse, yet one where I could see most of what was happening.

It was as if with the coming of darkness a calmness settled upon that village. There was no more laughter or wild gestures. Those who spoke at all spoke in the softest whispers. When they moved about, the pace was slow, the movements languid. Most sat around fires kindled throughout the village—each hut having its own fire. They sat close together as if pressed for space, yet there was room enough for twice their number. Later, when my eyes got used to the dimness, I saw the reason for this closeness. Each picked lice from the other, a task which never ceased. A boy who could not have been more than twelve knelt before one of the fires, while a withered Indian whose sex I could only tell by her apron, cut furrows into his cheeks with a bit of sharpened shell. And it was as if the boy felt nothing, for he did not flinch, did not cry out, and showed in his back and shoulders a relaxed posture. When the old woman finished each furrow she filled it with hot ash. Later I learned that this was one way a boy proved himself ready to be a man. The greater his unconcern as he underwent the torture, the more he proved his manhood.

In the dim light of the fires, sitting cross-legged as they were, the Indians appeared less fierce than when I first saw them. It was this diminished fierceness which caused me to approach the group huddled around the fire where the boy was proving his readiness for manhood.

I might have been one born and raised in their village instead of Estevan, a black man of far-off Azemmour, from the way they made room for me. With soft grunts they provided a sufficient space and then, to my amazement, those on either side of me started searching in my hair for lice. How shall I describe the strange feeling that passed through me as their careful fingers explored my hair? A lifetime earlier my head rested in my mother's lap as she gently searched my scalp. "You must taste sweet, my pretty boy," she had whispered as she teased away a tiny creature, "the nits and lice favor you over all my others, so you must taste sweet." Their fingers might have been the fingers of my mother.

The old woman who had been cutting furrows into the boy's cheeks stood in front of me, the bloody bit of sharpened shell between her swollen fingers. She grinned, and pointed at my face. All the other Indians leaned a little in my direction. With a quick movement she flicked the shell against my skin, drawing blood, and I pushed the hag away. My actions caused the Indians amusement, and their laughter brought others from nearby fires. The old woman came at me again, but this time I kept her from getting close. Then, with clicking sounds of her tongue, she pointed at the scars of the warriors sitting on either side of me, and then gestured toward my manly parts; this brought fresh laughter from the Indians. Then for several seconds I considered letting the old woman have at my cheeks—if a boy of twelve could bear the torture . . . I forced the thought away, and pointed to the saber-scar that crossed my cheek from ear to chin. The old woman ran her finger-tip along the scar. Then I showed her the shackle-scars on my wrists and ankles, the branding-scars on my shoulders, the whip-scars on my back. Each scar she tested with her fingertip. Then, as if I suddenly had ceased to exist, she turned away and again directed her attention toward the boy. And so it was with all the other Indians, I might have been a stone or a stick for all the attention they paid me as they continued their never-ending search for lice.

Later that night as I lay, still unable to sleep, in the darkness of the hut, I wondered at my actions—would I have let the hag furrow my cheeks had I not already owned scars enough? "Estevan," I whispered, "beware lest you become a savage little different from these pagan Indians."

XL

If any one of us truly believed he had already experienced the full weight of slavery that first day of our capture, the second day he was to learn how foolish had been this belief. For the Indians, with kicks and blows, drove us into a defile choked with thorny scrub, where we were forced to labor under the full rays of the sun. Thorns tore at our hands and feet, and then, when we carried the bundled sticks back to the village, they bloodied our backs and shoulders. Scorpions and poisonous snakes with their plague-rattle sound dwelt in that defile, and great caution must be exercised lest we receive a fatal sting. With a choked cry Diego de Huelva, struggling under his load of sticks, collapsed and lay senseless. After several kicks with no response, judging him dead, the Indians left him where he lay. But he was not dead, for after a little time he moaned for water, which I brought him despite blows from their fists. We worked on, and there was no respite for us at noon, for those savages took food only in the morning and evening.

Our tasks ended at sunset, and I was forced to carry Diego de Huelva back to the village, for he had again fallen senseless. And Andres Dorantes must support his cousin Diego, that one having fallen ill of the shakes and vomits. But, once back in the village, it was as it had been the night before. The Indians shared their poor provisions with us, and appeared not to care where we wandered. Those of us who so desired could lie with their widowed women. It is my belief that darkness in some mysterious fashion softened these savages, for as long as we stayed with them, they never showed us any harshness after sunset.

This second evening, after making Diego de Huelva and Diego Dorantes as comfortable as possible, Andres Dorantes and Alonso del Castillo joined me for a walk throughout the village—Valdevieso remaining in the hut in case he should be needed.

"Another day of laboring beneath that sun and I despair of Diego de Huelva's life," muttered Andres Dorantes. To this Alonso del Castillo nodded. "But in his condition, how can we risk escape?"

"Escape to where, my captain?" I carefully asked. "The time is past when we should talk of escape. Better that we consider ways of softening our condition." At these words, Andres Dorantes frowned.

"As the black man says," said Alonso del Castillo, laying his hand on the other's shoulder. "We waste our energy when we talk of escape, when it cannot be done. Perhaps in a month . . . And we may gain much from Estevan, who has a long experience of slavery, if we will listen to him." To this, Andres Dorantes grunted. "Tell us, my friend," Alonso del Castillo went on, "from your experience, what would be best?"

Nearly a minute passed before I could make an answer. I was not yet used to having an officer address me as friend. With my face turned half away, I finally said, "It is best for the slave to please his master, yet never to forget that he is still a man. It is best for the slave to accept his slavery, yet never to forget that there still is freedom. It is best for the slave to live each day as if it were his last one, yet never to forget that there still are many years."

Suddenly I turned and faced both men. "We will not escape after a month, my captains. I have spent most of my life in slavery and I hunger for freedom more than you can ever know. But I will not delude myself. I will not entertain false hopes. We are lost. Never have I known of men more lost. Even those who wander the African deserts, which is my home, know the direction they must wander if they are to again find civilization. This we do not know. Thus, if we escape, we escape only to wander in the wilderness where we may be taken by Indians even more savage. Or, we may wander until starvation and exhaustion leave us easy prey for marauding beasts." Pain showed in the faces of the two captains. "These Indians," I nodded toward the center of the village, "despite their harshness, do not kill us, and we are fed no worse than they feed their own. Forget escape for now, my captains, and let us learn to live and labor as if we were Indians. Let us learn to please our hosts—only in this way will our burdens be lightened."

Blows from my fists could not have hurt the two captains

more than did my words. In a voice drained of all passion, Andres Dorantes cursed me: "It is your black skin—the color of the skin of Satan—that has brought this evil down upon us. If we were in Christian lands, I would have you flayed and your carcass burnt. . . . My father warned me not to keep a black man as a slave. . . . " I listened, and remembered all the years we had together, then turned away and walked alone through the moonlit village.

Children who had thrown stones and offal came up and touched me gently. These same children who would again belabor us could not have been more gentle as they came up to me that evening. And again the men made room for me at the fire and started searching my hair for lice. An old man, toothless, with eyes reduced to slits by folds of wrinkled skin, crossed from the other side of the circle and sat down before me. Snorting and spitting, he drew a large uneven square on the ground, whose shape resembled an animal skin. Then, with twigs and bits of grass he constructed in one corner tiny structures—almost perfect likenesses of their huts. He then drew trees and animals in the area surrounding these huts; and in the center of the square he placed a disc of wood stained yellow. As he constructed this rough map, for I soon guessed the meaning of his labors, a large number of Indians of the village left their fires and crowded close. Then, having completed his work, the last of which was drawing the figures of men on different parts of the map, showing a huge grin, he handed me the drawing stick.

I understood what he wanted from me, yet I hesitated to give an answer—there was something dangerous lying behind his grin. Waving one hand before my face, he pointed with his other hand toward the drawing. I waved my hand back and shrugged. Then he addressed me, part of which I understood, yet pretended I did not. His grin was gone and in his faded eyes I saw flashes of cruelty. "If we are to love you, man with fire-blackened skin, we must know from where you come," his speech, although harsher, was not unlike that of the Indians on the island of Malhado. "To show our love, we will burn fish so that your departed holy men can satisfy their hunger, but first we must know from where you come." All the gathered Indians made sounds deep in their chests, and there was much coughing and spitting. "Point with the stick, fire-blackened-skinned man, to the place where you and your pale companions were born." He pulled my hand toward the ground. Again I shrugged and grinned. Puzzled, the old Indian turned and whispered to several whose shell ornaments showed them to be of higher rank. Then, motioning me to stay where I was, he went into his hut, where he remained for a time.

If I pointed with the stick to a place on the far side of the map, what would be the harm? I asked myself. What would be the harm if I showed them we came from across the water? I was puzzled at my reluctance to give the man his answer.

Emerging from the hut, his grin restored, the old Indian presented me first with a strip of dried venison, a thing I had not tasted in a long time, and also with six dolls of rough manufacture, five of which were rubbed white with chalk, the sixth blackened with ash. Such coughing and spitting then erupted from the Indians that they must be judged suffering a deadly contagion. Not certain what would be best to do, I examined each of the dolls carefully, handling them with great delicacy, as if they were made of the finest ivory instead of sticks tied with grasses. As I examined these rude creations, the Indians pressed in close to me. Then, having determined what would be best, I tried to distribute these dolls to those who crowded closest. It was as if I had offered them hissing adders, for they leapt backwards, gibbering, their faces showing a deathly pallor. Where one moment I had been so crowded I could scarcely breathe, I now found myself with room enough; the only one staying within ten paces being the old Indian, who again had lost his grin. That one then poured out such a torrent of words that I could not understand more than three in ten, but I understood that he berated me. I had come near killing different ones with my offer of the dolls; I had caused several such fright that it must take days for them to recover; I was a very foolish man . . . other things he said whose meaning lay beyond my understanding.

With repeated shoulder shrugs, and a forced grin, I listened to the old Indian. Then, when breathlessness caused him to pause, I gave one last shrug, dropped the six dolls on the ground, and started to move away. And it was as if I had suddenly become invisible, for not one of the Indians so much as glanced at me as I walked away from the fire. All their attention was concentrated on the six dolls. Finding a place in the shadows, I turned and watched.

They stood as if frozen. Dogs trained in the art of hunting birds stand as did those Indians—their heads pointing. I watched carefully, and it was as if the Indians each moment drew a little closer to the dolls, yet I could not see that they moved. Soon they were separated by no more than the length of a man's arm. Then, suddenly, they rushed in. Had the six dolls been six vipers, not so much as a scrap of skin the size of the tip of a child's finger would have been left after the Indians ceased their beating. Had the six dolls been six lions, they could not have made defense, so savage was the attack. Then, as suddenly as it started, it was over, and the Indians settled down again about their fires.

It must have been a madness caused by the fullness of the moon, how else can I explain my leaving the shadows and venturing once again to join the Indians? Somehow I knew—how, I cannot say—I knew that had I pointed to the wrong place on the map, had I done other than drop the dolls, they would have destroyed me and my five companions. Yet, as if a member of the tribe since birth, I eased down amongst them. Fingers again searched my hair and the gentle tugs sent throbs of pleasure down my throat. "Estevan," I murmured, "if ever there was one who suffers lunacy, you are that one." Yet I did not care. A chorus of wolves howled in the distance; owls and other night birds called in the woods. Like a shawl of gossamer drawn across a rising bosom, a fine cloud passed over the moon. Then the bosom-moon again was bare. A woman, whose skin hung from her bones as does the skin of a hanging man left to rot, stepped from a nearby hut. So shriveled was her bosom that I shuddered. She moved slowly toward the fire, dragging her swollen feet as if they were of stone. Not a hair showed on her parchment head, and her eyes were so far sunken that from where I sat they could not be seen. As she moved into the circle different Indians whispered, "It is the woman of the dream; the woman of the dream."

This woman dwelt in her hut alone, I later learned, and no one, not even the chief or medicine man, dared look into her face. Even the littlest children lowered their eyes when she passed. And always it was the same, when she emerged from her hut different ones would whisper, "It is the woman of the dream." I watched her as she shuffled into the circle, her lips moving but with no sound. I watched her as she squatted before the fire and roasted a fish—although old and without children or a man, she never lacked for food. I watched her as she picked away the steaming flesh with trembling fingers and stuffed it into her toothless mouth. Never had I seen a more lonely creature—as certain as I am of death I knew she was lonely, and this drew me to her.

She had been taken from another tribe when only half grown, I also later learned. It is the custom of these Indians to give their own females to the dogs as soon as they are born, for the men of the tribe cannot marry them, this being a thing disgustful. Thus it is that all their women are taken or bartered from other tribes. This woman, I also later learned, was given as wife to the son of the chief, she being judged of all the women most handsome. But in time he put her aside, for she proved barren. Then, as is true of every barren woman in this savage land, her condition was little better than a slave. All the hardest work was hers, and any man could have her at his pleasure. But

293

in her third season of laboring, during the time the prickly pears are eaten, this woman dreamed of the spotted tiger. Of all the people in this world, none take dreams more seriously than do these Indians. The woman had awakened screaming the name of the spotted tiger, a creature so terrible to these savages that even a whisper of its name will cause their warriors to cower. Great fires were quickly lit for protection. Sacrifices of fish, nuts and skins were offered. All weapons were held in readiness as they listened to the woman tell of her dream.

The spotted tiger had come from a place far across the bay. His claws sharper than the sharpest flints, his teeth longer than a man's finger, and his breath choked like smoke from green wood. As the woman told of the dream, the medicine man and several of the older ones of the tribe shook rattles and scratched at their skin with sharp stones until the blood ran. The eyes of the spotted tiger had burned the woman's flesh and its dripping saliva had set fire to the grass. She had lain helpless, waiting for the beast to consume her. But instead of teeth, she had felt its manly parts as the creature mounted. It was as if her loins were being filled with boiling water. It was as if glowing coals were being thrust up into her abdomen. In her ears she heard the storming ocean. Her eyes filled with wind-blown sand. Then she awoke from the dream, screaming.

So great was their terror of the spotted tiger that these Indians dared not kill the woman. Yet they feared that in time a tiger would emerge from her womb. Not one could look the woman in her face. Even after she ceased to flow, eyes would dart toward her abdomen.

I watched the feeble old creature as she picked the steaming flesh from the roasted fish. Her lips kept making talking movements, and from time to time they tightened into a grin that was not a grin. She raised her head, and the many pairs of eyes that were watching her turned away—all eyes turned away except mine.

It is said that if a creature stares into a serpent's eyes, it will

294

lose all power of movement and thus becomes its victim. And so it was with the old woman. Staring into her hollow eyes, I grew numb. But this numbness was not of fear, as with the serpent; it was the numbness of despair. All the pain of that woman's life, in a single moment, touched all the pain of mine. Perhaps, for the first time since the night she had the dream her eyes met the eyes of another human being. She held my eyes without wavering, then she turned her head away and released me from my numbness.

I watched her shuffle slowly with stone feet toward her shelter. Only when I could no longer see her withered form did I find strength to depart that circle of savages and seek relief in the darkness of my hut.

XLI

To detail our life with that tribe of Indians for the next several weeks would be to give an account of savage treatment and pitiless labor in the worsening summer heat. I, who had been hardened by years spent chained to an oar in a galley, suffered. How then should it have been with my companions? After several days I gave up all hope for Diego de Huelva, so weak and shrunken had he grown. Yet he and Diego Dorantes, whose condition was very little better, refused to succumb. Knowing their fate if they could not work, they dragged their bodies from the hut each morning and somehow managed to survive until dusk. Despite the beatings they suffered for their slowness, and despite attacks of fever and trembling, they were determined to survive. Yet had we not, the second week of our slavery, gained a day's relief from a violent thunderstorm, which these primitive people deathly fear, I cannot see how those two could have stayed alive.

As a slave in the galley, I learned to read a man's fate in his features. Certain changes told me of coming death, others were guarantees of life. By the end of the third week, I saw those changes that spoke of life in the faces of Diego de Huelva and Diego Dorantes, and thus no longer feared for their survival. Yet in their eyes I also saw that their sanity had been affected.

It must have been the end of the sixth week or the beginning of the seventh, I found it difficult to keep track of time; it was the evening of the day when two large deer were taken and we all feasted on roasted flesh, that Diego Dorantes made his escape. For several days he had muttered about finding Asturiano, the clergyman, that he might be shriven.

He came up to me after the evening meal as I sat in the shadows, as was my wont. Then, in a strong voice that was not yet an order, he said, "Come with me, Estevan, and we will find Figueroa and the clergyman." I listened, but made no answer. "I have been slave to these Indians long enough," he gestured toward the village. "I mean to be shriven and then to escape." In the man's voice I heard a strange shrill sound. "I have thought about this carefully, Estevanico," he lowered his face so that I smelled the harshness of his breath. "I cannot tell the others; only you can understand." He softened his voice to a whisper. "The clergyman hears many things in confession," he touched his finger to his lips. "He will know the direction we must take." Using almost no breath he began to laugh. "As certain as I am that there is a God in Heaven, I am certain that Asturiano has gained this information from the Indians." As if I were about to make an answer, he quickly shook his head and again brought his finger to his lips. "We must be careful, Estevanico, if they should learn of this . . ." he suddenly broke off and appeared to listen.

296

Fearing for the safety of the man, I agreed to go with him. Then, offering as an excuse a need to gather my few belongings, I went to find the other men. Not ten minutes had passed when I returned with Andres Dorantes and Alonso del Castillo, but Diego Dorantes had already gone. "He said that a clergyman hears many things in confession," I repeated the man's words. "He said that he will learn from Asturiano the direction to escape."

"My cousin believes that the clergyman gained this information from the Indians?" asked Andres Dorantes. I nodded. "From their making confession?" Again I nodded. "Then he has grown mad!" I hesitated, then nodded for the third time.

It took all of Alonso del Castillo's strongest arguments to keep Andres Dorantes from going after his cousin. Had I still been his slave I am certain he would have ordered me to go with him and could not have been dissuaded. But when faced with following a madman through the jungle alone and at night . . . "He carries a sword, Andres," said Alonso del Castillo. "And they say madness gives a cat's vision to a man—and there is no moon!"

How deeply Diego Dorantes' madness and sudden departure affected the three of us, words cannot say. I counted him as one already dead, and from his cousin's sighs and from Alonso del Castillo's constant hand-movements across his eyes, I had little doubt but that they were of my opinion.

Although physicians will say that madness is not a pestilence, I have known it to be a virulent contagion. And so it was with Diego de Huelva when he learned of the departure of Diego Dorantes. "How can you know the Indians have not made confession?" he shouted. "When I served with Hernan Cortez we converted thousands—I have seen them lined up a full league waiting for confession." So powerful is this contagion of madness that for several seconds I listened and half believed. And from their faces, so did the others.

"If Diego learns the direction we must travel to escape, he will return and tell us," Valdevieso said, to calm the man whose eyes were darting wildly. But these words, instead of calming, further inflamed him.

"I have seen them lined up a full league, waiting for confession!" Diego de Huelva repeated, in a voice that was near a scream. He drew his sword, which he began to wave wildly above his head. "I mean to join Diego, and will kill the man who tries to stop me." He started backing towards the entrance to the hut, and I waited for that moment he would have to hunch down to go out the door. Then, with a single blow of my fist to his temple, I felled him.

"You have killed him?" asked Valdevieso, for the blow had been well placed, and the man dropped as if shot. I shook my head, yet was not certain, and began chafing his wrists. It was then that I came as close as I have ever been to death. Perhaps it was all the past hatred Diego de Huelva had for me; this added to his madness that caused the man to take hold of his sword with his one hand as I, unaware of his action, chafed the other. It was as if my brain exploded—the sword struck my skull, tore my neck, and bit into my shoulder. Had the man had another hand's breadth of room to swing his weapon, he must have dispatched me. As it was, I lay senseless for an hour.

I opened my eyes and saw the troubled features of Alonso del Castillo swimming darkly before me. "How does it go, black man?" I grunted, then sank into darkness again. It was almost morning before I was sufficiently recovered to so much as raise my head. On the far side of the hut lay Diego de Huelva, trussed like a pig prepared for slaughter. The light of the fire cast patterns of yellow and orange on his sleeping face. He had come closer than any other man to killing Estevan—Estevan, whose strength and quickness had preserved him again and yet again—he had almost brought him to the mystery that lies beyond the shadow. I examined his coarse features. Should I ease over to the man, who had such hatred for me, and with a single squeeze to his throat relieve myself of the danger of his hatred? I wondered. It would only be the matter of a single moment. Then Diego de Huelva's eyes opened and stared into mine. He knew what I had been thinking. I started across the hut. His eyes filled with fear. My lips not a finger's width from his ear, I whispered, "Must Christian kill Christian?" He closed his eyes and slowly shook his head. With trembling hands I then loosed his bonds, and we sat together until dawn, arms around each other.

XLII

How I survived that day after being wounded by Diego de Huelva, I do not know. Blood kept oozing from my gashed head and torn shoulder. Waves of dizziness caused me to stumble and tear my hands on the sharp flints that filled the arroyo where we worked. The Indians, angered at my condition, beat me with sticks. And insects drawn by my open wounds, allowed me not a moment's peace. Yet it was more than my physical condition that caused that day to be a torture. For Diego de Huelva, in his madness, now counted me as his only friend and would throw rocks at the other Spaniards when they drew too near. Yet this was not all of it, for he kept muttering about killing our Indian warders, who were already upset by the disappearance of Diego Dorantes—thus it was that I must constantly watch him and at different times restrain him. And I will confess it was only my fear that the man's wild actions would bring the Indians' retribution down upon all of us that caused me to interfere. For if I prayed once I prayed a hundred times that he follow his original inclination and escape. How close I came to reminding him of Asturiano, as for the dozenth time I turned him away from the Indians whom he started to curse, only the Lord God can ever know. The coming of night brought a gradual lessening of the man's frenzy, until at last he grew as docile as a nun. Whether this was feigned to provide him an opportunity to escape and join with Diego Dorantes once our vigilance relaxed, or whether it resulted from a cooling of the fever to his brain, no one will ever know. For upon entering our hut, we were greeted by Diego Dorantes.

He had crossed the bay, seeking Asturiano and Figueroa, and once there learned that they had escaped to the south ten days earlier. "The clergyman gained the Indians' affection by curing different ones of a distemper," he recounted. "So grateful were those savages, they gave him bows, dried venison and other things—thus he was able to escape." At this, Valdevieso lowered his face into his hands and groaned as Diego de Huelva muttered curses softly. "The Indians sent a party of warriors after them," Diego Dorantes continued. "But after three days the warriors returned, fearing to travel too far south, for there are different tribes of their enemies to the south. They tried to keep me as their slave, but I told them I was already a slave to others."

"The clergyman gained his information from the Indians, just as you said," Valdevieso muttered, his face still in his hands. "He learned the way from giving them confession—and now he and Figueroa travel toward Spanish lands."

"And they did not come back for us, the whoresons!" Diego de Huelva snarled. "If ever I meet up with them. . . ."

"How should they come for us?" Diego Dorantes interrupted. "The warriors of their tribe would have seized and killed them. Escape is to the south, and we are on the north shore of the bay. But I know the clergyman," Diego Dorantes' face softened. "He did not come for us because he could not—

300

yet I will risk my chance of salvation if he and Figueroa do not wait for us somewhere to the south!"

"Why should they wait for us?" asked Valdevieso, lifting his face from his hands. "It is ten days since their escape—they are already far to the south. Why should they wait for us?" he asked again.

"Because Asturiano is a holy man," Diego Dorantes answered.

"Asturiano may be holy, but what of Figueroa?" Valdevieso took hold of the man's arm. "What of Figueroa?"

"They wait for us for reasons other than Asturiano's holiness," Diego de Huelva said with a sly laugh. "If the holiness of priests were meat we must sup on water. They wait for us because they must. How should two men, alone, travel through nations of hostile savages? And do you not remember the look of Figueroa . . ."

"He followed his Indian like a whipped dog," muttered Valdevieso.

"They wait for us because they must!" said Diego de Huelva.

To this, Diego Dorantes vigorously nodded. "The priest will have left some writings," he added. "We will find his writings and know where to meet. But if we do not hurry . . ." he made a cutting motion with his finger across his neck.

Neither Alonso del Castillo nor Andres Dorantes said a single word during this exchange. But when the exchange had ended, after several throat-clearings, Alonso del Castillo offered as his opinion that it was doubtful the clergyman had gained any information from the Indians. "Do masters tell slaves the way to escape?" he said in an even voice.

"The clergyman knows the way!" Diego Dorantes hissed. "Is it that you are afraid, Alonso? Or is it that you have come to love your slavery?"

"Be careful, cousin!" Andres Dorantes, seeing Alonso del Castillo's features darken, stepped between the two men.

"From the disorder of your thinking I must judge you not in full possession of your reason—but to charge one like Alonso with cowardice. . . ." Diego Dorantes, scowling, turned away, muttering softly under his breath.

Despite my fatigue, I stayed awake after the others were asleep. My shoulder so pained me I could not find even a moment of relief. After an hour of suffering its throbbing, which worsened each minute, it would have taken very little provocation to cause me to lay violent hands on Diego de Huelva, who sprawled in the middle of the hut, softly snoring. I forced my eyes closed and saw streaks of red—red from the fire in my shoulder. I opened them and saw Diego Dorantes on all fours, crawling toward the entrance to the hut. "Take your whoreson friend with you, and may you both rot in the jungle," I wanted to say to the man. But instead I forced myself to stay silent, and pretended that I did not see him. He took a skin, several dried fish and all our dried berries, then, with an insulting gesture toward the sleeping form of Alonso del Castillo, left the hut. This was the last I ever was to see of the man.

Weeks later from a wandering Indian who traded ochre from tribe to tribe we learned that, not yet a league from the village, Diego Dorantes had been taken. Then, after certain tortures, he had been dispatched by having his head broken with a stone. Would that we had known of the man's unfortunate end earlier. For Valdevieso, after mooning about nearly a week, left to join him. The next day he was taken and immediately dispatched. Diego de Huelva, by now completely bereft of his reason, left two days later. But he traveled in the wrong direction. The warriors of the tribe captured him before an hour, and thinking he was seeking to join another tribe, brought him back to the village, tightly bound. Then, as if he were a sack of wheat and not a man, they hoisted him up by his feet and hung him from a pole raised for that purpose. He hung all day in the

302

sun and we could hear his howls down in the arroyo where we worked. Just before sunset, the children of the village gathered around the man and mercifully relieved him of his suffering by beating him to death with sticks.

It was also from the Indian who traded ochre that we learned the fate of Esquivel. A woman of the Mariames tribe with which he dwelt dreamed that her son attacked and killed Esquivel. Knowing of these savages' belief in dreams, Esquivel tried to escape the village, but was easily taken. Then, as it had been in the dream, the woman's son pierced his chest with arrows, and so he was killed.

XLIII

After we heard the account of the Indian who traded ochre—who showed a certain glee in imparting his information—other than an occasional necessary word, we fell into the habit of silence. Perhaps it was I more than the other two who brought about this change. For I had nothing left to say, and found it almost painful to speak. Yet, strangely, I also found a certain peace in the days and weeks that then followed.

It being the height of summer, the heat worsened until I found it difficult to breathe, working as I did down in the arroyo where there was much dust; yet it did not matter. From eating poisoned fish, I suffered an affliction of the bowels which can only be likened to having a sword thrust in the abdomen then twisted; yet this, too, did not matter. Nor did it worry me when the Indians, fearing that we made ready to escape, threatened us with sharp arrows pressed against our necks. Days would pass, and it was as if the sleeping and waking hours were but moments of a dream. I would awake in the early morning, then, only minutes and I found that it was already evening. And there were times when moments lengthened into days.

I remember a certain moment, as I was chopping at a tree, when the stone ax in my hand took a full day to descend. In that day made of a moment, I begged the tree to forgive me for causing its death. Perhaps it was from the Indians that I grew aware of the spirit of the tree—of all living things.

Another time, as I searched with my fingers beneath the water for roots, I looked up and saw the Indian who was our warder. He sat in the shadow cast by a boulder, his chin pressed against his chest, nearly asleep. How is it to be a savage Indian? I wondered. How would it be if, instead of being Estevan I were him? If that were so, how many things I then would have no knowledge of. Faces and names and scenes tumbled wildly through my mind. "How sad it would be, not to be Estevan," I whispered as my fingers continued with their search for roots. Then I whispered, "If he were me, how sad it would be for him," and my words for the moment had the sound of madness, but only for that moment. For the next moment I began to gain an understanding of things no words can explain. "I am Estevan," I turned and addressed the Indian, who grunted. "And you are not Estevan; you are you." Again the man grunted. Not if I had the learning of the wisest bachelor in all of Fez would I have the words to describe what I then knew, as I addressed that Indian. And there are no words for what I saw as I sat before my hut that night and listened to the stars. Singing crystals, they danced in the distant heaven, yet within my being I could also feel them dancing. As I look up at them, do the stars look down at me? I wondered. "What do you see, you diamond spangles of God's velvet vestments?" I whispered to the sky. "Can you see this one, shrouded as he is by darkness, or does his black skin keep him hidden from your vision?" Does it matter if I am seen by the stars? Is it not enough that I see them? "And if I am forgotten?" I then whispered. "Is it not enough that I have been?" Then all the heavens began to blaze, and the moon became the sun, and it was day again.

XLIV

As the summer's end approached, our condition of slavery worsened. Perhaps it was the weeks of merciless heat that shortened the tempers of our captors so that they would kick and beat us with little provocation. Perhaps it was the poorness of the catch of fish, or that they snared no game. Whatever the reason, our lives with these savage people grew ever more cruel.

It was after we suffered a beating from their fists for not having secured sufficient roots that Dorantes, without saying a word, slipped away and went to join the Mariames—the tribe with which Esquivel had dwelt. For several days before his departure he had shown in the hollowness of his eyes and in the sallowness of his complexion an increasing distress. It having become our habit for each to leave the other alone, neither I nor Castillo approached the man, yet we both knew of his suffering. Thus it was painful but no surprise when we found him gone.

"Will we see him again, black man?" Castillo asked, in a voice grown unused to talking.

"If not in this world, then in another," was my studied answer.

"Shall we escape and try and join with him?" All passion was gone from Castillo's voice. "Why escape?" he answered his question with another question, then shrugged. "Our Indians kick and beat us, yet they do not kill us, and we lie with their widowed women—although the Almighty knows how little energy is left for fornication. Who would have thought that Alonso del Castillo, not yet twenty-three years of age, would bemoan his loss of desire." The man tried to grin.

"If not to have them pick my lice and cook my food, I would not lie with them," I said. I laid my hand for a moment on the young man's shoulder. "I too have lost my passion, Alonso." He raised his eyes to mine. It was the first time I had called him by his given name."

"If certain of my companions in Spain should ever learn that Alonso—that Alonso who had gained no small reputation for his nice way with women—if these ones should ever learn that I moaned about demands made of my manhood . . . I could never face their mockery."

"Satan himself, with all his tortures, will not draw a single word from me," I promised the man. "And what of those who knew Estevan? If it were ever broadcast that he had so far descended that he would only share the blanket of a willing woman to be relieved of lice . . . I, too, am no lover of mockery."

"Even if racked by the Inquisition, your secret is safe with me—as I know mine is with you, black man." The little levity passed out of Castillo's voice, and it took on its hollow sound again. "You have already proved your ability to keep a secret." I raised my eyebrows. "That day in the swamp, when I tested my manhood in the slime-covered sump—have you forgotten, Estevan?" I shook my head. His features took on a troubled look, and he fell silent. "I have not always treated you with the kindness you deserve, black man," he finally said. "There were times when I used rough words with little cause." I nodded, but not for the truth of what he was saying but for the friendship he was showing.

Although we labored side by side, and at night lay in the same hut, each blanketed with his woman, except for a few words exchanged it was weeks before we spoke again. As I now stretch my mind back to that time when we labored like beasts for that tribe of Indians, I can say with a near certainty that had it not been for one single event we might have stayed with that savage nation until relieved by death, so dispirited had we become. It was the death of the woman of the dream, and what then happened that awakened my desire to be free again.

We were laboring in the arroyo, naked except for breachclouts, the season having mysteriously grown hot again, when our warder, with an excited shout, suddenly turned and ran up the hill toward the village. Although not bidden, we followed him, and found every inhabitant down to the smallest children gathered in a great circle in whose center the woman of the dream lay thrashing on the ground, struggling to catch her breath. Not one made an effort to aid the suffering creature, and when I started forward I was pinioned by half a score of steellike hands. Only in the galleys had I seen human beings die with no attempt made to offer them a moment's comfort. Even condemned felons are offered the solace of a priest; and when hoisted up there is always one or more who will pull on the dying one's feet that he may gain a quicker release from his tortures. The old woman twitched and gasped, her gaping mouth filling with earth and bits of dried grass. Slowly the great circle tightened. Her twitchings threw her on her back, where she lay shuddering.

Although violent in her dying, at the moment of her death the woman of the dream grew calm. It was a red ant, crawling into the creature's eye with her not blinking, that told us she was gone. All had seen the ant, and for several seconds there was silence, and then a roar, as the Indians rushed in. Separated by many years from that terrible day, I now can see that what they did was because they still feared the spotted tiger. But at the time, I could only see the horror. They stamped upon the creature, all two hundred of them, until she was no more—her very substance having been ground into the earth.

"If it costs us our lives, we cannot spend another night in this village after such an abomination," I whispered to Castillo as we knelt, side by side, in the darkness of our hut.

"Even her bones were ground into the earth, even her bones, Estevan," the man gripped my arm with cold fingers which he dug deep into my flesh. "A hundred times would I rather rot in the jungle or be devoured by some wild beast, than be served as was that poor old creature."

Disdaining to carry so much as a handful of berries or a mouthful of dried meat, we left our hut and circled the village toward the bay. We held our swords unsheathed, but this proved to be unnecessary, for it was as if we had not been seen, although we passed dozens of inhabitants of that village.

If the Indians later pursued us, it must have been with little passion, for they never came near us, although hunger and exhaustion forced us to make frequent stops.

As we struggled through thick underbrush and clambered over boulders and fallen trees, each day we grew more like brothers than friends. Those times when we could walk upright, it was always hand in hand, and the few words that passed between us were said softly, with nods and smiles of understanding. I could not help remembering how harsh-voiced and unsmiling this same Alonso del Castillo once had been, nor could I help remembering there was a time Estevan would have recoiled from the touch of a white man's hand. We traveled a total of eleven days, four of which were beyond the furthest inland reaches of the bay, and became so broken by exhaustion that we grew confused, and several times changed our direction. What little nourishment we had was gained from grubs, snails, ants and other such loathsome creatures. At night we gained warmth by burrowing under rotted leaves and lying tightly wrapped in each other's arms. And it was in such a condition that we were discovered by a tribe of Indians called the Yguazes.

Had I been found in this condition by Christians, I might have suffered some uneasiness. But to be so viewed by pagan Indians caused me not a moment of concern. With Castillo it was otherwise. He stumbled to his feet, blushing, then turned away from the staring Indians and, like the child who expects a beating, bent his back and hunched his shoulders. Perhaps the man's reaction came more from the ill usage we had suffered than from embarrassment. Yet, had he not turned away, he would have seen that these savages feared us more than we feared them.

Although armed with stout bows and stone axes, and outnumbering us ten to one, they retreated, as Castillo arose. Then they crouched partially hidden by the tall grasses gibbering and trembling. It is my guess that when they saw us lying in each other's arms they judged us to be a single strange creature, white on one side, black on the other. Then, when the white side suddenly separated itself and arose from the ground and they saw that the creature was no creature but two men they were frightened, never having had experience with men whose skins were colored different from their own. These Indians were shorter by half a span than those we left. Although their features were coarser, their bodies were of a fine symmetry and in the way they moved they showed an agility more like that of a deer than a man. Their underlips and nipples were bored, as were the lips and nipples of the Indians with whom we quartered on the island of Malhado.

Having gained considerable experience of the savages who dwell in this part of the Western Indies, from the months I dwelt with them, and trusting my judgment, I quickly gathered up a quantity of small stones, then slowly walked with my hand outstretched in their direction. Several leapt up and made a show of putting arrows to their bows, and I stopped and waited until they crouched again. Behind me, I heard Castillo whispering uneasy warnings, but then, as he saw that the Indians only threatened, he too started moving slowly in their direction. They received the stones I had gathered as if they were pearls, or nuggets of gold. As I placed the stones in their hands, one to each man, they made soft murmuring sounds, then moved their tongues and lips in such a way that had my eyes been closed I would have sworn I heard the flutter of linnets' wings or the sound of a distant swarm of locusts. As had the Indians of Malhado, these Indians easily showed their emotions and they started weeping after receiving the stones. Although I should have been used to such displays of feeling, I found myself deeply moved, as I saw tears coursing down the scarred faces of savages. As they wept, they rubbed the stones I had given them over their foreheads, pressed them against their breasts, and at different times placed them inside their mouths. Castillo, who had also learned much about the way of Indians, not to be outdone by me, quickly gathered a number of small sticks, which he distributed to the Indians. This second gift brought fresh tears, which I will confess also did not leave me unmoved.

So different are the ideas of value of these simple people from those of Christians that when they presented us with bows, arrows and stone axes in return for the sticks and pebbles, they hung their heads—ashamed that their gifts were of so much less importance than ours. For they viewed us as powerful sorcerers or wizards, and in our presenting them with what Christians might judge worthless trifles, we transferred a portion of our power to them; their bows, axes and arrows were nothing more than weapons.

During the three days of travel to their village, our spirits lightened more than they had at any time since being shipwrecked on this savage land. The contrast between the harshness of our former captors and the gentleness of these people

310

produced within us a near intoxication, yet I could not help but
wonder what would happen when we reached their village.
How would we be received by their women, their chief, their
medicine man? Several times during the three days we traveled,
I had to force myself not to share my uneasiness with Castillo.
But when we reached the village, I was glad I had not interfered
with my companion's growing happiness, for we were received
in the gentlest of ways. From the moment of our arrival it was as
if we had been a member of this nation our entire lives.

XLV

If either Castillo or I had any doubt that we were to be
accepted as members of this Indian nation—other nations had
shown gentleness at first toward Christians later followed by
savagery—whatever doubt we might have had was dispelled
when we were included in a hunting party that went out to hunt
deer the very day of our arrival. We had scarcely rested an hour,
and had not yet fully digested the meal of venison and nuts they
provided, when we were given spears, spear-throwers and
pouches of powdered meat as provision, and ordered to join
with the other hunters of the village.

If there are better hunters anywhere in this world than
those Yguazes, I have never heard of them. I am second to no
man I have ever known in strength, and not unused to exertion,
yet after a day and night of loping alongside those Indians, I lay
trembling with exhaustion when we made camp. Castillo early
fell out of the party, along with several of the half-grown boys,

and joined us later, for the direction we took was a great circle. How I managed to keep up with that hunting party for the four days we were gone, I cannot say. At times I found myself half-blinded from exhaustion, yet pride provided a sufficient goad so I forced myself on. On the morning of the fourth day, we came upon a herd of grazing deer, and then the race began in earnest. Three hours or more we chased that herd in an ever-diminishing circle, different ones of the Indians running at varying speeds and in this way relieving one another. From time to time a hunter would pull alongside a doe or an older fawn and skewer the creature with his spear, but the greater number of deer kept ahead of us. Had it not been late in the season, had the sun provided more than the littlest warmth, I am certain that I could not have survived that three-hour run. Yet I ran among the slowest runners in the outer circle, and only rarely relieved the faster-running men.

Not one of that herd of more than two-score deer escaped. The strongest fully-horned bucks were the last to fall, and in their final struggles, two of the hunters were impaled and killed as they thrust their spears.

To those hunters who had run the circles was granted the honor of carrying the fallen deer. Although I had not joined in on a single kill, I was given a share in this honor. Castillo, who had not run the circles, was denied, yet despite what may be judged a blow to his pride, at different times I saw him wink and grin as, sweating, I struggled with my burden the four leagues back to the village.

After such a bout of work—except for brief rests we had been on the run more than four days and nights—any other men except these Yguazes would have collapsed in exhaustion and slept. But with the sight of their village and of their excited waiting women they were all restored. Thus, after eating portions of the still-smoking livers, and consuming the hearts of the horned bucks, the hunters (excepting this one and Castillo) joined in a night of uninterrupted celebration. The forty deer,

312

whose spleens and livers had provided the feast for all of the members of the village, were piled in a great heap around which were lit a circle of fires. Blood dripping from the carcasses formed puddles into which the children dipped their fingers. They then painted their faces in imitation of the adults, who had streaked their cheeks vermillion. The dance, joined by every member of the village, even the oldest women, appeared to have no beginning. One moment they all were wandering about, the women displaying the manly parts of the slain deer, the men waving their bloodied spears, the children weaving in and out in a sort of random game; the next minute three circles formed around the pile of carcasses just beyond the fires, and these circles started to move; the inner and outer circles in one direction, the middle circle, composed of the hunters, in the other. Except for irregular foot-stamps and bursts of handclaps, this circular movement was all there was to their dance.

As had all the nations of Indians we had come to know, these people also partook of a potion concocted of certain cactus buds, roots and mushrooms. Perhaps it was this potion that provided them with the energy for their dance, which continued until morning. Yet, with Castillo and with me, the potion, several sips of which we shared, produced such a lassitude that our bones felt as if they had turned to jelly, and whorls of colors so filled our eyes we could scarcely see.

"Are we in Heaven, Estevan?" Castillo softly asked, after taking a second sip of the potion. "There are the bodies of all the holy martyrs." He pointed at the pile of deer. "And there are their spirits, changed to angels." He waved in the direction of the moving circles. "And there the seraphim," he nodded to the children. I was about to reply that what he saw were carcasses and lousy savages, when I also had Castillo's vision.

I opened my mouth to agree with the man, but could not form the words, so dazzling were the angels and the seraphim. Then my eyes cleared and I watched the circling savages and noted that their number appeared to have grown greater since the dance started. "Have the number of angels increased?" I asked Castillo. His answer was a shrug and grin. I closed my eyes, counted to a hundred, then opened them—the number of circling savages had increased again.

Knowing how thin the line between madness and delusion, the increasing number of savages made me fear madness. I turned away to relieve my eyes with the darkness, and saw, easing from the shadows one by one, other savages I later learned were of a neighboring rogue nation. These savages, as they emerged from the shadows, fell into the rhythm of the dance, moved easily into the circles, and, what was strangest of all, appeared not to be seen.

I was puzzled, but not alarmed, as I witnessed this peculiar happening. At the time, how could I have had knowledge that these newcomers were rogues; and I judged them to be of a neighboring friendly tribe. Only when I saw these newcomers slip from the circles, still dancing, and two by two carry surely a score of carcasses into the darkness, did I realize that something strange was taking place.

These thieves, for that was what they were, other than continuing their dancing movements, made no effort to conceal their actions, yet it was as if they were invisible, for not one member of the village tried in any way to stop them. Yet, in the morning, when the dance had ended, the Indians bemoaned the loss of half their hunting spoils and sat around much of the day bowed with dejection.

Although at the time confused, I later learned that this was the way of many of the Indian nations. Few people in this world are greater thieves. Even in a single village, individuals freely steal from one another. Yet, why those Indians could not see the thieves that stole their deer is a thing I still cannot understand. The next night the Indians of the village took good caution to conceal the remaining portion of their catch before again starting their dance.

Being much restored, Castillo and I joined this dance, de-

314

termined to continue all night if need be, but unlike the night before, the dance lasted scarcely more than an hour, and ended when the medicine man, without warning and in a piercing voice—in contrast to their usual sighing sounds—started telling the story of Bad Thing.

A split moon struggled to rise from the thickening eastern mists. To the west came the faint barking of hunting foxes. Occasional gusts of wind swirled smoke and dust and bits of dried grasses into our faces. From a place in the darkness at different times came what might have been the sobbing sounds of a little child.

"Never in the memory of even the oldest ones now long departed was there a time when Bad Thing did not wander through this land," the medicine man began his story. "With these two eyes I have seen that one," he touched his eyes, "and so have others of this village." He pointed a carved bone at different older members of the tribe. "Although stronger than the strongest warrior, Bad Thing is no bigger than a boy," the medicine man continued. Turning the carved bone around, he pointed the rounded end at a half-grown boy not more than ten years of age. The medicine man hesitated, grinned, then pointed the same rounded end at Castillo. "Bad Thing's face is covered with hair, as is that one—so much hair his features are hidden." The medicine man's voice softened almost to a whisper. "No hut is safe from his visit." He made stabbing motions in the direction of the huts with his finger. "When he comes to your house, your hair will stand up." His voice rose. "You will tremble. Never has there been a hunter so brave that he did not tremble at the visit of Bad Thing." The medicine man paused, and the listening Indians shifted uneasily. "When Bad Thing comes to your door, you will see a blazing torch." The medicine man crouched down. "To Bad Thing, no door can be barred, and he will enter your hut and seize whom he chooses. Three deep gashes in the side will Bad Thing give to the one he chooses." As he said these words, an Indian on

315

whose face was pasted grasses to resemble hair stepped from the shadows. He walked hunched over, covered by a deerskin, and although he made no attempt at concealment, it was if not one of the listening Indians had seen him. "Into the three gashes Bad Thing will put his hand and draw forth the entrails." The medicine man's voice cracked as he spoke, and the skin-covered Indian hesitated at the edge of the circle, his head darting in all directions. "Bad Thing will cut a portion of these entrails the length of a palm and throw it on the embers." The medicine man tossed a piece of deer-gut into the fire as the skin-covered Indian, still crouching, rushed over to an older boy of perhaps twelve or thirteen and with a piece of flint gave him three slashes in the side, which began to bleed. "To the one he chooses, Bad Thing will then give three gashes to his arm, the second cut on the inside of the elbow which must sever the arm." The skin-covered Indian slashed the boy three times on his left arm. These slashes also began to bleed, yet it was as if the boy felt nothing. The medicine man moved slowly in the direction of the bleeding boy. "A little after the limb is severed, Bad Thing will unite it, and will put his hands upon the wounds, and these at once will become healed." The skin-covered Indian dipped his hand into a pouch and rubbed an unguent on the youth's wounds, and the bleeding ceased.

Suddenly, as if he had been swallowed by the earth, the skin-covered Indian disappeared. "It is not only to your hut that Bad Thing will come," the medicine man continued in a voice grown shrill. "He will appear among you in the dance, at times in the dress of a woman, at times as a man. If it pleases him, he will take a house and lift it high and in a little time throw it down in a heavy fall." At this, a sighing sound, like the wind passing through the branches, came from the listening Indians. "Do not think you can tempt Bad Thing with victuals, for no matter how rich the meat, he will not eat." Again the sighing sound. "I have asked him where he comes from, as have others, and he showed me a fissure in the earth and said that his house was there, below."

316

The medicine man then fell silent, and after the passage of a little time, several of the oldest warriors arose from their place, moved slowly and with great deliberation toward the boy who had been slashed. They then suddenly rushed upon the boy and carried him quickly to the furthest point that was illuminated by the firelight and, with a mighty heave, cast him out into the darkness. These older warriors then returned to their places, but they had scarcely settled down when the boy, whose elbows and knees were badly bruised, came from out of the darkness and, instead of seeking the place where he had been amongst the other boys, walked to the section occupied by the warriors and settled down among them.

Then, despite increasing gusts of wind which brought in chilling air, the Indians remained where they were, silent and unmoving. Afraid to offend them, Castillo and I also remained. Again, from the distance, came the sound of foxes barking, and again, from the shadows, the child's whimpering. A shift of wind caused the whimpering sound to grow clearer, and I could hear between the sobs short gasps of fear. Castillo's face tightened, and then, with a shrug, he made his way into the darkness toward the sobbing child.

A girl of no more than four years it was and he carried the child close to a fire, where he squatted down and started to rub its cold-stiffened limbs. The child had been taken in a raid from another nation and it sobbed in fear. For more than an hour Castillo ministered to the little creature until an old woman came up and demanded her, and for that time the hands of Alonso del Castillo, whose reputation as a soldier was second to none, were as gentle as those of a nursing mother.

"They steal their children, yet had it not been for you, that child would have frozen," I muttered as we settled down in our shelter. To this, Castillo only grunted. "It is a savage custom that these pagans practice," I continued. "Why they find women born of their own loins disgustful . . ."

"They are savages!" Castillo hissed. "They give their newborn females to the dogs.

317

"To kill grown men . . . even women . . ." the man's voice broke. "I have killed women, Estevan. At different times I have killed women."

I made a sound, to let him know I understood—I, too, had killed women . . . in battle . . . a thing I am ashamed of. "How can we know we did not kill children?" I asked the man. "When we stormed a town, how can we know we did not kill children?" I covered my eyes with my hands.

"My father was a physician, Estevan," said Castillo softly. "I have seen him struggle half a night trying to preserve life in a newborn child. I have gone with him when he was summoned to repair the work of some whorish midwife, or when the infant was so placed it could not pass out its mother's loins. I have seen him blow his own breath into the mouth of a child judged dead, and in this wise restore it to life."

"He must have been a great physician," I murmured.

"I learned from him many of his arts. Had I so chosen, I, too, could have been a physician. There are different ones who call themselves by this name who know less of the art than I. But instead of letting blood with a lancet, I have let it with the sword. And before tonight, I never gave thought to this matter; may the Lord forgive me." I reached out my hand in the darkness and laid it on his arm. "If I ever return to Spain, black man," he whispered, "if I ever return to Christian lands I might yet take up the scales of the physician."

XLVI

So great was the contrast of our lives with the Yguazes with what it had been with our former captors that we eagerly fell

318

into the routine of the village. Although not at all times content, I experienced much peace in the months that followed. True, we were not free to depart. Had we strayed beyond the furthest limits of the village, I am certain they would have followed and inflicted a heavy punishment—even death—yet, of all who inhabited that village, who was free to depart? Custom stronger than the strongest laws found anywhere in Christendom declared not even the chief could leave the village alone lest he somehow be taken by another nation who would then use his power to destroy the village. And these uneasy people suffered from a thousand fears. Powerful spirits were believed to lurk everywhere. Before doing the most simple task, care had to be taken not to offend these spirits. So powerful was the Yguazes' belief in magic that I have seen the fiercest warrior show uneasiness as he picked up a stick or knelt down to drink at a stream of water.

Again, unlike our experience with our former captors, our tasks in this village were no harder than those of the other members. Thus it was that we found leisure time, for the winter which we entered was much milder than the year before, and good fortune brought an abundance of game. Despite this leisure, for there were days when I could wander about freely in late afternoon with no task which must be done, Castillo and I engaged in little conversation. He had fallen into the habit of caring for the hurts of the children, and was rarely to be seen without half a score of them closely following him. I, on the other hand, during these free times, would find a place where I might sit alone and study the way clouds move across the sky. During the rare moments we spoke, we never mentioned Dorantes by name, yet I know Castillo often thought of the man, as did I. Was he still alive? I wondered. If alive, would we ever see him again? And there were times I thought of Alvar Nuñez, and at those times I felt a great heaviness.

We had been with the Yguazes five months when a sudden scarcity of game and the exhaustion of our supply of nuts and roots caused the old ones of the village to determine on a great

319

hunt. It was as we readied our weapons that Castillo let it be known by laying aside his bow and spear and joining with the women that he would no longer do the work of a man. Although in Christian nations such an action must have cost a soldier the cruelest scorn, and would have brought rough usage, among these Indians it was a thing not uncommon. Half a score of men of the village worked amongst the women—although why they chose the labor of women, which was far more difficult than that of men, always puzzled me.

Had I been able, I would have asked Castillo why he had determined on such an action. But I was unable, for had I joined with him as he squatted among the women, the warriors would have judged this action to mean I, too, had given up the ways of a man. Ten days later, when I returned from the hunt and saw that he wore a woman's apron, I judged it best not to question him.

Winter had given way to spring before Castillo and I spoke again, for we no longer shared the same shelter, and with these Indians there were many rules governing the conversation between men and women. When we finally spoke, it was because amazement caused each of us to forget himself.

Two wild cattle had been taken the day before, and as a part of the celebration the medicine man started to tell a story. I had heard him tell the tale of Bad Thing five times, and I settled down with my eyes half closed, prepared to hear this tale again. But his tale was not of Bad Thing:

"Far away," the medicine man began speaking as he gestured to the south, "further than a warrior can travel if he started walking at the time of his first hunt and continued until grown so old his arms cannot string the bow; far away," the medicine man repeated, again gesturing to the south, "there lives a serpent taller than the tallest tree, and this serpent, unlike any serpent you have seen, wears feathers and has wings." The listening Indians shifted uneasily. "All who live in the land of this great serpent must fear him, for at any time he may descend from the sky and even the strongest warrior cannot resist his sting. So feared is this serpent that even his wife, a great white bird, must escape from him." The medicine man held out his arms in the manner of a bird and turned around slowly, his body rising and falling. "If she be captured by her husband, he will sting her and kill her." The medicine man made a hissing sound and caused his tongue to dart in and out. "Thus it was his wife flew higher and higher. Below, she heard the beat of his wings and if not for her friend the sun, her husband must have come up to her. But the sun sent down his strongest rays, which the snake hates more than any other thing. So her husband, the snake, returned to earth and hid in a dark cave. Although the sun was the white bird's friend, she had flown so close to him he could not find a cloud to cover her from his heat. So it was she sickened and grew faint." The listening Indians scratched at the ground with their long fingernails, and the sound they produced was that of a multitude of gnawing rats. "Her sickness caused her breech to open and out fell a great white egg." As if at a signal, the scratching ceased. "To such a great height had the white bird flown that the egg fell for a greater time than is spent among the prickly pears when they are ripe, so that by the time the egg reached the earth it was hatched." At this, all the women who had not yet had children, puffed out their abdomens as the older women made the sign of a man and woman mating with their fingers. "A party of warriors came up to where the egg had fallen, and found the fledgling, which was half-black and half-white, lying on the ground. Even as they watched, the fledgling broke into two pieces, and each piece then rose from the ground and was a man. Then the man who was black offered the warriors holy stones."

"It is of us that he speaks, Estevan!" Castillo blurted out from the place where he sat, some twenty paces distant. "Until this very moment I thought he spoke of some ancient ones."

The tale ended as the medicine man told of how the white

321

man handed the warriors holy sticks, and how both then accompanied the warriors to their village.

I, too, was certain that this tale was about us, yet the listening Indians did not so much as glance at either one of us, nor did the medicine man give the slightest suggestion that the two men he spoke of were amongst those who were listening to him. Hearing this tale reminded me of how different these Indians were from all other people I have known. Yet there was to come a time when the ways of these people no longer seemed strange to me.

XLVII

Months passed and it was summer. Then autumn and the season to depart the village and go to the fields where the ripe prickly pears could be eaten. And it was as if I had dwelt with these people called Yguazes for many years. If I thought of escape at all, it was only a dull yearning, and it is my belief that with Castillo it was the same.

Great excitement affected all the members of the village, as we prepared to go south to the fields of ripe prickly pears. "You will stuff your belly until it is swollen, Tall Black Skin," said the medicine man. "From full moon to full moon you will not know a moment's hunger, Tall Black Skin." Surely a dozen times in the several days before we departed the village, the medicine man addressed me in this way—each time grinning to the roots of his blackened teeth and clapping his hands together. Although I already had experience of prickly pears, and remembered how my mouth was puckered by their juice and how griped I later became, each time the medicine man approached me I put on a good face and also clapped my hands, which gave the man much satisfaction.

It was the afternoon of the second day that we traveled southward toward the fields of prickly pears that we met up with Dorantes. So gaunt had the man grown—his face was more that of a death's-head than a living human—so broken his manner of walking, so hunched his shoulders and bent his back that at first I did not recognize him. Had Castillo, who was close by, not shouted out a warning, he would have suffered rough usage, for his sudden appearance from behind a boulder startled and frightened the Indians.

The two officers wept in each other's arms until Castillo, remembering his woman's apron, grew ashamed and retired. I then embraced the man, and he murmured, "Estevanico, my Estevanico." His tears and piteous condition caused my tears to flow. And the joy that swelled inside me at being joined again with this one with whom I had spent so many years caused me to kiss his sunken cheeks again and again. And the Indians, seeing the depths of our emotion, squatted down and, to a man, joined us in weeping.

Later, when we camped and prepared the evening meal, Dorantes said over and over, "I despaired of ever meeting again with Christians; I despaired of ever meeting again with Christians." How he remained alive the months he had wandered since escaping the Mariames, the Lord God alone will ever know. I questioned him, but he could not make an intelligent answer. He muttered about devil-demons with forked tails and cloven hoofs; he muttered about savages whose nakedness was not covered by so much as a breechclout, and who gained their nourishment from worms and rotted wood. He spoke of hearing about a man who had risen from the dead, then spoke about being fed manna by white-robed angels. What he had suffered while a slave of the Mariames, and how he escaped, I never learned. Whether he would not or could not speak of these matters, I cannot say.

If Dorantes slept at all that first night after he joined with us, it was only for brief moments. For even as I tried to question him, he grew fevered and began to show great agitation, so that at different times he must be restrained. Had deprivation not robbed him of his strength, he would have caused me, and the Indians who rendered assistance, great harm. So violent did he become that at last we were forced to bind him, and this brought a stream of shrieks and terrible curses.

It was nearly a month before Dorantes was sufficiently restored that he need not be restrained, and all during that time Castillo, still wearing his woman's apron, cared for him.

Having lost Castillo as a companion, and hungering to talk again in the Spanish tongue of matters these Indians could not understand, I awaited Dorantes' recovery with impatience. Yet, when the madness at last went out of his eyes, he was not restored to the Dorantes I had known, but rather to a crafty, violent man whose ways were little different than those of the most savage Indian.

"Have I, too, grown savage?" I wondered as Dorantes joined with the warriors who whirled their thundersticks, which is their way of praying. "Am I still a Christian?" I asked in a whisper. I knelt down and drew the cross, and then the fish, and tried to calculate which day was the Sabbath. Then I again whispered, "I no longer pray, and I have forgotten the Sabbath; can such a one be a Christian?"

A story brought to our village by an Indian who traded flints and ochre for skins, answered my question.

It was four months, a few days more or less, from the time we feasted on prickly pears, that this Indian who traded for skins came to our village. A raid upon another village that had had a successful hunt relieved us of a scarcity, which had caused the deaths of several older ones and the swelling of the children's bellies. Although the raid had cost many wounds, none had fallen—thus it was we held a great celebration. After we stuffed with the rich meat we had captured, and after those who had been wounded displayed their wounds, of which number I was one, the Indian who traded skins was drawn out into the center of the village, and was offered presents of arrows and axes in exchange for his story. Ignoring the proffered gifts, which, however, he took with him when he departed, the one who traded skins walked slowly around the circle, as if searching for something. Several times he picked up sticks and pebbles, then laid them carefully down again. Finally he came to a patch of bare ground which appeared to suit him, and there he stood, without moving, for all the time he told his tale.

Except for the weather being much colder, the night was the same as it had been a year earlier when the medicine man first told the story about Bad Thing. In the distance, I heard the bark of hunting foxes. In the shadows, a child who we had captured on our raid whimpered. Rising mists dulled the light of the half moon struggling over the horizon, and at times there were sudden gusts of wind. Has a year really passed? I wondered. It all feels so much the same. Am I awake, or is it a dream? If a dream, I might awake and find that everything has been a dream. Yet even as I teased myself with these thoughts I knew that I had not been dreaming, and that more than two years had passed since our shipwreck.

With fingers that fluttered like those of the people with whom we quartered on the island of Malhado, the Indian who traded skins drew our attention. From his manner, I thought he must be of that nation, and grew excited, as I wondered if he brought news of Lope de Oviedo. But when he started speaking and his words were not formed of sighs, I knew he was of a different nation.

"Deep down," the Indian who traded skins pointed at the earth, then stamped his foot, "Boy Who Weaves Reed Baskets

To Carry Water one day gathered many tall reeds and started to weave. It being very hot, the sun forgot to move and fell asleep, and the moon would not wake him. Thus it was that Boy Who Weaves Baskets continued to weave, gathering more and more reeds. Soon the basket was so big it contained all the sea, and then the land grew dry. Seeing what he had done, Boy Who Weaves Baskets ran away, until he reached a far, far place where he thought he would be safe. There the warriors found him, and, because they could not fish, they killed him. Afraid of a punishment, they hid his body in a cave, which they sealed with a great stone." All the listening Indians sat wide-eyed and silent. Not even the youngest dared to make the slightest movement. "Although they had killed him," the story went on, "Boy Who Weaves Baskets did not die. After a certain time in the cave, he pushed the stone aside and the warriors who had killed him trembled with fear." A shudder passed through the ranks of the listening Indians. "But they need not have feared him, for Boy Who Weaves Baskets did not harm them. When they saw that they were safe, they followed him and watched how he restored the dead and cured sick ones by blowing his breath and making certain signs over them." The Indian who traded skins moved his finger in such a way that it drew the cross. Seeing this, I was overcome with such a powerful emotion I no longer heard the man, and although the night was cold, it was as if a fire burned my skin.

"He speaks of the Christ!" I gasped. "This savage pagan knows of Jesus!" It was at that moment I knew with certainty that I was still a Christian.

Because of my emotion, I did not hear the story's end. But when I saw the Indian who traded skins squat down and rest his head in his hands, I went up to him and asked where he had heard this story of the Christ and how he had learned to make the cross. Although I spoke his language, he appeared not to understand, and when I pressed him, he grew uneasy and offered me a fine flint as a present if I would go away.

326

Still filled with emotion, I turned to Dorantes, forgetting for the moment how changed he had become. "You heard the savage speak of the Christ? You saw him make the cross?"

"The cross . . ." Dorantes laughed. "You are mistaken," the man's voice took on a cruel sound. "Do not trouble me again, black man, with this talk of crosses—do not trouble me again." Seeing the man's tightened features, I turned away.

Refusing to let doubt dampen my emotion, I determined to approach Castillo for confirmation, although I knew if I went among the women the warriors would laugh and point their fingers at me. Ignoring the laughter, I went up to the man and asked the question—after a little hesitation, he shook his head, mumbling that he had not seen the Indian make the sign.

Had I been able, I would have asked other questions of the man, but the women started laughing, and different warriors gathered about, hooting and pointing.

Later, as I lay beneath my blanket, unable to sleep, I wondered if I had really seen the pagan make the holy sign. Doubt teased me. If Dorantes had not seen it, if Castillo had not seen it . . . Fighting a heaviness that began to settle on my chest, I left my shelter and slowly walked about the sleeping village. I stopped several times and listened, as if for a message, but except for the distant barking foxes, the night was silent. Each minute the heaviness in my chest increased, until it was as if a great stone dragged me down. Cold numbed my toes and fingers. Gusts of wind brought in bits of snow and ice, yet despite this cold I yearned to stretch out on the ground and lay there until the heavy weight within my chest was gone.

An image of a man whose brow dripped blood, a man dragging a great burden, formed before my eyes. His hands were torn, and the burden bore him down and at different times he stumbled, yet did not fall. How can such a one carry such a burden without falling? I wondered. The vision faded, and I found myself kneeling on the ground, bent over, my forehead pressed against a stone.

327

"Rise to your feet, Estevan," I whispered. "He did not fall although burdened. Get to your feet, black man." And it was the vision of that other One, whose brow dripped blood and whose hands were torn, that caused me to rise again.

XLVIII

Knowing what I must do, I neglected no opportunity when I might speak to Dorantes and Castillo about the tortured One and His burden. I stayed alert to the chance of finding Castillo engaged in a task away from the women, and always I observed Dorantes' features to see if he was enraged or calm, sane or in a state of madness. When we suffered a season of scarcity, Castillo would listen; when we had enough food, he would turn away. With Dorantes, scarcity or plenty made no difference. With that one it was the boisterousness of the weather or the fullness of the moon that controlled his nature; thus it was I could never know what would be his actions. I approached each man not less than fifty times in the year that followed. Not only did I speak to them of the tortured One, but I urged Castillo to cast off his apron and warned Dorantes that he faced damnation if he would not cease worshiping in the manner of these heathens.

For that year, each morning brought a renewal of my passion. Yet, when the year had passed and both men still refused to change their condition, and I could not see how we would ever escape from these Indians, there were days when I was almost conquered by black despair.

Finally, there came a day—almost three years had passed since we joined with these Indians—I found myself so weighted with depression that I wondered if there was any reason to go on. We had just returned from a raid on a neighboring nation, where we captured several of their children, also a quantity of provision; I had suffered a severe griping of the guts from a spoiled fish I had eaten, and the woman with whom I shared my blanket had just died. Like a spring of water whose source is choked with rotted matter, my flow of prayers had dried. I knelt down and tried to force the words, but they would not come—nothing mattered, everything was emptiness. Yet it was as if by *not* praying I had prayed, as if the Lord God has ears for prayers unsaid. For that night the Indian who traded ochre and flints for skins returned to our village.

The first sight of the man eased my depression, and then when he spoke of how Bad Thing had been driven from the land by a new one called Good Thing, I began to fill with an excitement as great as any I had ever known. For this Indian swore he had seen Good Thing, whose radiance he described as being that of the rising sun.

Offering the man a present of polished beads and a fine knife I had fashioned from a bone, I questioned him about the one named Good Thing. When I asked from where Good Thing had come, he shrugged, and grinned, laying the presents I had just given him at my feet, together with three reed arrows of his own. Having gained sufficient knowledge of the ways of Indians, I returned the arrows to the man, and added to the beads and knife a score of quills. "Good Thing came into the land riding the back of a great red bull," he then said. "Whenever nations war," the man lowered his voice to a whisper, "Good Thing comes and then there is peace. Deer and game follow him; thus it is that even the most savage nations welcome him."

"You have seen Good Thing?" I asked the man.

"Tall as you are, Tall Black Skin, Good Thing is yet

329

taller," the man measured with his hand over his head. "And his skin is whiter than foam. So white is that one, and so dazzling the light that shines from within, if you do not turn away your eyes you will be blinded as was the medicine man who one time challenged the sun and stared up at him." With that the Indian turned away refusing to answer any further questions.

"Wherever he travels he brings peace to warring nations," I repeated to Castillo what I had learned from the Indian who traded for skins. "To look at him longer than a moment will bring blindness," I went on. "And the one who told me this is the same Indian who told us about the One who was killed and placed in a cave sealed with a stone—the One who after a certain time was alive again! Can you not understand, my friend? Can you not understand?" As Castillo listened, his jaw tightened and he frowned. It was as if he struggled to control a rising anger. Chancing the man's wrath, I seized his hand, which he had passed again and again across his eyes, and begged him to cast off his apron and join with me in Christian prayer.

As I held his one hand, his other hand tightened into a fist. "If you strike my one cheek," I lowered my voice to a whisper, "then I will turn my head and offer you the other." Swollen veins quivered in the man's neck and the knuckles of his fist turned white. "Strike me if you must!" Tears formed in Castillo's eyes, and his fist began to open. The hand which I still held grew limp as the tears spilled from his eyes and rolled down his cheeks.

A little time then passed, during which a number of the women gathered around us, laughing, and certain warriors came up, hooting and pointing. Suddenly, Castillo freed the hand I was holding, stood up, his body quivering, and ripped away the apron, which he cast in the direction of the warriors, throwing them into much confusion. Then he turned on the women, who were no longer laughing, and with a single sweeping gesture of his arm drove them backwards.

330

"I will pray with you, Estevan, I will pray with you in the manner of a Christian." Castillo's voice cracked as he spoke. "I have been sleeping, but you have awakened me from this sleep, black man." He threw his arms around me and embraced me, repeating again and again, "I have been sleeping; I have been sleeping."

We prayed together on our knees until the cold forced us to seek shelter, then in the darkness of my hut we repeated the words of the Pater Noster until overcome by fatigue.

In the morning we approached Dorantes, and knowing that he was in the grip of Satan, for he picked up a club and hissed a warning as he saw us come, we knew we must struggle with the man to free him from the Evil One.

All the Indians in the village gathered as, weaponless, we circled Dorantes, who shrieked curses as he brandished his club. "One step closer, Négro, and you will not live to grow an hour older!" said Dorantes, lunging forward.

"We are come because we love you, Andres," Castillo shouted. "We are come to save your Christian soul from Satan."

"Get back among the women," Dorantes shrieked as he spat in the man's face. The watching Indians began stamping and clapping.

Willing to risk whatever wounds might be inflicted by his club, and determined not to injure the man, I rushed in unarmed. Had the blow Dorantes then delivered not been deflected, it must have broke my head, but Castillo grabbed the man's free arm, pulling him around; thus it was that the club glanced off my shoulder, tearing the skin and numbing the arm, but otherwise doing me little harm. A second blow from Dorantes' club found its mark in Castillo's abdomen, doubling him up. But a third blow, aimed again at my head, I was able to duck; and then with a careful kick I disarmed the man and wrestled him to the ground.

Castillo, gasping and suffering too much pain to rise, crawled up and hugged Dorantes. And this so inflamed the man that he almost broke free as he thrashed and struggled, digging his nails at us until we bled, and trying to bite us. Yet we continued to hold him, careful not to hurt him, each of us as we recovered our breath saying prayers and offering him words of endearment.

It was just after Castillo escaped being bitten on the cheek as he again prayed for help in freeing Dorantes from the grip of Satan, that Dorantes suddenly went limp. For a moment I feared that, despite all our caution, we had somehow killed him, so limp had he become. But then I knew Dorantes lived, for from deep within the man I heard a soft whimpering.

I stroked his brow, and Castillo held his hand, which he brought to his lips from time to time. Gradually the whimpering sound grew louder, until at last it filled Dorantes' being and then he wept.

With all the Indians, now grown silent, watching, the three of us began to pray. How can I describe the sweetness of the words as they rose from my chest, flowed across my tongue and out my lips? The perfumed wine mixed with honey sipped by rich merchants in the bazaar of the city where I was born could not have tasted any sweeter. And how shall I describe the love I felt for Dorantes? Never in my life, not even toward a woman, had I known more tender feelings; and my feelings for Castillo were almost the same.

We prayed, and the power of our prayer drew the Indians closer, until we were pressed within their midst. Then, as if in response to a secret signal, they all knelt, and although not one understood a word of our language, they all tried to imitate its sound.

Taking from my pouch several ashcakes, still on my knees, I moved amongst the Indians, placing in each man's mouth a small portion. Castillo and Dorantes, after a moment's hesitation, took ashcakes of their own which they distributed in a like manner to the remaining scores of open-mouthed begging Indians.

332

When we finished and tried to rise from our knees, the Indians, as if angered, pulled us back down and then, much to our amazement, we suffered rough usage. In a little time we were so pummeled we could scarcely move. And after the Indians left us, at different times, one or another would come up and scratch our skin with their sharp nails, kick at us, and spit.

"We are become martyrs for our faith," whispered Castillo, his eyes shining.

"They revile us because we are Christians," Dorantes, whose face showed a mass of lumps, was smiling. And truly we had suffered for our faith, for I came to understand that by passing out the ashcake in the manner which we did, the Indians took this as a transfer of all of our power to them, and since we had neglected not a single one of them, this left us the weakest of the village. Because of this, we then began a season with these Yguazes during which our condition can only be described as piteous.

It was as if the three peaceful years we had spent with them were as nothing. It was as if we were again with our former captors. For we were forced to carry heavy burdens, and were beaten with little provocation. At times the children pelted us with stones and offal, and the women made no scruple about abusing us, grabbing at our manly parts and taking other like liberties of a vile nature. Yet, through all of this we were strengthened by the knowledge that we were Christians. Christians who suffered for their religion. And each of us held the belief that the Almighty, when it was a proper time, would grant us His relief.

XLIX

If not for our faith, we would have perished that winter. Although conditioned to every manner of hardship by the more than four years already spent in this savage land, the circumstances of our existence during those cruel months were beyond anything we had known. In the severest weather we were forced to dig for roots, protected by no more than a single skin, and always we received beatings and always we were reviled. Yet it was as if our religion was an invisible cloak that kept our bodies warm even when we were whipped by the north wind, or forced to walk waist-deep in freezing water. And this cloak softened the blows we received—we felt them, but it did not matter.

It was about two months after our change in condition—I was in a thicket of thorny bushes, trying to cut wood while shielding my eyes from sand, for the wind blew in severe gusts—when Dorantes suddenly cried out. Fearing that he had been injured by a falling branch, or that something even worse had happened to him, I ran in his direction. But he had not been injured. Unprotected from the wind he stood pointing at the western horizon. I was joined by Castillo, and we both questioned the man. His lips moved as if he tried to answer our questions, but for all the time we remained in that thicket, he could make no sound.

"I raised my ax to strike at the tree," he later whispered as we huddled within our hut, "and the ax became a tongue of fire which burned my hand, and then all of me was aflame." There was a look of joy on Dorantes' face such as I never saw on his face before. "The fire burned my skin so I must scream in pain! Then the flame rose into my eyes and burnt away all the clouds that dulled my vision." The power of the man's words caused me to tremble, and, noting this, he reached out and gripped my arm. "Descending to the earth from Heaven was a ladder made of fire, and I saw men, and I saw angels climbing up and down," he went on. "That ladder rose from the earth to the very Throne." The flesh of my arm felt as if it was searing in the man's grip. "And I know, as I know the meaning of His suffering on the cross, I know He will descend that ladder and walk again upon this earth." I have no words that can describe my emotion as I listened to Dorantes tell of his vision. How little it mattered if we suffered. How little it mattered if we waited for our liberation one year or ten.

Each night, after our work was done, Dorantes would again tell us of his vision, and no matter how severe our exhaustion, we were restored. And during the day, each time we met we greeted one another with, "He is coming," and from this greeting each of us gained new strength.

The warming winds of spring caused the Indians to temper their harsh treatment of us a little. Not that we were granted the freedom we had known before, and not that we did not still know their mocking laughter and experience beatings, yet, as the first buds appeared, we could not help but notice a gradual improvement of our condition. And it was in these early days of spring that we heard again of Good Thing.

Having suffered the loss of half a score of women and as many children from a savage raid, we were forced to raid a nation two days' journey distant. We captured seven of their women, three of whom they had earlier captured from another nation in a raid of their own. It was from these three women that we heard about Good Thing.

Where Good Thing camps there is no winter, the women

told us. If he but sets foot inside a shelter, any barren women who dwell there will be barren no longer. If he walks along the shore, fish will leap out of the water onto the sand, and wherever he travels, even amongst the most savage nations, there can be no war until he is gone. As had the Indian who traded skins, the women swore they had seen Good Thing.

From the day Dorantes saw the fiery ladder, I had prayed that I too might be granted a vision. And after listening to the three women, I prayed again. But it was not a vision I was granted, but a dream:

It was bright sunlight, so bright my eyes were dazzled, and there was a great circus around which were seated thousands of laughing people dressed in white togas. Passing amongst them were baskets of fruit, and pitchers of wine, and it was as if they enjoyed a great celebration. Then, down on the sand of the circus, I saw a group of people carrying crosses, and despite the approach of savage lions it was as if these people, too, were at a celebration. Then, as the beasts came up, the cross-carriers threw themselves into the lions' mouths, waving and laughing as they were eaten. Soon they all were gone, and the celebrating Romans, shaking with mirth, asked one another, Why are these Christians so eager to be eaten? And I answered, "To prove their faith."

"If they truly believed, they would have no need to prove," was the response of the Romans as they laughed harder.

"They are holy martyrs!" I screamed.

Then, in one voice, all the Romans answered, "They are martyred not for what they believe, but for what they doubt."

I awoke trembling and drenched with sweat. The darkness of the hut lay heavy as earth that fills the grave. Although my eyes were open, I still could see the Christians throwing themselves at the lions. The words of the gleeful Romans still rang in my ears. "Could it be that they suffered martyrdom because of doubt?" I asked myself.

As I returned to sleep and to that dream, suddenly it was I

336

who was on the sands of the arena. Thousands of white-robed Romans sitting in tiers looked down at me—I was alone. From the far side of the arena came three lions. Their terrible mouths were open, and I stared into the darkness of their throats. For several moments I hesitated. Then I turned and ran. As I ran, I heard the voices of the Christians coming from the throats of the pursuing lions. And these voices called, "If you have faith you will not run, Estevan." I ran faster. "If you truly be a Christian you will gladly suffer for your religion." Behind me, I heard the howls of the pursuing lions, and I ran still faster. Then I awoke to the darkness of my hut.

Lying there in the darkness, the vividness of the dream still with me, I gained an understanding that I cannot describe with words—but it was from this understanding I knew there is no need for suffering in this world. No need to suffer.

The next day, and for days and weeks after, it was as if I had found a priceless gift, a gift so precious I feared to share it with Dorantes and Castillo. I was afraid that if they did not understand its meaning their lack of understanding might in some mysterious way rob me of this gift. So I sought out places where I could be alone, where, with only the trees and sky to hear, I might shout, "There is no need to suffer!"

L

Glorying in the knowledge I had gained, I found the days of spring slipping easily past. At different times the medicine man gathered the people of the village around him and told the story of Good Thing, Bad Thing having been driven from the land. And then it was summer.

337

It was as we were gathering walnuts in a grove of trees, two day's journey from our village, that we again saw the Indian who traded for skins. He turned from the medicine man, with whom he had been talking, and nodded, as I and my two companions came up. Then, placing in each of our hands a likeness of a fish carved from bone, he muttered, "Good Thing sends the message, 'I am coming.' " And then each time I happened upon the Indian who traded for skins during the several days he camped with us, he would say, as if for the first time, "Good Thing sends the message, 'I am coming.' " Yet, when I tried to question the man, he would only shrug and again repeat the message.

It was the day that we prepared to leave the walnut grove and return to our village, a day during which lightning had flashed across the heavens and there was a constant roll of thunder, although no rain, a day of oppressive heat without the relief of wind, when two boys sent to fetch water returned running, crying in excited voices, "Good Thing comes! We have seen him! Good Thing comes!"

Dorantes, who worked on the far side of the grove closest to the river, upon hearing the cries of the two boys, turned and moved cautiously in the direction from where they had come. Castillo and I started to follow, but our way was barred by the chief warrior of the clan with whom we worked. This man, called One Eye—like his father before him, he had lost an eye in a raid on another nation—had justly gained a reputation for cruelty, and it was he, together with other members of his clan, who treated us with the greatest harshness. Spitting at us and scratching our chests with the point of an arrow until we bled, he pushed us backwards as he ordered several of the warriors to go after Dorantes. It was only when One Eye heard the sound of approaching men that he let up from his scratching and spitting, and then for a time we were forgotten as he turned in the direction of the sound.

Flanked by more than two score armed and painted Indi-

338

ans came Dorantes, hand in hand with another man. One Eye and the warriors of his clan slowly moved backwards as the band approached. The glaring sun hampered my vision, and the heated air danced, causing a distortion. I strained my eyes— it was Alvar Nuñez who held Dorantes' hand. . . .

Had ten score warriors holding strung bows with arrows notched stood in my way, they could not have stopped me as I rushed forward, calling his name. And so it was with Castillo. We fell upon the man, weeping, and if I kissed his lips and cheeks once, I kissed them a hundred times. And as I kissed him, he kissed me, murmuring, "Estevanico, my friend, Estevanico." I then hugged Castillo as Dorantes took Alvar Nuñez into his arms. Then it was Dorantes I hugged, then the four of us together. Since a boy, I had not done such weeping, and I tasted the others' tears, and the taste was sweet. In this way many minutes passed, each unable to speak except to call the name of the other.

"You are not dead?" I was finally able to ask Alvar Nuñez. He smiled, showing his missing teeth, so I knew he was not dead.

Then, in a rush of words, he told us how he recovered from the pestilence, and how he later escaped from his tribe and lived as a free man, trading amongst the Indians up and down the coast. Each year he had returned to the island of Malhado to urge Lope de Oviedo to accompany him to Pánuco, whose direction he was convinced lay to the south. For four years Lope de Oviedo had refused, but then, his woman having died, he agreed to come. They had traveled south until they reached the bay on whose shores we lived with our former captors, and there learned from the Indians of three Christians living with a nation several days' journey inland. These Indians had described our condition as being that of slaves, our lives harsh to the extreme. He told us how Lope de Oviedo, despite all importuning, then deserted.

If we forgot that we were slaves, our masters, the Yguazes,

had not. On first seeing Alvar Nuñez, they were cautious, and for a time hid amongst the trees, but, also being a curious people, after the passage of some minutes they left their hiding places and gradually drew close. Then they stroked his hair, touched his skin, examined his dress, which was of bark and feathers, yet they still showed signs of uneasiness. The coming of darkness increased the uneasiness of the Indians. It was then that we remembered that we were slaves, for as they separated from Alvar Nuñez we were forced to go with them.

The next day, when Alvar Nuñez came up, seeing how delicate was our position and how uneasy our Indian masters, he approached carefully, offering One Eye and the other warriors of the clan presents of a certain pod whose seeds these Indians value above all things. These presents for a time softened the savages, and, knowing we faced a problem of the greatest urgency, we put aside talk of past happenings and entered into serious conversation.

At first Alvar Nuñez strongly urged that we escape and the four of us travel south until we reached Christian lands. But we explained to him that we were certain to be followed and we told him of the fate of the three who tried to escape from our former captors. After we described the prowess of the Yguazes—there are no finer bowmen in the world—and informed him that the land to the south was barren, with very little cover where we might hide, he agreed that escape at this time was too hazardous. After further discussion, it was determined to wait until the season when the tribe went to the fields where prickly pears are eaten. There, with the help of the Almighty, we might be able to join with Indians of another tribe, since many nations go to eat prickly pears when they are ripe.

Fearing that we might be separated from him during the several months we must wait, or that if not separated, that the Indians might grow uneasy at his continued presence and cause us mischief, Alvar Nuñez then decided to join with us by offering himself as a slave to One Eye, which, despite our protests, he straightaway did.

340

As it had been from the day we left Spain, it again was the case of will being no match for fate. For, instead of causing us to stay together, Alvar Nuñez, by offering himself as a slave to One Eye, gave to that one so much power that he, and all the members of his clan, at once broke from the rest of the Yguazes to become a nation of their own. So sudden was this break that, except for a quick oath that we would all escape when we met in the fields of prickly pears, we were unable to gain another word of the history of the man or to tell him of the fate of different ones who had traveled with us.

It would serve little purpose to detail the pain we felt at this sudden separation from one we loved. Nor would there be any gain to describe the increased cruelty of our masters—it was as if they blamed us for the loss of One Eye and his clan. It is enough to say that the more than two months we were forced to wait until the prickly pears were ripe was a difficult time; each day passing with the slowness of ten, a time when I and my two companions constantly struggled against being overwhelmed by depression.

Yet, upon arriving in the field of prickly pears, we again faced a situation where fate triumphed over will.

LI

The new nation formed of the clan of One Eye was already in the field of prickly pears when we arrived, and Castillo, Dorantes and I trembled with excitement as we saw Alvar Nuñez in their midst. Yet, despite our being no more than the distance

of an arrow-shot from the man, ten more months were to pass
before we had the chance to speak to him. For, upon our coming into the fields, various warriors of the two nations started
quarreling over certain women taken by One Eye at the time of
separation. And, although no one was killed, there was much
blood spilled, and One Eye's tribe was driven from the field.

Only the certainty of our being pursued and taken restrained us from immediately following after Alvar Nuñez. Yet
such was our despair we would have abandoned caution and
risked almost certain death that night had not an Indian of
another tribe brought us the message: We will meet in the
prickly pear fields next season.

"To wait until the prickly pears again ripen—another
year," Castillo murmured, "and if we should not survive . . ."

"We will survive—if we have faith enough, we will survive," Dorantes' words rang hollow, and as he spoke he shook
his head.

"Even the prophet Job," Castillo looked up at the cold
night sky, "even that one had a limit to his patience—how then
should we go on another year?"

Yet we did go on, the days slowly passing one by one, until
they gathered into months. At different times we heard rumors
of Alvar Nuñez. We heard that he had escaped and we grew
excited. We heard that he had not escaped but had become a
medicine man and had healed his tribe of a pestilence. Other
rumors. And so the months passed, and there was an early
spring and an early summer, and soon it would again be the
season to eat prickly pears, which we learned were ripening
before their time.

And if the warriors of our tribe and the warriors of the tribe
of One Eye should again quarrel when we meet in the fields,
what then? I thought as we started southward. And this
thought came to me again and again. The night before we arrived at the fields of prickly pears, I sweated and trembled. And
then, in the morning, when we entered the fields and there

342

ahead was the tribe of One Eye, my heart pounded and my mouth grew dry.

But the passage of time had cooled passions, thus it was, instead of quarreling, the warriors of both tribes grinned and grunted, then, squatting side by side, started stuffing their mouths with ripe fruit. Soon all was contentment, as hands, faces and chests were stained with juices, the bellies of the gorging people distended.

Fearing to excite the suspicions of our masters, we scarcely greeted Alvar Nuñez as we came up to him, and he, in his turn, if he glanced at us at all, it was for a single moment. Only when we had eased away from the others and were hidden by a wall of vegetation did we exchange greetings. Yet so cautious had we become that we did not embrace or kiss, and after hurried whispers quickly separated so that we could be seen again by our masters before they should grow suspicious.

How the three of us managed to lie in their midst for that long afternoon, and how we managed not to show excitement and in this way reveal our plans, only the Lord God Himself can ever know. Yet, somehow the afternoon passed and it was night.

As great hunting cats edge across the ground on their bellies, the four of us moved silently through the fields of prickly pears after it grew dark. Yet, unlike the cats, we were not hunters, we were prey. And thanks be to God the Indians' dogs had no bark.

Once past the prickly pear fields, we rose up from our hands and knees, which had suffered from the thorns, and, hunched over, we began a slow run in the manner of wolves, moving westward, drawn by the last traces of red flickering on the far horizon.

It was Alvar Nuñez who led us, then came Castillo, then Dorantes. I followed, twenty paces to the rear, a spear in one hand, a club gripped in the other, and, except for quick glances behind, I kept my eyes on the ground, searching in the darkness for roots and stones. But when we left the last bushes and came out upon a barren plain, I raised my eyes to the dark figure of the man we were following. His thick shoulders rose and fell, his head, thrust forward, moved from side to side. I strained my vision. His form blended with the night, and it was as if I ran blind. Then there he was again, but this time his skin gave off a golden glow, as if a thousand fireflies had settled on the man. Streams of light seemed to radiate from him. The ground beneath his feet turned golden. And the light he cast fell upon Castillo and Dorantes, softening their faces until their features were those of angels.

We came to a rise where, if we were pursued, we would be seen outlined against the sky. So we no longer ran in the easy manner of wolves, but as escaping deer. The years spent with the Indians had strengthened us, and the fear of capture gave wings to our feet. Crossing the rise, three of us were brothers tied together by a sacred bond, and the other—the other one, our father. Never would we have escaped if not for him. If not for him, we would have lived and died slaves of the Indians. Had he run the length of this earth, I would have followed; I would have followed him, as would have the others, until our lungs burst.

We ran all that night. Only when the eastern sky began to brighten did we dare to rest. And this was only for a moment, as we picked thorns from our bleeding feet, and soothed our throats with gulps of water. Then we ran again.

Guided by the rays of the rising sun, we finally reached a high place. There, off to the west of us, we saw smoke from fires.

Escape from Slavery and the Journey Westward

LII

Crouched more like dogs than men, panting, we rested on the rise. From the many fires, we knew we had reached the land of another nation, thus were safe from pursuit. It was then that the years of slavery showed their effects, as the three of us dumbly shook our heads when Alvar Nuñez urged us forward. So we camped on that high place without fire, and the day passed slowly as we slept by turns, stared at the curls of smoke in the distance, and listened without response to the patient arguments of Alvar Nuñez that we should push forward—strongest of which was that he had traveled amongst more than two score nations without ever an attempt being made to capture him. The arguments of Alvar Nuñez were powerful, yet so deep had slavery scarred my being that the thought of entering that strange village caused me to sweat and tremble. And if I, who had been hardened by years in the galley, was so affected, how then should it have been with Castillo and Dorantes?

"I would follow you into the very waters of the ocean, my

346

Governor," said Dorantes, his chin pressed against his chest, his eyes lowered to the ground. "I will follow you anywhere except to that village—to be captured and again be a slave to Indians. . . ."

"If these Indians be friends to the Yguazes," Castillo spoke hoarsely, covering his eyes with his hands, "if they be friends to them and then return us—" Yet even as he spoke he knew his words were hollow, for the Yguazes had no friends.

"If we do not go to the Indians, how shall we eat?" Alvar Nuñez asked gently. "Each day the weather grows more severe, and except for breechclouts, we are naked. We have no salt, no vessels, no fire—how are we to survive without the Indians?"

With the coming of darkness, I could no longer resist Alvar Nuñez's arguments, and I separated myself from the others and, until overcome by fatigue, prayed for guidance.

Although I had been convinced, with Dorantes and Castillo it was different. It was as if they could not hear the man. He would address them and they would answer him with grunts and shrugs. But, just before morning, when he offered to go forward without them, fear changed their minds.

As I knew there was a God in Heaven, I knew, to survive, one of us must go forward to that village—so why not I?

I then told Alvar Nuñez of my decision, and after fashioning a cross of the club and spear I carried, after commending my soul to God, and after receiving Alvar Nuñez's blessing, I descended from the rise and made straight for the village, an hour's journey distant.

The chilling thought of again being pressed into slavery so troubled me that surely a dozen times I brushed against bushes or stumbled over stones, tearing my skin and suffering painful bruises. Then, once upon the plain, as an antidote to the fear that urged me back to my companions, I ran forward with my eyes nearly shut, the cross clutched in both hands and held out before me.

Thus it was I came up to an Indian, sent out from the village to meet me, without seeing him. The first I knew of his presence was when I felt his gentle touch as he ran alongside me. And the gentleness of this touch gave me hope.

Only a member of a victorious Roman legion could have ever known a reception such as the one I received as I was led into that village. From the oldest to the youngest, the Indians came out of their huts shouting, their bodies and faces decorated with fresh paint, their arms loaded with gifts. And as I stood in the midst of the village surrounded with presents while half a thousand savages pressed close laughing and clapping, I filled with exultation as I knew with certainty I was free again.

All the inhabitants of the village, not excepting the youngest children, followed me across the plain as I returned for my three companions. How they viewed this multitude from their position on the rise as they saw us approaching I never knew, for they would not ever speak of this matter. All I knew was that when we arrived they were hidden and although Alvar Nuñez quickly appeared when he heard my shouts, the other two took much convincing.

If Castillo and Dorantes still had any doubts as they emerged from the crevices in which they crouched, these must have been dispelled as they saw me, festooned with fine skins and feathers, Alvar Nuñez similarly arrayed, surrounded by the leading warriors of the village who showed with their every gesture that they made us obeisance.

Had we not forcefully discouraged these Indians, they would have carried us like emperors the entire distance to their village. Not that our bruised feet would not have benefitted from such a mode of travel, but it was as if each of us separately felt—we did not share our thoughts—that to walk showed a greater dignity, for we were soldiers of the King of Spain, not royalty.

Although as impoverished as any of the nations we had

348

known, the Indians of that village offered us such a celebration that, until we discovered that they went hungry to provide us an abundance of food, we believed that we had happened upon one of the richest tribes of all the Western Indies. Yet had our eyes not been clouded by the richness of the celebration, we must have noted that their houses were of flimsy manufacture, their naked children showing bones sharply through their skins. But who is there who will not forgive us for not seeing during that day and night of celebration? We had suffered so many years of harshness, such privation . . . The taste of their dried venison was so sweet, my mind emptied of all thought. Each of us had our fill of meat, washed down with a mild beer brewed of nuts. And as we ate, the Indians kept clapping and cheering.

If any one of us had fears that after being so lavishly fêted we might be set upon as had been the case years earlier when we still traveled with the expedition of Pánfilo de Narvaez, with the arrival of morning and with our being offered yet another banquet such fears must have been dispelled. But that banquet was to be the last with this tribe of Indians, for after again being lavished with an abundance of meat and other good things to eat, their supply was completely exhausted.

One might expect four companions again united after such a time of separation to forego sleep and use every moment of the night and day that followed for conversation; yet such was not the case with the four of us as we lolled at our ease in that Indian village. For me it was enough that the other three were there. In time I would learn more of Alvar Nuñez's history, of that I was certain. So why sacrifice the perfect joy of the moment? Each of the other three had his private reason for silence. And our years of wandering had made us great respecters of privacy, for when our condition was most severe, only in the deep recesses of the mind did we find peace.

LIII

The second night with the Indians of that nation (called Avavares), having enjoyed sufficient rest and having been much restored by the lavish feasts, we might have engaged in conversation—the four of us having settled down in a quiet place—had the chief not ordered preparations be made to leave the village and travel south to a field of prickly pears whose fruit was just coming ripe. With these people, unless someone makes objection, when a thing has been decided upon, it is done at once. Thus, all was packed and ready within thirty minutes of the order.

It was as we moved out that Alvar Nuñez first suffered a sudden indisposition of bowels brought on, no doubt, by the quantity and richness of the food he had consumed. By midnight, although our forward progress was slow, burdened as we were by children and provisions, he could not keep up with us so griped had he become. Seeing the severity of his condition—although the air was cold he had cast off his clothes for he was drenched with sweat—the chief ordered a halt that Alvar Nuñez might relieve himself. When after half an hour he had not returned, the chief determined to move out again leaving behind markings.

I might have tried to search for Alvar Nuñez had I not remembered that those times when I had known the colic it was privacy I most desired. So I restrained myself, confident that after he had a sufficient time to purge, he could easily find the markings and come up to us. Perhaps I should have been more concerned, for the weather, each hour, was growing colder.

But neither Dorantes nor Castillo appeared concerned—
Dorantes enjoying the attention he was being given by different Indian women; Castillo working his art as physician and
curing the headache, an affliction common among these
Indians.

With the coming of morning and Alvar Nuñez having not
reappeared, a concern I should have felt during the darkest
hours of night came upon me. It was then that I remembered he
had cast off his clothes because of sweat; it was then that I
thought about how it was when I had suffered a like condition—
more than once I had grown so weak from the force of purgings
I could not walk. When the sun had risen and in the direction
from which we had come we could descry no movement, the
concern that was taking a heavy grip on me began to affect
Dorantes and Castillo. We approached the chief and, instead of
relieving our anxiety, he fell to weeping, saying that the man
must have suffered a sting from a viper, for the countryside
swarms with these poisonous creatures.

The chief being reluctant to halt the forward progress of
the expedition (for he judged Alvar Nuñez already dead), and
unwilling to order any of his warriors to search for the man (for
fear of an attack by marauders), it fell upon the three of us to
succor our captain.

After gaining promises from the chief that he would leave
sufficient markings and after promising that we would rejoin
him within two days the three of us separated from that nation;
Dorantes taking a westerly direction, Castillo moving to the
east while I retraced the course we had traveled.

At different times during the first few hours of our search I
could hear one or the other of the captains shouting out the
name of the Governor. To these I added shouts of my own.
Then as the distances between us grew greater the shouts grew
faint. Then silence except for the rustle of grasses and at different times the plague-rattle sound of vipers.

I searched behind every boulder and peered into every

gully. I descended into arroyos when needs be, exercising great caution not to be stung by vipers. I mounted each rise I came up to that I might have a better view of the distance. Thus it took me until dark before I reached the village. Except for a sick dog the Indians had abandoned, the place was empty.

The next day I continued my search circling the village in ever widening rings taking care not to neglect any crevice or depression, any stand of bushes—even the shadows cast by boulders might be places in which a man lay hidden. By night, not having found a trace of the Governor, I feared that any further exploration would be useless. Yet, in the morning I searched again.

The three of us rejoined the nation called Avavares in the early afternoon. Neither Castillo nor Dorantes had discovered a trace of Alvar Nuñez.

"To have been reunited with the Governor after so many years and then in such a senseless way to have lost him," Castillo wiped at his eyes to stop his tears. "Had I been more concerned with one whom I have grown to love as if he were my own father than in the smiles and winks of their disease-rotted women as I showed off my prowess as physician, I would have recognized the seriousness of his condition . . ."

"May I be struck dead if I ever again touch one of their women," Dorantes interrupted. "To rut with their whores, I neglected a suffering companion—so hungry for their caresses I did not have eyes to see his suffering. And now he is lost. Naked and sick in this icy weather how could he survive?"

"He survived five years among the Indians with no help from his companions," I then offered.

"He was not naked, black man!" Dorantes turned on me. "For those five years he was not naked in this frigid air—nor was he doubled over with the tortures of colic . . . "

"In a land swarming with vipers and other terrible creatures," Castillo joined in. From the way the two men looked at me it was as if I had been the cause of the Governor's

352

misfortune—as if they believed I had poisoned him. But then their faces softened; first Castillo, quickly followed by he who had one time been my master.

"As you say, Estevanico," Dorantes nudged me with his elbow, "Alvar Nuñez did survive a full five years with no help from us and here we mourn the man not gone three days."

If Dorantes and Castillo had any further thoughts, they kept them to themselves, for that was the last word we shared until we reached the field of prickly pears late afternoon of the next day. But no matter how hard I tried, I could not keep my head free of painful thoughts. As had Dorantes and Castillo, for those few moments, I blamed myself for Alvar Nuñez's disappearance. But unlike them I could not soften. By his attack of madness Dorantes had shown that, despite the broadness of his shoulders and the strength of his arms, he suffered an especial weakness; and Castillo when he put on the apron of a woman revealed a fragileness that gave lie to the severity of his expression and the quickness of his temper. Thus of the three only I retained the vigor of my mind and body unimpaired. And thus it was my responsibility to be aware of the nature of Alvar Nuñez's sickness—this responsibility I neglected.

If I retained any trace of hope that I might see Alvar Nuñez again it was lost as the weather turned so cold frost formed on the ground and the pears froze hard and must be thawed before they were eaten.

The three of us camped by the bank of a modest river separated by the distance of a quarter of a league from the Indians who continued to gorge themselves with fruit. There we built a fire, but our spirits were such that its heat could not warm us. There was no wind and the sound of the ravenous Indians, grunting and spitting, came down to us. Although fatigued from the rough march, we could not sleep. Several times I tried to close my eyes, but an image of Alvar Nuñez, naked, struggling in the dark would appear, and I had to open them. With Dorantes and Castillo it must have been the same. So it was that

353

we stared into the darkness motionless except when we tossed dead branches into the leaping flames from time to time.

"As Estevanico says, Alvar Nuñez survived five years of wandering among the Indians," Dorantes murmured. It was as if I had just spoken that very minute instead of more than a day ago.

"We will search for him again in the morning!" declared Castillo. "I cannot bring myself to believe that we will not see those broken teeth, that battered nose again." He threw a branch into the fire and in the burst of flame I could clearly see his features. A hundred times, a thousand times I had looked at Castillo in the years of our wandering, but this was the first time since that day so long ago when I followed the man into the Florida jungle to search for water that I truly saw him. Then he had been of delicate features with an unrelieved frown to hide his beauty from the soldiers who served him. Then, despite all his gruffness and quickness of temper, he had been still a boy. Now in spite of his uncertainty and the tears that swam in his eyes, he was a man. And his features had coarsened, not that he was not handsome, but he was no longer pretty. I turned my gaze to the one who had been my master. A burst of flame illumined his face for a single moment, but it was enough for me to see that he still suffered traces of his madness, for his eyes were hooded and uneasy; the corners of his mouth tightened with a smile, yet there was no smile.

"We will search for him in the morning," Castillo repeated. "I will not believe that I am not to see Alvar Nuñez Cabeza de Vaca in this world again."

These words had scarcely left his lips when we heard a rustling in the trees and saw a light. We started to rise but got no further than our knees when the branches parted and Alvar Nuñez, naked, his feet bleeding, his hands gripping a burning brand, stepped into the clearing.

So chilled was the man his jaws were frozen so he could not speak; his hand gripping the burning brand so stiff his fingers

354

would not open. We chafed him, the three of us at once, and if our kisses had any warmth they must have brought fire to his lips and cheeks. How we did not rub the skin from his legs and arms from the vigor of our chafing I shall never know.

At last he found his voice and cried out: "Enough!" And although we let up with our chafing, our hugs and kisses only ceased when he struck at us with his fists, roughly but not too roughly. "Have you mistaken me for a woman, you thick skulled ox?" he croaked at Dorantes. "Are you so blinded by your passion you attempt fornication with your captain?" Dorantes laughed and released the man from a great hug with which he was holding him. "And, Alonso, where is your reputation as a despoiler of virgins—to attempt your captain and he scarcely recovered from his little walk through some of the most safe and pleasant country to be found anywhere in this friendly land?" Castillo let go of the man and joined Dorantes in laughing.

"And you, Estevanico," he shook his head as he looked at me still straddled over his legs, "are there not Indian women enough to satisfy your appetite—must you relieve your ardor with a man and he your captain and of a different race? If the Viceroy should ever hear of this . . . " Phlegm brought up by laughter prevented him from going on.

Each of us, as if bidden by some unseen force, then gave the man as a gift the most precious thing he owned. With Dorantes it was a strip of dried venison a palm in length he had saved from our feasting. Castillo's gift was a pouch of herbs of wonderful medicinal power he had carefully collected. My offering was a single stone in whose luster could be seen the moon. Each gift Alvar Nuñez accepted without protest and with grave nods, for he understood our need to give them.

LIV

With the reappearance of Alvar Nuñez I was completely restored. Not a trace of the crushing fatigue that had lain on my shoulders like lead was left. And so it was also with Castillo and Dorantes. Only our concern for the weakness of the man prevented us from showering him with questions as he slowly chewed on his piece of venison while Castillo salved and bound his injured feet. But finally when his cheeks infused with color and his lips had lost their bluish tinge, without our urging, he began to speak.

"For the first hours of that colic, I was certain the Indians had fed us poison and I expected to hear groans as each of you was forced to find a private place to relieve your purgings. Then I grew so weak that unless stepped upon I could not have given notice of my presence. Then the weakness grew less and the sweats were gone." Picking up a corner of the blanket that covered his legs and feet he continued, "For this blanket or even for one half its thickness I would have given title to all the land I own in Spain. Ice formed on my skin and the air grew so chill it felt as if my throat and lungs were freezing. If I did not find warmth I knew I would be dead by morning. So, trusting the Lord, God to guide me, although my legs were loose, I forced myself to my feet and started to run. I ran all through the night and then into the morning. How many times I stumbled . . . Twice I doubled up with colic . . . But if I did not run it was certain I would freeze. Yet had the Almighty not led me to a tree that was cleft by lightning and still smoldering, with the setting of the sun I must have expired.

356

"With whatever little breath I had left I blew on the places that smoldered until there were sparks. These I teased into a mound of dried leaves, then there was flame. I remembered, as a boy, listening to my tutor telling of the ancient one who risked his liberty to steal fire that those who dwelt on earth might be warm. As the flames rose from that pile of leaves, I understood the meaning of this story—I understood why that noble Titan was willing to suffer a vulture each day tearing at his liver. 'If the world was cold,' I whispered as I fanned the flame, 'and by offering myself as a sacrifice I could make all men warm, as I know Christ died for us I know I could do no less than did Prometheus.'

"Being too weakened to travel any further that afternoon, I stayed next to that smoldering tree, trusting that after a night's rest I would be sufficiently restored to find the trail. But if I thought the first night cold, it was like a spring day in comparison with the night that followed. Even the great fire I built could not provide enough warmth, my condition being naked; and if I was to regain my strength I must sleep. Accordingly, I dug a pit which I filled with grasses. I then built four fires around the pit. After making certain there was enough fuel to last the night, I crawled down into the pit, covered myself with leaves and grasses and in little time was warm.

"Except to replenish the fires two times, I slept that night as I have not slept since a child, nestled between my father and mother. Yet despite the deepness of my sleep I was not restored in the morning. The purgings had robbed me of my energy and other than some few berries of a poor quality I found, I had nothing to eat.

"Carrying a burning brand before me for its little heat, together with enough dried sticks so that I would not lose my fire, I started to search for the trail as soon as it was light. But my wild run during the first night had taken me in the wrong direction. Thus it was I hunted all through the day yet could find no markings. If my spirits sagged at different times, I forced myself to remember I had been guided to the smoldering tree without which I would now be dead and I gave thanks that although freezing cold there was no wind. Had there been wind, I do not see how I could have survived.

"I camped that night as I had the night before. But having grown careless I placed the fires too close to the pit and when a sàp filled branch exploded it showered sparks on the leaves and grasses I used as my cover and set me afire, singeing my eyebrows, beard and hair, but fortunately doing nothing worse. Taking care that it should not happen again, I crawled back into the pit, but although I trembled from fatigue I could not sleep. So filled with thoughts was my brain, that they crowded out any chance of sleeping. And not one of these thoughts contained so much as a single element of despair."

A smile softened Alvar Nuñez's face as he stopped speaking for a time. In the distance a pack of wolves broke out with their baying. When Alvar Nuñez started speaking again the cold light of the rising moon illumined the eastern horizon.

"Never had I been more certain of anything than I was that the four of us would be reunited," Alvar Nuñez spoke slowly. "Too many things had happened for me not to know certainty . . . The smoldering tree set afire by a bolt from the Almighty was just another proof that my destiny rested safely in Divine hands. How did I survive when I lay struggling for each breath after I had been carried by the Indians of Malhado over to the main? How did I remain alive, a single Christian among that tribe of pagans? When I learned that the Christians who quartered to the north of the island had crossed over to the main and had then departed, when I learned that I would not be succored I gave up all hope and turned my face to the wall of the hut in which I was quartered to wait for death. But I did not die, I could not die. I could not die although I wished for death." Alvar Nuñez paused for breath.

"All the myriad things that had happened to me in my life came back to me as I lay out there in that pit staring up at the

358

listening sky—a tapestry of the life of Alvar Nuñez Cabeza de Vaca. Never have I experienced a night of such great length—like a bridge stretching from the past across the present to eternity, it was. Although only two days since, I know that should half a hundred years pass and I still live I will retain within my mind a remembrance of that night of certainty.

"Not even a bachelor whose life is spent in doing writings would have the words to describe what I felt as I lay there alone and naked yet in such peace—how then should I, scarcely able to more than read or write, have the words? I felt a closeness to the Mother's Tortured Son—a closeness I first knew when, still a boy, I knelt in church three days before the gilded statues mourning for my servant, Niño." From the luster of Alvar Nuñez's eyes and the way his face was tilted upwards I knew that although we were the audience these words were not only for us.

"Niño, another proof of my destiny. . . . My father, that I might sooner become a man, ordered me to hunt the boar on horseback with a spear as my only weapon—I lacked three months of my thirteenth year. Taking a spear fashioned of lemon wood with little Niño astride a great plow horse as my companion, I set out after promising my father a feast of wild pig meat before the world grew three days older.

"It was as if every boar that roamed those hills knew of our coming; we hunted two days without sighting a snout or tail. Niño, who knew the ways of wild beasts, said we must fail in our hunt for all the signs were wrong. But my promise to my father to serve a feast of pig so filled my ears, Niño's words might have been the wind. The third morning as the sun was level with my eyes, blinded for the moment by its light, my horse surprised a great boar in the thicket. With a rush the boar cut the horse's strings, tumbling him, then with a sweep of his tusks, gutted him. I fell clear but had lost my weapon. Seeing my movements as, dazed from my fall, I crawled on my hands and knees searching for my spear, the boar turned from the open belly of the horse in which he had been rooting and made for me. Had Niño not rode his old plow horse between us I would have been split like a goat prepared for roasting. As it had been with my horse so it was with Niño's—a Damascus sword could not have gutted the creature more cleanly than did that boar's tusks. Then it turned on Niño who struggled to free himself from the weight of the dying beast. The first slash Niño escaped as he twisted to one side causing the tusks in which were tangled bits of gut to rake against the horse's ribs. The second slash I deflected as I rushed at the creature with my spear which I had recovered. The third slash hooked the man below the chest and opened him to the chin—I could see his heart beating. But that pig never slashed in this world again, for I pinioned him through the throat and despite his struggles held on until he lay dead.

"My father never had his feast of pig, for it was not the swine I dragged down the mountain on a litter made of sticks, but the corpse of little Niño.

"Three days I knelt in the church nave praying for the soul of Niño. Three days during which all that passed my lips was water. I thought to take a holy order—one whose oath was silence. I begged guidance from the Virgin as I gazed at Her face glowing in the colored sunshine; Her gown glistening from rows of votive lights.

"The third day, my limbs trembling from the fast, my skin damp with sweat, I turned away from the Woman to a great cross from which hung Her Son. I gazed at Him; at the thorns; at His tortured eyes; at the wounds. And I saw that the wounds bled. And from this blood came a light which wrapped around His wracked body until it glowed.

"I had prayed to the Mother, yet from the Son came my sign. And I knew mine must be the way of men—arms not Orders. As I knew that He who had given the sign would guide me; as I knew that Niño's gift of his life in exchange for mine was for some purpose.

360

"All this I knew as I knelt in the nave of that church, but a score of years and a dozen battles caused what I knew to grow dim until in time it was nearly forgotten. Yet, that day in springtime, five years since, as I lay in that Indian hut wishing for my death, and did not die, the memory of Niño's sacrifice came back to me as did the bleeding wounds of the Tortured Son.

"As if the memory of Niño and the light cast from the bleeding wounds of Christ together formed a balm, my breathing grew less labored and my fever lifted. By morning I had gained such relief that I could take food. Within a week a portion of my strength had returned and I could walk about the village. It was then that the Indians reminded me that, although of all the Christians I alone was left, my condition was still that of slavery.

"Had it not been for the determination of the woman who had taken me as her husband I am certain I would have fallen sick again and a second bout of that malady no man could survive. As soon as they saw I could walk, the Indians ordered me to join with those who searched for roots beneath the water and then struck me across my shoulders with sticks when I hesitated. My woman rushed to my defense. Those who were beating me she tore at with fingers used like talons. Her feet, hard as hoofs from a lifetime without shoes, struck at their faces and their parts—had there been a dozen belaboring me instead of only three or four she would have scattered them, so savage was her attack. That the widow of a chief had chosen me—had nursed me, then had saved me, was this not another sign of my destiny?

"As I lay in my hut that night feeling the strength of that woman's arms around me, as I strained to see her seamed and pitted features in the little light from the glowing coals, my feelings and my thoughts flowed together; I gained meanings about which I was certain, yet they had no words.

"As it was in that hut with the woman, now five years dead,

so it was as I lay naked after my purging. Each beat of my heart told me again the truth of what I knew—that every happening in my life was for a purpose, that it all connected leading outward beyond the limits of the sky to the throne of the Almighty before which stands the Son.

"It was the death of the woman who had taken me as her husband that caused me to flee from that tribe of Indians. When she sickened with the bloody vomits and, despite all the care I could give her, I saw that she could not survive, I made my preparations, gathering a store of food, flints, ochre, and other things I could use to trade with the Indians who dwelt inland.

"So deeply did that woman love me that, dying, she whispered for me to cover her face with skins so the others of the village should not hear her rattle. 'Do not let them know I am gone, my husband,' she gasped with the little breath left. 'Stay with me until all are asleep then escape to the Charruco who live two days journey inland from whom I was taken as a child. Walk into their village bravely and seek out their chief who you must then wrestle; if you do this, my husband, they will know you have the knowledge of their ways and will not harm you.' These were her last words. With eyes streaming I covered her face with skins and in such a way that her death was not prolonged." Alvar Nuñez fell silent and except for the soft hiss of the fire and the murmur of the river there was no sound. Then the wolves, whose skulking forms could be seen in the light of the risen moon moving amongst the trees on the far side of the river, started their howling again.

"I traveled two days inland then searched another day north and south for the nation of the woman who had taken me as husband," Alvar Nuñez went on. "And when I found them, I did as she had instructed: Offering no gifts, brushing past the warriors, I sought out the chief and, without a word, started wrestling him. Had I not regained every scruple of my strength—six months had passed since the last of the fever left

362

me—and had I not acquired from my father some skill in the art of wrestling, I would have been rendered helpless by that chief before two minutes. As it was I could not beat him. But I was strong and quick enough so that, despite his greater skill with which he threw me to the ground not less than a score of times, he could not pinion and thus beat me. But I suffered bites on my arms and shoulders, twice kicks to my groin just missed my parts but bruised my thighs, one eye he closed tight with a thrust of his elbow and only when I caught his hand and twisted it in such a wise that his wrist was broke did he let up from his attack. Then he stroked me with his sound hand, as did all the men of the village who crowded close, sighing and murmuring.

"With these Indians with whom I dwelt for many months I was not a slave, and because I came to them as a trader I was permitted to go from one tribe to another, a thing forbidden to all except this one class of beings.

"Because of the color of my skin and because of my profession as a trader—one who brings both commodities and messages which to these Indians is of the highest importance—I was treated with great honor while amongst these Charrucos, as I was by every nation to which I traveled as far distant as fifty leagues north and even a greater distance south. Then when I employed the little skill I had gained of the arts of the physician together with providing the sick with crosses fashioned of sticks and showing them how to make the holy sign, my reputation so increased that I was given greater honor than the medicine man or chief and sat with them and the ancient ones even at those special times when they told their sacred stories.

"Although my intention, as I traveled, was to find out the way by which I should go forward and to gain information as to the presence of any Christians, the peacefulness of my existence and the honors which I was shown caused my intention, I must confess, to grow dim. There were whole months together when scarcely a thought other than matters of the moment passed through my mind. And there came a time, except for the lighter color of my skin, there was little to distinguish me from the Indian, so accustomed to my existence with them had I become.

"It was a sacred story I heard as I dwelt with the Aguenes as they celebrated a great victory that caused me to again consider my destiny. A nation three days journey to the south called the Guevenes had attacked the village during the night killing three men and capturing several women. Then the warriors of the Aguenes gathered together and stealthily followed the enemy through the woods. I accompanied the warriors not as a soldier but as a physician to offer them my services if needs be. The warriors of my village attacked just before sunrise and so great was the surprise of the Guevenes, who thought themselves safe having traveled more than three leagues, that five of their number were killed before they could make defense and many wounded; also they lost most of their weapons and the several women they had captured. I remained hidden during the battle, but not so hidden that I could not observe the action.

"Of all the Indians I have ever known these Aguenes are the most warlike and the most skilled with their weapons. They fight in a crouched position and dart from side to side in a manner marvelous to behold and while they fight they talk to one another, and they whistle as they dodge the arrows of the enemy, discharging their own arrows with deadly accuracy. More than any other soldiers, Turkish and Spanish not excepted, they can detect fear in the enemy and are quick to take advantage of it. And unless pierced through some vital organ they will not quit the battle.

"Whirling sticks attached to thongs which makes a sound that can only be likened to the bellow of a maddened bull, the Indians returned to their village carrying the bodies of the five they had slain and the great quantity of weapons. After eating portions of these corpses—the heart, the liver, other organs, a thing I found painful to witness although this was not the first time I had viewed such a practice—and after consuming great

364

pots of foaming beer prepared by the women in expectation of their return, the younger warriors, and these were much the majority, retired to their huts while the older warriors and certain very old women gathered in a special place to continue the celebration. Because of the high esteem in which they held me I was included in this gathering.

"Posting three or four of their number as guards so that no one should get close enough to listen—for there was much anger and grumbling from those not included and it was not uncommon for a young warrior to try and gain intelligence by crawling stealthily through the high grasses—the medicine man and the chief started drawing sacred symbols in the sand. Watching from my place of honor I could not help remembering the picture of the great white beast drawn by that other medicine man and chief of the island of Malhado. You three must remember, I am certain you do." This was the first time since he had started his narration that Alvar Nuñez addressed us. The first time he had so much as looked at us.

"I remember," Castillo answered. "I remember how the chief told his story of the great white beast and its struggles with the terrible crocodile and I also remember, my captain, how at different times the Indians began to spit . . . "

"And how when he was finished with the story he must tell it over again," interrupted Dorantes with a grin.

"And how there was a third telling," added Castillo. "And I remember those five whore-sons who, if not reminded it is not nice to leave a celebration without permission from the host, would have tramped out belching and farting . . . "

"Gonçalo Ruiz, Diego Lopez, Palaçios, Corral and Sierra," Dorantes counted off the five names on his fingers. "How did it go with them?" he asked Alvar Nuñez. "Did you have further difficulty with that scum of the expedition?"

His voice reduced almost to a whisper, his eyes staring into the deep of the fire, Alvar Nuñez recounted the fate of the five men.

" . . . found the body of Gonçalo Ruiz and the bones of the other four roasted black and split for their marrow," Castillo repeated the Governor's final words in a hollow voice.

"Worse than the vilest of pagan savages," Dorantes muttered, droplets spraying from his lips, both hands balled into a single fist. "How can such things be?"

"The pagan Indian will eat portions of the enemy for their strength," Alvar Nuñez said so softly his words were almost lost in the hiss of the fire. "But will die of starvation before consuming the flesh of their own."

A breath of wind stirred the bushes and caused us to draw our blankets closer. "As I sat amongst the Aguenes at their sacred celebration and watched the chief and medicine man drawing those powerful symbols in the sand," Alvar Nuñez went on with his narration, "as my mind went back to that other celebration on the island of Malhado I could not escape thoughts of the five, thoughts I had tried to keep buried in the deep of my memory. Thus it was as I sat there pressed close on both sides by sour smelling savages whose faces yet showed traces of the special food they had consumed, thoughts of the five dead Christians tugging at my brain, the savagery of the battle I had witnessed still before my eyes, I prepared myself to hear a tale of cruelty and viciousness—of some terrible raid made by warriors of the tribe in past years, or an account of tortures inflicted slowly on helpless captives with those who told the story writhing to show how terrible had been the pain. But this was no ordinary celebration, for the victory had come at the time of the new moon and one of the victims had been the enemy's chief. Thus, what I heard that night was no ordinary story, but one reserved for the most sacred of occasions. A story last told by the father of the present chief when even the oldest of those gathered to listen was judged too young to attend such a sacred gathering. Only the chief and the medicine man had ever heard this tale before.

"As the medicine man added red sand to the likeness of the

366

sun, yellow sand to that of the moon, the chief commenced his story. 'In a place that is no more, the sun and his wife, the moon, one time had their home. Thus this place where those two lived never could be dark, although when the sun went out to hunt he took with him his heat. (It was only then that those who lived there were cool enough to sleep.) And everyone in that place were their children. For the sun never failed to mount the moon on his return from the hunt, and then when he was gone again she would open up her loins and without a sigh give birth.' At this the old women present made sounds of wonder and softly clapped their hands. 'And in this land there was no war, for everyone was of one tribe.' The listening men made angry sounds as they heard this and slapped their thighs. 'And because there was no war and because those of the tribe could not form clans and fight (all being brothers and sisters), there were no weapons—their father the sun bringing home enough meat so there was no need to hunt.' At this the angry sounds of the men grew louder and they started pounding the ground with their fists. 'To prove your manhood, there were foot races and wrestling, throwing stones for distance and high jumping. Thus, in that place that is no more, there was little difference between the least and the greatest warrior.' The chief paused until the angry sounds grew less. 'And in that place that is no more, except for their aprons, the women were no different from the men. For the women wrestled, threw stones, told stories, and when the food must be cooked it was who was closest to the fire pit that took the task even if the one closest was a man.' The listening women showed impassive faces and offered no sound while the men glared at them and made threatening gestures. 'Yet those who dwelt in this place that is no more had knowledge of many things, things of such great power that if even a chief or a medicine man of our nation were to know them he must be struck dead: How a seed becomes a tree; where their father the sun goes when he hunts; the face of the creature whose breath is the wind; why water turns to stone in the winter—other things, many other things. And to gain this powerful knowledge each one, when he is ready, must go from that place that is no more to where he can be alone and there, alone, he waits for the understanding even if he must wait many seasons. Once it is given to him he returns and shares it with all the others not only the older ones.' At this statement all who were listening, men and women, broke out with angry mutterings which quickly increased in volume until it was a roar. And it was many minutes before the chief could continue with his story, these minutes he employed by drawing a circle of armed warriors around the pictures of the moon and sun.

" 'For more seasons than there are trees in all these forests that place that is no more was as I have told you,' the chief continued with his story. 'But then one of the men, when it came his time to be alone, hungry to gain an understanding of matters not given to any man to know, traveled too great a distance. He crossed mountains and rivers, struggled through canyons and across deserts until he reached the top of the world and there he sat alone for as many seasons as there are fingers on both hands. But because he sat at the top of the world, a great warrior of the forests saw him as he hunted and, seeing that he was like no man he had ever known, for he carried no weapon not even a knife, the great warrior together with all the men of his nation followed that one when it came time for him to return home.' At this the listening men began snapping their fingers and grinning, the women clapping their hands and nodding their heads. 'Not knowing he was followed he led the band of warriors to the place that is no more. And seeing that those who dwelt there were weaponless the warriors who had followed descended.' The grins of the men turned into laughter as the claps of the women grew faster. 'Not knowing how to fight, the men of that place that is no more ran to the moon who is their mother and hid behind her—the sun their father being away on his hunt. All their women the warriors captured so that each warrior had more women than there are in this nation.' So violent had grown the men's laughter tears ran down their cheeks, but the clapping of the women lessened. 'Then the warriors started shooting arrows at the moon so that they drove her and her great brood of weaponless sons up into the sky. After that, the place that is no more was no longer light. Then, driving the women before them, the warriors made their escape before the sun should return from his hunt. And the men of that place that is no more had been driven too high to return and all that could be seen of them were their eyes which can still be seen.' The chief made a sweeping gesture upwards. 'The sun, not knowing of the raid, returned home and started searching for his children. But his heat was such he set fire to the land, for he must needs cool his heat in the loins of his wife the moon and she was gone.' "

Alvar Nuñez paused for several moments. "What these savages took as the meaning of this story I never learned. For that was the only time I ever heard it. But later as I lay on a bed of leaves, the night being warm, staring up at the sky, this sacred story brought a special meaning." Alvar Nuñez paused. "That there could be a place without war or weapons . . . that all could be peace . . . how could such a story have been born unless there had once existed such a place—these were my thoughts. Was peace not the message of The Son? Was not Prince of Peace His name? If pagans with no knowledge of the One who died on the twisted tree, who have never knelt before a priest, if such savages have in their history, however dim, a remembrance of a land of peace, is this not proof that upon His next return such a place again can be?

"By morning I was determined to pursue the way of peace in imitation of the Christ as did our Seraphic Father, St. Francis. Never would I raise my hand against a man again. If I must live out my years amongst these savages, the years would be employed in bringing amity to warring villages." Then, as if Alvar Nuñez had taken a draught of laudanum whose full effect

369

had suddenly come upon him, his jaw dropped, his eyes fluttered shut, his breathing deepened and he fell into such a sleep that it was afternoon of the next day before he awakened.

But although his three companions also felt fatigue, we could not sleep.

"The Governor is much changed," Dorantes was the first to speak.

"How should he not be changed, after five years of wanderings among these pagans—and alone," Castillo answered.

"We all have changed, Alonso," the sound of Dorantes' voice was such that I could not tell if these changes were to his liking or not. "Even Estevanico with all his great size, thick muscles and scarred features no longer appears so fierce."

"Although, Andres, if one who did not know him, should come upon him suddenly in the forest they might see him otherwise." Both men laughed softly.

"Did you know, my little Estevanico, that for all the many years we were together, although you were the slave and I the master I never felt easy with you; did you know that, my gentle Estevanico?"

I hesitated several seconds then answered, "Yes, Andres, I knew this. I am not a pretty man and I am of a size greater than most—and I am black. Few men that I have ever known have been easy with me."

"Alonso, do you hear how he who for half a score of years was my slave now calls me Andres—if I am granted as many more years as I already have will there ever be a time I do not wince?"

"Andres, Andres, after so many leagues traveled together, after such adversity how should such a little thing yet matter?" said Castillo.

"It is not that I do not love Estevanico, it is not my lack of love, but my pride, Alonso. Leagues, adversity and years have not robbed me of my pride."

"And Alvar Nuñez, has he less pride? Yet even when this

370

expedition was young I have seen him with my own eyes put an arm around the shoulders of this black man; and he second-in-command."

"Call me Andres whenever you wish, Estevanico. And if through the grace of God we return to Spain I will steel myself to this familiarity even if it be in a tavern in the presence of my friends, even in my father's house. You have proved yourself a friend; I will sacrifice a portion of my pride."

"May the four of us be together when he calls you by name in that Spanish tavern," said Castillo with his eyes half closed. "To roll a single drop of wine pressed from the grapes from Castile on my tongue I would put on the skin of an ass and walk on hands and knees, so little have I come to regard pride."

Dorantes bit his lip then pulled on his beard. "For a sip of your wine, Alonso, if it really be Castilian, for such a sip—now as I consider it—for such a sip I too would play the ass, even allow this great black ox to ride me." As he said these words the man delivered a blow to my arm the pain of which gave me pleasure.

"With Alvar Nuñez to lead us, as certain as I am that there is a God in Heaven, we will again see Spain." Castillo's face filled with color. "I cannot believe that we could have survived so much adversity unless to fulfill a destiny. If it had been the will of the Almighty that we die in this desolate place, we would have perished long since as did all the others."

"As Alvar Nuñez said," Dorantes pulled his beard with such force it brought tears to his eyes, "he stayed alive for a reason; so it must be for the three of us." The same look of wonder as had transformed his features that day while slaving for the Yguazes when he gained certain meanings again showed in his face. "That each of us survived is no less a miracle than it was with him! So close to death has each of us come that it is as if we were dead and are risen." Dorantes clasped his hands as his eyes rolled upwards. "Steeped as you are in religion, how say you, Estevan."

"That Andres Dorantes, Alonso del Castillo, Alvar Nuñez Cabeza de Vaca and a black man of Azemmour survive, four of three hundred who landed six and more years ago on the coast of Florida, that we survive when so many died must be counted as a great miracle!" I answered.

LV

I was awakened in the mid morning by hunger and the sun's rays as were the two captains; Alvar Nuñez, whose fatigue was greater, slept on. Upon opening my eyes, I saw ranged around us scores of warriors of the Avavares together with warriors of other tribes unfamiliar to us. Although it is not uncommon for more than one nation to visit a field of prickly pears at the same time (even if they are warring, they will call a truce), still to see men of different tribes carrying weapons and standing so close to one another yet not fighting caused the three of us much amazement. How long they had been waiting I cannot know, but I do know they waited in such silence that had hunger and the rays of the sun not awakened us we would not have known of their presence. It was for Castillo's services as physician that they waited, a reputation gained by curing headaches as we marched. This reputation having spread to other nations in the region, five Indians paralyzed and very sick had been brought to him for his services.

Sleep still clouding his eyes, Castillo arose and made his way to the sick whose skins were the color of corpses. Then after making the holy sign over them and laying on each one's breast a cross of sticks he began praying that they be restored.

372

And it was as if his words were a healing balm, for even as he uttered them the sick ones' faces grew less pale, their eyelids fluttered and within minutes they made efforts to sit up.

Bows and arrows and skins were piled as payment at Castillo's feet. And when, in a little time, all five appeared to be completely restored, the depth of amazement of the Indians and the boundlessness of their gratitude was a thing beyond description.

Although I have heard it said that of all news, bad news travels fastest, and was inclined to believe this, the speed with which intelligence of these miraculous cures was broadcast throughout the land was such that I was forced to change my mind. By the time Alvar Nuñez opened his eyes in the early afternoon two more nations had arrived carrying with them certain sick ones; by nightfall there were another five. And it was not only the sorely afflicted we were begged to cure but those with headaches and bruises, eruptions of the skin and watery eyes, even some who suffered from bad dreams. The task being too great for Castillo alone he begged my assistance. Then he turned to the other two as more and more Indians arrived. Alvar Nuñez, who had regained much of his strength and who had enough experience as a physician, willingly joined in, although Dorantes stood aside. It was not only prayers, crosses of sticks and holy signs we used, but washes made of powdered antimony which Castillo had found, unguents prepared of certain leaves and roots, poultices of bark and a fine white earth, and for those with the most severe headache, bleeding.

If ever there were physicians who effected more cures than we did that day, I have never heard of them. For many of our patients a single touch of the hand was enough, although there were a few who had grown so infirm or whose condition had reached such pitiable proportions that despite their claims to have gained relief from our ministrations I could not see that they were much improved.

With the arrival of the five new nations at nightfall our

tasks grew so heavy that Castillo again begged Dorantes to join in. He shook his head but from his expression it could be seen that he wavered. And then when Alvar Nuñez urged that he try his hand he shrugged and, with a wide grin, walked up to a groaning Indian and drew the cross on the savage's forehead with the nail of his thumb. If ever a man has been cured of his pain faster than was that one, I have never heard tell of it. After that Dorantes needed no further urgings, and, if anything, worked with even greater vigor than the three of us.

If we found any sleep than night it was only a few broken hours, for two more tribes arrived with their afflicted and in the morning still another. And we were informed that all through the country they talked only of the wonders which God our Lord worked through us and that yet more Indians were coming.

We labored as we had the day before, effecting cures no less miraculous, but by late afternoon the four of us had grown so exhausted we could not continue and laid down to rest. The Indians, believing that we must replenish our power from contact with the earth, made no protest, but formed a circle around us consisting of not less than six hundred. And while we rested, different ones would leave the circle and come up with gifts— we already possessed enough bows and spears to arm a regiment, enough blankets and skins to clothe a village. Just before dark as we prepared to resume our tasks, a band of warriors of the Susolas came up to ask Castillo to go with them to cure their chief who was dead. Of all the tribes in that region the Susolas are the fiercest and, although they came in peace, the warriors of the other nations gave them much room and kept their faces hidden. Hearing that their chief was dead, Castillo refused to go, saying his skill would be better employed on the living. But the Susolas would not accept this refusal and kept insisting, offering him a rich variety of presents if he would go with them. And when he again refused they began to show an ugly humor spitting and hissing and notching arrows to bow strings.

Seeing that Castillo was unyielding in his refusal and not wishing to urge the man to do a thing against his will, Alvar Nuñez offered to go with these Susolas, which offer they quickly accepted, he being our chief; and then Dorantes and I insisted that we accompany him.

The band of Susolas traveled in a near run, but this caused us no exhaustion, for in respect for our reputation they carried us on litters. How they could survive such exertion is a thing for which there is no explanation. But when we arrived after three hours, although drenched with sweat, they were not winded, for they chattered excitedly with the crowd that came out to meet them.

Their chief lay covered by a mat with all his wives and children kneeling about him weeping, and his house had been torn down, a sign amongst these people that the one who dwelt in it is no more. From the look of the man he was dead; his eyes were rolled up, his skin cold and he had no pulse. Alvar Nuñez removed the mat and supplicated the Lord as fervently as he could to give health to the chief. Then he blessed the man and breathed on him many times as he made the sign of the cross.

For his efforts the Indians gave Alvar Nuñez a bow belonging to the chief and a basket of prickly pears. Then they prepared a place for us to sleep. But we had scarcely closed our eyes when we heard shouting in the village, for the dead chief had got up whole and walked, and had eaten, and had spoken to those who came up to him. This caused great fear of us among them and they drove us from their village. Thus, without gaining any more sleep we were forced to return alone to the place from which we came.

LVI

Intelligence of the miraculous cure somehow preceded us and the place where we camped by the river swarmed with Indians who, upon viewing us emerging from the forest on the far bank, set up such a shout as they beat on drums and whirled their sticks that to preserve our hearing we were forced to cover our ears. Every Indian, man and woman, struggled to touch us—there could not have been less than two thousand—so that by the time they had finished we felt more mauled than loved and refused to do any further cures until we had rested.

Castillo who labored diligently while we were gone, bringing relief to scores, upon our return stood to one side, ignored. From the cast of his features as the Indians pressed in all about us it could be seen that he was displeased at this neglect. Yet it is to his credit that after the Indians let up with their caresses he joined us.

It was as we tried to catch our breaths after this display of the Indians' affection that we determined to set limits on the hours we would practice as physicians. We decided also to demand of the chiefs and principal warriors that they regulate those who sought our services, so that another incident such as the one we had just suffered through could not occur.

So it was that we fell into the regular routine of healing and we never lacked for cases—even in the most inclement of weather dozens, if not scores, waited patiently.

Because of the quantity of food we received as payment for our services, most of which we shared with the Avavares, there was no need to leave the place where we camped near the field of prickly pears even after the fruit had been exhausted. Some fish were secured from the river, a little game snared, and this together with what we earned was enough to support the tribe.

For Dorantes, Castillo and the one whose account this is it was the best life we had known in many years. So it was that time slipped away, until we had been with the Avavares more than half a year. At those times when we talked about continuing with our journey, it was always Alvar Nuñez who urged that we soon move on. Castillo and Dorantes, although agreeing, found reasons why it should not be yet. I was content to wait until the three others reached agreement. Gradually an understanding developed, that as soon as it should be spring we would move on.

After this understanding, our meetings grew more frequent until a day could not pass without some discussion of what direction we should take, how long we might expect to travel before reaching a Christian land, and what would be the hazards. With each discussion, Dorantes and Castillo grew more strengthened in their determination to risk the journey. Yet when the day arrived when Alvar Nuñez came up to us with a branch on whose twigs were green buds, the two captains showed uneasiness and found reasons not to discuss details of departure.

"It took the Israelites forty years to recover from their scars of slavery," Alvar Nuñez said softly as the two men walked away.

"Some never recovered," I answered, "but lived out their lives wandering in the desert. It may be that Moses waited all those forty years not for the most sorely afflicted to recover but to die!"

"It may be," Alvar Nuñez murmured in reply. "From this I take it you are angered at Alonso and Andres." I considered what he said for several seconds then nodded. "Yet who is there that understands slavery better than you, Estevanico."

Alvar Nuñez had known of my anger before I did, for as I

377

listened to his words my gorge started to rise until my throat felt swollen. "They are Spanish captains, not whipped dogs," the words, as if they had wills of their own, forced themselves from my lips. "Patience is a blessed thing, but there is a limit to patience." Almost at once I began to regret my words.

"Are not Spanish captains men, Estevan? And who should blame men who have experienced years of adversity for fearing to exchange a life which in many ways is good enough, for the risks of the unknown."

"My impatience, for the moment, robbed me of my Christianity, my Governor," I said in apology. "They have suffered, and are true and brave men. . . ." Alvar Nuñez put his arm around my shoulders, and once again although half a head shorter, he was the taller man.

We then decided to leave Dorantes and Castillo temporarily behind while we made some explorations. This would help prevent any uneasiness of our hosts who, we concluded, might make objections if they suspected those whom they worshipped as holy men were about to desert them.

So, after telling the two captains of our intentions we left the Avavares, giving as our excuse a need for solitude to regain our strength which had been much diminished by so much healing.

We had made friends among the Maliacones who lived a day's journey to the northwest; so we went in that direction and were received by them with many marks of honor. Once there, we learned they were planning to travel several days west to where there were roots and fish that could be taken from the river. Having been importuned by their chief, medicine man, and principal warriors to join with them in this journey and not having any better plan, we decided that at least for the present our way was west. Accordingly, Alvar Nuñez sent me back for Castillo and Dorantes with the understanding that if I could not persuade them to come he would return.

So that the Avavares should not have any suspicion of my intention, I vigorously engaged in healing almost from the moment I returned to the campsite. And it was while I was laying crosses of sticks on the sick ones, making holy signs and doing things of a curative nature that I engaged the two captains in conversation, for they were working close beside me.

"Our friends the Maliacones beg us to join with them on their journey west to a place where there is an abundance of fish," were the words I used to open the conversation. Castillo raised his head and glanced for a moment in my direction; Dorantes grunted. "The Governor, this very moment, confers with them and they show him every mark of respect—he sits between the medicine man and the chief." To this Dorantes shrugged, while Castillo grew more busy treating a boy with an ulcer of the leg. "The Governor asks you to leave this nation as soon as it is dark enough and join with him—it is his intention to reach a land inhabited by Christians before summer." This last, if not the Governor's words, were his thoughts.

"Pánuco lies to the south, not west," Castillo muttered; Dorantes grunted his agreement.

"In our travels south, my captains, as you must remember, each day brought us to a place more savage than we had been the day before. How then is south the direction toward civilization?"

Both Castillo and Dorantes looked up. "Yet you were the one who most vigorously insisted Pánuco lay to the south," Castillo answered in a voice that contained a rough edge.

"And now you tell us the way is west," Dorantes added, also in a voice that held elements of harshness.

"It may be that Pánuco does lie to the south, my captains, but how great a distance? And are there not other cities inhabited by Christians, other cities than Pánuco?" I hesitated several seconds then went on. "Have we not gained better treatment, by far, from the Avavares than we did from the Yguazes and do not the Avavares live to the west?" To this the two men made no answer. "And when Alvar Nuñez traveled inland—which is west—after he escaped from his nation, was he not received as a free man by the inhabitants of that region?" The strength of my arguments forced both of the men to nod their heads, although I could see they did so reluctantly. "We will follow the sun, my captains, and before summer will find ourselves in Christian lands—then after enjoying a little sport, board a ship for Spain."

If some of the things I said were speculations although presented as facts I must be forgiven, for it was of the greatest importance that Dorantes and Castillo be strengthened. Yet as I listened to my brave words, each ringing with the deep bell tone of truth, I found it increasingly difficult to continue.

Seeing doubt still etched into both men's faces it suddenly came to me that rather than continue my efforts to convince them, why not allow them to convince me?

I let up with my ministrations on a woman with a swollen abdomen whom in gratitude stroked my hands and blew her breath upon me, gesturing toward a younger woman with whom, as payment, I might take my pleasure. Then I reached over to a pile of food we had received as gifts and selected a piece of venison. "We have enough food," I murmured, but not so softly that I should not be heard. "And we have the pick of their women." I nodded and smiled at the woman I had been offered. "Even noblemen do not receive as much respect as we." I started chewing my venison making smacking sounds with my lips. "Now that I think on it," I addressed a log of wood that lay several paces away rather than the two men, "it may be that hidalgos and officers know a better life than this in Spain, but will a black man?" Both men strained to hear, for I kept my voice almost at a whisper. Then speaking a little louder I asked the log of wood, "Why leave this pleasant life for what may be months of difficulty, even danger?"

"You fear to face danger, Estevanico?" Dorantes took hold of his beard as he asked the question.

"It is not that I fear danger, my captain," I said slowly putting special emphasis on the word captain, "I have given sufficient proofs of my bravery. But there comes a time—," I hesitated, "there comes a time, my captain, when it is better to be prudent. Although not an hour ago I was of a different opinion, I now wonder what advantage it would be to me to leave all this," I gestured at the food, the piles of gifts, the women; "to leave all this for another journey that may take months . . ." again I hesitated. "Then should it be the will of the Almighty that I reach Spain, what will be the nature of my life there . . . the best I can expect is hard work and little pay . . . and can I be certain that I will not be pressed back into slavery?"

"May the Lord God be my witness, if I must die for it, you will not again suffer slavery, Estevan," as he said these words Dorantes crossed himself then kissed his fingers, one laid crossways on the other. "And you will not be ill paid if you choose to accompany me to the house of my father where the work, I promise you, will not be hard."

"I remember your father's house," I said softly. "I remember cutting cork from the great oak trees he has growing there."

"As Andres has sworn so I swear," Castillo held his hand just before his eyes but without touching them. "The man who attempts to press you into slavery, even if he be of the highest rank, must first contend with me. For your years of service, Estevan, you will be granted a pension, I promise, so you can take your life at ease. If not from the king's coffers then from the inheritance my father left me."

I listened to the two men, but took care not to show any expression, keeping my eyes fixed either on the log or on the piece of dried venison I gnawed from time to time.

"It is Alvar Nuñez's belief that civilization lies to the west?" questioned Castillo, yet it was not a question. Instead of answering I shrugged. "You doubt Alvar Nuñez?" Again I shrugged.

"Black man," Dorantes forced his voice to sound rough as

he pointed a thick finger in my direction, "do you dare to doubt the Governor!"

"But if civilization is to the south or to the north what then," I answered in a soft voice. "To again face danger. . . ."

"To hear Estevan simper like a woman . . ." Dorantes snorted. "From the way you talk I must conclude you are about to put on an apron . . ." the man broke off what he was saying, glanced at Castillo, then started vigorously carving on a stick with the flint knife he carried.

"Each of us has known days when difficulty of travel and prospect of yet more danger became so painful that giving up and letting what will happen, happen seemed preferable to going on," Castillo spoke gently—it was as if he had not heard what Dorantes said, or that it did not matter. "If I have doubted once, I have doubted a thousand times, my friend; but now, this moment here in my chest," he laid his hand on the place between his sun-blackened paps, "this moment I am certain. Even if it takes year, I am certain we will reach a place inhabited by Christians—we could not have survived this long unless it was for a purpose. After guiding us nearly seven years would the Almighty now desert us?" Having seen how successful were my shrugs, I shrugged again.

"When it is dark enough we will leave these Avavares, black man, and you go with us!" Dorantes turned the point of his flint knife in my direction. I raised my head and looked at the man—he scowled, and his knife still pointed, yet from a tiny crinkling in the corners of his eyes I gained a suspicion he knew what I had done.

The several hours that still remained until darkness I employed, as did Dorantes and Castillo, in using all my skills as physician. And as did the other men, I selected those cases that appeared to be the gravest even if they were slaves or women.

382

And although my hands were busy relieving distress, my mind was occupied with other things.

Why do we travel west? I wondered. Does Alvar Nuñez possess information he has not shared with us?—It was my defense of his direction that had raised the question.—Then I began to consider the nature of the life we led here among the Avavares. What had been intended only as a goad to stimulate the two captains' reaction now pricked me. Life with these Indians, all in all, was better than any I had known since leaving Spain. Since leaving Spain? No. Better than any I had known since taken from the city where I was born. Where else had I been held in such high honor? And the food—not that of Europeans—but I had grown used to this food of which there was a ceaseless supply. And the work—hard but useful and when I wish to rest there is no one I must needs ask. And if my loins cry out for relief are there not scores of women waiting to welcome my embrace? Then my thoughts turned to the day we should again be in a land of Christians. How would I a black man with scarred features whose countenance has always been judged as fierce be received? How much love will a Moor who has once been a slave gain from men of Spanish lineage? And should my grant of freedom be revoked? So heavy grew my thoughts that my hands for a time lost their gentleness and I was forced to leave my labors and seek relief in a quiet place on the bank of the river.

I found a rock and dipped my fingers into the moving water feeling bubbles and bits of twigs flowing between them. "Why leave this place of safety to again face the hazards of travel?" I asked in a whisper. But in the murmur of the water and rustle of the grasses I could hear no answer. Everything I had said to the two captains for purposes of manipulation had grown real. The feigned fear of danger was no longer feigned. "If it is my determination to stay, it will take more than the two of them to make me go," I muttered.

Sitting there by the river, of all the dreams I had had of what would someday be, the only dream left to me, and that was dim, was of returning home. I tried to form a picture in my mind of the city where I was born, but it would not come. Then I tried for the faces of my parents, my brothers, but they were gone. All I had were the hands of my mother shaping the flat bread, grinding spices with pestle and mortar, cleaning the sweet fish called shebel taken from the river Habid. And then the river into which my fingers dipped became for a moment that other river. And then there were skiffs with billowing sails skipping across the water with fishermen with sun-seamed faces casting their wide nets and pulling on the tiller. In which of those vessels is my father? In which my brothers? Then the moment was gone and I was again on the banks of this nameless river. And sitting there, my fingers still feeling the flow of the water, I knew I would go on.

LVII

Not ten minutes after our joining with Alvar Nuñez, the Maliacones, having completed all their preparations, started their journey. The three of us had slipped away from the Avavares after dark and in order that we might travel quickly, other than several bows, we did not take any of our possessions. Thus it was we arrived as poor as we had been before our months of practice as physicians. But if we were poor, these Maliacones were poorer. For we at least showed enough flesh over our bones and we each carried a blanket while most of them were the perfect picture of starvation. Yet the tribe we were next to meet made these Maliacones look prosperous in comparison.

When Castillo and Dorantes saw the condition of the Maliacones they both darted questioning looks in Alvar Nuñez's direction, but he just continued assisting the principal warriors of the village with their final preparations.

Such is the chance which is life; the passage of a single day can reduce sufficiency, even abundance, to want. If there was a morsel of food among that entire tribe of Maliacones other than some pitiful dried berries of a sour taste and a few moldy nuts, we did not learn of it. Within twenty-four hours our old adversary, hunger, the strength of whose arms we had almost forgot, had us again in his embrace. After a second twenty-four hours of difficult travel over a land choked with thorny vegetation with little water and fierce heat, having almost nothing to eat, I was sorely tempted to desert this expedition and return to the Avavares. And although they said nothing, from their expressions I doubt if Dorantes and Castillo felt other than I did.

"In another day of travel, no more than two, we will have fish," Alvar Nuñez offered us encouragement as we rested during the hottest portion of the second day. To this Dorantes and Castillo scarcely more than grunted. "They say that there is a field of sweet fruit growing near the place where they fish, fruit of such delicacy that its perfume alone is enough to satisfy hunger."

"It will take more than some smell to satisfy this one," Dorantes responded in a gruff manner. "More than smells, more than fruit, more than a few miserable fish!" Castillo's expression was such that it was difficult to tell if he even listened. Although I made no response out of respect for Alvar Nuñez, I felt exactly as Dorantes did. Yet two days later when we arrived at the river which proved to be no river but a stream of thin mud, and found there were no fish and the field of fruit had not come ripe, so that their milky juices burnt our throats and caused severe thirst, we would have rejoiced at a handful of prickly pears, even a snake or a lizard that we might roast.

There being nothing else to eat, we were forced to sup on this green fruit, pressing out as much of the bitter juice as possible. But not one of us, Indian or Christian, did not suffer purging that night so in the end we gained less from eating than we would have if we had continued with our fast.

"Is this the perfume of which you spoke, Alvar Nuñez Cabeza de Vaca," asked Dorantes as a shift in the wind brought in proofs that the several hundred Maliacones suffered as much from their meal of fruit as we did. "Truly if one breathes it deeply it does satisfy hunger."

Castillo opened his mouth as if he were about to join in, but instead turned his head away and remained silent. Forming each word carefully, his mouth being thick from the burning juices of the fruit, Alvar Nuñez then began to speak. "As distressed as the three of you must be, I am more distressed—for it was my urgings that made you join with this pitiful band of Indians." He paused and licked his lips. "I go forward, of that I am determined. But it may be the better course for you to return to the Avavares." In the fading light he looked into each of our faces for several moments. "From this poor beginning I must conclude that even greater adversity may lie ahead—how can I counsel hunger and suffering when no more than four days travel back to the Avavares there awaits a life of pleasure and abundance. If it should be your decision to turn back, I will not think any less of you. Each of you has given more proofs of his manhood than have entire companies of the finest soldiers. Who in all this world would blame you, after all you have endured, for now choosing certainty over chance?"

Visions of the mounds of food we had left filled my mind. Why not return to the Avavares? Another season might bring us in contact with a nation traveling to the south—a nation of greater prosperity than these Maliacones; what would prevent

386

us from joining with this nation with whom we would have an easier time?

"I did not think I would ever say this thing," Castillo started speaking, "and if at an earlier time any had said of me what I now say of myself, such a one would have had to kill me to prevent his own death on my sword." Although it was dark, I could see that Alvar Nuñez and Dorantes watched the man intently. "I know fear." Castillo's voice dropped almost to a whisper. "I know fear this minute and have known it every minute since leaving the Avavares. Even during the worst time of slavery with the other Indians I did not know such fear; certainly not in battle." Both of Castillo's hands rested on the ground and his eyes were cast downward. "Even as I speak now my bones are filled with ice. Estevan with his cleverness made it easier for me to break with the Avavares. For his little pretense which called upon my manhood I must thank him, for in all my years I have not done a thing as painful. Every step we take away from the Avavares I judge to be a step toward death. And now, Alvar Nuñez Cabeza de Vaca, you suggest that we retrace our steps. If you were not one whom I love better than myself, I would challenge you even if it must be with flint knives for this terrible threat to the little that is left of my manhood. So passionately do I want to return to the Avavares I can think of little else. Not five minutes have passed since leaving them that I did not consider going back. If you have any of God's mercy in your breast—as I know you must have—do not mention such a thing again."

Morning brought another tribe, the Arbadaos, to the field of unripened fruit. In all my travels, before and since, I have never seen a band of more miserable human beings. Had they walked on all fours they must have been taken for a pack of mangy, starving brutes—jackals in my native land made a better appearance than did these ones.

387

The arrival in the field of these Arbadaos, as if a signal, caused the Maliacones to start back to the place from which we had come. So sudden was their decision to depart that we were given no more than five minutes to consider should we go with them or remain. It was our determination to remain. But I will confess to a certain uneasiness as I watched the Maliacones file out of the field to the east leaving us alone in the company of this nation of near beasts.

Although a few of their words had a familiar ring, perhaps these were words gained from other nations, I could not understand their language—and I am one who has great facility with languages. So we stood separated by the distance of a dozen paces staring at one another—their children who resemble nothing so much as rats cowering together with their mothers to the rear. Then as if they all at once lost interest in us, they turned away and attacked the green fruit with savage voracity.

I doubt if hyenas or scaly vultures who delight in the ripest carrion possess digestions to equal these Arbadaos. Neither the bitterness of the milky juices nor the lack of ripeness appeared to bother them. They gorged. From the littlest ones to their grizzled chief whose body was a mass of scars they stuffed. They stuffed until their bellies were distended, their faces, necks and chests dripping with the sticky juices. Then, when they lay down to rest, different ones, without any attempt to seek privacy, fornicated—the men and women on all fours in the manner of beasts.

Of all the nations we encountered on our journey this one alone appeared to have no interest in our skill as physicians. Not that they did not suffer. To a man they showed ulcers, boils or carbuncles. They constantly coughed, spit and sneezed. Their breaths were so foul that should one unleash it full in your face, you would be hard pressed to keep your eyes from tearing. And their bodies were alive with lice which, when they had nothing else, they picked from each other and ate.

Had they possessed weapons other than clubs and stone axes, or had they been less afraid of us I am certain we would
388

have been enslaved then eaten. For it appeared there was nothing which these brutish humans would not eat, and unless I miss my guess all who were not of their tribe were looked upon as meat. But we had bows, which we took care to keep in readiness, and they were enough afraid of us and kept their distance. Still, more than once during the course of several nights we stayed in their company when fatigue caused us temporarily to relax our vigilance, different ones began to edge towards us; these were sent scurrying with whimpers as we brandished our weapons.

Had it not been for our loss of strength from our famished condition, made worse by the bouts of purgings, we would have separated from these Arbadaos immediately. But in the field of fruit we at least had shade, some little water and if we searched hard enough here and there could find a root that for a time would dull our hunger.

The fourth day of our stay in the field together with the Arbadaos, the four of us experienced such weakness that we grew concerned lest we become helpless and then be overrun. It was then that Alvar Nuñez, noting that their chief possessed two little dogs which he was fattening, offered our blankets in exchange for these dogs. Such wealth the chief was unable to resist, so he handed them over and we roasted and ate them and in this way regained some of our strength.

As I remember the relish with which we consumed these little creatures, I cannot help considering how vast the chasm had become that separated us from the nice ways of civilization. Not only did we relish the flesh of dogs, but when we could get them we would roast grubs, grasshoppers, moles and mice whose taste we did not find unpleasing. And our appearance in no way resembled that of civilized men. Much of the time we went naked exposed to the wind and sun which caused us to shed our skins two times each year, like snakes. Yet for all our appearance we were Christians, better Christians even than we had been in the early days of the expedition.

So, strengthened by our meal and being in agreement that

we should press forward, we separated from the Arbadaos after first soliciting from them the trail west that would lead us to the next village. Although we had paid for this information by the gift of a flint knife, the route we had been put upon quickly got us lost. A violent rainstorm then drove us from a creek bed along which we had been traveling so that had we wished to retrace our steps to pick up the trail we could not have. Night-fall found us in a stand of timber where we huddled soaked by the teeming rain until it was light.

Try as I would, I could not keep bitter thoughts from sting-ing my brain as I struggled against the gnats and mosquitoes made bolder by the rain. The little relief I had gained from the meal of the dogs was gone and I found myself with a cough. If I slept at all, it was for brief moments, for if I let up fighting the insects they quickly covered my skin—some seeking to enter my ears and eyes. But such is the miracle of existence, even the darkest night gives way at last to the light of morning. And with morning came an end to the rain and a fresh wind which helped drive away some of the insects.

Although I had no way of seeing myself, from the swollen faces of my three companions—even their lips had been stung—I knew my features must be no less distorted. But if I had any doubts, Dorantes' expression when he first saw me gave me confirmation. "These insects, in the manner of certain Portuguese I have known, prefer their meat dark," he said with a grin, giving me a friendly slap on the shoulder. "Yet now that I think about it, the ones that those rutting boars of Lisbon hungered after were not as hairy as our Estevan, and if I do not disremember, showed some slight difference in their anat-omy."

"Perhaps it is that these insects are all ladies," Castillo, whose eyes had been so stung they were swollen into slits, joined in.

"Yes, that must be it," said Dorantes. "My acquaintance is only with Portuguese gentlemen." Both men began to laugh.

390

"Tell us, Estevan," Dorantes then asked, "do you have amongst your many admirers any Portuguese women?"

I pulled a grave face, stroked my chin and answered, "I am ashamed to admit—you will not broadcast it among my friends—that I have known no more than fifty, and there were three, if I do not disremember, or was it four, who were not virgins."

"Estevan, when I consider how many years I invested in your proper training . . ." Dorantes shook his head. "And with such a one as your former master to set you an example . . . Perhaps it is that you have little interest in worldly matters and should really be a hooded monk copying sacred manuscripts in a quiet monastery."

"If what I have heard of monasteries be true, I have little doubt but that Estevan would fit in," Castillo forced his voice to sound light, but from the way his body drooped I could see he felt no levity.

"Let Estevan enjoy those delights of his monastery served up nicely wrapped in mantillas and laces; I'll take the ones prepared with wheaten crusts and savory sauces," Dorantes swallowed as he spoke. "For a little goat who has never known food other than that which it takes from its mother, for such a gentle creature prepared with a stuffing of bread and herbs moistened with just enough wine and then carefully roasted over a slow oak fire, for just a portion of such a preparation I would take the oath of celibacy and if granted an hundred years of life never violate it."

"Such an oath must cause no less than a thousand Spanish mothers of maiden daughters much relief," said Alvar Nuñez as he stepped out of a thicket which he had been exploring. "And if I could gain the blessings of that thousand by offering you your roasted kid I would gladly do it. But, my friend, all I can provide for your feast is as many ripe prickly pears as you can eat."

Not a hundred paces from where we had huddled through

the night was a field of fruit which Alvar Nuñez had discovered, a field either unknown to the Indians of this region or forgotten. Thus we were able to enjoy the largest and ripest and even snare some birds who came to the field to feast.

After eating we lay in the shade trying to find the little sleep denied to us during the night.

"There were moments during the night just past that I struggled with depression, Satan's subtle poison," Alvar Nuñez abruptly started speaking dragging me from the edge of sleep. "Why after all the proofs I have been given, I should allow myself even a moment of depression. . . . And now with this field of fruit offering us sustenance when we needed it; another proof. Such is the frailty of man that we still doubt when we should be certain."

"But did not even our Lord doubt when He cried out in anguish from the cross," Castillo offered in a sleepy voice. "Would you be more than the One whose suffering was for all men?"

Some time then passed. I slept, awakened, slept again; then came into full wakefulness when Dorantes asked, "Why do we travel west, my Governor? Do you have certain information?"

"West is the way of the sun," was Alvar Nuñez's answer.

"The way west will lead to civilization?" Dorantes asked staring at the man. "Do you know in which direction lies civilization?" How long then passed between the question and the answer I cannot be certain; it felt like minutes although it may have been only moments.

"West is the way toward the unknown," Alvar Nuñez responded. "We are not here to search like lost dogs only for a means to return. We are here because there is work that must be done."

"Work, my Governor?" Dorantes' voice was forced, yet there was something in its sound that told me he was not without understanding of what was being said.

"How far this land stretches out toward the west we do not know," Alvar Nuñez started intoning. "During the years I traveled among the Indians I heard stories of mountains whose tops are never free of snow, of grassland that thirty days travel is not enough to traverse—grassland on which graze hairy cattle whose numbers can only be compared to great swarms of bees or to the leaves that cling to each twig of every tree in the forest. And I heard stories of arroyos of such depth a full day is not enough to descend and then climb up again."

"Stories!" Dorantes spat out the word. "If stories were gold we should be the richest men in all these Western Indies—yet we own not a single blanket among the four of us."

"And in all this vast land," Alvar Nuñez continued as if deaf to Dorantes' words, "a land that may yet stretch a thousand leagues to the west, there are Indian nations without number—nations that may have need of us."

If Alvar Nuñez still had more to say or if he had finished speaking I have no way of knowing, for a shift in wind from the west brought in the sound of drumbeats which abruptly ended our conversation.

Gathering as many prickly pears as we could carry we started in the direction of the sound and by early afternoon, emerging from a stand of timber, we came upon a party of Indian women digging for roots. At the sight of us they fled hiding behind trees or beneath bushes, but they could not control their frightened gibbering; and then when we came up to different ones it was as if they were frozen. Offering our prickly pears as gifts we calmed them and when they saw we did not intend to harm them they led us to their village where we were received with a great celebration—the principal warriors having gained some knowledge of our reputation.

Although with the many Indians we had encountered up to this time a celebration consisted of consuming all the food that was available, followed either by the telling of stories or dancing, with these Indians it was different. Instead of gorging

393

on food they filled their stomachs with a liquid brewed of the leaves of trees resembling holm oaks. These leaves were first toasted over a fire, then boiled until the liquid was a deep yellow; this they drank as hot as could be endured. Their celebration lasted three days during which time no other food was eaten. Their women, who were not permitted to partake of this drink, were forbidden to move under pain of death while the drinking was going on.

Our condition was such we would have been much better pleased had we been offered a celebration of food—a roast of venison is what I most yearned for—in order not to offend these Indians we joined in their drinking. I have experienced drunkenness; what man who has served as a sailor and a soldier has not, but never have I been as drunk as I was after drinking that yellow colored potion. My ten fingers crawled from my hands and lay writhing on the ground like snakes. Both of my eyes fell out of my skull leaving me blind. And I could feel the tissue of my brain dripping from my nose and ears.

Had I drunk a tenth part of the quantity that these Indians regularly consume I am certain my guts would have burst, for I felt such a fire running through my abdomen it could have been a pot of boiling lead I had just quaffed. Then the lead congealed and pinioned me with its weight to the ground. Yet it must be said, when this drunkenness lifted there was no lingering distress as is the case with beer or wine. But it also must be said that afterwards one's thinking shows areas of confusion for quite a time. Thus it is I cannot remember how long we stayed with this Indian nation—several days, a week, two weeks.

When our minds had finally cleared we ministered to these Indians, their principal complaints being dizziness and ulcers of the legs and feet. Our skills, although unused for several weeks, were unimpaired and the cures effected with the Almighty's help can be given no other name than that of miracles.

As it had been with the Avavares and with the other nations who visited us while we lived with them, these Indians showered us with presents. "If my father had been paid in like proportion for his services during the years he worked as court physician," laughed Castillo as an Indian we had just cured came up and laid all his possessions before us on the ground, "if he had been paid a tenth part in like proportion, he would have died the wealthiest man in all of Christendom."

"To be the friend of one to whom will come such an inheritance," Dorantes nudged Castillo, "to be a friend to such a one must guarantee a wagon load of costly gifts. If I have had questions as to why I offered you my valuable friendship, a friendship more properly shared with dukes and princes, I now have my answer; you are to make me rich."

"If we are to travel a thousand leagues," Castillo glanced in the direction of Alvar Nuñez, "and if in these travels are to encounter tens of scores of nations and if each bestows upon us this quantity of gifts, you will have no need for a share in my inheritance, Andres, you will own more bows than are possessed by all the troops of England and France together—you will be able to have your own war."

"And skins, Alonso," Dorantes pointed his thumb at a pile of skins—all that this nation owned—"when we have completed this little walk of a thousand leagues, we will have skins enough to clothe all Spain, even a few left over for friends of Estevan in Morocco," he winked at me.

Not to be outdone I joined in, "But how are we to transport a hundred thousand bows and a like number of skins, my learned captains? We do not own a wagon."

"We will build a wagon, black man," Dorantes wagged a finger at me. "And then you will have the chance to prove your strength."

"One mule never pulls as well as two," Castillo winked at the man. "And you are one, Andres, not averse to showing the might of your muscles."

"And two mules, Alonso, no matter how well matched cannot do the task of three," Alvar Nuñez offered with a laugh.

"Now that I think on it," Dorantes made a show of pulling his beard, "there is a lack of balance in three except in such as the Trinity; four is a nice number."

Just then a woman, whose boil Dorantes had opened and cleaned of pus, came up and placed several flints and a bundle of sinews at his feet. She was hollow eyed and her fingers were swollen and bent, her head except for a few tufts of hair bald and scabby. "She gives me all her wealth." All the mirth suddenly went out of Dorantes' voice. "A widow with no son and now the few possessions that stand between her and starvation she lays at my feet for five minutes of work."

"We will wait until we reach a nation of great wealth before we build our wagon," Castillo said softly.

"If we took all these Indians offered us," Dorantes stared down at the gift of flints and sinews, "they could not hunt or fish and would starve to death." I glanced for a moment at the man's face and never had I seen it so softened. And late that afternoon during a time taken for rest I gained further proof of his gentleness.

We had separated, each to his private place for an hour or two of sleep when an indisposition of the bowels caused me to seek a retreat of even greater privacy. I had done what was necessary and was about to return to my bed of leaves when I heard a sound I judged to be from a wild animal, but of a species unfamiliar to me. Being curious, I moved cautiously in the direction of the sound until I reached a place protected by a growth of cactus where I could see without being seen.

Resting on his haunches, his hands and arms spattered with blood Dorantes leaned over a small wolf to whom he was making deep throat sounds. These, the creature seemed to understand and its labored breathing grew more easy as the man searched with careful fingers into its wounds. It had somehow gotten tangled in the cactus, for I saw tufts of fur and bits of blood clinging to a nearby clump of that cruel vegetation. Dorantes extracted a thorn from the creature's flank greater in

396

length than my middle finger; then a second thorn. The beast shuddered and bared its fangs but Dorantes, showing no fear, gently stroked it between the ears again making his deep throat sound. This appeared to comfort the animal who lowered its lip and softly whimpered. From the appearance of its eyes and from its thinness—it must have been trapped for several days— I judged the creature close to death and wondered why Dorantes would risk a bite when it must surely die. Remembering my bed of leaves and a strip of dried venison I had, I was about to turn away when the man started speaking.

"Try to live, my little brother, for life is good and death is cold and forever." He leaned close to the beast and spoke to it as if it were able to understand human speech. "Do you not want to run again and bark at the yellow moon?" he asked the wounded wolf. "Do you not want to lie stuffed with mice on the sun-warmed earth in the long afternoon?" He stroked the creature with his hand. Despite my reason, I half expected the wolf to rise to its feet, still bleeding, and lope away. But it only quivered and its breathing grew more shallow. "Let me make you sound again, my little brother," Dorantes said softly, so softly I had to strain to hear. "Let me share my breath with you." With that, using great care, he forced the beast's jaws open exposing its yellow teeth and purple tongue and breathed into its mouth. The wolf struggled scratching with its feet, then Dorantes blew first into its one ear and then the other and the beast grew calm. The wolf's eyes were opened wide and looked in such a wise into the eyes of Dorantes that I had no doubt but that it understood the man. Then it coughed, and its tongue lolled out, and it stiffened and it died. Dorantes laid his hand on the creature's heart; after some moments, he took a grip on its two front legs rose up and with a mighty heave hurled the corpse into a thorny thicket ten or twelve paces distant. He then quickly walked away.

I remained where I was crouching for many minutes, perhaps as much as an hour after Dorantes' departure. Insects

397

quickened by the smell of blood swarmed over the place where the wolf had lain. A bird drawn by the sight of these tiny scurrying creatures skimmed down and began to feast. I glanced at the bushes half expecting to see a wild cat ready to pounce upon the bird. Then a remembrance of how I sat before the still, green waters of the poisonous pool in the Florida jungle, my mind weighted with visions of my insect covered corpse lying unattended, came back to me. Seven years had passed since that time I revisited the place where Castillo, challenged by himself, had been forced to prove his manhood. And here I was as sound as I had been that day. "Not yet," I murmured to the swarming insects, whose numbers, despite the attentions of the bird, grew greater. "Be patient and in time you will have your turn with me, but not yet." I suddenly burst out laughing; it all seemed so funny. I looked up to the sky, a single cloud showing the face of an old man moved toward the sun. The force of my laughter grew greater. I thought of the dead wolf lying in the thicket and of my three companions resting on their beds of leaves and tears began to course down my cheeks, so great was the force of my laughter. Just as the cloud passed over the sun I winked at the old man, and I am ready to take my oath that he winked back at me.

LVIII

To describe how this nation of Indians pleaded with us not to leave them, how they offered every advantage of which they were capable even to serving us as slaves, to give an account of this and of the deep sadness that came over them as we grew ready to depart would fill many pages. It is enough to say that they would not eat and sat around bowed with dejection, tears wetting the cheeks of every one, as we completed our preparations.

Leaving all the rest of their gifts untouched, Dorantes, Castillo and I each selected a bow together with a handful of stone tipped arrows. Alvar Nuñez watched us, but did not come forward to select his weapon. After several moments of hesitation Dorantes asked, "You go unarmed, my friend?" Alvar Nuñez nodded. "And should we again meet with a nation such as the Arbadaos what then?"

"I will tell them we come in peace," was his soft answer. "I will tell them that if they let us we will love them and cure their afflictions . . ."

"But if they are like those brutish Arbadaos and cannot hear us!" Dorantes interrupted.

"I will make the cross and draw the fish and say Christ's name."

"But . . ." Dorantes took several steps toward the man, his bow in one hand, his arrows in the other, "those savages whose breaths are like sulfur, who rut like beasts know nothing of the cross and the fish."

"We will teach them," Alvar Nuñez answered.

"And if they will not learn and overrun us?" Castillo asked carefully.

"We still will love them and will pray."

"To wander weaponless through this land . . ." wonder sounded in Dorantes' voice.

"Did the Carpenter and fisherman carry weapons?" Although Alvar Nuñez addressed the men, he gazed beyond them. "And were there not dangers enough in the land through which they traveled?"

Almost as if they responded to an unseen signal, Dorantes and Castillo turned back to the pile of gifts and placed their bows and arrows alongside the many others. I hesitated.

"How shall we hunt?" I asked Alvar Nuñez already knowing what would be the nature of his answer.

"Were not the Israelites, when they hungered in the desert, provided with sufficient manna? If those many thousands, children and old ones amongst them had faith—how then should four men in their prime have doubt?"

With a deep sigh I cast my weapons on the heap. And then it was as if I had let go of heavy stones.

So it was that weaponless, naked except for breach clouts, each carrying a modest pouch of food we continued our journey, and after many months of moving westward during which we cured thousands, we at last came to a nation where we gained information that men like us dwelt ten days travel to the south.

Accompanied by scores of Christians met along the way and hundreds of Indians, we entered Mexico City July 25, 1536, eight years, two months and twenty five days from our landing on the coast of Florida. Word of our survival had reached the capitol city weeks earlier and a tumultuous welcome awaited us, the like of which was never before seen in the Western Indies. Had we been members of the Royal Family we could not have been received with more thunderous shouts— the bells of every church rang without ceasing and on the last portion of the way to the center of the city, we were accompanied by Viceroy Mendoza and Hernan Cortes who presented each of us with clothing from their own wardrobes and many fine and costly gifts.

The following day a great feast was held and a celebration which included a joust of reeds with bulls. Hundreds, including many noblemen came up to touch me, to offer their prayers

400

to God for having saved me and my three companions from so many calamities, to press gold and silver coins into my hands. Then Viceroy Mendoza came up and, after presenting me with a likeness of Christ's Mother, Mary, done in gold and jewels, declared that he was claiming me for his household. Although I forced my face to give no sign, within my chest my heart turned to ice. Nothing Alvar Nuñez, Dorantes or Castillo could say altered the Viceroy's determination. Thus despite the silks I now wore, the gold and silver coins that filled my pockets, I was again a slave.

AFTERWORD

Alonso Castillo settled down as a citizen of Mexico City, practiced as a physician, married a widow and was granted, for life, half the rents of the town of Tehuacan.

Andres Dorantes served Mendoza in the conquest of Jalisco. He then married a widow by the name of Doña María de la Torre, fathered a large family and became one of the richest men of New Spain.

Alvar Nuñez (Cabeza de Vaca) returned to Spain where he found his wife waiting for him, never doubting his return through their ten years of separation. He subsequently became governor and captain general of the provinces of Rio de la Plata (now Paraguay) where he engaged in further explorations. After some successes and reverses he again returned to Spain where he spent the remainder of his life, a living legend, handsomely pensioned by the Crown.

Estevan, again a slave, served the Viceroy of Mexico. In 1539 he was assigned as a guide to the exploration headed by Fray Marcos de Niza. Traveling a hundred leagues in advance of this exploration which was to find the seven fabled cities of Cibola, Estevan was the first non-Indian to enter the areas now known as Arizona and New Mexico. In the area now known as the Gila River region, in the Indian city of Hawikuh, he was captured by the Zuni Indian inhabitants and after three days of torture was put to death.

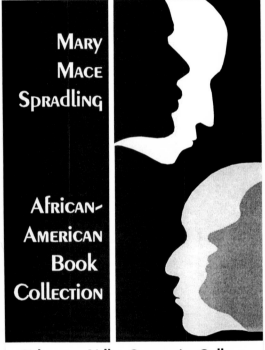

MARY
MACE
Spradling

African-
American
Book
Collection

Kalamazoo Valley Community College